TO WAKE A KINGDOM

WAKE TO A KINGDOM

NISHA J. TULI

THIRTEEN CROWNS PRESS

TO WAKE A KINGDOM

Copyright © 2022 by Nisha J Tuli

For information contact: http://www.nishajtuli.com/

Cover design by Miblart.com

Editing by Jennifer Herrington, Nina Fiegl

ISBN: 978-1-7781269-2-5

First Edition August 2022

10 9 8 7 6 5 4 3 2

This book is for Matthew.
Thank you for picking up my slack while I follow my dream.

AUTHOR'S NOTE

As an author, I do think it's my job to let you know if there's anything that might be problematic for any readers. With that in mind, content warnings are listed below. If you prefer to go in without them, then you can skip right ahead to Chapter One.

For those who'd like a heads up, this is an adult novel that involves a fair amount of death and blood and people killing each other. There are two non-graphic scenes of sexual assault that don't happen. There is some swearing... you're unlikely to read a book of mine where there aren't several F-bombs because in real life, I tend to swear like a sailor. There are also on the page, detailed sex scenes. Everything between the main love interests is consensual.

Happy Reading!

Love,

Nisha

CHAPTER ONE

T HE FIRST THING I noticed was the sweetness of roses, twisted
with the violent scent of blood. The second was the sting
of an icy breeze that whispered of winter. The third was a man
hovering over me, a leer on his face, his sour breath clinging to
my skin.

I blinked through a syrupy fog of recollection.

Flowers in a spectrum of colors nested around my face as if
I'd grown from a garden. A soft pillow cushioned my head, and
my hands lay crossed over my heart. Like a corpse laid to rest.

But I was not dead. At least, not yet.

The man kneeled on the bier where I lay, the glint of bloodied
steel flashing in his hand. I blinked again, trying to untangle my
confusion.

Where had he come from? Who let him in here? Could no one
have bothered to protect me?

Our gazes locked, shock carving into his ruddy features.

My heart thumped as understanding fused into iron. I screamed and did the only thing that made sense—lifted my knee and drove it between his legs with every ounce of strength I had.

With a howl, he clutched his groin, his head thrown back.

Skirts tangling around me, I flipped off the platform and landed in a crouch.

The man rolled on the ground, writhing, his eyes watering. "You bitch." He rocked back and forth, gulping deep breaths. "You fucking whore!"

Spinning on my heel, I plunged through the door and entered the adjacent room where twelve women lay slain. Not women—Fae.

I remembered them.

I was slowly remembering everything.

Their gossamer dresses ripped and shredded, they lay bent and broken like discarded dolls with dull glass eyes. Some had slid to the ground, while others remained seated upon the thrones where they had once argued, schemed, and plotted.

Death crawled across the stone floor like afternoon shadows.

Bile rising in my throat, I covered my mouth, shudders stamping into my skin. The man with the sword had killed every one of these Fae.

What else had he done? The vile possibilities expanded in my mind. I was to be his thirteenth victim before I'd woken up.

But why was I awake?

Behind me, the murderer roared again, and I ran.

Through the hallways of the castle I'd grown up in, I ran. Every passage familiar, my soft slippers pounded against the dark stones as I scattered around corners.

I knew with the confidence of the bricks in these walls that the man would kill me if he caught me. Only death lingered on his shoulders. Attempting to block his pursuit, I knocked down vases, suits of armor, and tottering candelabras. Given his age and girth, he was inconveniently nimble. He kept close behind, shouting obscenities that would make even the merpeople blush.

My chest constricted from lack of use, bands tightening and squeezing. I careened into the throne room—the heart of my home—and came to an abrupt stop. Sunlight winked through stained glass windows, painting the walls in rainbows.

My mother and father sat asleep on the dais, dressed in furs and silk, exactly as I remembered them. Around the massive room, guards and courtiers and servants slept. Some leaned against the walls. Some lay on the ground. Some swayed where they stood—towers ready to topple from the force of a stiff breeze.

A breath, sharp and bitter, scraped the back of my throat.

A curse.

I remembered that too. How could I ever forget?

The man roared again, and I snatched the sword lying across my father's lap.

With a sneer, the man prowled deeper into the room. "Put that thing down. You don't want to cut yourself, Princess. I won't hurt you. I just want a taste."

As though *a taste* wouldn't hurt me.

Beady eyes glittered as his gaze pitched over me and he licked his lips, the scant contents of my stomach threatening to rise.

"Stay away from me." My voice was coated in cobwebs. It had been a very long time since I'd uttered a single syllable, so I cleared my throat and tried again. "Stay away from me!" This time, my words trumpeted with more certainty, despite the tremble I hoped he couldn't hear.

As the man stalked closer, I noted his fine red jacket worked with scrolls of golden thread. His graying beard was neatly trimmed, and his polished leather boots reflected the sunlight. This man was no bandit or thief. He was a man of stature. A nobleman, perhaps. What was he doing here?

The sword in his hand glittered with life as though it possessed a heartbeat melded into the steel. Nearly losing myself in its pull, I couldn't peel my eyes away. The sword in my own hand seemed inadequate in comparison. Like a cheap toy, instead of my father's most lethal weapon.

The man lurched, and I snapped back to the present. Barely able to lift the blade, I swung it wildly, its weight throwing me off balance. When I stumbled, the man barked out a cruel and mirthless laugh, delight in his eyes.

Then he was on me, his sneer morphing into a guttural snarl. Grabbing my hair, he pulled me upright and pressed my back against his broad chest. My scalp burned as he twisted harder, and I felt the heavy weight of his stare drifting down my body. Spinning me around, a meaty hand encircled my throat.

He knocked the blade from my hand, and I watched it clatter to the stones along with my fleeting courage. Pinning me against the wall, the man smiled, showing off two rows of clean, white teeth. The scent of blood and sweat coated the inside of my mouth, choking me like wet rags stuffed down my windpipe.

"You can make this easy, or you can make this hard." He leaned in closer, his breath burrowing into my skin. "For your sake, I'd choose easy. But for my sake, I like it *hard*."

With a grunt, he jammed his body against mine, trapping me to the stone. My breath rushed out in quick gasps as he crushed my throat. I had little doubt he cared if I was unconscious for this.

"That's right," he said in my ear. "Be a good girl and do as you're told." Hot and heavy, his breath wormed across my cheeks as tears slipped from my eyes. Black spots mushroomed in my vision when he gripped my throat harder.

I was going to die.

After everything, how could *this* be my ending?

Then I remembered something else.

It was taking time to unravel each buried memory from the snarl of chains locking them down. But as he shoved his knee between mine, a tendril of recollection unfurled like a feeble blossom of hope. I clung to it, bruising the stems.

My father's captain of the guard believed a princess should be able to defend herself. I wasn't offered many useful lessons in my pampered life, but Andrick had gifted me this.

I slid my hand into my skirt, searching for the opening cut for exactly this reason. Down the side of my leg, I reached for a lifeline of polished steel, and *there* it still was.

The man had failed to notice it in his fury. Or maybe he saw me as so meager an opponent, he'd dismissed it. Desperation made me quick. I yanked the dagger from the strap around my thigh and thrust it between his ribs.

Stunned, we both watched blood gush out of him and onto me, coating my hand and arm and chest. Warm splashes pelted my chin and cheeks, my eyelashes fluttering at the impact. He met my gaze, outraged, as if he couldn't believe I'd had the nerve.

I didn't give him the chance to reach for the dagger. Desperation also made me decisive. I jerked the weapon away and slammed the sharpened point into the side of his neck. A fountain of blood spurted, bathing us in a robe of scarlet. Suspended in time, everything went quiet but for the shreds of my panting breaths. His knees then crumpled, and he dropped to the ground. Blank eyes stared at the ceiling. Dead.

I just killed a man.

A sob ripped from the back of my sternum as I slid down the wall, cradling my head in my arms, and dropped the bloody dagger. I trembled as my heart battled my lungs. Condensing myself into a ball of cemented limbs, I cried and cried until my cheeks were raw and my chest had drained out into a hollow chamber.

Eventually, I forced my chin up and surveyed the room. With a pool of blood congealed beneath me, I peeled myself off the floor. Black and silver banners hung from the high stone walls, the points ending above where my parents sat. Their bodies were relaxed, and they slouched against their silver thrones, hands hanging off the armrests as though they'd still been clasped when sleep took them.

On wobbly legs, I stumbled over and reached for my mother, circling my hands around her delicate shoulders.

"Wake up," I whispered.

With a gentle shake, I searched her face for any flutter of consciousness. She remained placid—dead to the world, for all it mattered.

"Wake up." I shook harder, her arms flopping like a scarecrow's. "Wake up!" I screamed it this time, my plea desperate and wretched. "Wake up! I need you to wake up!"

Nothing happened as my voice echoed off the room's high corners. My mother's head, garlanded with glossy black curls, had fallen forward, chin resting on her chest. "Please, wake up." I hiccupped a ragged sob and laid her back, carefully arranging her in the same position. Blood covered the arms of her white dress and the fur stole hanging around her shoulders. I stared at my hands in horror.

I killed a man.

Already knowing it was pointless, I stood in front of my father, hoping that if I screamed loud enough, someone would come and fix this.

None of them were supposed to be asleep.

No matter how loud I yelled, my father remained silent. I laid a hand on his dark hair and thought of the deep brown eyes concealed by shuttered lids. I would give anything to feel the warmth of his gaze. To feel his trust and his confidence. He would have known what to do.

It was then I snapped—the tether binding me to the earth, loosing me like an errant cannon. I ran from person to person, trying to wake someone. Rattling them, shouting at them. "Wake up, wake up, wake up. Someone, wake up!"

Tears blurred my vision, and I wiped them away with my sweaty palms. The air in my chest was as thick as tree sap. The guards, the courtiers, and the servants all slept on, oblivious to me. Oblivious to the blood coating the floor and my hands. Oblivious to the twelve Fae lying upstairs, murdered as they slept.

Thirteen bodies.

I had thirteen bodies to deal with and not a soul to help. But this was my home, and that man could not remain as a reminder of his sins in what had always been the sunny yellow center of this castle.

Beyond the throne room lay a wide stone hallway ending in a massive set of doors that stood several feet over my head. One stood slightly ajar where the man had entered my sanctuary.

Shielding my eyes from the bright light, I stepped outside, my slippers crunching on a pile of thick brambles littering the path. Brittle and black, they were covered in sharp, deadly spines. Growing up around the walls and over the top of the battlements, spreading with a thousand extendable limbs, they covered the entire castle. Was this part of the curse? They were too dense and ominous to have grown by nature's will.

My breath caught as I saw a man—or rather what was left of one—trapped in the brambles as if he'd tried to climb his way to the top, only to be rendered fleshless into bleached bone.

How long had I been asleep?

I picked up a bramble, its end severed cleanly with a blade. Others had tried to transgress my resting place.

I thought of the way the man's weapon had glittered with a preternatural glow. Like I could have pressed two fingers to the hardened steel and counted the beats of its heart. Why had he succeeded where others had failed?

Further down the wall, more skeletons sat trapped in the brush, and I swallowed the burning lump of coal in my throat.

A neigh caught my attention. I spun to find a white horse in a polished leather saddle, tied to a tree. It could only have belonged to *him*. With trembling hands, I fumbled with the rope, untying the beast and leading it toward the stables. My mind spun with calamitous thoughts, but these mundane, insignificant tasks calmed my galloping heart and gave me something else to focus on.

I killed a man.

The stable's massive sliding door sat closed, and I hauled it open. Rusted tracks shrieked in protest to reveal a dozen stalls. My slippers crunching on a layer of hay, I found a stall to store the horse. The air was thick and damp, clinging like a second layer of skin. I walked to the third stall on the left, where my mare, Blizzard, lived. My throat knotted as I peered over the partition. Bones. Nothing but a dry husk left of my old friend.

A boy no older than twelve, wearing dark breeches and a thin shirt, lay asleep against the back wall. He sighed, his narrow chest rising and falling. A spattering of freckles bridged across his nose, his shaggy blond hair falling in his eyes. Propped up against the wall next to him was a shovel.

Thirteen bodies.

With the shovel slung over my shoulder, I walked deeper into the forest. Royal birch grew in dense formations, their trunks wide with the confidence of age. Bright green leaves fluttered in the breeze, their edges coated in creeping borders of white. Winter was around the corner and soon they would turn silver, forming a glittering canopy.

Under normal circumstances, it was one of my favorite sights.

My long skirts tangled around my ankles, stiffening with dried blood. Heart beating in my throat, I walked through the forest until the castle disappeared behind a curtain of foliage. The air was cool, a nip biting against my fevered skin.

Continuing deeper, I found a clearing surrounded by royal birch and apple trees. Rotten fruit littered the ground, their cloying scent filling the air. How many years had these trees provided for a harvest that never came?

Slowly pushing the breath from my lungs, I walked to the center of the clearing. Closing my eyes for a moment, I listened to the stillness of the forest, trying to coax a sliver of relief from my splintering nerves. Shovel gripped so tight my hands ached, I swung it off my shoulder and plunged it into the earth.

Then, I began to dig.

CHAPTER TWO

B EFORE ME LAY THIRTEEN jagged holes. They weren't deep, but
they would have to do. With winter's brittle kiss brushing
the edges of fall, the ground had hardened, making it impossible to dig more than a few feet.

Drenched in sweat and covered in a strange man's blood, I
made my way back to the castle. Shock coursed through me in
needle-sharp bolts. My limbs were hollow and weightless from
exhaustion, the fatigue muffling my fraying nerves.

Back in the chamber where the twelve Fae lay dead, tears
blurred my vision. Today, rivers had flowed from me, snaking in
endless currents. My throat constricted, the pressure so heavy
it almost severed my breath.

The scene before me had been plucked from the worst pages
of every fairy tale ever written—that moment when all seemed
lost, only to culminate in a tearful, happy ending. But I already
knew there would be no happy ending for me.

That had never been my destiny.

Naomi lay closest to the door, her body sprawled on the black and silver rug that ran the length of the narrow room. The dark stone walls were punctuated with wide arched windows, brambles obscuring the view outside.

Doing what I could to cover her, I pulled the front of her diaphanous dress closed, trying to wrap it so it wouldn't pop open. When I was done, I grabbed her by the arms and dragged her toward the hall. Yellow wings scraped the floor, and I winced at the sound. Shredded, their delicate membranes had been ripped from their frames, blood spattering them with crimson tattoos.

Naomi had been beautiful, as all Fae were. Thick copper curls were matted to her blood-soaked skull. Deep and red and gaping, her pale, creamy throat had been slashed almost to her spine.

What would possess a man to do this?

"I'm so sorry," I whispered. "You deserved a better end than this, and you deserve a better burial, too. I'm sorry this is the best I can give you."

With the back of my hand, I scrubbed more tears from my cheeks and then tugged on Naomi's arms, dragging her further. Though she was slight, we lurched, inch by laborious inch. This was going to take forever.

My stomach growled. Whatever enchantment had kept my body suspended for so many years—requiring neither food nor water—had worn off. The sensation of nausea and hunger collided, threatening to dredge up the lining of my stomach yet again.

But I forgot my inconvenient human needs when a groan echoed from the far side of the room. One of the Fae rolled over, and I gasped, dropping Naomi's arms.

"Are you okay?" I called, running across the room and dropping to my knees.

A shallow wound on the Fae's ribs oozed red, as did a cut on her forehead. Blood coated both the side of her face and the expanse of her minty green, shimmering dress. They were superficial wounds, and I breathed a sigh of relief. If just one Fae had survived, perhaps everything wasn't lost.

Kianna raised a slender brown arm, placing a hand against her forehead. Her warm, dark skin glistened in the weak sunlight filtering into the room.

"I think so." Her shaky voice was high and musical. "What happened?"

I helped her sit up, and her eyes grew wide as she took me in.

"Princess Thorne, what happened to you? Is that your blood? Are you hurt?" Her eyes then expanded even further into dark orbs of surprise. "You're awake? The curse! It's broken!" Light beamed from her expression, but a glance at my face made it dim as quickly as it had come.

"I'm fine. This isn't my blood."

Kianna then let out a soft cry as she surveyed the room, a sob pressing from her throat. "What happened? My sisters. What happened to my sisters?"

I recounted the tale of the man in the red coat. "I'm awake, but the rest of the castle is asleep."

Kianna pushed out her bottom lip, eyes shifting to the side. "Then my spell didn't work."

She had been the twelfth Fae. The one to counteract the curse her sister Mare had placed on me—instead of enslavement, an eternal sleep. I'd never figured out why that was meant to be better.

"We need to get out of here." She clutched my arm, nails digging into my skin. "That man may come back."

"I killed him." My words were matter-of-fact. They had run through my head on a loop, over and over, as I attempted to distance myself from what I'd done. *I killed a man.* But as Kianna bore witness to my sin, they became part of me, etched in indelible ink.

A killer. Now and forever.

He'd deserved it and, given the chance, I'd do it again. I had never taken a human life, and I wanted to cry and vomit all at the same time, but I had work to do.

"You killed him? How?" Kianna asked.

"With the dagger Andrick gave me." I shrugged as Kianna squeezed my arm again. "It was still attached to my leg." Scanning the beautiful Fae from head to toe, I asked, "Did he...use you?"

Kianna's face went blank for several long moments. "I don't think so," she finally replied.

It was only a sliver of hope, but I allowed it to prick my skin and slide under the surface. Slivers were all I had.

With her hand still on my arm, Kianna spoke as if to herself. "This was not how it was supposed to work."

"How was it supposed to work?"

She turned, her mouth open, as though she'd forgotten I was there.

"You were very brave." Awe filtered into her voice as she canted her head and pierced me with keen brown eyes. "Bravery is not one of your gifts."

I blinked. *Right.*

Eleven gifts befitting a princess had also been granted the same day as the curse.

Bravery was not one of them. Killing a man wasn't, either.

"I was going to bury them." I gestured to the surrounding bodies.

Kianna studied the slain Fae, silvery tears lining her eyes. She nodded and stood. Her wounds were healing already, thanks to her Faerie blood.

"I can do it." I placed a hand on her shoulder. This felt like my responsibility, though I wasn't sure why.

"No, Your Highness, they were my sisters. I will help you."

Together, we carried the eleven Fae to the forest clearing, gently laying them in their graves and crossing their hands over their hearts. It was hard and strenuous, and neither of us said much, lost in a labyrinth of thoughts that twisted and folded in on each other.

Now, we stood in the throne room over the body of the man. He was much bigger than me, and at least twice the size of Kianna. I picked up the sword he had brandished, studying the blade. Beautifully rendered, it was decorated with intricate scrollwork and embedded with an array of pale jewels. But its primordial energy was gone. Maybe I had imagined it, giving it significance when it had threatened my life. It was nothing but an ordinary blade, with no more power to hurt me.

I tucked it in the back of my belt and bent over. "Take his arms." I gestured to Kianna. "On the count of three, let's try to shift him."

We heaved as hard as we could, only dragging him a few inches.

"Damn," I said, pressing the heel of my hand to my eye socket. Kianna's gaze widened at my language, and I snorted. "Oh, don't be so shocked. We're going to have to roll him."

Little by little, we shoved the man's body out of the castle. By the time we'd rolled him into the clearing, the sky glowed in hues of orange and pink, pale stars winking overhead.

It was a beautiful sky for an ugly day.

We heaved the man into his assigned plot. His stomach—born of too little activity and too much gravy—protruded above the ground. But I was beyond weariness, and I couldn't dig anymore. It would have to suffice. I dropped his sword next to him, kicking dirt over it.

While the sun set, we filled each of the holes. Kianna moved between her sisters' graves, bloodied green tulle trailing in the dirt behind her, its edges ragged and torn. As she passed the graves, flowers sprouted, forming patches over each Faerie's resting place.

"What about him?" she asked as we stared at the man's humped burial plot.

"Fuck him. He can rot in hell." I spat on the earth. Again, Kianna regarded me with wide-eyed wariness. Ignoring her, I turned back to the castle.

The sky was dark now, silver embers reflecting off midnight blue. I rubbed my arms, wincing at the burn of cloth against my flayed palms.

"I'm starving. Let's hope the food slept, too." Exhausted, hungry, and furious, I stomped to the castle.

Kianna flitted behind me, saying nothing as we entered the dark building. Sconces lined the walls, but I didn't know how to light them. Kianna flicked her wrist, and they flared to life as flames sparked, casting shadows across every surface. I nodded to her and pulled the castle doors shut, sealing us in.

A thick beam sat propped against the wall, and I slammed it into the brackets. Staring at it, I chewed my bottom lip, deeply mistrustful this bit of wood would protect us. What I wouldn't have given for a few guards. Inside the throne room, I picked up my father's sword.

"Which way are the kitchens?" I asked Kianna.

"Don't ask me." She stood on her tiptoes in front of a guard, nose pressed almost to his before she poked him in the cheek.

"Stop that! They won't wake up. Your spell is a disaster."

An unnecessary comment—I felt guilty for it immediately, especially seeing the hurt that crossed Kianna's face. But I was also in too foul a mood to apologize. I wasn't wrong, and my relationship with the Fae had always been complicated. Today had changed nothing between us.

Reasoning the kitchens must be near where we ate, I headed for the dining hall. My already cloudy mood grew even darker as I realized how incapable I was. I'd been coddled and protected like a delicate glass rose. I didn't even know how to find the kitchen in my own home. It had never been required of me—someone had always been there to see to my every desire. The uncomfortable truth was this: no one had expected me to be here long enough for it to matter.

A servant's hallway ran parallel to the dining room, ending in a staircase that opened to an enormous kitchen. Dozens of people—an army of cooks, bakers, and servers—slept in corners and flopped over furniture, faces pressed to any surface that had been nearby. Whatever fire burned in the large stoves had long fizzled out. Silence permeated the walls and the floor, a reminder of how alone we were.

Everything was suspiciously clean and free of dust. Like it had been only yesterday they had gone to sleep. Was this part of the magic, too?

After poking around in cupboards and wooden boxes, I found bread and butter and jam, a bottle of wine, thick links of salami, and hunks of crumbly white cheese. I was used to feasts served on fine plates with even finer silver. Delicate bites and nibbles, like a princess was meant to eat.

Picking up a piece of bread, I tore into it with my teeth, following it with a sizeable chunk of cheese and stuffed it all in. My mouth slightly open, crumbs sprayed out while I chewed with vigor, savoring the saltiness. Savoring the freedom from polite manners. No one but Kianna was here to scrutinize me, but I was making her nervous. She watched me as if I were an animal testing the bars of its cage.

"Eat." I pointed to the food. "And stop looking at me like that."

With a nod, Kianna slipped onto a stool across from me and nibbled on a corner of cheese, her gaze flitting about the room like a fly trapped in a jar. I poured the wine, filling my glass to the top and taking a large, slurpy gulp.

A line of concern formed between Kianna's perfectly arched brows.

Done with the food, I stood, taking the bottle of wine with me in one hand. In the other, I held my father's sword, dragging it behind me as I stalked upstairs. My bedroom sat at the back of the castle, overlooking Lake Ravalyn.

A huge bed sat in the center, draped in dark blue velvet and adorned with silver embroidery. The stone floor was covered in thick blue rugs. I kicked off my dirty slippers, feeling the fibers squishing beneath my feet. My black hair was plastered to my forehead and cheeks, and blood and dirt streaked the backs of my brown hands. A glimpse in the mirror revealed more of both on my face.

Inside the bathing chamber, I stared at the empty marble tub. I wanted a bath, but this wasn't something I'd ever done for myself, either. Nothing happened when I turned the polished silver taps. Whatever water once ran through the castle's plumbing had long since dried. With no one to bring me hot water, my hands balled up, frustrated at how incapable I was.

"Kianna!" I called over my shoulder. "Kianna! Come here!"

A few moments later, the Fae came running, her steps tiny and delicate. "What is it, Your Highness?"

"Can you make me a hot bath?" I didn't understand the full capabilities of her magic, but surely it had some use beyond curses that didn't work.

Kianna nodded, waving a hand over the tub. It slowly filled with soapy water, steam curling off the surface.

I stripped out of my dress and stepped into the water. Sinking down into the tub, I closed my eyes and rested my head on the edge of the basin.

"Enjoy, Your Highness," Kianna whispered before leaving.

Guilt burned in my chest. She was the only one I had right now, and I'd have to plow through the years of resentment I had built up around me. Though she was to blame for messing up this damn curse, I'd been too short with her today.

After all, it wasn't her fault she'd needed to cast it in the first place.

CHAPTER THREE

MY BIRTH WAS HERALDED across our small kingdom to fanfare and fireworks.

Unable to bear children, my mother had pined for me for years. Desperate with longing, she had sought the aid of every witch, sorcerer, Fae, mage, or purveyor of magic she could scoop from the land. Carted to Ravalyn, they came from kingdoms that dwelled in the furthest reaches of the continent. From across the widest and most ferocious seas. From every shadowed corner where rumors whispered of gifts that could bequeath a child to a woman who desired one above all else.

She guzzled tonics and potions and slumbered with crystals and stones, potent with spells, beneath her pillow. She ate cheese strained through lamb intestines, drank wine brewed from the rarest of fruits, and even stuffed herbs into her teeth every night, hoping to conceive. But none of it yielded her heart's yearning.

It wasn't until my mother was walking through the woods one day that a Fae—resplendent and shimmering—appeared before her. My mother's face was stained with tears, and the Fae asked what troubled her. My mother then regaled her with the whole of her woeful tale. How she had tried everything to conceive, and nothing had worked. How she had prayed to every deity in the heavens, but her pleas had gone unanswered.

The Fae clasped my mother's hands in her own. "I will grant you the child you seek. Return home. Soon, you will bear a daughter of surpassing beauty, grace, and light."

My mother was hopeful about the Fae's claim but had suffered through countless disappointments already. If so many others had failed, how could this Fae be the one to finally grant her wish?

Nevertheless, my mother did as the Fae had asked and, much to my parents' delight, she fell pregnant. Nine months later, I was born, fists clenched and wailing, to a world that had been waiting for me for a very long time.

Word went out across Ravalyn and to our neighbors. Thousands came to the unveiling days after my birth, including thirteen Fae bearing gifts for a princess. One by one, they presented me with virtues befitting my role as the heir to the kingdom.

Elegance. Poise. Chastity. Fastidiousness. Patience. Gentleness. Modesty. Humility. Grace. Refinement. Cheerfulness.

After the eleventh Fae had imparted her gift, the twelfth stepped forward and threw back her hood. My mother recognized the Fae who had promised her a child. No longer gentle and kind, she stood forged into a ruthless nightmare. The benevolence of her promise was now twisted and shaped into a dagger pointed straight at my mother's heart.

"I gave you this child. And on her twenty-first birthday, you will return her to me to spend the rest of her days in my service. *Your* suffering will be my greatest reward."

And then Mare disappeared in a haze of fog, much to everyone's shock. A ripple of chatter ran through those in attendance, confusion stirring the air. My mother nearly fainted, my father holding on to her tightly.

But there had still been one Fae left to grant her favor, and it had been Kianna. She stepped forward and then, with a wave of her hand, marked me forever. "On the day before your twenty-first birthday, you shall fall into an eternal sleep, so that my sister may never enslave you or claim you as her own."

And thus, I grew up under the shadow of not one, but two curses.

For many years, my parents pretended nothing would happen. That it was all a cruel trick and none of what Mare or Kianna had foretold would come to pass. And for a while, I believed them. I think we all did. We became masters of disassociation, separating the truth as it was from the truth we all hoped for.

The twelve Fae remained at my side in the castle, declaring themselves a line of defense wrapped in gossamer. Perhaps it was a misplaced sense of guilt that kept them here, feeling responsible for Mare's actions. Whatever it was, they stayed to ensure I grew up fit to rule Ravalyn as they tried to find a way around their sister's curse.

We never heard from Mare again.

A tear ran down my cheek, weaving an itchy path down my skin. It splashed into the bath with a resonant plop. The Fae hadn't been my friends. Not really. Their job had been to protect me from Mare. But they had also been a constant presence in my life and losing all but one today punched a hole in my heart.

Finished with the bath, I wrapped myself in a towel and padded into the bedroom. From the closet, I dug out a pair of buttery calfskin leggings and a dark tunic. I braided my long black waves into a single plait and pulled on a soft pair of brown boots. Too restless to sleep, I picked up the bottle of wine I'd brought from the kitchen along with my father's sword and stalked through the halls. It was fully dark outside now, but the torches were lit—thanks to Kianna, I presumed.

Tomorrow, I would have to figure out what to do next. I had killed a man, and his clothes and his horse suggested he would be missed.

But tonight, I needed a moment to breathe.

I entered the throne room and kneeled before my mother, arranging her midnight curls over the bloodstains I'd left so they were no longer visible. The only other sign of today's violence was the dark stain of blood against the far wall. Tomorrow, I would have to clean that up, too.

Like a scared child cowering from ghosts, I leaned against my mother's legs, wrapping an arm around her calves. She was warmer than I'd expected. Sitting like this, so still and lifeless, it was easy to forget she wasn't dead. Though our relationship was complex, my parents had always been loving, even if they'd expected a daughter who was more of a proper princess than the one they'd gotten.

Still, they'd never made me feel too bad when I couldn't quite master the correct dance steps or figure out which fork was which. Maybe it was because they knew none of it would matter in the end. They had accepted my flaws in the face of my cursed existence. My mother had wanted me so much, and I loved both of my parents, whatever their faults.

The wine warmed my blood, my head spinning in a languorous arc like a pinwheel through fog. I wasn't accustomed to more than a small glass with dinner, but after waking from an enchanted sleep to be assaulted and almost murdered by a feral stranger, I was allowed to indulge tonight. It felt good to let myself release. Increment by increment, the fist clamped around my ribcage slowly relaxed.

My grandparents stood off to the left of the dais, leaning against each other, my grandmother's head tipped against my grandfather's shoulder. I missed them, too. Some of my happiest memories were in their chalet, deep in the woods.

Most of my family had come for the occasion. All here to bear witness to my eternal slumber. There were aunts, uncles, and cousins, and the heads of noble houses, too. I wondered what had become of the rest of their families.

On the steps off to my right lay Adrian, his head cradled in his arms. A small smile crossed my lips as I remembered the last time we'd kissed, hidden in the forest. How different everything had been then.

Soft footsteps drew my attention to Kianna. She, too, had found a bath and a clean dress. The green layers of chiffon floated around her like layered tulips. Her opalescent wings twitched as she approached. Tight black curls stood up around her head, forming a halo that framed her delicate round face.

"Kianna, I'm sorry. I shouldn't have been—"

She held up a hand. "Your Highness, do not worry about it. It has been quite a day." She sat down on the step next to me, pulling her knees up and wrapping her arms around them.

"How long has it been?" I asked her.

Kianna slowly studied the sleeping bodies, her mouth pursed in a bow. "One hundred years," she said with a sigh. "To the day."

"How do you know?"

She shrugged her slight shoulders. "It's my magic. I can tell."

I pondered that for a moment. "What happened? Why is everyone asleep, Kianna?"

"That, I don't know. I must have made a mistake when I cast the spell."

"What about the brambles? Where did those come from?"

"Another side-effect of the curse. A protection from the outside."

I huffed out a derisive laugh at that, and Kianna winced.

"Do you think they were all broken?" I asked.

"What do you mean?"

"I mean, your sisters said I was to be poised and patient and elegant. I am none of those things. I was never any of those things. Maybe none of it worked the way it was supposed to. That's what you said this afternoon, wasn't it?"

Kianna chewed her lip, caution in her eyes. "But you did fall asleep on the day before your twenty-first birthday."

"Yes, but so did everyone else. Was that the plan?"

"It wasn't. I don't know how that happened."

"Could it have been Mare?"

Kianna shook her head. "No. My sister wanted you very much."

"Why did she want me? Why give me to my parents only to take me away?"

"I don't know that, either," Kianna said. "Mare was always...different from the rest of us. More ambitious. More ruthless. More cunning than me and my sisters."

I snorted. "So it would seem."

We sat in silence for a moment. I held the bottle of wine out to Kianna, who gave it a careful look. Then something flicked in her expression before she smiled. She grabbed it and took a long gulp, tilting the bottle back.

"So, tomorrow is my twenty-first birthday, then."

"Yes, I suppose it is, Your Highness."

"Stop that." I scowled. "We're the only two people here. Call me Thorne."

Kianna nodded, that wary look in her eyes returning. "What do you want to do for your birthday?"

I bent my leg and pressed my chin to my knee. "I don't know, Kianna. Maybe we should have a party. Just you and me, in a castle full of cursed humans. It can be the most depressing celebration ever."

CHAPTER FOUR

S TILL CRADLED ON THE stone dais at my parent's feet, I awoke. Kianna lay nearby, breathing softly, her head pillowed on top of her hands and her knees tucked up to her stomach. She'd stayed here with me last night, instead of finding her bed, and something soft condensed in my heart, like clouds whipped from the finest cotton.

We had never been close. None of the Faeries had been here for companionship, but the thought of losing the one person I had left stuck in my chest like tar.

The air in the room was frigid, the wind battering the windows. Once the snow fell, the enormous fireplace along the wall would need to be lit or we'd both die from the cold. She must have been freezing lying on the stone floor. I pushed myself up and shook her gently awake. Kianna blinked, her large brown eyes dreamy with sleep.

"You should go to your bed," I said. "You'll be more comfortable."

She nodded and stood, padding out of the throne room on bare feet.

I watched her leave, summoning my strength to face another day with all the potent ferocity of a wounded lion cub, and then headed to the kitchen. I dug into the bread and cheese from last night. A cup of tea would have been nice, but I didn't know how to light the stove. Maybe Kianna could do it later.

After eating my fill, I picked up my father's sword and headed back through the castle, stopping in front of a sleeping guard. A shock of red hair sprouted from his head, his trim body slumped against the dining room wall.

Careful not to disturb him, I untied his sword belt and wrapped it around my waist, sheathing my father's blade. The heavy weapon pulled on my hip like a weight, dragging me to the bottom of a turbulent ocean. Andrick had only taught me to use a knife, but that didn't feel like enough. A knife could kill a man—I'd already proven that. But premonition told me men would become the least of my worries.

Soon, I would have to face down monsters.

I also pilfered several knives and daggers off the guard, tucking them into my belt and tunic. Branded with my skirt of steel, an insignificant sense of security wrapped around me, as flimsy as a cage made of wheat. I had no idea what lingered outside the castle walls, but I couldn't sit here waiting for it to come find me.

Exiting through the large castle door, I stepped into the morning light. Frost clung to the grass, delicate white tips sparkling in the sun like sugared emeralds. The sky was an icy blue, wisps of clouds streaking across it. As I made my way down the path, I rubbed my arms against the chill, my breath fogging the air.

Peering into the trees toward my haphazard graveyard, I was satisfied I couldn't see my way to the clearing. Stands of royal birch grew thick, preventing anyone from witnessing something I couldn't afford. Set into the castle wall was a wide-open gate, and I passed through it into the village that lay beyond.

Everything was quiet, the air distended with heavy apprehension. Drips of fear beat a steady pattern in my chest. After a pause, I took a deep breath, gathering the shreds of myself. One foot in front of the other, I continued walking, balancing on a razor-fine edge. I peered into the window of the first house I passed, the glass warped and cloudy. It sat empty, as did every house, belongings carted away along with whatever hope I'd kept clamped in my fist. Of course, everyone who'd lived here had abandoned this place while we slept.

The reality of our absolute solitude coalesced into a flash of electrified panic. My pulse quickened, spurred to life by the stark understanding that Kianna and I were completely alone.

Where had everyone gone? To nearby towns? Or had they deserted Ravalyn entirely?

This had been only a small village, sitting at the base of the castle and home to a few hundred people. Most of Ravalyn's citizens had dwelled in the towns and cities surrounding it. Farmland—the source of our wealth—stretched over these miles, golden and lush.

What had happened to those cities? Were they still there?

No one was asleep here, so I assumed the curse had only affected those on the castle grounds.

It was only another sliver of hope, but I held onto it as if it were a jewel plucked from a pirate's bounty.

There were so many things I needed to figure out. Mostly, how to wake everyone in the castle. Kianna didn't seem to have a clue, and I needed answers. But caution was crucial. It had been one hundred long years. Enough time for the world to have changed beyond recognition. I didn't know what I was up against.

And who was the man I'd killed?

Footsteps crunched in the gravel behind me, and I turned.

A woman with inky black wings prowled toward me. Her skin was marble white, and hair blacker than cursed shadows fell in sheets on either side of her face. She moved with sinuous grace, a viper slithering over a nest of twisted satin. Her lips were painted blood-red, and her eyes gleamed like golden lanterns while she stared me down through a curtain of thick, dark lashes.

Mare.

I'd been only days old when I last saw her, but the certainty of who I faced cratered deep into the marrow of my bones. I didn't need to remember her to know this was the Fae who'd sworn she'd take me for herself when I turned twenty-one. The Fae who had given my parents everything they'd desired and then snatched it away. The Fae who wanted to enslave me for a reason no one understood.

I pulled the sword from the sheath at my hip.

A slow smile spread across her crimson lips, forming a bloody slash against snow-white canines. "Well, well, well. Isn't it a *delight* to see you up and awake? My sister's talent for spells has never been very good."

"What do you want?" I pointed the sword at her.

Hands on her hips, she sauntered closer, coming to a stop right in front of me. The tip of my blade sat an inch from her heart. Head tilted, she considered me as though I were an ant sizzling beneath a magnifying glass in the sun. "Why, I'm here for you, my dear. Surely your mother told you that you belong to me."

"I belong to no one." I gritted my teeth, tightening my hold on the sword.

Mare laughed, the light and lyrical sound entirely at odds with her appearance.

"Oh, you are even more of a fool than she was." She gutted me with narrowed eyes. "You have always belonged to me, Thorne. You were simply...on loan. It's only because my sister got in the way that I've been forced to wait a very, very long time for what is mine. And I am *done* waiting."

She leaned forward, the tip of my sword now touching her breastbone. Sweat beaded on my forehead as I shook with the effort of holding the blade. Mare put her hand on the sword and pushed it down. The sharp edges pressed into her skin, and I tunnelled into my strength, trying to resist as blood welled up between her fingers. She didn't even flinch. Each one of her fingers was tipped in a silver metal claw, sharpened to a throat-slitting point.

With more laughter, her head arched back, exposing the expanse of her smooth white throat. "My dear Thorne. Do you think you can stop me? Your time is up."

Eyes flashing like twin pools of melted gold, Mare released the blade and flicked her hand. She had waited one hundred years for this moment, and her wings fluttered with the promise of a prize long withheld.

My limbs snapped into rigid lines as I braced myself, waiting for the tide of fate to sweep me away.

But nothing happened.

We stood on the same dusty road, the village as silent as ever.

Fury dulled Mare's eyes for a heartbeat before she recovered, gracing me with her simpering smile. "It seems my sister's magic is still keeping you here. No matter—there is a very simple way to deal with that."

Without another word, she spun and strode away, her midnight wings flaring, skirts billowing like inked sheets left on the clothesline.

Stunned, I watched her retreat before I suddenly understood her plan.

I slammed the sword back into its sheath and started running. Only she was faster. Her wings lifted her into the air as she hurled a piercing look over her shoulder. We both knew I couldn't hope to catch her, but I ran anyway, my legs churning against the dusty road.

"Come back here!"

Mare laughed, and I ran faster. I couldn't let her reach Kianna. We passed through the gates, my arms pumping as Mare raced ahead of me, a murky streak on the horizon. The dark Fae disappeared through the castle doors, and I held my breath, fearing she would lock me out.

But I skidded against the door, fingers gripping the edge as I flipped myself around. Mare was nowhere to be seen, and I ran down the hallway.

"Kianna! Hide!" I screamed through the halls. "She's coming! Hide!" She had been sleeping when I'd left her.

Why did I leave her?

"Kianna!" I kept screaming, hoping she was awake and would disappear.

I turned a corner and crashed into a wall of green tulle and silk.

"Mare is in the castle." Panting heavily, I pitched my voice low, hands wrapped around Kianna's shoulders. "Your spell... It's preventing her from taking me, and she's coming to kill you to break it once and for all."

"Oh." Kianna's mouth formed a circle, her eyes spreading into rings of fear.

"Come on. You need to hide."

Hands clasped, we ran for the throne room. She could hide in the kitchen. We tumbled into the large chamber and both skidded to a stop.

Mare stood in the center of the room, a hand on her hip, waiting as if time moved only for her.

"Aren't you two adorable? Thinking you can run from me?" Her golden gaze swept over Kianna. "It's such a delight to see you after all these years, sister. Where are the rest of the nattering hens? I shall have to pay them a visit before I leave."

As I held my father's sword in front of me, Kianna clutched my arm, trembling like a wind-blown leaf skittering across stone. "Mare, stop this. Killing me isn't a guarantee the curse will break. You know that."

"True." Mare tapped her chin with a slender clawed finger, the metal filigree beautiful despite its clear and intended purpose. I imagined her using them to shred through my organs, relishing each slice as if carving up a perfectly seasoned roast for dinner. "But it doesn't hurt to try, does it?"

She was so fast; I didn't have time to react. With a flick of her wrist, the sword was wrenched from my hand and hurled across the room. As Mare rushed past me, she pinned Kianna against the wall, her shimmering wings spread like a dragonfly fossilized in amber.

Kianna whimpered as Mare raised a metal-tipped hand to her face.

I ran at them, wrapping my arms around Mare's tiny waist, and attempted to pull her off. Mare whipped out a hand and sent me flying across the room. I landed on my back, the breath hammering from my lungs. My shoulder and ribs smoldered from the scrape of stone on my skin. Teeth bared, I launched myself up and hurtled toward the two Fae.

Mare had Kianna's throat gripped in her fist, and it must have finally occurred to Kianna that she could defend herself because, a moment later, it was Mare who went flying. But she flipped in the air, her wings beating as she righted herself and hovered several feet from the ground—an angel of death, delivering judgment from the heavens.

Delicate as a dandelion seed, she drifted to the floor, hands on her hips, and sighed with the weariness of an exasperated mother. "I'm not going to hurt you, Thorne." She tossed me an irritated look. "I just need to deal with this little problem, and then we can live together, happily ever after. As it was always meant to be."

"I am not going anywhere with you." Feet planted, I steeled myself for her next attack.

"This would be so much easier if you'd accept your fate. There is no running from this."

As she raced toward me, I rushed in her direction, too. That caught her by surprise. It was only for a moment, but it was enough to knock her over. My shoulder made bruising contact with enough force that she went skidding along the floor, crashing into the wall.

Kianna and I both ran for her. I leaped on Mare, wrapping my hands around her throat, and she let out a scream so loud, so piercing, and so soul-jarring that it shocked me into letting go.

Mare kept screaming as I stumbled back, the walls rattling and blood pounding in my ears as she lurched to her feet. A long gash had appeared, traveling from her shoulder to a spot above her heart. It was a gruesome and gaping thing. She clutched at it, blood gushing through her fingers as her scream finally died.

Blood dripped down the front of her dress, soaking into the midnight fabric. "You cannot escape me, you filthy brat." Her dark eyes glittered with an incandescent rage so visceral it shifted the air in the room. "You are *mine*. You will always be *mine*."

In a puff of black vapor, she vanished, and I stared at the spot where she had stood, my heart galloping and my breath shuddering.

"You got rid of her," I said to a shaking Kianna. "Sit down." She eased to the floor, my arms wrapping around her. Mare's words cycled over and over in my head.

You are mine. You will always be mine.

She truly believed that. Believed it with every tick of her starving heart.

Kianna had saved us this time, but Mare would try again.

I leaned against the wall, pulling my knee up and tipping my head back, eyes drifting to the ceiling. Kianna didn't let go of my hand as the shaking in her limbs ebbed. Neither of us knew what to say.

Eventually, I broke our silence. "So, this is it, then. We either break this curse, or Mare is going to kill you and then take me."

Kianna nodded slowly, eyes edged in silvery tears.

I pressed the heel of my hand to my forehead, pressure building in every crevice like water against a dam. "Well, that's just fucking perfect."

CHAPTER FIVE

B *ANG.*

Another book slapped the wall with a crack, dropping
to the floor like a butterfly knocked unconscious. Books stood
in unbalanced towers, strewn about me where I sat in the castle
library, legs crossed on the floor with my back against a black
velvet sofa.

The room was small and cozy, with dark wooden shelves that
lined the walls and a large arched window filtering in the light
by which I was furiously flipping through pages. My movements abrupt, I'd already ripped more books than I'd saved. I'd
been here for hours, waking up while the sky had been dark,
my dreams punctuated with metal-tipped claws and blood-red
lips twisted into macabre sneers.

It was here Kianna found me, amongst the toppling ruins of
my paperbound frustration.

"What are you doing, Your Highness?" Her voice was cautious as she wandered the room and picked through the stacks.

Pain throbbed behind my eyes as I hunched over the book I was currently assailing with my thumbs.

"Researching curses and spells," I said, not looking up.

"You are trying to find a way to break it."

I glared up at her. "Yes, I'm looking for a way to break it. Don't you want to? Or are you keen to end up with your head mounted over Mare's fireplace?"

A hand fluttered to Kianna's mouth. "The things you say, Highness."

Issuing a grunt, I slapped the book shut. "This library is useless. There are hardly any magic books, and the ones I have found don't tell me anything. They're full of pointless spells on how to hex your mother-in-law or enchant your neighbor's pig. Nothing about breaking curses."

Kianna slid onto the plush sofa, picking up a slim volume and flipping through the pages. "Curses can be tricky things. Sometimes they demand an impossible price, one you might not be willing to pay."

"What is that supposed to mean?"

Kianna shrugged. "Magic doesn't always work the way we intend. Hence, why we're here now. Magic this powerful won't break with the flick of a wrist. It will require a sacrifice or a profound and immutable alteration of your life's path."

"What kind of sacrifice? What sort of alteration?"

She placed the book back on the table and stood to look out the window, brambles slashing across the view. Her voice was distant when she finally answered. "I don't know, Princess. I'm sorry."

Resentment fractured inside me, releasing a billowing fog of yearning. This wasn't only about saving Kianna from Mare. I wanted to speak with my parents. Feel the warmth of my grandparents' love. Relive the stolen moments of Adrian's kisses.

My life had been experienced in segmented pieces. A wall of impenetrable granite had spliced the years, dividing the time before the curse would fall and after. But the impossible had happened. I'd woken up on the other side, and this was a second chance at a life none of us had ever dared dream could exist.

Using both hands, I hurled the book against the wall, where it hit with an echoing crack. Kianna flinched, her forehead furrowing. I stood.

"Well, that's extremely helpful," I said as I stormed out of the library.

In need of air, I headed to the back of the castle, finding the rear courtyard doors. They stuck as I shoved against them, brambles barring the way. With my father's sword, I sliced them down like paper streamers.

Why had anyone tried to climb up if they were so easy to cut down? Had they lost their power when I awoke, too?

More brambles snapped and tumbled at my feet as the door swung open. Stepping over the detritus, I entered the courtyard banked against Lake Ravalyn. The glassy surface stretched for miles, disappearing over the horizon. It would freeze over soon. Already, I could see the edges of frost forming on the rocky shore.

Here was where my father's guards had trained. Racks of gleaming weapons still lined the walls. His sword came with me everywhere now—a lifeline to my survival. Faced with Mare's threats, brute strength was my only defense. Though she possessed magic I could never match, yesterday had proven she could still bleed. When she returned, she would be more furious than ever. I had to be ready to strike without hesitation.

I dragged one of the sparring dummies into the middle of the courtyard and whacked it with a practice sword. It teetered and then righted itself, mocking me. This was so stupid. I couldn't learn how to use a weapon by myself, against an opponent who couldn't fight back. Maybe I could convince Kianna to train with me, though I imagined that would be a hard sell. I didn't remember the Fae ever getting their hands dirty.

A bow and quiver of arrows caught my eye, and I retrieved them next. Across the courtyard, I faced the dummy, one eye closed. The bow was stiff in my hands. My arms protested when I pulled the string with an arrow nocked and let it fly. It went wide. Extremely wide as it plunged into the lake with an impertinent plop.

A memory came back of a day when I had stood in this same spot, watching my father's soldiers train as a young recruit was reminded to shoot with both eyes open. So, I tried again.

This time, the arrow still went wide, but stayed within the boundaries of the courtyard. Okay—this was something I could work with. So I kept firing arrow after arrow until I managed a shot straight through the dummy's heart. It wasn't much, but at least it was something.

Drenched in sweat, my arms and back ached from the effort, but for the first time since I'd woken up, I felt some sense of control over this situation. Maybe I could do this.

A breeze blew off the lake, chilling my flushed skin.

Ready for a break, I headed down to the kitchen.

Kianna stood in front of the hearth, palms held up to a merrily crackling fire. "I thought we could have something hot for supper," she said.

With a nod, I moved to examine the ice boxes that were still cool, the raw meats stored inside still fresh. I wondered how long they would stay that way. The food hadn't spoiled while Kianna and I slept, but we didn't know how time moved in this post-slumber existence.

"I think we should cook all of it." I mentally catalogued the meat and offered silent gratitude to whoever had already skinned and cut the animals. Going from never having set foot in a kitchen to plucking my own chickens felt too much like tumbling down a flight of stairs on the way to self-sufficiency. "It will be edible longer, in case—"

As my words broke off, Kianna dipped her chin. She, too, had considered the precariousness of our supplies.

"Do you know how?" Kianna asked with a helpless look.

I sighed for the both of us, the sound brittle with dejection. We were a pair of newborn colts, abandoned by their mother and left in the wilds. It was a wonder we'd even lasted the night.

I tossed pieces of rabbit, chicken, and venison on the smoking grate. Together, we watched the meat char, fat sliding off and sizzling in the flames. Pale nuggets of flesh turned crispy and ochre, the heady scent of a feast filling the air. Maybe I'd underestimated myself. This didn't seem that hard.

A while later, we sat down with our dinner, the meat no longer a reassuring gold but blackened and dry. I'd overcooked it. Sinking my teeth into a morsel of rabbit, I tore at it. My jaw ached as I chewed, the texture rubbery and dense. This was nothing like the food I was used to, and a vague despair stacked itself onto my shoulders.

"This is terrible," I croaked, sucking in a big gulp of water. My mouth twisted as I faced down a chicken thigh like it was my last meal before being ushered to the gallows.

Kianna watched me with a dubious look, and then let out a delicate snort that blew through the chain of my pessimistic thoughts.

I blinked.

She covered her mouth, gaze glued to the table like it might save her from my glare. She was laughing at me. Her slender frame shook as she tried to hold in her giggles, but she was failing miserably. The sound was so contrary to the silence and stillness, it took a moment before I smiled, too.

It was the first one I'd cracked in over one hundred years.

And then my laughter snapped, bursting into a shower of sparks. It welled up out of me as the traumatizing events of the past two days gathered and dispelled.

But it wasn't only these two days that flew at me. It was one hundred and twenty-one long, terrifying years of tightly bundled fury and apprehension. It released, spinning from me like threads of fraying rope, unwinding in a heap at my feet. My eyes watered while Kianna lay with her face down on the table, her body shaking and her wings twitching with glee.

After a few minutes, our snickers tapered off, and we stared at each other as reality crashed in like a boulder dropped from the sky. Our situation was untenable. We were trapped here. I wouldn't leave my family unprotected and we couldn't wake them up. Mare would return soon, bearing the full and merciless weight of her wrath. Whatever magic Kianna had conjured wouldn't keep Mare away forever.

"Kianna," I whispered, my words digging a hole in the silence where I wanted to bury myself and hide. "What are we going to do?"

She reached across the table and took my hand, squeezing it. "We are going to be okay, Your Highness. We'll figure this out. You'll see."

Our eyes met, and I knew neither of us really believed that.

CHAPTER SIX

APPREHENSION STIRRED ME FROM sleep, tingles plucking the fine hairs on my arms like cello strings. The only illumination came from moonlight streaming through the windows of my bedchamber. The air pulsated with a thick promise of catastrophe. Something wasn't right.

Shoving back the covers, I swung my legs to the floor and slipped out the dagger I'd stashed under my pillow. Knife gripped in my hand, I walked across the thick carpet, my bare feet making no sound. Dressed in only my thin nightgown, I shivered in the cool night air.

A scream echoed outside my room, and my stomach liquified into an acidic sinkhole.

Kianna.

Though her bedroom was in another wing of the castle, she had moved to the one across the hallway from mine.

Another scream pierced the silence, and I hurtled for Kianna's room. Huddled in the corner, her arms covered her head. Mare hunched over her trembling form, a white, clawed hand stroking Kianna's black coils.

"Oh, good." Mare struck me with an ugly sneer. "I wanted you to be here to witness this."

"Don't do this. Leave her alone." I pointed the dagger at Mare, my arm shaking like the pathetic thing it was. "Please, don't do this. You don't even know if her death will break the curse."

"No, but I know keeping her alive won't, since it appears she is incapable of undoing her own magic. Isn't that right, my dear, idiot sister?" Mare gripped Kianna's chin and lifted her head. Kianna let out a squeak, squeezing her eyes closed. With her other hand, Mare dragged a metal tip down Kianna's smooth brown cheek.

"You were always the most pathetic one, weren't you? Such an embarrassment. Such a tragedy. Your death is a chance I am more than willing to take." Mare offered me a malicious smile before turning back to her sister. "You are going to make such a divine trophy. Perhaps, one day, I can collect the entire set." Her hand levered up, poised to strike.

"I'll go with you!" The words escaped in a thundering rush of ill-conceived intentions. Mare went still, arm halted in mid-air as she considered me. "If you give me time to break the curse, I'll go with you willingly once it's done. Please. I can't leave them here like this. Let me wake them up, and then I'm yours."

"No, Your Highness!" Kianna shouted, finally finding her voice. "You cannot!"

My focus on Mare, I ignored Kianna's pleas.

"I give you my word." My shoulders fell back, and my chin tipped up. I hoped I sounded surer than I felt. Mare's expression turned inward as she tapped her chin with a pointed claw. "Surely a willing captive is much easier to deal with than an obstinate one? You've already waited this long. What's a little longer?" I spread my hands in a helpless gesture.

Mare placed her hands on her knees and rose. A puckered scar ran across her chest. Red and angry, it had only partially healed. I reminded myself that whatever power she held, Mare could still be cut. At least Kianna's magic had managed that much.

I met Mare's gaze, trying not to tremble under her piercing golden stare.

"I do admit I am intrigued. *Can* you find a way to break it?" She tilted her head and scanned me from head to toe. "Very well. You have exactly thirty days. Break the curse yourself, wake up your miserable family, and then you come willingly with me."

"And you won't touch Kianna. Now or then or ever."

"Now or then or ever," Mare mimicked, her eyes narrowing. "But don't think you can trick me. I could kill her now and take you, anyway."

I acquiesced with a small tip of my chin.

"We shall see what you are capable of, little princess."

My lip curled as she took a step toward me, trying to force me back, but I stood my ground. A light winked in her eyes as if a thought as delicious as honey-soaked cakes had materialized in her hands. "And if you fail, I will not only kill her—I will kill every person who sleeps in this castle."

"Why?" The word lumped out in a gasp and sagged to the floor.

She patted my cheek and gave me a simpering smile. "Because I can, my dear Thorne."

My heart stilled in my chest, the air emptying from my lungs in a soundless scream.

What had I done?

Mare bared her teeth and checked an imaginary pocket watch, giving it a shake as if to spur a sluggish mechanism. "Tick, tock, Princess. I'll be keeping my eye on you."

Then, with a tight smile that didn't reach her eyes, Mare disappeared into the air, and I collapsed in a shaking mess. Pressing my forehead to the ground, I wrapped my arms around my head as I rocked back and forth. I couldn't breathe, my neck caught in an ever-tightening noose.

Kianna rushed to me, stroking my back with a delicate hand until I found my breath. Her voice was soft when she asked, "Why did you do that? You can't go with her. Do you know what she'll do to you?"

Abruptly, I sat up and turned a sharp gaze to the Fae. "I couldn't let her kill you, could I?"

Mare's last threat clanged in my ears like a dirge, a hammer smashing through the ephemeral future I'd constructed for myself. I'd thought this was a second chance for me. For all of us. My parents. My grandparents.

Every person I'd ever cared about was somewhere in these castle's halls, and Mare had already taken them from me the day I'd been born. This was no second chance. It was just another curse.

How many could I endure before I crumbled to ash?

Kianna's eyebrows knit. "You should have let her. That would have been easy compared to whatever she wants from you."

"Then you would be dead, and she would still have taken me. What good would that have done?"

Kianna nodded, though I could tell she wasn't convinced. The dagger still gripped in my hand, I clutched it to my chest. "At least this gives us time to figure something out."

CHAPTER SEVEN

30 DAYS LEFT

I COULDN'T KEEP HIDING here. Until last night, I'd been using the castle's thick stone walls as a shield, but Mare's threat had rooted into every corner, forcing me into the cold light of day.

The library had turned up nothing of use, and Kianna still didn't know how to undo her spell. I also wanted to learn what had become of the kingdom my family had once ruled. I needed so many answers. And I needed them fast.

Somehow, I would figure a way out of this. And when that happened, I wanted the life I'd dreamed of. One where I was the heir of Ravalyn, happy and secure with my family. I could marry a prince from a neighboring kingdom, and we'd form an alliance to protect and watch over our people until we withered with age, surrounded by the children and grandchildren we'd borne.

Besides, even if the food in the kitchen didn't spoil, eventually we would run out.

There were rows of spices and bags of flour and blocks of butter, but neither of us knew how to make anything using them. I was so tired of my helplessness. I'd learned how to needlepoint and play the piano and curtsy—utterly useless things that didn't matter to anyone except a privileged princess.

"I'm going outside," I said, peering into a bag of salt. "Find someone who knows how to break this curse and a town where we can buy more meat and bread and cheese. Hopefully, Tenby still exists, and if not, that man came from somewhere."

The castle's coffers were well-stocked, and the one thing we had was gold. The mechanics of commerce were one thing I understood, at least.

"No, Highness," Kianna said. "It is too dangerous. We must stay here."

I rolled my eyes. "And do what? Eat the rats?"

Kianna pouted, her face turning as green as her dress.

"We need information, and we won't find answers sitting here. Anyway, it isn't safe here either, is it?"

Not waiting for her reply, I donned my traveling cloak. Clad in a simple gray dress, I hoped it made me as inconspicuous as possible. For now, I wanted to remain anonymous in my kingdom. I didn't know what changes had transpired during my family's absence. No one had claimed my castle, but I thought of the skeletons caught in the brambles and wondered if someone had tried. That man in the red coat had arrived with some nefarious intention.

A small bag filled with gold coins hung from my waist, along with a dagger that wouldn't attract notice. My long black hair was tied back, and I'd removed all my jewelry—the diamond earrings and gold rings I'd always worn. It would only draw attention and, more importantly, it felt like clinging to some version of a life that no longer existed. One that might never exist again.

After lifting the barrier to the castle door, I headed outside, Kianna close on my heels.

"Are you sure about this, Your Highness? What if there are more men like *him* out there?"

"There will always be men like him out there, Kianna. Staying here won't change that. We need to eat, and we need to break the curse. You stay here and watch over my family. If I don't come back, then I guess you're free of all of this." I shrugged.

"Your Highness, don't say things like that."

I offered her a wan look and then stalked to the stables. I knew tending to the horse had been a good idea. I glanced at the boy asleep against the back wall. I was doing this for him, too. If I didn't break this curse, Mare would kill this child who was absolutely innocent of everything. I could not let that happen.

Leading the horse outside, I turned to Kianna. "Go inside and bar the door. Don't open it for anyone but me. Do you understand?" I didn't like leaving her behind, but a Faerie would only attract attention, and I was reasonably sure Mare wouldn't meddle until my time ran out. She wanted to watch me squirm.

Eyes wide, Kianna nodded as she studied me with trepidation. Lips parted, she appeared on the verge of speaking.

"What?" I asked.

"You are very different, Your Highness. Than before, I mean."

I stared at her, a memory surfacing of a day when I'd been fourteen, and Kianna and her sisters had been trying to teach me the finer points of attending a royal state dinner. Viviane had rapped my hands when I'd picked up the wrong fork for the salad and chosen the wrong glass for the apéritif. Eleven more Fae had loomed over me, correcting my every misstep. The way I had sat, the way I'd picked up my napkin, the way I had rolled my eyes at everything. I'd hated every minute.

"Poise!" one had shouted at me, followed by "Elegance!" from another. My gifts. The treasures they had so selflessly bestowed hurled like cannonballs as I'd failed to live up to their standards over and over.

I gave Kianna a look hard enough to compress coal into diamonds. My relationship with the Fae was not one I ever thought of fondly, more often than not rueing their presence in my life. They'd claimed they were protecting me, but all they had done was make me miserable. In a life already cut short, they had stolen so many seconds I'd never get back, wasting them on lessons I would never need. Time I could have been soaking in the tiny drops life offered a girl like me. Being stuck here now, with one of the Fae as my only companion, seemed like another cruel twist of fate.

"I'm not different, Kianna. You've never actually seen me before."

Before she could respond, I mounted the saddle marked with the same crest the intruder wore on his tunic. He'd carried no provisions, and I hoped that meant he hadn't come from far. There were once towns and villages nearby, but I worried about how much had changed in a hundred years. Time had stood still behind these walls, but the same couldn't be true of the rest of the world.

Reins gripped in my hand, I spoke softly to the horse, rubbing its neck. Kianna continued to hover, wringing her hands.

"Lock yourself inside. I'll be back as soon as I can."

"Be careful, Your Highness."

I nodded and trotted away.

Passing the abandoned village, I rode into the dense forests that surrounded the castle, thick with pines and silvery royal birch, their leaves almost completely white now. I looked behind me. Once visible from the road, the castle was now obscured by a hundred years of growth, and I breathed a little easier.

There was something permanent about this moment. Something that marked me forever, so deep it formed roots in my limbs. From the day I'd been born, Mare's hand had written my future. One I couldn't escape.

But all of that had fallen away, and suddenly, anything was possible. Even with her threat still hanging, at least a fork had appeared in the road. One that might lead to a happy ending if I chose the right path. Good or bad, potential glimmered like a beacon. I had woken up. I was here and in control of my destiny. As the horse trotted forward, I couldn't shake the feeling I'd taken a step from which I could never go back.

After several long hours of riding, I saw signs of an approaching town. Farmland transformed into homes and cottages lining the road. Before long, Tenby's stone wall came into view. Its enormous gates stood open as a stream of people and carts and horses passed in and out of the city.

No one marked me as I entered. Even before the curse, I had spent little time beyond the castle walls, and being here all alone gave me a curious thrill.

Along the busy streets, vendors sold fruit, bread, cheese, and wine. I got down from the horse, buying as much as I could fit into my pack.

As I tightened the straps over the horse's backend, I asked him, "What did that bastard call you? How about I name you Slumber?" I snorted at my own joke, but no one was here to care it wasn't all that amusing.

I spent the afternoon wandering the streets, enjoying the bustle of life and activity. Whatever this was, it was still all a second chance at something. What would happen if I disappeared and hid myself away forever? How hard would Mare search for me? Maybe she'd assume I was dead and give up. But I knew that path was impossible. Mare would kill Kianna and everyone in the castle; I needed to break this curse.

In front of a bookstore, I tied Slumber to a post. Inside the shop, crammed shelves ran through every inch of space, so crowded I had to shuffle sideways to fit through them. At the back of the store sat an old man at a desk piled with even more volumes.

"Hello?"

He pinned me with a watery blue stare. "Heh?"

"I'm wondering if you could help me?"

"Heh?"

"Can you hear me, sir?"

"Did you say something?"

"Do you have any books on breaking curses?!" I shouted.

He jumped in his seat and glared. "Why are you shouting at me, girl?"

"I, uh..."

"Curses? You want a book on breaking curses? It's not a curse, dearie. Go see the midwife. She'll help you take care of your little problem."

He gestured at my midsection, where I had my hands pressed to my stomach.

"No," I said. "That's not... What? No, a magical curse. I need to break a curse."

The man peered over the glasses perched on his nose, interest now piqued. "Is that right?"

I nodded, looking around me at the hundreds of books, reasoning there must be something more useful than what I'd found in the castle.

"That kind of knowledge isn't kept in books," he said, and my chest crumpled.

"Where is it kept? Please, I need your help."

The man tapped his temple with a bony finger. "Secrets like that are kept up here."

"So, you know? How to break a curse?"

"Bah! Not me. Whoever cast the curse. They'll know."

My jaw clenched as I summoned my patience. "No, she doesn't know. It didn't work the way she'd intended it, and now it seems to be...stuck."

The man gave an exaggerated shrug of his shoulders, as if my problems were of little consequence. "I'm only telling you what I know. Ask her again. Make sure she isn't holding out on you." He resumed his work, pen scratching along his paper.

"Please." I wasn't above begging.

With an exasperated huff, he pushed himself from the desk and disappeared into the rows of shelves. A few minutes later, he appeared with a shiny leather book in his hands.

"Like I already said, those kinds of answers aren't found in books. But if you insist on spending money in my store, don't let me stop you."

He handed me a thick volume titled *Common Magical Cures*, and I paid him extra, despite his assurances I was wasting my time. Even if that were true, the idea of leaving empty-handed sat like a stone in my stomach.

After I was back outside, panic shimmered on the edges of my vision as I clutched the book to my chest. If this man was right, no one could help me, and I only had thirty days until Mare returned. It wasn't enough time, though I got the sinking sense even a thousand years wouldn't be enough. I pressed my forehead to Slumber's saddle and let out a ragged breath.

Shouts rose then, drawing my attention to a large plaza where a crowd was gathering. Fists raised in the air, they seemed excited about something. I untied Slumber and pulled myself onto his back to gain a better view. The crowd had amassed around a wooden platform in the center.

On it stood two men dressed in black leather armor, chased with scrolling silver details. One had pure black eyes and silver hair the color of pewter, that hung to the middle of his back. His light brown skin appeared dusted with gold. The second man's bright blue eyes and fiery red hair stood out against pale white skin that shimmered pearlescent in the sun.

As the silver-haired man turned his head, I noted the telltale pointed ears. *Fae.* The redhead smiled at the furious crowd, displaying a set of sharp white canines, and my stomach lurched. Something terrible was about to happen.

My fears were confirmed as a group of men were escorted through the crowd and led up onto the platform. Thin and dirty, their clothing hung in rags, and raw wounds covered almost every inch of exposed skin. Their hair had been ripped out in clumps, and their eyes bore the haunted emptiness that came from long periods of torment.

The two Fae smiled as the ten prisoners were pushed in a row to their knees, their hands tied behind their backs. The iron-haired Fae walked around the men, his gaze assessing, mouth set in a hard line. He was magnificent. Wide shoulders and narrow hips descended into powerful thighs, every inch of him hewn from muscle that flexed beneath his armor. The redhead was pandering to the crowd as if this were the daily entertainment.

I realized that was exactly what it was. They chanted, their fury mounting to a point of explosion. The redhead raised his arms and, suddenly, every voice in the square went quiet.

At that moment, I noticed a small group of soldiers in the corner, dressed in similar armor as the Fae, though they were all human. Their ears were round, their skin absent of the same ethereal luminescence. Their demeanor spoke of authority and confidence, though a guarded wariness flickered in their eyes as they watched the Fae, hands never leaving the swords at their hips. I got the sense they were here to keep order, even if they weren't entirely sure how.

"For crimes of treason against His Majesty King Winston Avery Hammond Goldraven, these men are hereby sentenced to death!" shouted the silver-haired Fae, and my attention returned to him, forehead wrinkled. Who was this king? The name Goldraven was familiar, though I couldn't recall why.

The redheaded Fae raised his arms again, and this time, the crowd roared in ecstasy. Dozens more soldiers filed into the square, standing near exits as the Fae finally turned their sharp attention on the trembling prisoners.

"Liar!" one man on the platform shouted, his voice raw but impassioned. "Liar!" he said again with more force. "You are liars, and your king is a liar—"

His protest was silenced as his body cleaved in two, splitting right down the center from the top of his head to his groin. He collapsed on the platform in a mass of blood and viscera, spraying the rest of the prisoners and the audience below. My hand slapping over my mouth, I gasped at the wanton exhibition of violence.

"Does anyone else have something to say?" The silver-haired Fae asked, a splash of blood on his cheek. As the crowd jeered, he regarded the nine remaining prisoners, who watched with terrified expressions. Even from where I sat on the edge of the square, I could see them quivering. "I didn't think so. Not that your silence will save you, either."

Without further warning, the nine other men were similarly ended, the two Fae moving from prisoner to prisoner as blood coated their armor. The prisoners were each split down the middle in a scarlet haze of shrieking. The smile never left the Faes' faces, and the crowd cheered louder with every body that collapsed on the wooden platform.

The scene burned my eyes and my chest as though I'd been encased in a white, hot iron shell. Who was allowing this to happen? What kind of king delivered justice this way?

Once all ten men were dead, the silver-haired Fae spoke again, his voice molded from whisky and windstorms. "Let this be a reminder to the former subjects of Ravalyn should they try to deny the will, the word, or the rule of Estria and their true king."

At that, I almost fell off my horse.

Former subjects of Ravalyn? But my father was the king of Ravalyn. Embarrassment trickled in, slow drips singeing my cheeks at this monumental miscalculation on my part. Did I really think my father could disappear for a hundred years and his kingdom would remain unchecked?

Estria. A kingdom two weeks' ride from here. Now, I understood why the name Goldraven had been familiar.

My task had suddenly become so much more dire. More urgent. If I didn't wake up my family, I would lose not only them but everything that belonged to me. My birthright. My future. *My* kingdom. I could not fight another king with only a single Fae at my back.

The soldiers stationed throughout the square had dispersed the frenzied crowd into the streets. It was a practised maneuver. This wasn't the first time a demonstration like this had occurred. Some were angry, but most were tired and defeated, their protests weak and brushed away as easily as footprints in the snow. Whatever collective fury gripped them earlier had drained away.

The silver-hair Fae was staring at me with those deep, black eyes reflecting like an inky lake in the sun. There was a mixture of curiosity and menace in his expression, marred by the spattering of blood coating his burnished skin. A strange heaviness skipped in my chest as his gaze lingered a moment too long before he turned away.

The two Fae jumped down from the platform, their movements lithe and effortless, like waves gliding over shifting sand. They left the ten massacred bodies behind. A reminder to the people of Tenby of the cost of rebellion. For remaining loyal to Ravalyn. I watched as the Fae disappeared between the rows of buildings, the silver-haired demon flashing one final fleeting glance in my direction.

CHAPTER EIGHT

THE DAY HAD PASSED in a blur, and now the sun was setting. I considered turning back to the castle, but riding at night didn't seem prudent. Instead, I steered Slumber down a wide, cheerful street lit with lamps and bustling with people.

It was such a direct contrast to the horrific sight I'd just witnessed that it took me a moment to orient myself to the abrupt shift in tension. A tidy inn sat at the end of the block, and I directed Slumber toward it. Though I knew a woman traveling alone would raise suspicion, one roaming the roads at night would only invite trouble. I had more than enough of that to contend with at the moment.

Pulling up on Slumber's reins, I dismounted and entered the Whitefeather's spacious common room. A stout woman wiped the shiny bar counter lined with stools.

"A room for the night," I said. She regarded me with a raised eyebrow, wringing the cloth in her hands. "Please," I added.

Here, I was not a princess. Here, it was imperative I remain no one.

"Just you?" She wiped her hands on the rag, watching the door as if expecting a companion. A husband or perhaps a brother.

"Just me. I'm traveling to my aunt's in Kenthon. She is very ill." I plucked the name from my memory. A city a day's ride from here. The woman nodded, apparently satisfied with my explanation.

"Very well." She reached under the bar and pulled out a large iron key. "Third floor, last door on the left. It should suit you well."

"And my horse?"

"I'll have it seen to."

I took the key, nodding gratefully, and made my way upstairs.

As I descended from my room a short while later, the inn's common room buzzed with low conversation. I'd cleaned myself up and found a quiet booth in the corner that offered a wide view of the room without exposing me to prying eyes. What I'd heard in the square earlier left me feeling exposed. If King Goldraven had claimed Ravalyn, he wouldn't welcome my family's return.

Verna, the inn's landlady, had taken it upon herself to see I was cared for, fussing over me and bringing me a hearty stew, a loaf of soft white bread, and a large tankard of ale. I suspected she hadn't believed my lie about visiting a sick aunt, but she said nothing as she left my table.

I took a hesitant sip of the foaming cup; I'd never had ale before. It was bitter and made my tongue curl, but it also tasted like a tentative kind of freedom. I'd never been on my own like this, responsible solely for myself. I took a bigger gulp, wiping the froth from my upper lip. A small belch hiccupped from my mouth, and I snickered. If only Kianna could see me now. Maybe I'd bring some of this back with me.

A constant hum of noise was subdued by the memory of the slain prisoners. Who was this tyrant who had claimed my kingdom? What kind of man would allow such a demonstration to keep control? The prisoner had called the Fae liars, and I wondered whose truth the people of Tenby believed.

The tavern door opened, letting in swirls of frigid air. A light snow was falling, and I wrapped my shawl tighter as I wriggled into my seat.

The same armored soldiers I had noted at the execution entered. Two men and one woman, all armed and brimming with authority. My attention slid to the tall and muscular man standing in front, who must have been only a few years older than me. His black hair fell past his shoulders, the sides lined with two thick braids running along each side of his head. A pair of intense green eyes were set between a straight nose and high cheekbones that mirrored the lethal cut of his jaw.

My reaction straddled the line between flustered and captivated as I stared at his full mouth and the way he filled out the lines of his armor with the power and grace of a lion. He stood separate from his surroundings, more vivid and his edges crisper, as if someone had glued him to a blank sheet of paper. As he surveyed the room with the focus of a hunter, several other patrons stole secret glances his way.

This was stupid. I didn't have time for distractions, no matter how beautiful and chiseled they might be. Still, I couldn't take my eyes off him and enjoyed the view from a distance as he signaled to Verna and the three soldiers slid into the booth next to mine.

Hidden in the corner, I didn't think they'd noticed me. A moment later, a fourth person—an older man with graying brown hair and dressed in light brown leather—joined their table. Verna ambled over with tankards of ale for each, slamming them down on the surface. She chatted for a few minutes, clearly familiar with their presence.

"Enjoy," she said with a wink directed at the handsome one. Though she was old enough to be his mother, she was definitely flirting, and I smiled into my cup.

The four companions sat silently for a few minutes after Verna left, taking sips of their ale. Then the handsome one—in a low voice, clearly meant to be concealed from eavesdroppers—said, "This is where the trail goes cold."

Though I felt guilty for listening, I also scooted in closer so I could hear better. This man intrigued me. There was no harm in learning something about him.

"His guards claim he took a room and were stationed all around it, but in the morning, it was empty. His sword, his boots, his horse—all gone. No signs of struggle or foul play."

"He wouldn't have wandered off on his own, Ronan," said the pale woman sitting to his left. It was surprising to see her in armor—my father's soldiers had never included women. She was beautiful in a ferocious way, like a panther coiled to strike. Her long red hair was shaved along one side of her head, the rest plaited in an array of braids of varying thickness. Her light gray eyes wandered the room, assessing everything.

"It seems like that's exactly what he did," Ronan replied as he looked thoughtfully into his cup. "No one has come forward to claim a ransom or declare war. None of his guards saw anything. It's like he did indeed decide to walk away, but that makes no sense. That, or he disappeared into thin air."

Frustration in his voice, whoever he was talking about mattered a great deal to him.

"Let's knock on some doors," said the man sitting across from Ronan who I couldn't see, his voice guarded.

"And then what, Noah? Alert everyone that my father is missing? That the King of Estria has *disappeared?*"

Air seized in my throat. The king who'd ordered those deaths today was missing? The man who'd claimed my birthright? My hand curled against my glass, squeezing it. Perhaps with him gone, it would be easier to reclaim my lands.

"No one can know he's gone." Ronan's tone took on an edge that made me lean in closer. "The noble houses would begin plotting against us immediately, to say nothing of the neighboring kingdoms. They'd love a reason to march on Estria and an empty throne would be a very good one. This needs to be kept quiet."

The woman spoke again. "What about his royal asshole, Erick?"

"They won't recognize Erick without my father's approval or confirmation of his death," Ronan said, his face grim. "He'd keep them in check for weeks at best."

The four of them fell silent. I waited for them to say more, but their discussion appeared to be over. Nibbling at my stew, I waited for them to leave, worried they'd notice I had been close enough to hear if I left now. After another stretch of tense silence, they finally drained their cups and stood. Watching their backs as they departed, I slid out of the booth and headed to the bar where Verna was pouring drinks.

"That was delicious." I placed a gold coin on the bar top. "Will this cover it?"

Verna's eyes went wide.

"My lady, that is far too much," she said, her voice low. "Don't flash gold around like that in this town. That will get you killed, or worse." Her eyes flicked away and then back to me.

I frowned. I'd been handing these out to merchants all day. No wonder they'd behaved with such bewilderment, though none had thought to refuse me. I was such a fool. So much for my knowledge of trade and commerce. I'd been taught to trade grain for lumber, not coppers for bread.

"Thank you for your honesty. Please take it and hide it away, then."

Verna glanced past me, and I looked over my shoulder. The black-haired warrior stood right next to me, and I jumped, surprised to find him so close. Ronan glanced at the coin, still on the counter, and then over to me.

He didn't seem like the type to slit my throat over a bit of gold; his father was a king. But I swallowed a string of nerves as Verna made the coin disappear.

Ronan studied me, his bright eyes kindling with curiosity. His proximity wasn't exactly unnerving, but the look he was giving me felt like tender touches pulling up gooseflesh all over my skin. This close, he was even more beautiful to look at, the shape of his mouth and the line of his jaw worthy of an artist's canvas. Our eyes clashed, locking in place as my limbs hollowed out.

"Good night," I said to Verna, prying my gaze from his and forcing my leaden feet to move. As I brushed past him, I noticed the crest embossed on the chest of his armor. Slightly raised with a sheen, it was only visible in the right light.

It was the same crest the man I'd killed had worn. A circle, pierced with a flourished arrow. I'd sleep for another hundred years and never forget it. It *had* to be a coincidence. The man must have been someone in the king's employ who'd wandered off. It couldn't be the same father Ronan was searching for.

Panic expanded in my ribs. But deep in my gut, I knew the man buried in my forest was the missing king.

"Are you all right, my lady?" Ronan stared down at me from his warrior's height, a mixture of questions and concern. "You've gone very pale." Something inside of me shriveled like a flower in winter, sure the truth was splashed across me in vivid red paint. My harmless attraction turned to dust as he swept me with an appraising arch of his eyebrow. I had to get away from this man. My throat had turned to powder, and I couldn't force words from my mouth.

With a shake of my head, I hurried past him and clattered up to my room in a rush of swelling alarm. Unlocking the door and flinging myself in, I slammed it shut behind me.

I'd killed the king of Estria. I'd stuck a knife in his throat and killed him. The ruler of my rival kingdom.

He'd deserved it. I didn't feel one ounce of remorse for saving my life, nor for avenging the deaths of the Fae. But no one else would see it that way. *I killed a king.*

And his son—a warrior with an abundance of muscles and weapons—was going to kill me next.

I sank to the floor, taking down all my grief and worry with me. Wrapping my arms around my knees, I balled up all my emotions, squeezing them into a knot that burned in my chest like an ember hot from the fire.

Nothing seemed possible right now. Nothing was going right. I was going to lose everything and everyone I loved. I had been such a fool. There were no second chances for me—only an endless labyrinth of baited traps, waiting for me to make every wrong move.

CHAPTER NINE

29 DAYS LEFT

IN THE EARLY HOURS of the morning, my eyes flew open, a cold sweat boiling under the cotton of the dress I'd fallen asleep in last night.

The horse. *The king's fucking horse.*

If Ronan saw it, he might recognize it. Especially given the king's saddle was still strapped to its back. I'd been so distraught last night that I hadn't considered I was carting around a literal hand-painted sign pointing to my crime. I might as well have composed a song and performed it for the entire town.

I had to get out of here immediately.

With controlled movements, I slipped out of bed, hoping Ronan and his companions hadn't spent the night at the Whitefeather. But he was a prince, and Verna's appeared to be the nicest inn in town. Cursing a streak of colorful words that would have made Kianna blush, I laced up my boots and secured my cloak.

The room still dark, the sun was just peeking over the rooftops. When I made my way downstairs, the common room was empty save for Verna, who was polishing glasses behind the bar.

"Can I get you some breakfast?" she asked cheerfully, and I resisted the urge to shush her in her own inn.

"I need to be off. Thank you for your hospitality." I placed three more gold coins on the counter. It was far too much, and now we both knew it, but I hoped it would convey my urgency for a swift departure. After glancing at the coins, she gave me an understanding look and nodded as she pushed open the door behind her.

"Meet me out front," she said as she disappeared through it.

Verna was already bringing Slumber toward me as I stepped outside. A thin layer of snow covered the streets, and only a handful of villagers were about.

"Thank you," I said, taking Slumber's reins and pulling myself up, before heading through the city. As we exited out the gates, I signaled the horse into a gallop, and we sped away into the forest. With any luck, Ronan and everyone else in Tenby would have already forgotten I was ever there.

When the road leading to the castle appeared, I nearly collapsed in relief. After I dove into the cover of the trees, I finally let out a serrated breath. Since last night, my heart had been loping in my chest, sweat pooling in my lower back, thanks to the truth about the man partially buried in my forest.

Directing Slumber to the stables, I dismounted and unbuckled his saddle, hoisting it over my shoulder. A firepit, where the stable hands once gathered after the day's work, sat piled with logs. I dumped the saddle on top with a grunt. Inside the stable, I found a box of matches and lit one, holding it to the dry logs.

A neat stack of chopped wood was piled nearby, and I grabbed a log with each hand to bank the fire. It surged to life, the flames consuming the saddle. As I settled on the bench, I watched as the leather dissolved, releasing a distinct and unpleasant odor of roasting flesh.

My head dropped into my hands, too heavy to hold. I was no closer to breaking this curse, and someone had stolen my kingdom while my family slept. I'd killed a king, and his royal son—who carried a very big sword—was searching for him.

At a soft neigh, I glanced up to find Slumber watching me. I should slit his throat and bury him too, but I'd seen enough blood and death to last me many lifetimes. With resignation, I stood and clicked at the horse to follow. He trotted behind me with misguided faith, the poor, hapless beast.

We walked deep into the forest, passing through the clearing with the Fae graveyard. Kianna's patches of flowers bloomed with color, their cheerfulness belying the brutal deaths of the women they covered.

King Goldraven's grave was visible through the mound of dirt that protruded above the ground. The glistening white leaves of the royal birch trees formed a canopy that protected the earth from the thin covering of snow that had fallen last night. Frozen for a few moments, I stared at the king's grave and then shook my head. The foray into Tenby had shaken me. My problems kept mounting like bricks patched with scant layers of crumbling mortar.

Slumber continued to follow as we moved deeper into the forest, my feet crunching over the frosted leaves and branches. The sparkling canvas of winter had always been one of my favorite things. When I felt we'd gone far enough, I slapped the horse on his hindquarters and shouted at him to leave. Slumber cocked his head, and then did as I asked, walking into the trees. I hoped a pack of wolves would finish the task I was too cowardly to complete.

I'd need to find another way to return to Tenby, should the need arise. We only had twenty-nine days, and I was reasonably sure we could make the food last that long if we were careful. After that... Well, I didn't want to think about it right now.

Returning to the stables, I tossed the full saddlebags over my shoulder. Regardless, I had reason to avoid Tenby. How long would Ronan hang around the city, hoping for a clue to his father's whereabouts? I was even more grateful the dense forest shielded us from prying eyes.

"Kianna! It's me! Open up!" I pounded on the castle doors and held my breath, expecting her to have fled or died in some gruesome way while I was gone. A cord unhitched around my heart a moment later when I heard the beam shifting on the other side of the door.

Kianna yanked it open and peered out at me. "Any luck?"

I held up the bulging saddlebags. "Hungry?"

She grinned as I entered. We headed to the kitchens, where I unpacked my purchases. This had become my favorite spot to linger. Kianna kept the hearth burning on a low flame, and it was warmer and cozier here than in the rest of the castle.

I was quiet while we ate, lost in my thoughts.

"Something is troubling you, Your Highness," Kianna said. "Did something happen while you were out there?"

"My father's kingdom. *My* kingdom—it seems Estria has claimed it for its own." This was something I needed to unburden myself with.

"That is not surprising. They have always been ambitious, and with your father no longer able to defend his lands, they were bound to take what was left unchallenged for so long."

"I saw Fae in the town square," I said, and Kianna visibly reacted to that news, her shoulders bunching to her pointed ears. "Do Fae normally work for human kings?"

"What did they do?" She tremored as I recounted the horrors I'd seen. "They are cruel and unfeeling creatures, Your Highness. I don't know where their allegiances lie, but you'd do well to stay far away from them."

"Aren't they your kin?"

Kianna shuddered as she took a nibble of her bread. "Faeries come in many forms, mostly related to the strength and affinity line of their magic. Fae like me can perform various tasks but usually have no singular tie to any one kind of magic. That's why my sisters and I have wings. It marks us as those who descended from the union of the Fae queen and king of the Pixies thousands of years ago. The ones you saw in Tenby are pure Fae. Given what you described, they are probably aligned with blood magic."

Kianna didn't say much about the bookseller's proclamation that methods for breaking curses couldn't be found in books. I showed her the one I'd purchased, but she didn't look at it as she asked me about the inn and the tavern. I told her about Verna and the ale and my ignorance with the gold coins.

Kianna, too, had spent many years inside the castle, the human world outside a mystery. Before getting saddled with the care of a cursed princess, she had lived in the Faerie realms to the south. "Maybe I'll come with you next time," she said. I could tell the idea made her nervous, but I nodded.

If there was a next time.

I left out what I'd learned about the man buried in the forest, not ready to face it. I also didn't mention Ronan. I didn't want to worry her more than was necessary. It wouldn't solve anything. My first and only priority was to break the curse and free us from Mare.

I'd worry about dead kings and their royal sons later.

CHAPTER TEN

28 DAYS LEFT

K IANNA SAT ON A log, her face cupped in her hands and elbows planted on her knees, eyes tracking me like cynical metronomes. I'd begged her to learn how to fight with me, but she'd categorically refused. Instead, she supervised me by traipsing out to the forest where I would dance in circles, feinting and dodging against an invisible, and therefore, impossible to kill, opponent.

"You know this would be a lot more helpful if you took part," I said as my shallow breaths fogged in the cool morning air. My daily routine had included waking up with the sun to train with any weapon I could get my hands on. I derived immense satisfaction in hearing the *thunk* of my arrow as it sank deep into a tree from a hundred paces away, like I was arranging the broken pieces of a pattern and gluing them back together. I'd also practised my knife throwing, recalling the lessons Captain Andrick had drilled into me.

"Not happening," Kianna replied with a shake of her head, dressed in one of her usual sleeveless green dresses. She didn't seem to feel the cold. Her only concession to the onset of winter was a pair of white fur boots she'd dug up from the recesses of her closet.

"Why not?" I asked, swishing the sword. "We could practise against each other."

"I don't like getting sweaty." She wrinkled her nose as she scrutinized the line of perspiration running down my face. "Besides, I don't fight with weapons. It's undignified."

I grunted but didn't press her further. In the absence of any other plan, this was still my best defense against Mare. I had no intention of honoring my side of this bargain without a fight.

Still, I'd struggled without an opponent and had contented myself with reading books and performing practice drills, sometimes attacking trees when I was feeling particularly foul.

I thought of the red-haired woman who had been traveling with Ronan. How strong she had seemed. Surely *she* knew how to fight. Knew how to bring a man to his knees. She was a soldier. A woman who hadn't been left helpless, with nothing but a dagger to protect herself.

While I continued to move about the clearing, practising the footwork sequence I'd found in a book on sword fighting, I thought maybe I was improving. Maybe I could hold up in a real fight. I shuffled for a tree, slashing the heavy blade and scoring two gashes into the bark. "Ah-ha!" I cried in triumph, my arms raised.

A snort was followed by several deep voices bursting into laughter behind me. Startled, I spun around so fast that my heel caught a root, and I crashed to the ground, landing on my ass. The laughter doubled as my audience bent over, slapping their knees and holding onto their sides.

"That tree certainly has met its match," one of them said as I scrambled to my feet, rubbing the spot where a bruise would be tomorrow.

Was I surprised it was Ronan and his companions? Not really. At least the waltz with my nebulous fate was consistent.

My sword held aloft, my gaze flicked to Kianna, who was clutching her hands and staring at the newcomers with alarm.

This was it. They'd uncovered my secret. They knew what I had done to their king, and they were here to take their revenge. Arrest me. Throw me into confinement. String me up to the gallows and watch my neck stretch. Maybe they'd deliver me to the blood Fae to be sliced into a thousand fleshy pieces.

Except they were all still laughing and didn't seem like warriors bent on vengeance.

"Who are you?" I demanded, pretending I didn't already know.

Ronan was the first to regain his composure. "Forgive me, my lady. It's not every day you see someone fighting a tree. What exactly are you doing?" He crossed his muscled arms over his chest and tilted his head at me, those piercing green eyes finding all of my softest places. The forest sprang to life as he studied me, my senses thawing like a stream in the earliest days of spring. I'd never been so aware of the air in my lungs, the thump of my heart, nor the blood flowing in my veins. Shoving away my dizzying thoughts, I opted for righteous indignation to mask the heat sawing at my nerves.

But I was also sure there was still mud on my ass.

"I asked who you were," I said, not lowering the sword.

Ronan offered a formal bow. "I am Commander Ronan Goldraven." He then gestured to the bearded man with tanned skin, brown eyes, and dark blonde hair, half of it tied in a knot at the back of his head. "This is my second in command, Lieutenant Commander Noah Tallhelm."

Next, he pointed to the woman with fiery red hair. "This is my third, Lieutenant Emmaline Nilsen, usually known as Em. And finally, I present Gideon Baldsa." The fourth man, the older one dressed in brown leather, offered me a kind smile that crinkled the corners of his soft brown eyes, and I decided I liked him the best of this lot.

"What are you doing here?" I asked, trying to seem intimidating. The way Ronan was smiling at me, the corner of his mouth crooked up and his eyes sparkling, suggested I was about as threatening as a hedgehog.

A knot of panic formed at the base of my neck. Though they didn't appear to be intent on arresting me, they'd still found the castle through the overgrown forest, and their presence couldn't signal anything good. What were they doing on my doorstep?

Ronan's searing gaze raked over me, my throat swelling like I was trying to breathe underwater. I shook my head, dislodging the muddled wreath of my thoughts. What was wrong with me?

"We were passing through when we saw you and couldn't resist such a fearsome foe facing off against the forest." Now he was mocking me, and my feelings transposed into irritation.

"You're lying," I said. "What are you doing here? How did you find this place?"

"You were at the inn the other night," Ronan said, his demeanor sobering as he bestowed me with a serious look. My lips pursed into a line scratched into hardened concrete. *Shit.* He remembered me. "And as I said, we were passing when we saw the castle and hoped we could stop for shelter. It is a long way to the next town, and we won't make it there by nightfall. It appears a storm is brewing."

"No." I forged iron into my voice, hoping I sounded firm and in control of this rapidly deteriorating situation. "Absolutely not. You cannot stay here. You must leave this instant."

Suddenly, Kianna was standing at my elbow. I hadn't even noticed her move. "Your Highness." She pinched my arm, and speculation flicked in Ronan's eyes. I stifled a groan of frustration, wanting to pinch Kianna twice as hard for calling me that. "Don't be so rude. Of course, these gentlemen and this lady should stay and join us for dinner. I hope you'll forgive the simple fare. But you are welcome to what we have."

Incredulous, I flayed Kianna with a glare hot enough to melt glaciers.

She ignored me as she dipped into a quick curtsy, so I dragged her behind the tree. "What the hell, Kianna? We can't invite them inside. They're going to see everyone asleep and start asking questions."

"Maybe they can help," Kianna said, her hands clasped over her heart, her expression as bottomless as a well full of wishes.

Fingers pinched to the bridge of my nose, I asked, "How can they possibly help?"

"I don't know, but didn't you say you have no idea how to break the curse? What harm could it do?"

Maybe she had a point.

"Just dinner, Your Highness."

"Is everything okay? Should the rest of the trees in the forest be worried for their safety?" A deep voice drifted to our hiding place, accompanied by more snickers.

I tossed Kianna a dark look to convey the unending depth of my disapproval, and I stalked back around the tree, planting my hands on my hips.

"We would appreciate anything you can offer," Ronan said now, his hand pressed to his heart. His words felt sincere, even if the corners of his mouth were turned up in amusement.

Five pairs of eyes watched me, expectant, waiting for my verdict.

"Fine," I snarled at them. "Dinner, but you are not spending the night. Is that understood? I don't care if you freeze to death. That isn't my problem."

Kianna nodded as I pinned her with another glare, her eyes dropping to her feet. I was about to turn away when Ronan reached for the sword at his hip. Kianna let out a small screech that mirrored my own, and we both jumped back as I shoved her behind me.

Ronan held up his empty hands. "Sorry, my lady. I didn't mean to scare you. I thought you'd like a sparring partner who can fight back?" He glanced at the tree I'd been attacking and then arched a dark eyebrow that had me warring between thinking it made him even more devastating and wanting to slap him for his impertinence. "I may know a trick or two."

There was no doubt this man knew more than a trick or two. A scar bisected his eyebrow, and his large hands bore the marks of someone used to fighting. By his physique alone, no one would mistake him for anything but a seasoned warrior. He was almost a head taller than me, his broad shoulders filling out his armor like he'd been born with it on.

Still, I'd also learned a trick or two since I'd begun schooling myself in the fine art of swordplay. With a confident step forward, I nodded and pulled out my weapon. He did the same, and we circled. He blocked me with ease when I lunged. I tried swinging again and, as we sparred, it became rapidly clear he wasn't even trying. I couldn't get anywhere near him. I had learned nothing and was as helpless and useless as I'd always been.

Fury curdled thick in my limbs, and I was about to call a halt to this nonsense when he lunged for me, spinning the sword from my hand. To add to my humiliation, I tripped on the same fucking root and went down, a bolt of pain shooting up my spine and my teeth cracking so hard I felt it in the lining of my skull. It took every ounce of will I possessed not to throw a toddler-sized tantrum.

To his credit, Ronan didn't gloat. I wasn't sure if it was good manners or an attuned sense of self-preservation. The rest of his companions weren't so considerate, each of them staring at the ground, their shoulders shaking with tightly restrained laughter. Kianna gave me a smile that was one part apology and one part apprehension, knowing I was furious. Ronan offered a hand, but I ignored it and stood, picking my sword up and sheathing it with an irritated grunt.

My shoulders squared, I turned and marched toward the castle, not waiting to see if they followed. Of course they would. If the world had any sense of justice, they would all dissolve into the ether, but nothing in my life was that easy. The pounding ache behind my eye had returned, wearing a scourge on my patience.

Snippets of conversation drifted to my ears as Kianna laughed at something one of them had said. At least someone was having a good time. After I entered the castle, I briefly considered barring the door and leaving them all outside. Even Kianna. If she was so eager to have dinner with them, she could do it in the snow. Instead, I left it open and made my way down the wide central hallway to the throne room.

My muscles seized with tension when they approached. They couldn't fail to notice our circumstances. I was going to throttle Kianna for inviting them inside.

A few moments later, their heavy, booted steps accompanied a low whistle. I wanted to cover everyone in the throne room from their gazes. My family wasn't here to be gawped at like a three-headed goat at the circus.

Out of the corner of my eye, I watched Ronan, wondering how he would react. "It's real," he said, momentarily speechless, a touch of awe in his voice. I sensed he was a man who wasn't surprised by much.

"What's real?" I asked as he stared at my parents—not in judgment, but with glimmers of concern and curiosity.

"The stories. As children, we were told tales of the sleeping princess inside the castle. How people tried for years to get inside but eventually had to give up when the enchantment killed everyone who tried. Are you..." His gaze shifted to me.

"I don't know what you're talking about. I'm not a princess. And I'm clearly not asleep."

Inside my head, I was screaming so loud blood vessels popped in bright crimson bombs of apprehension. These men were dangerous. They belonged to the king who had stolen my kingdom. To the man buried deep in the forest, a wound from my dagger in his neck. If they knew what I'd done, everything I was holding would dissolve between my fingers. My plans were as fragile as a tower of champagne flutes. One wrong move, and the entire thing would topple and shatter.

"She called you 'Your Highness'," Noah said, pointing to Kianna as though he'd solved a great riddle. He took a small step back as I glared at him with the heat of a thousand bonfires.

With a turn on my heel, I headed for the kitchens. The sound of boots on stone followed me as my ardent wish for them all to dissipate into a puff of smoke failed to materialize.

Inside the warm, bright space, they all started pulling stools around the large central table. Ronan glanced at one of the kitchen staff asleep in the corner and raised that soul-destroying eyebrow again. Wisely, he said nothing.

"Would we not be more comfortable in the dining room?" Kianna asked, but the acrimonious look I gave her silenced any further comments on the matter.

"This will do," said the older man, Gideon. He started digging into our stores, pulling down bags of flour and butter as he grabbed a large bowl and an array of cooking utensils.

"What is he doing?" I whispered to Kianna.

Gideon must have been some kind of manservant who traveled with the prince and his companions. Ronan hadn't introduced himself as a prince, though, only as a commander.

As I was about to comment on how they couldn't travel without help—who was I to talk?—the rest of them got up and started pitching in, too.

Noah poured wine for me and Kianna while Em found jugs of ale, passing glasses around. Ronan brought over a stack of plates, laying them out on the table. It was a sight filled with warmth. One borne of countless nights and days spent in each other's company, the banter teasing and comfortable.

Ronan sat down across from where I stood. "Your Highness, please sit. You seem tense."

"I don't need an invitation to sit at my own table."

Ronan's answering grin was full of wry amusement that lit up his face like he was a gift from the sun.

What was so damn funny?

Still, I couldn't fault the artfully cut platter of cheese and cured meats Gideon had placed between us. It looked delicious, and I was starving. Trying to make it seem like it was my idea, I slid onto a stool while Kianna parked herself next to me.

"Kianna, was it?" Ronan gestured to her. "I haven't met many winged Faeries. The tales of your beauty are vastly underestimated."

She blushed with a coquettish giggle, and I rolled my eyes.

"And what may I call you, Your Highness?" Ronan looked between us. I considered the request and couldn't think of any good reason not to tell him my name. Other than I didn't want to.

"'Your Highness' is fine." I picked up a cube of cheese and popped it in my mouth, daring him to argue.

"She is Princess Thorne," Kianna piped in, followed by a squeak as my boot connected with her shin. She glowered at me, and I returned the look with amplified intensity.

"Thorne?" Ronan said, his expression somehow becoming even more entertained.

While I was losing myself in a haze of useless emotions, he apparently found me as hilarious as a court jester. Noah snorted, choking on his ale, and I noticed Em cover her mouth and look down as if trying to hide her smile.

"A fitting name for another beautiful woman." Ronan smiled again, and now I was positively sure he was mocking me.

Before long, the smells of spice and roasting meat filled the air. Gideon placed a tureen with poached fish swimming in a creamy sauce on the table alongside a tray of glistening roasted chicken legs and rounds of fresh, unleavened bread.

"Where did you find all this?" I stared at the bounty before me.

"In the cellar, Your Highness." Gideon sat down as everyone doled food onto their plates.

I'd never even thought to look for a cellar. Of course, there was more food. This castle was home to almost two hundred people. I was such a fool, but everything smelled amazing, so I stashed away yet another blunder and focused on the feast.

As I took a bite of the fish, I realized all my mistakes in the kitchen. A lack of seasoning, and I overcooked everything. Idly, I wondered if Gideon could teach me a few tricks, except these soldiers were leaving as soon as they were finished with supper.

But it was at that moment the wind picked up, howling so loud it whistled through the walls. Snow battered the glass like handfuls of gravel. I groaned as Gideon pressed his palms to the table.

"I'll see to the horses?" He hesitated, his eyes going between me and Ronan.

I'd said I didn't care if they had to go out in the cold. That it wasn't my problem if they froze to death. The wind roared again, rattling the panes, the whole castle sighing at the gale's ferocity. I'd be a monster to send them out into this. Despite my endless list of reservations, I resigned myself to their company for the night.

"Kianna, please show Gideon to the stables," I said, a collective breath releasing around the room. Kianna nodded, jumping up. I threw her a scathing look. This was still her fault. She shouldn't have invited them in the first place.

Ronan remained at the table, lifting his cup, triumph in his expression. My gaze traveled the line of his mouth, his lips full and soft, moving to the scruff of his jaw. Lost in the idea of it brushing my face, an involuntary movement had me touching my cheek. He wasn't just handsome, there was something luminous about him, like the sky had given up its favorite star and dropped it into my kitchen.

As his bright green eyes met mine, my body threatened to melt into nothing. Biting the inside of my mouth, I centered myself back on the earth and pushed away from the table. The room had become too warm, the air stifling.

"There are guest rooms in the west wing." I stood up so abruptly that the stool fell from under me. It clattered to the ground, and I winced. "Kianna can show you where they are when she returns. Help yourselves to whatever you need."

"Thank you, Your Highness." Ronan stood then too, walking around to the other side of the table. He righted my stool before stopping inches in front of me.

I had to crane my neck to look into his perfect face. He took my hand, his fingers warm and gentle, my skin firing like ceramic in a kiln. The brightness in his eyes darkened to the color of night-shaded pine trees, his nose flaring.

Then he pressed his mouth to the back of my hand, something awkwardly emotional stirring in me. "You have rescued us from a miserable night on the road. Your irrepressible generosity knows no bounds."

But the spark in his eyes suggested he was mocking me again, and I yanked my hand away. "Bastard," I muttered under my breath, spearing him with narrowed eyes and spinning away. His low, dark laughter followed me out of the kitchen as I dashed to my room.

The wind continued to howl as fat white flakes rained from the sky. After changing into my nightgown and robe, I paced the floor, stopping every now and again to watch the world fall under a cover of white. I'd always loved the snow. The way it rendered everything into muffled silence, coating the landscape in a shell of sparkling purity. But I couldn't fall asleep with Ronan in the castle. He was the son of the man who'd murdered eleven Fae in my home. I didn't want him here.

A knock came at my door, and Kianna called softly, "Your Highness?"

"Come in." I kept pacing as she eased the door open.

"You are unhappy with me."

I whirled on her. "Yes, I'm unhappy! Why did you invite them to stay? Don't you realize how dangerous this is?"

"Why is it dangerous?"

"Don't you remember what happened the last time a strange man found his way here? Or have you already forgotten your sisters?"

She recoiled as if I'd slapped her, but I was too angry to care.

"I have not forgotten," she said, picking at the silver beading on her dress. "But I thought it would be nice to have some company. You aren't happy here with just the two of us."

"Happy? What do I have to be happy about? There is nothing *happy* going on here."

"You're right. I thought..." Her voice dropped to barely a whisper. At her trembling bottom lip, the fight in me died.

My shoulders slumped as I sank onto the chest at the foot of my bed.

"I don't think it's a good idea to have them here. We don't know who they are or why they're here. I don't even understand how they found us. The forest should have kept them from seeing the castle." I looked at her. "What were you thinking?"

"I thought they could help?" Kianna's voice pitched up a note at the end.

In search of patience, I looked heavenward, hoping answers would fall from the sky. Why had I been saddled with the most incompetent Faerie in existence?

"Why can't you undo this, Kianna? The man in the bookstore said you could fix this. He was right when he said the book he'd sold me was useless—there's nothing there either. Surely you must have some idea."

Kianna shook her head. "I'm sorry, Your Highness." Her big, dark eyes shone with unshed tears. After a moment, she spoke again as she sat down next to me. "I think they are good people. They do not strike me as the sort who would harm us."

"I suppose you're right." I felt as defeated as a worm curling over the toe of my boot. It was so lonely here, and it wasn't awful listening to their comfortable banter during dinner. It felt like things had almost been normal.

"And they're all so attractive." Kianna fanned her face, a sly glint in her eyes, and I couldn't help but smile. "The commander especially—though he carries himself more like a prince, wouldn't you agree?" I wondered what she thought she was keeping from me.

I sighed. "Yes, he's very handsome, but that is completely beside the point. They can't stay here. As soon as it stops snowing, they need to leave."

Kianna gave me a grave nod, her curls bobbing. "Of course, Your Highness. As soon as the snow stops, they're gone." She placed a delicate hand over her heart. "You have my word." The words rolled off her tongue, and I dropped my head in my hands and built a bridge made of sighs.

CHAPTER ELEVEN

27 DAYS LEFT

The wind continued to howl through the night, dusting the world in an ocean of snow. Great cyclones swept past the windows, obscuring the forest from view. The temperature dropped and Kianna lit the castle's fireplaces, her magic ensuring they never went out.

Gideon bustled through the kitchen, preparing breakfast where Kianna and I sat at the long wooden table. *Common Magical Cures*, the book I'd acquired in Tenby, was spread in front of me as I flipped through it, trying to parse out something useful. Thick as my arm, it was taking forever to read through all the thin, nearly translucent pages, the script so cramped I'd hunted down a magnifying glass to relieve the strain on my eyes.

With a hot mug of tea sitting next to me, Gideon placed a dish piled with glazed fruit pastries on the table.

Snatching one, I bit into it with a moan. "This is the best thing I've ever tasted."

"That's what you said about the fish last night, Your Highness," Gideon said, a huge smile on his face.

"Well, now it's this. A princess may be fickle," I said as I bit into the center and a burst of raspberry melted on my tongue. "You are a genius, Gideon. What's Ronan paying you? I'll triple it."

"Thank you, Highness," he said, returning to the oven.

If we were stuck with their company, at least we'd dine in decadence until the storm abated. I peered out the high squat window, watching the darkened sky, wondering when that would be.

Ronan and Em entered, taking a seat at the table. Gideon brought over pans of scrambled eggs, crispy bacon, and thick slices of buttered toast.

"How did you sleep?" Kianna asked. "I hope everything was comfortable?" She was watching Em, who gave her a bright, lopsided smile.

"Fantastic, thank you."

Kianna's cheeks flushed as she poured Em some tea.

"And you, Your Highness?" Ronan asked me. "I hope your dreams were filled with only satisfied pleasure."

My eyes narrowed, sure there was some intended meaning in those words. He winked, and the skin on my neck flushed. Why did he have to be so gorgeous?

"I slept well enough," I said. "Considering vagrants made themselves comfortable in my home last night."

Ronan snorted. "That's the third pastry you've eaten. It can't be all bad having us here."

I stuffed the remaining bit in my mouth. "Gideon is welcome to stay forever. What have you got to offer, Commander?" The words came out muffled, a shower of crumbs landing on the table. Kianna threw me an incensed look that I ignored.

Ronan leaned forward, a suggestive tilt to his lips as he gave me a once-over that would make a fallen angel blush.

My thighs pressed together, and I ground down on my teeth. No. This wasn't what I needed right now.

"I could teach you how to use that?" He tipped his head in the direction of the sword propped up against the next table. That...wasn't what I'd expected him to say. I blinked as I was once again forced to stitch up the seams of my equilibrium.

"Why?"

"Because a lady, even one with the disposition of a hungry lion, should know how to protect herself," he countered, an elbow on the table, the hand of his other arm braced on his knee.

Ignoring his insult, I warmed at the memory of Captain Andrick saying something similar a very long time ago. He'd felt the same way, even if my Fae guardians hadn't. Andrick had taken my protection personally. It had all started when I was twelve and a daughter from a neighboring kingdom had gone missing. She had been the second youngest of eight princesses. One night she had gone to sleep, and the next morning she had disappeared.

They'd spent months searching for Carissa, but she was never found. Two years later, her older sister Madeline had suffered a similar fate, and it was then Andrick had insisted I learn at least the basics of self-defense.

"You're going to teach me?" I gave Ronan my most skeptical frown and looked at Em. "What about you?"

"Me?"

"You're a woman."

"She's very observant, isn't she?" Ronan said to the rest of the room, and I glared.

"Are there other women in your army?" I asked, desperately curious now.

He shrugged his wide shoulders. "Some. Anyone who wants to put in the training necessary to join my ranks is welcome."

"Why?" I'd never heard of such a thing.

"Why not? Women are more than capable of learning to fight. Em is one of the best in Estria with a sword."

I considered that for a moment, his words thrilling me. An army with female soldiers felt like a bridge to an entire world I had no idea existed. How might my life have been different if I'd ended up like Em instead?

"I'm no teacher," Em said, biting into a piece of bacon. "Don't have the patience for it. Besides, everything I know I learned from Ronan."

Ronan's beautiful face broke into a shit-eating grin. "I'm a *very* good teacher."

"And rather arrogant." I sat back and crossed my arms, though I was definitely warming to the idea.

Unfazed, his smile didn't falter. "Do you want to learn or not? Or shall we find you another tree, Little Lion?"

"Yes. I want to learn," I said, biting out the words like I'd torn them from marble. "And don't call me that."

"Say 'please'." He mimicked my stance, arms folded. My glare should have melted him into the ground, but alas, there he sat, looking smug and sexy and exactly like what I didn't need right now. But, if I had any hope of besting Mare, I needed more than a knife and the clumsy swing of my sword. Ronan might be my only hope. I could control my thoughts around him. I wasn't an animal.

"Please," I muttered through gritted teeth.

"Now, was that so hard?" He stood and scooped my sword in his large hand. "First lesson: don't leave your weapons lying around for anyone to take and use against you." He headed for the door and then stopped. "Coming?" Not waiting for a reply, he left the room, forcing me to scurry after.

"Where are we going?" I asked when I'd caught up.

"We need space. Gideon will have our hides if we mess up his kitchen."

For now, I ignored the implication that my kitchen had somehow become Gideon's. Ronan continued walking, stopping in the throne room and spinning to face me, sword held aloft.

"No," I said, shaking my head. "This way." This time, he followed me to the castle's ballroom. The floors were covered in creamy marble, shot through with pink and teal and purple. One wall was taken up by a single mirror that ran the entire length, while the opposite one gleamed with intricate gold inlay. A dozen sparkling chandeliers hung from the ceiling, their pewter arms cradling hundreds of creamy candles. Large arched windows looked out at each end of the room, filtering in blue light as the snow continued to fly.

"Will this do?" I asked, planting my hands on my hips.

"This will do." Ronan looked around. "I don't suppose this room has seen too many sword fights."

I shrugged. "Actually, my Uncle Baylor used to get drunk here all the time and challenge everyone to duels. Even my ninety-eight-year-old grandmother." Ronan lifted an eyebrow as the corners of his mouth ticked up. "Besides, there are no rules anymore." The words slipped out unintentionally, rippling through the atmosphere like a magic spell. My world had been turned around. Everything had changed. Even if I stopped Mare and got my second chance, nothing would ever be the same. A warrior standing in my ballroom, teaching me how to use a sword, was proof enough of that.

He watched me, perhaps sensing I needed a moment to collect myself.

But I began to wilt under his intense gaze, green eyes lighting me up like a torch. "Well, stop staring at me, and let's get on with it." I intended for it to sound breezy and teasing, but the words came out breathless. As I flicked my braid over my shoulder and squared my stance, I was rewarded with a smirk that did everything it could to weaken my carefully assembled resolve.

For the rest of the day, Ronan pummeled and battered me through drills and exercises, insisting I repeat the thrusts and parries over and over until my limbs grew shaky and every cell in my body hummed with energy.

It became clear he was as good a teacher as he'd claimed, and it didn't take long before I could block some of his blows and even fight back.

Noah and Em drifted into the ballroom, calling out pointers and correcting my form as they shouted ribald remarks to their friend. It was obvious how much they all adored each other, and I sensed a fierce, unwavering loyalty bound them.

"Show her how you handle a sword, Ronan," Em called, shaking with laughter.

"I think it's the lady who wants to handle the sword, don't you think?" Noah asked, in the snooty way of noblewomen out for an afternoon stroll through the garden.

"If by 'sword' you mean 'cock', then yes, Noah, that's exactly what I think," Em replied, and they both collapsed into hysterics as Ronan rolled his eyes at them.

They were trying to embarrass me, and it worked, the truth of their jesting too close for my comfort. But I'd also hung around Captain Andrick enough to overhear similar teasing among my father's guard and understood they were trying to include me in their circle. The gesture warmed me. I had always been the cursed girl existing on the edges, a ghost preparing for her inevitable departure. There'd been no point in getting too attached to my presence, and no one had ever included me like that.

Under normal circumstances, I was sure they'd never talk like this around me, but no one was under any illusion these were normal circumstances.

"Who taught you to stand like that?" Ronan asked after several more hours of training. The snow was still flying, but the sun had set, the windows now a row of black holes lining the walls. The chandeliers glowed with golden light, stretching our shadows along the floor.

"My father's captain taught me a few things," I replied as Ronan brought down his blade and I blocked it.

"I'd say you're a natural at this, Little Lion." I shouldn't have enjoyed his praise as much as I did, but the admiration in his eyes did erratic things to my pulse.

"You really think so?"

"Maybe you should give up this princess thing and join my army."

He flashed me a smile of perfect white teeth as I snorted. "I haven't hit my head *that* many times today." Ronan let out a laugh, and it sang through him as he tipped his head back.

I admired the column of his throat, covered in a layer of day-old scruff. He'd long ago undone the top laces of his black tunic, exposing an expanse of taut, tanned flesh that had distracted me for much longer than I would ever admit.

"We'll have you bringing down your deadliest foes in no time," he said, and I tucked those words into my pocket for safekeeping. How I hoped he was right. Maybe he was flattering me, but he couldn't know how close to the truth he'd come.

CHAPTER TWELVE

25 DAYS LEFT

MY BODY WAS ONE giant pulsating bruise. For three days, Ronan had been relentless with my training. I ached in every muscle I had and ones I hadn't even known existed. If I'd thought he'd go easy on me because I was a princess, I was sorely mistaken.

Ronan had barely broken a sweat. He was so damn competent it almost made me hate him, except he had been nothing but patient and kind through every one of my clumsy and artless fumbles. Teaching a useless princess how to hold a sword couldn't have been high on his list of priorities. He hadn't mentioned his father, but there were moments I sensed him withdrawing into a veil of troubled thoughts.

"I think I need a break," I said, arching my back, seeking the relief of a stretch.

"So soon, Your Highness?" he taunted, rocking from foot to foot.

I glared, hobbling toward the door, when I summoned a reserve of strength and lunged for him. Catching him off guard, I finally got in a hit, slamming my blunted sword into his ribs with a satisfying thump. He grunted as he brought the pommel of his weapon down on my wrist, causing me to drop my blade. When I dove for it, he snatched me around the waist, pulling me up against him. His deep laughter brushed my ear, raising a map of goosebumps over my skin.

"Well done, Little Lion. You've taught me an important lesson about never underestimating my opponent." Once again, I preened at the respect in his voice. His opinion shouldn't have mattered, but I couldn't stop the smile he'd coaxed from the hard knot of anxiety that had taken up residence in my chest.

His strong, sculpted arm flexed where he held me, his large palm spread over my ribs. Drawing me closer, I wasn't sure if the movement was intentional or if he was finding his balance. Whichever it was, he didn't let go as his breath split into a forest of tendrils that wound around my limbs, setting off another wave of shivers that vibrated straight to the floor.

We went entirely still, both of us turned into crystal, afraid to shatter if we made too sudden a movement. The room was silent but for the sound of the howling wind. His hard, muscled chest pressed against my back, his powerful thighs against mine. Every place he touched me came alive in a congestion of senses. Over the past three days, he'd touched me countless times—the clinical touches of a student and teacher—but this was something entirely different. This touch slipped us into another dimension.

"Thanks," I whispered, my throat too tight. "I had an excellent teacher."

After a huff of laughter, he slowly dropped his arm. When I turned to face him, we both remained caught in the spell sucking us under. His smile died, playful green eyes shifting into a dangerous place. I needed to get it together. Focus on my task. The luxury of distraction wasn't something I could afford.

He cleared his throat. "It was my pleasure, Your Highness. I had an equally talented student." He dipped his head as I turned to leave the room, my heart sprinting away.

Twelve chairs lined up in two rows, facing each other, six on each side. I walked through the chamber where the Fae had once planned to keep vigil as I slept, still hoping to find a way around Mare's curse.

Kianna and I had cleaned up the blood, but nothing could ever wash away the stains of so much violence. They would remain here forever, forged into the walls and the floors like a brand seared into skin.

After I'd left Ronan in the ballroom, I'd returned to my bedroom to peruse *Common Magical Cures*. But after re-reading the same page three times, I'd conceded defeat for the day.

This room had been calling me, a tattered song whistling through the castle's halls. Though I'd tried to ignore it, I could no longer shut out the melody that haunted my dreams.

Constructed of large gray stones, the round room was lined with arched windows overlooking Lake Ravalyn. As if a lakeside view would have mattered while I slept. Still, it had been a nice thought. Ice crystals grew in the corners of the glass, the ledges covered in snow. The wind had died down, and a pristine white sheet sparkled under the moonlight.

Still limping, I approached the bier where I'd slept. Flowers cascaded along the walls, reminding me of funerals. The irony wasn't lost on me. Though I hadn't died in the literal sense, I'd left in every way that had mattered.

Arms braced against the frame, I lifted myself onto the platform, my sore muscles protesting. I lay back, crossing my hands over my heart, just as I had for so long.

Though my parents had spent many years pretending neither Mare nor Kianna's curses would be my fate, they'd constructed this shrine, anyway. My head nestled on the soft velvet cushion, I stared at the ceiling, remembering the day before my twenty-first birthday. The Fae had escorted me here while my mother, claiming she couldn't bear to watch, remained in the throne room, surrounded by her family and friends. *My* family and friends.

In the silence, I watched the gently falling snow glittering like tears from the sky. Footsteps clicked on the stones, and I turned to watch Ronan as he approached. As he took in the strange room, I sat up on the equally strange bed where I lay.

"You shouldn't be in here," I said, but there was no heat in my words. I was tired of pretending, and he would figure out some of the truth, no matter how much I tried to fight it.

"I missed you at dinner—I mean, we missed you at dinner." His gaze shifted to me, curious and considering.

"I must have dozed off."

"Is this where they kept you?"

"They didn't *keep* me, but yes. This is where I slept."

"For how long?"

"Exactly one hundred years. I woke up the day before my twenty-first birthday."

He drifted around the perimeter of the room, looking out of the windows.

"Why did you wake up? Why not anyone else? Why Kianna?"

I'd deduced it must have been his father's interference that resurrected me and Kianna, but I couldn't tell him that.

"I don't know," I lied. "Kianna said the spell has gone wrong, and she doesn't know how to fix it."

"Why did you have to sleep for so long?"

"That's a long story."

"I have time," he responded, his gaze challenging.

I rolled my eyes. "I suppose you won't relent unless I tell you."

"You would be correct. I'm not sure how much longer you expect me to pretend we aren't in a castle full of enchanted sleeping people."

I sighed dramatically, catching the hint of a smile as he leaned against the windowsill, one ankle crossed over the other. He'd been asking questions for the past three days, trying to unravel my secrets, but I'd dodged them all with the grace of an acrobat. As he watched me now, there was an openness in his face. Something that told me I could trust him, and I found I wanted to unburden myself with at least some of the truth.

Legs crossed beneath me, I sat on the bier and told him the story of my mother, the Fae who'd helped her, and Mare's threat. I told him about the gifts the Fae had given me and the curse Kianna had tried to stop with her ill-fated spell.

When I was done, he was stunned, eyebrows high on his forehead. "That's a hell of a story, Princess."

I offered him a tight smile.

"What happened to the other Faeries? Twelve Fae—there are twelve chairs out there."

Damn. He didn't miss much, but the circumstances around their deaths would lead to questions I didn't want to answer. So I lied a bit more.

"Gone," I said. "I don't know where they are." I made a mental note to fill Kianna in on my deception. I also kept the deal I made with Mare to myself. That felt like one truth too many. Ronan was still a stranger, and I had yet to understand his intentions.

"I have a question for you," I said. He tilted his head, waiting for me to continue. "How did you find the castle? It's hidden by the forest. What made you come here?"

He looked out the window, the snow-capped pines standing like chilled sentinels. "I'm not sure, to be honest. We were passing by, and something tugged at me, so we turned off the road." He gave me an inscrutable look. "And then it was hard to miss a castle entirely covered by brambles. How did you get past them?"

"I think they must have lost whatever magic was in them when I woke up." What I didn't add was that I didn't understand how the king had breached them in the first place. "What do you mean, you had a feeling?"

"It happens to me sometimes. A sense that guides me, and I felt it that day." We both fell silent, lost in our thoughts.

"There's no one else here," Ronan said a few moments later.

"What?"

"They left you alone here. No one stayed with you when you fell asleep?"

Hurt speared down the center of my body in a hot burning line. It was a truth that had been nibbling away at my heart since the day I awoke. All those years ago, I had been too overwhelmed to process it. But now, I had nothing but time to think.

My mother had been so distraught that she couldn't bear to watch. So saddened, she had taken everyone with her for support. She'd simply said goodbye and walked away, and I wondered now if she'd really said goodbye to me much sooner. My mother, who had wanted me so much. As though this had been only about her. As though only her feelings had mattered.

There had been no last words of comfort from the Fae. I'd saddled them with twenty-one years of burden. They'd fulfilled their duty, said goodbye, and then closed the door, but that was how it had always been between us.

I wondered how often my family would have visited me had they been able. Here, in this room, so far away, in a spot where few would ever wander unless by choice. A sleeping princess, forgotten in her sepulchre of flowers.

"No," I said, finally. "No one else was here."

CHAPTER THIRTEEN

24 DAYS LEFT

THE SOUNDS OF FIGHTING drifted into my room, steel clashing against steel as I cracked open my eyes. The sun was out, the sky the color of bluebells in spring and the sun hanging like a bright, white snowball. Ronan, Noah, and Em were in the courtyard training.

I'd slept late, my body sore and sluggish, every limb aching and every joint creaking like a rusty hinge. Ronan's lessons were partly to blame, but the pressure of all my worries added so much weight to my shoulders that it felt like I was dragging around a sack stuffed with lead.

Kianna drew me a bath, and I took my time, watching the soap weave glistening tracks along my brown skin. The warm water soothed my tired muscles, releasing some of the tension coiled in my limbs.

As much as I ached, there was something satisfying about putting my body to work, pushing it to the limits of what it could do. I felt a little less helpless. A little less useless.

After my bath, I put on a simple blue dress that trailed to the floor and stepped into a pair of golden slippers. My dark hair hung unbound in loose waves to the small of my back. Kianna hovered in the room as I spread *Common Magical Cures* over my knees, still trying to find something useful in its pages. I couldn't give up until I'd skimmed through them all. Then I'd go back to the library, or maybe to Tenby, and try again. Mentally, I tallied the days I had left, watching the numbers fall through time like a sundial collapsing in on itself.

"Here, this says it's a cure for drowsiness. Do you think this might work?" I pointed to the cramped writing on the page.

Kianna sat down on the bed next to me and leaned over, scrunching her nose. "Perhaps?"

"Navitas." The sketch depicted an herb with clumps of small white berries. "We need to find some. It's winter, though." I pushed out my bottom lip.

"There are some patches in the forest, Your Highness. It's still early in the season. We may find a few stems." Kianna nibbled on her fingernail, not meeting my eyes.

I threw up my hands. "Kianna! Do you not want to solve this?"

She jumped at my outburst. "Yes, of course, Your Highness. I will show you after lunch. I was just going to help Gideon." She thumbed in the kitchen's direction, and I nodded. Grateful to escape, she leaped up and scurried away.

I stepped out onto my balcony, overlooking Lake Ravalyn, covered in a thin layer of ice.

Ronan and his crew had gone out this morning, claiming they wanted to check if the roads were safe to travel. I suspected the real reason was to continue their search for the king. Ronan still hadn't mentioned him, and I pretended I hadn't overheard their conversation in Tenby. My gaze wandered in the direction of my graveyard in the forest, wondering how it had fared in the storm.

The flash of a sword flicked in the corner of my eye. Someone had cleared away the snow, and they were circling each other. Ronan had stripped to his pants, the sun's feeble warmth beating down on the expanse of his warm, bronzed skin.

My appreciative gaze traveled the bulk of his shoulders, veins popping in his forearms. It traced the bricked wall of his chest and the planes of his stomach, voyaging to the dark trail of hair and the vee of muscle that disappeared into his low-hanging waistband.

But these were pointless and unproductive observations. I had far more important things to worry about. Things I should have been getting on with right this very moment.

Yet I kept watching as igneous fire stirred in my treacherous stomach.

Ronan knocked Noah on his back, sword flying from his grip. Noah grinned at his commander, dark blonde waves shining as Ronan helped him up. Em stepped up next, tossing her mane of red hair over her shoulder. I marveled at her lithe and graceful movements. I swore I'd keep training until I looked even half as powerful.

As they circled, Ronan's back turned toward me, and I sucked in a sharp breath. A mass of scars covered his skin, tangling and twisting like a canvas of branches sculpted with ruined flesh.

Who had done that to him?

They sparred while Noah shouted insults at Ronan and Em that they did their best to ignore. After several minutes, Ronan took Em down too, both their chests expanding with shortened breaths.

Seeing the way he'd flattened Noah and Em, I felt better about never besting Ronan. Not yet, at least. I shook the thought away. The storm had passed, and they needed to leave. Ronan had taught me what he could, but our lessons were over.

As if feeling my stare, Ronan looked up to where I stood, his eyes bright, as the heat of dragon flame scalded my bones. It raced from my heart and down through my stomach, pooling somewhere below my navel. My lip caught between my teeth, I stood up straight, mortified he'd caught me staring.

He gave me a crooked smile that hooked into my skin, drawing me in like a spool of thread. As if sensing my indecision, he held my gaze for several fire-laced heartbeats before turning back to his companions. Taking it as my cue to disappear, I retreated to the warm darkness of my room.

My hand pressed to my heart, I took in several deep breaths to calm the way my pulse barreled through my chest like a cannon blasting through plywood.

They had to leave. I was too caught up in something that had no chance, no matter how much I hoped for it. This was not my fate. *He* was not my destiny. Ronan's presence had already diverted me too far from my task.

Down in the kitchen, I found Gideon standing in front of the stove, a large pot and a frying pan sizzling over the fire. Kianna chopped herbs at the counter.

"Your Highness." Gideon turned his warm smile to me as his brown eyes twinkled. "Lunch will be ready soon."

"Gideon, you don't need to cook for me and Kianna."

"Ah, Your Highness, I know that. However, I do need to cook for the commander and the others. It is nothing to feed you and Lady Kianna, as well. Besides, she's a very good helper." Kianna flashed him a grin.

"Will you teach me a few things before you all leave?"

Gideon's face lit up, and his smile tugged at my heart.

"Your Highness, it would be an honor." Eyes shining, he retrieved an apron and handed it to me with such reverence, I had to look away from the outpouring of emotion. He set me to work, demonstrating how to season the fish, slice and fry onions, and how to measure and knead the bread.

Much like training with Ronan, this too was gratifying. Getting my hands dirty and learning to fend for myself dispelled some of my despair. I'd believed myself entirely helpless, but maybe I was more capable than I realized. Covered in flour and grease, I felt lighter than I had in weeks.

Gideon was preparing a sauce for dinner, and I sampled the glossy, dark gravy. It was buttery and rich, and I groaned. "Marry me, Gideon."

Ronan, Em, and Noah all filed into the room then, laughing at my proposal.

"What are you up to, old man? Stealing the princess's heart?" Noah asked as he sat at the table.

"That would be most improper, Your Highness," Gideon stammered, his face crimson.

"There are no more rules, Gideon," I replied with a smirk. "This is the best thing I've ever tasted."

"You say that about everything." The pride was evident in his voice.

"I can't help if it's true," I said, taking another taste.

"C'mon, Gid, you two would make an adorable match." Ronan grinned, slapping the older man on the back.

"Sir, I—"

Ronan laughed and reached a hand toward me. I flinched as I gave him a suspicious look. Eyebrows lifted, he touched a finger to my cheek, and it came away with a drop of sauce on the tip.

Why was there sauce on my face?

"You had something there, Little Lion."

Ronan's eyes fused to mine as he placed his finger in his mouth and sucked off the sauce, teasing me with a wicked gleam in his eyes. The movement sent a shivering pulse across my skin, vibrations making my nerves spark and flare like candlewicks. He had put his tunic back on, muscles straining against the thin cloth, and I shoved down an inappropriate surge of disappointment.

"What's for lunch? I'm starving," Em asked, pouring herself a glass of water.

"Gideon is showing me how to cook, so we aren't helpless after you leave."

Darkness swirled in Ronan's eyes, his demeanor shifting to the predator I remembered from the night I'd first seen him in Tenby. All dark shadows and hard angles, his lightness fell away. He didn't want to return to Estria without news of their king, but perhaps he was hiding more. I didn't know what was at stake for him if he failed. Regardless, I couldn't let him find the answers he sought. It was better if they all left as soon as possible.

A bell dinged, and I jumped up. "My bread!"

A puff of black smoke greeted me as I opened the oven door. Coughing and waving it with a potholder, I pulled out the pan. The loaf wasn't exactly black, but it was considerably darker than intended. I exchanged a glance with Gideon, feeling defeated. Not two minutes ago, I'd been so sure I could do this. Gideon must have registered the devastation on my face, because he summoned a beaming smile.

"I'm sure it's delicious, Your Highness. Slice it up, and we'll all try some." Gideon gestured to everyone like he was conducting an orchestra. "Princess Thorne's very first loaf of bread."

After cutting it into thick slices, I passed the plate around. Everyone took a tentative bite, nibbling quietly. I noticed the looks they shared across the table as Kianna slipped in next to Em.

"Is it very bad?"

"No," said Em, taking a big gulp of water. "It's terrible."

"Oh," I said.

"It was your first try," Gideon said, his hands folded in front of him and his expression soft. "You'll get it right next time."

I took a furious bite and then choked as it lodged in my throat. It tasted like the inside of a fireplace and had the consistency of a charred log. "Oh, my God. That is awful," I muttered through a mouthful. Everyone burst out laughing, and I gave them an annoyed look. Crossing my arms, I dropped onto the bench next to Ronan, sitting sideways, my back toward him. He nudged me with his shoulder, and I turned my head, noticing his stormy visage had been replaced with a luminous smile. It was beautiful, and he was beautiful, and I mentally slapped myself for the useless observation.

He had to go. Right. Now.

Mouth so close to my ear, I felt his breath on my neck where it snaked down the front of my dress. Tiny hairs stood up like stupid attentive soldiers as Ronan purred, "Smile, Your Highness. It's good to learn how to laugh at yourself." His arm pressed against my back, and I attempted to ignore the intense awareness this benign touch ignited.

This was ridiculous. It was his *arm*. When had I become such a swooning mess of butterflies? I didn't want him to move, but we couldn't really sit like this forever without it becoming awkward. Had anyone noticed me sink closer?

"Maybe princesses aren't designed for this kind of thing."

That did it. I glared and straightened my back, breaking our connection. "You are such an ass." He grinned, and I hated how I wanted to touch the ridiculously charming dimple that popped on his left cheek. "Anyway," I said, trying to get a hold of the conversation and the shreds of my dignity. "The sun is out, and the snow has stopped—it's time for you to be on your way."

"I just had an idea," Kianna said, leaping to her feet, her eyes shining. "Your grandparents' chalet."

"What about it, Kianna?" I bit out the words like they'd been soaked in lemons.

"I wonder how it's fared all this time?"

"What?" Had I fallen asleep again only to wake up in the middle of this conversation?

"We should pack a picnic and walk out there. It's not too far past the lake. What do you think, Gideon?"

My mouth opened and closed like a befuddled fish as Gideon lit up as well.

"I think that's a wonderful idea! We'll need a fire to warm the soup, and I've got some chicken already prepared. Oh, and the tarts will be perfect." He clapped his hands in delighted joy.

"What? No, why would we have a picnic at my grandparent's chalet? What are you two talking about?" I looked to the others for confirmation of how ridiculous this was, but Em and Noah were already helping Gideon pack food into a large basket. "Will you talk some sense into them?" Hands planted on my hips, I scowled at Ronan. "This is outrageous. Surely you have somewhere to be?"

Kianna interjected, grabbing my hands and holding them in hers. "I just remembered there are patches of navitas that grow in that area. We can see if anything survived the storm."

Again, my mouth opened but nothing came out, my words ground into fine powder.

Ronan leaned over. "See? You can collect some herbs and have a nice dinner with some scintillating company. You really need to relax, Your Highness." He sat back, sweeping me with an appraising look. "Though you are especially beautiful when you're angry." His smile was wry, clearly enjoying every moment of my increasing irritation.

"Don't tell me I'm beautiful, and don't tell me to relax. I *am* relaxed." Obviously, that wasn't true, and I was quickly losing this argument.

Gideon and Kianna had disappeared into the cellar, and Noah and Em had gone up to their rooms to change. Ronan pushed himself from the table and tipped an imaginary hat in my direction. I growled, and he let out a dark chuckle and then departed, too.

Finally, I was left standing alone in the kitchen, like a bristling fool.

About an hour later, we gathered in the courtyard behind the castle. I still didn't know how I'd been talked into this. Of course, I wanted to see how the chateau had fared and I needed the navitas, but Kianna seemed so intent on keeping everyone here, I could only assume she didn't want to be left alone with me again. I couldn't blame her. I wasn't entirely pleasant to live with these days.

We headed out of the courtyard, snow crunching beneath us. The air crisp, I cinched the thick fur collar of my coat around my neck. Noah and Gideon carried a large wicker basket between them while Em and Kianna walked behind, shoulders brushing, their heads bent together as Kianna let out a giggle and gave Em a playful slap on the arm. Perhaps Kianna had other motives for wanting them to remain here.

We were just past the castle, skirting the shore of Lake Ravalyn, when I noticed animal prints in the snow. Several handspans wide, they ended in three long toes, each crowned with a depression that suggested a long, sharp claw. They formed a trail along the east wall of the castle. Ronan dropped into a crouch.

"What are they?" I asked.

"I've never seen anything like it. They almost look like bird feet, but I don't know of any bird that large."

I shivered, wondering what nightmare this thing had escaped.

"Do you feel that?" My body tingled, like numbed hands and feet thawing after coming in from the cold, sharp and slightly uncomfortable.

Ronan nodded. "I do. It's similar to the feeling that drew me here. I've learned it signifies magic." He stood, scanning the eastern forest. Nothing moved in the trees.

"Don't worry, Princess. You have the greatest warrior in the history of Estria at your side. You've nothing to fear." He flashed me a smile, and despite my worry, I rolled my eyes.

"Shall I swoon in your presence too, m'lord?"

"You wouldn't be the first damsel to fall at my feet."

"I guess your *charm* is powerless in Ravalyn, then," I snapped. His grin grew even bigger at the insult. Infuriating man. I glared as I brushed past to follow the rest of the group into the forest.

"We can set out a watch tonight. Noah, Em, and I can take turns," Ronan said, catching up to me. "Keep an eye out for anything amiss." Only sincerity in the offer, I nodded, suddenly grateful for their presence.

It took about an hour to reach my grandparents' home. The forest sparkled, ice crystals and frost coating the trees and bushes. The royal birch leaves were white now, their surfaces faintly iridescent as they fluttered on a breeze.

Through the trees, the chateau became visible. Made from pale green stone like molded sea foam, it was adorned with whorls of white and cream and gold. The windows were broken, jagged edges glinting in the sunlight, and the gardens were overgrown, the tangle of weeds and gangly bushes now covered in a dusting of frost. Fountains that had once bubbled with sprays of water sat dry and cracked, filled with fluffy snow.

I wondered how long the servants and guards had waited before realizing their lord and lady weren't coming back.

Debris covered the wide front steps where bits of dried leaves and dirt mingled with the snow. One golden door stood slightly ajar, and I walked up the stairs. Even in a state of decay, the chateau was magnificent.

Inside, my boots crunched on broken glass. Black-and-white checkered tile covered the floor, and a grand staircase dominated the entrance. In the sitting room, more broken glass and furniture covered the once pale blue carpet. I proceeded through hallways littered with debris, finding myself in the salon where my grandparents had once entertained.

A piano sat in the corner, surrounded by smashed settees and chairs. Thick green velvet curtains lay moth-eaten on the floor.

The last time I had been in this room had been weeks after my twentieth birthday, when we'd gathered to celebrate the engagement of my cousin Isabelle. I remembered the sting of it even now. She was six months my junior, but there would be no engagement, no wedding, and no future for me. Proudly she had stood, hanging off the arm of her soon-to-be husband, Edward.

My parents had avoided meeting my eyes the entire night, their guilt hanging like iron chains around their necks. We'd broken our unspoken contract. The one where we'd all deluded ourselves into believing the promise of two curses wouldn't come to pass. But as the years had ticked by and the Fae had found no solution, the inevitable became harder and harder to ignore.

That night, we weren't pretending anymore.

I was the only heir. It should have been my engagement and my future as queen we were celebrating, but there were only two paths for me. An eternal sleep or a Fae's enslavement, and we were all powerless to stop it.

Kianna and her sisters had scolded me earlier in the day when they'd caught me moping in the castle's halls.

"A princess is gracious and selfless," Abigail said, glossy blonde curls hanging to the waist of her bright pink gown. Dutifully, I nodded, wiping away tears I didn't have the freedom to shed. Isabelle would succeed me as the daughter of the king's eldest brother, and that's all there was to it.

I trailed my fingers along the piano keys, pressing them one by one. It was out of tune, but I played a small medley, feeling the off-key notes flow beneath my hand. That night, the shadow of knowing I wouldn't be here in a year had hung over the room like a spectre. There were no more years left and no more places for me to hide.

A smile crept to my lips. It was also the night Adrian and I finally gave into the looks we'd been sharing across the throne room for months. I'd been drawn to his kind demeanor, as well as his athletic build, head of thick brown hair, and soft brown eyes. Given he was a member of the king's guard, a relationship was entirely forbidden, but that didn't stop my cheeks from flushing or my heart from tripping every time he walked in the room.

For months, I found reasons to run into him in the castle. It was teasing words shared in hallways or a light touch as we passed, conscious of anyone noticing.

Adrian wasn't stationed in the room during the party, so I slipped away after the toasts to look for him. I found him in the gardens, out of uniform, handsome and relaxed in a navy tunic. He sat with a group of guards, also enjoying a respite from their duties.

Lingering on the edges, I caught his eye, and he extricated himself from his companions.

"Your Highness," he said, approaching, concern on his handsome face. "Is something wrong?"

I shook my head. "It was lonely and boring at the party. I was hoping for some company."

Shy and inexperienced, I was nervous, but also emboldened by what I wanted. I was under no illusion the attention of a princess would be easy to ignore. It was wrong and would get us both in so much trouble, but I had less than a year left. I was collecting happy memories like precious stones. Something good I could take with me.

Bewilderment followed a look of understanding as his bronzed face lit up. I was sure he'd assumed the looks we'd shared were just that—only looks. I was a princess, and he was a guard. But I didn't care anymore. Let them all judge.

I walked deeper into the gardens, searching for a spot we could be alone. To my delight, I soon heard the crunch of gravel as he followed. We stole into the darkness of the trees, fireflies lighting our way. The sky was a blanket of stars, and the moon hung low and bright. We said little as Adrian drew me to him.

"Are you sure about this, Highness?" he asked, uncertainty in his voice.

My arms wrapped around his neck, I drew up on my tiptoes so our mouths were inches apart. "I won't tell. No one will care, anyway. I will be gone soon. They won't remember me."

He tucked a lock of hair behind my ear. "*I'll* remember you, Princess." He kissed me then, softly at first and then with more heat.

Pressed against a tree, the rough bark scraped my skin through the thin silk of my dress. Even now, I remembered the warmth of his hands and his lips. How much I wanted him to touch every part of me and make me his. Our breath came heavy and frantic in the moonlight, and I never wanted it to stop. A thumb swept across my breast while another slipped between the folds of my skirt, caressing the softness of my thighs, and I moaned as he pressed himself into me, our bodies grinding against each other.

It was Cybil, a Fae with spiked brown hair and an orange gown, who found us.

"Thorne!" she hissed. "What are you doing? This is no way for a princess to behave! What will the king say about this?" A delicate hand flew to her slender neck as she took in Adrian. "And with one of the king's guards? They will throw him in the dungeons."

I begged her not to say anything. Told her it had been my idea. I swore on every god ever named that it would never happen again if only she'd keep quiet. It had taken a fair amount of convincing, but she'd relented eventually, threatening all manner of consequences if we were to transgress again.

After that, Adrian and I didn't stop spending time together, but we were more careful about it. He'd figured out how to climb into my bedroom via the balcony, and there were plenty of hidden corners in the castle where prying eyes never found us.

I touched my bottom lip, remembering his kisses. It had been over a hundred years, but I still remembered how his attention had made me feel. He'd been the one person who hadn't been uncomfortable with my presence, just waiting for me to be gone.

There was a shuffle of footsteps, and Ronan stood at the door. "Supper is almost ready." He came to stand next to me at the piano. "Do you play?"

"No, not really." I shook my head, my voice hollow. "That was an old princess. One trained in politics and manners and activities suitable to a proper lady, who bore the divine gifts of eleven misguided Fae." Ronan watched me carefully. "I don't think that's who I am anymore."

CHAPTER FOURTEEN

24 DAYS LEFT

"That wasn't so bad, was it?" Ronan asked, his strides matching mine as we headed back to the castle after dinner, stuffed full.

Gideon had cleared out the dining room while Noah and Em helped shove the rotted furniture away, leaving a cleared space on the floor. Gideon had laid blankets, and Kianna had lit the fireplace where he'd warmed the bean and tarragon soup. We'd eaten tender grilled chicken glazed with the sauce he'd been preparing that afternoon and then finished with pear tarts encased in delicate lattices of golden pastry.

Kianna and Em had sat next to one another, and I hadn't missed the looks they were exchanging. Nor the way their hands and shoulders had touched, pretending it wasn't intentional.

After I broke this curse, maybe Kianna could move on. She deserved a happy ending, too. Despite the years of resentment I held for the Fae, I wanted that for her.

"I suppose it was tolerable," I said to Ronan. Though I refused to admit it out loud, I was more relaxed than I'd been in days. The sun was setting, washing the sky in ribbons of blue and gray. A basket dangled from my arm, stuffed with sprigs of navitas and tentative hope. Maybe this would work.

"It was nice to see the chateau. It's a shame it's fallen into such a state. Maybe I'll get it fixed up once I find a way to—" I regarded Ronan from the corner of my eye.

"Find a way to what?"

"Nothing." I walked faster to shake him off, but he wasn't deterred.

"Nice try." He gently grabbed my arm and pulled me toward him, the warmth of his body melting into the cold air that surrounded me. "What were you going to say?"

For a moment, all I could focus on was the way my heart stumbled, as if it had been tossed down the side of a mountain. I became painfully aware of the way he leaned into me, tempting as the forbidden fruit in a garden.

But I needed to stop forgetting my singular purpose. There was an entire castle of people counting on me, and this was only a distraction. I pulled my arm away. I couldn't think properly when he was touching me.

"Fine." I lowered my voice. "I need to break the curse. That's what I needed this for." I held up my basket of herbs.

"I figured that," he said dryly, and I resisted the temptation to kick him in the shin.

"I'm sorry my problems are so trifling to you." I tried to stalk away, but he followed close behind.

"That's not what I meant. Of course, you're trying to break it, but why are you being so secretive?"

I stopped and gave him my most withering glare. "Because breaking a curse is a rather big deal. A big, strong warrior might not have experience in this matter, but it's not like you can go, '*poof*—curse broken'." To illustrate my point, I snapped my fingers in his face.

Arms crossed over his chest, he tilted his head. "But what else aren't you saying?"

I flattened my mouth. Did he miss nothing? How could he see me so clearly when I could barely weave through the mud of my thoughts? I exhaled a river of drawn-out air and allowed a trickle of truth to spread over cracked, parched earth.

"You remember the Faerie I told you about? Kianna's counter spell is preventing Mare from taking me away." He said nothing, waiting for me to continue. "She threatened to kill Kianna to release it and almost succeeded, but I made a bargain. If she let me try to break the curse, I'd then go with her willingly and she'd leave Kianna alone. If I don't, she'll kill Kianna and take me away."

In recounting the details, I left out my rapidly dwindling timeline and that Mare had threatened to kill everyone else, too. I'd already said far too much. Even telling him this felt like I'd cut myself open and allowed him to rummage inside the meat of my exposed flesh.

"I'm not sure what to say," he said, and I gave him a shocked look. "Hard to believe, I know."

"I didn't want to point it out."

He smirked and then wrinkled his brow. "You have no idea how to break it?"

I shook my head. "None. I've read everything in the library and visited the bookshop in Tenby. The man there seemed sure questions like that can't be answered with books. He sold me something, but most of it appears to be useless, and I don't know where any of this leaves me."

The cozy comfort of the evening ebbed away, leaving a chilled imprint in its wake. Those warm memories of Adrian I'd pumped to the surface dispersed into particles of nothing. The dinner we'd all shared evaporated as the faces of the people asleep in the castle calcified into a terrible dream. Their lives were in danger. My mother and father. My grandparents. My cousin Isabelle and her husband, Edward. Adrian.

We approached the castle, and I scanned the clawed tracks we'd seen earlier, following the line as it disappeared into the forest. The tingle I now associated with magic permeated my toes and fingers.

Ronan's expression was so full of concern that it felt like my soul might fracture from the barest touch. Instead, I gave him a weary smile. "None of this is your problem. But thank you for listening."

"I want to help you," he said, stepping so close I had to look up to meet his eyes. His hand circled my biceps like he wanted to stop me from leaping off a cliff.

"Why? You've just met me. There's no place for you in this mess. You should go home. This isn't your chaos to clean up."

Nothing wavered in his expression as he lifted his other hand, the back brushing along my jaw. The gentle touch was so at odds with the ferocious gleam in his eyes that it set every hair on my body to attention.

"Something brought me to this castle. That feeling I told you about has always been the precursor to something important. It's never been wrong. Let me help you."

"That would be nice if you could," I said, meaning it with every fiber of my faltering soul. He felt so protective and safe. Like an impenetrable fortress of unyielding confidence. I allowed myself to fantasize about what it would be like to wrap myself in his arms and let him give me the ending I'd always wished for. Nothing was more appealing than the idea of someone taking this burden from me. But there was no one who had that power, and I was completely alone. "But there's nothing you can do."

As I turned to the castle, I weighed Ronan's declaration, but something about it felt wrong. Not Ronan himself. I was sure he believed he'd arrived here for a greater purpose, but I wondered if he'd gotten the meaning of his intuition wrong. That he hadn't been sent here to help me but had arrived for some other reason. He was looking for his father, and that father was buried so close, his presence hovered over my head, deadly and sharp as an axe. I could still feel his meaty fist gripped around my throat and the hot spill of his blood on my hands.

Eventually, I had to acknowledge the truth might come out, and I hated the idea of how Ronan might look at me then. It was probably better that way. This fantasy in my head was just that—it was nothing more than a dream.

I *had* to get him out of here.

Once inside, I headed directly to the throne room, laying out the navitas around my parents' thrones. The book said their fragrance helped stave off drowsiness. I buried my nose in the small white flowers, inhaling their earthy scent.

As I stared at my parents, I already knew this was ridiculous. This would never work. It was a desperate hope masquerading as progress, intended to soothe my need to feel like I was doing something.

Nevertheless, I nestled the herbs in their laps, wrapping their hands around the stems. For good measure, I tucked more around their heads and into the collars of their clothing. And then I waited.

Nothing happened, of course. Not even a flicker. Implacable, their eyes remained closed, and hopelessness pried open my ribcage and dug its taloned claws into my chest.

It was then I dropped my face into my hands and sobbed so hard a piece of myself severed and floated away.

CHAPTER FIFTEEN

23 DAYS LEFT

After my failure with the navitas, I spent the night flipping through *Common Magical Cures*. The tiny black scratches blended together, ink coalescing into a giant black hole, trying to suck me in. This was so utterly futile, but a week had already passed, and Mare's threats ticked so loudly they echoed through every corner of the castle.

Book pillowed under my head, I awoke to a darkening gray sky. Another snowstorm was brewing, the scent lingering on the tip of my tongue, crisp and sharp like fresh reams of paper. My sleep had been restless, filled with dreams of stolen kisses in a moonlit garden, fearsome creatures with enormous, clawed feet, and the haunting melody of unbreakable curses.

My late-night search hadn't been in vain, though. Before I'd finally caved to sleep, I found a recipe for a tincture used to rouse people from unconsciousness and it was the most promising lead I'd uncovered so far. Or maybe I was simply grasping at brittle straws. I was getting very good at kidding myself.

Book tucked under my arm, I headed downstairs to the kitchen for breakfast. Everyone was already eating poached eggs and waffles while drinking hot cups of tea and coffee. Grabbing a piece of toast, I sat down and flipped open the book with a thud.

"Gideon, can you tell me if we have these ingredients in the kitchen?"

He scanned the book, picking it up and wandering into the pantry, murmuring to himself.

Turning to Ronan, I pointed my toast at him, more determined than ever to get these warriors from my enemy kingdom out of my home. Ronan officially knew too much, and I didn't need him getting any closer to the truth about what else had happened inside these walls.

"So, you'll be off today?" Everyone turned to look at me. "What? You convinced me to have dinner at the chateau, but now it's time to leave as we agreed, right? It looks like another storm is coming, so you'll want to be well on your way before then."

"But, Your Highness," Kianna said, "Valentus is in just two days. Wouldn't it be wonderful to attend in Tenby this year?"

My eyes narrowed. What was she up to now? Why was she bringing up Valentus, of all things? To my knowledge, no one in the castle ever attended. The Fae had spurned such celebrations, claiming they were pale, bastardized human copies of the

Faerie versions. It was a night for the villagers. One meant for drinking and carousing.

Kianna exchanged a meaningful glance with Em. She clearly wanted to keep Em here, but Kianna didn't know how dangerous this was. The longer Ronan stayed in this castle, the more likely he was to discover my secret. Her flirtatious crush could spell untold disaster.

"Kianna, can I talk to you outside?" With gritted teeth, I threw her a pointed look. My temper threatened to burst, but I would do Kianna the courtesy of scolding her without an audience.

She ignored my request, simply turning away as though I hadn't spoken, like I was a vase sitting at the center of the table. My teeth ground so hard I felt it in my temple.

"I've always wanted to go," she exclaimed, refusing to meet my eyes. "My sisters never approved."

"I haven't been to Valentus in years," Noah said in a wistful voice. "We've been out in the field for so long, I'd forgotten it was coming up. You should see how wild it gets in Estria."

Em snorted into her mug and pointed to Noah. "Remember that year you ended up naked inside Old Lady Shimp's hay loft? She nearly tore off your backside, chasing you with that rake."

"Ah, but it was worth it for a night with her oh-so-shapely daughter, literally rolling in the hay." Noah winked at me, and I wrinkled my nose. Everyone burst into laughter. Noah continued, "Your Highness, it wouldn't be proper to attend alone. Surely a guard would be most suitable." His questioning gaze flicked to Ronan, who was watching me. "Ronan, come on. What's a few more days?" There was a pleading edge to his voice. "I promise we'll scout some of the nearby villages this afternoon."

Em chimed in as well, and after Ronan folded like a cheap paper fan, everyone returned their attention to me. Too arrogant to beg, Ronan's query came from that single, devastating raised eyebrow I was apparently helpless to resist, because my resolve was as solid as a house of cards in a windstorm. Finding those enormous, clawed footprints outside had shaken me, and these warriors provided a layer of security from what hid under my bed.

"Fine, you can stay here a few more days and attend, but Kianna and I will remain here." With a sharp look, I dared her to argue, but I wasn't sure why I thought I had any authority, because she did it anyway.

Pressing her hands together in front of her heart, she implored me with round doe eyes. "Please, Your Highness. Let's go. You could use a night of fun, for *all* our sakes. Please?"

I ignored Ronan's snort and looked to Gideon for aid. Just returned from the pantry, he wore an expectant smile. "What about you?"

"It is one night I usually get a break from my duties, Your Highness." He held up the book. "And, regrettably, we do not have everything you need. We can pick up the rest while we're in the city."

With a sigh, I rolled my eyes and put on my most irritated expression. "I guess I'm outnumbered."

A cheer went up around the table, and I smiled despite myself. I was doing this only to secure the ingredients I needed.

As animated chatter filled the room, Ronan's eyes locked with mine.

The noise melted away, and it was the two of us standing out on a ledge, a pair of magnets drawn by fate's meddling pull. His perfect, full lips turned up into a smile that mirrored the private thoughts I only allowed myself during the moonlit hours in my bed, as my heart stuttered and tripped on its face.

CHAPTER SIXTEEN

21 DAYS LEFT

THE SNOW KEPT FALLING, coating the forest in icy frost. We kept mostly indoors, haunting the hallways and listening to the howling of the wind. Kianna retreated to her bedroom to sleep while Gideon kept busy in the kitchen. In between scouting for the king, Noah and Em moved their training to the ballroom.

They grunted and punched and fought with their fists and their knives, and I insisted they teach me that too. After spending long hours practising with Ronan, I was improving. It wasn't enough to take down Mare, but it still catered to some flimsy illusion of freedom. This ability to defend and care for myself was something I hadn't even realized I needed.

Following a grueling session in the ballroom, I retreated to the throne room, as I did every night. Sitting amongst the people I loved calmed me as the sounds of their soft breaths filled the quiet space.

Adrian slumped against the dais stairs, his head cradled in his arms where a lock of dark hair had fallen across his forehead. I leaned down to brush it back before resting my hand on his warm cheek, caressing the rough bit of stubble. How I wished I could thank him for those final grim days. Thank him for being the only one who hadn't made me feel like I was covered in boils that would infect him if I got too close.

A bottle of wine placed on the floor next to me, I sat down between my parents. Leaning against my mother's legs, I recalled the day before my twenty-first birthday all those years ago.

Anxiety lingered in the castle, but it blended with an undeniable sense of relief. I had become a burden. Once we'd accepted the inevitable, everyone was eager to get this over with. Which, I supposed, was fair. After I was asleep, Mare would stay away, and she'd leave them in peace. The only thing anyone had to give up was me.

Soft footsteps preceded Ronan into the room. He wore a white shirt, the open collar exposing the hard planes of his chest, the sleeves fitted against sculpted arms. Fresh from a bath, his shiny hair hung past his shoulders, braids neatly redone, the top half swept into a knot at the back of his head. His pants hugged his hips as if they worshipped him, and I'd never been more envious of a piece of leather in my life. I took a large swig of wine to calm my nerves, which were in a permanent state of turmoil.

"You okay?" Hands stuffed in his pockets, he canted his head. "Drinking alone, Little Lion?"

With a defiant glare, I picked up the bottle and took another long swig, staring him dead in the eye. I'd drink alone, and I'd drink a lot if I damn well wanted. I was a princess with some serious issues.

"Is that a problem?" I asked, wiping my mouth with my sleeve. That won me a roll of his eyes.

"Would you like some company?"

I shrugged, but I also scooted over, making some room.

"What are you doing?" he asked, wrapping a hand around the bottle in my grip, but I resisted his pull. He gave it a small jerk and glared, tugging harder, and finally, I relented. He offered me a dubious look and then tipped his head back, taking a long swig. I watched the bob of his throat, mesmerized by the rugged lines of his profile.

"Wallowing," I replied, letting my head drop against my mother's knee.

"I don't see why. You're in the middle of a snowstorm, sitting next to the most handsome man in the entire kingdom."

I snorted. "Thanks, I needed a laugh. You should be a court jester if this whole commander thing doesn't work out." The sound of his deep laughter rattled something loose inside me before he took another sip from the bottle.

"Give that to me," I said, snatching it from his grasp.

He snatched it back and held it high over his head where I couldn't reach without standing up or leaning on top of him. Though I considered the latter option, I sat back with a petulant scowl.

"Fine, you win." A gloating smile spread across his face before he took another pull of wine. "But this isn't your kingdom." He stilled, the bottle poised in midair. "We are in Ravalyn. Tenby and all the surrounding villages once belonged to us, but your father stole them."

The words hung between us, thick as sugar-spun webs, the truth we'd been avoiding finally laid bare.

"How do you know the king is my father?"

"I heard you that night at the Whitefeather Inn. I was sitting at the table next to you. You are a prince, and your father—the king—is missing. I know that's why you go out looking every day. Also, I doubt most soldiers travel with a manservant."

It took all my willpower not to let my gaze wander toward the forest where the king lay buried under an inadequate layer of dirt and snow.

"Why are you really here?" I asked. "What are you hiding from? You didn't stay here because of a little snow, and you certainly aren't staying longer because of some silly festival. What aren't you telling me, *Prince* Ronan?"

"I am not a prince," he growled, and there were so many layers of unvoiced truth buried in that sound that I could dig forever and still not uncover them all. "My brother is the crown prince. I just command the king's armies."

"And why aren't you there commanding them now?"

Now that I'd started this, I couldn't stop myself. As he ran a hand down his face, his shoulders pinched together with tension.

"Because I can't go home without answers about the king. We've searched for weeks, but the trail is cold. No one outside Tenby remembers seeing him the day he left the Whitefeather. Our kingdom's rule is tenuous at best. My family's hold on the crown is fragile, and if my father's absence is discovered, it could mean war."

Since Ronan appeared to be in a sharing mood tonight, I pressed further. "From the noble houses?"

He flashed a glare at me. "You really heard everything, didn't you?"

I raised my hands in a gesture of mock helplessness. "You should be more careful when you have your top-secret meetings."

He narrowed his gaze but replied, "From them, yes, but the greater threat comes from outside our borders."

Quietly, I waited for him to continue.

"The true threat lies to the south. The Faerie kingdoms." I took in a sharp breath, remembering the two brutal Fae I'd witnessed in the town square.

"Why does your father employ them? I saw them that day in Tenby. At the...execution." Slaughter would be a more apt description.

"My father doesn't employ them. Humans don't employ Fae. They hang around, watching, spying, and doing what they can to torture us. Riding the confines of laws that bind them from exacting the brutality they once subjected on humanity. They are biding their time, waiting for their moment. Accords drawn between humans and Fae are a weak veneer for what still goes on in the Faerie realms. There are plenty who desire a return to the old ways, when humans were used for their entertainment or torment and nothing more."

He sighed, leaning against the leg of my father's throne.

"Those two you saw are of a particularly nasty breed. My reason for being in Tenby wasn't only because of my father, but to keep an eye on Maida and Alban. But it's futile because they recognize no orders from me—or the king, for that matter."

"Which is the silver-haired one?" I asked.

"That's Maida. Why do you ask?"

"No reason," I said, recalling the way he had stared at me, as if he wanted to peel off my skin and savor my organs between his sharp teeth.

"Then Ravalyn is in danger too," I added.

"Yes, we all are. And you're right—my father stole your kingdom because there was no one to defend it. But we had no idea you were alive. The stories about the curse of a sleeping princess were a legend. They said people tried to rescue you at first, but after enough time, it seemed impossible any of you were still alive."

Ronan's green eyes studied me like I was a puzzle to be cracked. "Many in Ravalyn still believe you're alive. It's part of the reason they're so restless—they think you're coming back for them."

That bit of news latched into my hopes, bolstering them like plaster smoothed over decaying walls. "And outside Ravalyn? What about in Estria?"

"I don't know. Possibly. Why do you ask?"

I shook my head, wondering if the king had believed us dead. If he had come looking, only to meet his end at the point of my dagger.

"Thorne," he said. It was the first time he'd said my name without a sarcastic 'Princess' attached to it. I liked the way it sounded coming from him, like it was shiny and clean, though I was neither of those things. "I'm sorry. On behalf of my father, I'm sorry we took your lands while you slept. If my father had known you were here—"

"What? He would have left them alone? He will give them back now that I'm awake?" My anger swelled, exploding through the thin shield of guilt I wore for what I had done to the king.

"No," Ronan said, as if realizing an important truth. "Not that."

"Was—" I caught myself. "Is your father a good man?"

I needed to know. Had it been one act of depravity, borne of a violence the king hadn't even known he possessed? Or was he a man wholly capable of what he'd done?

Ronan hesitated, and the silence in that momentary pause told me everything I needed to know.

"He is a hard man," Ronan said, finally. He opened his mouth when footsteps pounded toward the throne room, echoing along the corridor.

Gideon burst into the room, his chest heaving. "Your Highness. Commander. You must come."

Ronan and I exchanged worried glances as we stood to follow Gideon.

Was it Mare? The creature with the enormous claws? Or some other disaster?

He directed us toward a spiral staircase that wound into the dungeons.

"Gideon, why are you taking us down here?"

The man scrubbed a hand through his graying hair. "It would be better if you see it, Highness. Please follow me."

Gideon clomped down the staircase, and I followed with Ronan close on my heels. The temperature dropped as we descended, a chill stealing through my clothes. Sconces lit our way, illuminating the velvety darkness. The smell wafted up, and I gagged as shame heated my cheeks. It had never occurred to me there might be people down here, too.

We reached the bottom, and Gideon gestured for us to follow, his face ashen. "This way." Cells lined the walls, most of them empty. Gideon came to a stop in front of one, and Ronan and I approached, bracing ourselves.

What I saw made the air in my lungs turn sluggish and dense.

A man lay asleep on the floor. One half of him was whole, his face arranged into a peaceful imitation of slumber, while the other half was a decayed mass of bones and rotted bits of faded clothing, like something was eating him alive.

My gorge rose as I clapped my hands over my mouth. "The curse," I said, the words slinking into the blackness, coating the dungeon with their taint. "It's receding?"

And the truth of it hit us. Whatever magic had kept the people of the castle preserved in a suspended state for a century was retreating. As I went to explore further, Ronan grabbed me and pulled me against him.

"Don't." An arm banded around my waist. "What if you cross the line and you..." We both peered into the shadows of the dim hallway.

"What if I turn to dust?" My voice sounded timid and empty, swallowed by an impermeable silence. I felt him nod. "We have to move everyone." I spun around, my hands pressed against Ronan's chest, his arm still around me. "We'll move them to the throne room. It's at the center of the castle. They'll be safer there."

Bleak determination on his face, Ronan tipped his chin. "Get the others," he ordered Gideon, not taking his eyes off me.

Gideon took off at full speed.

I was shaking, my knees liquifying like melted butter. Ronan's strong arm held me up as he pressed me closer.

"The keys. We need the keys for the cells," I said into his chest. My skin was warm and clammy, and I couldn't stop trembling.

Ronan placed a finger under my chin, tipping my face up. "It's okay. We'll move everyone. Don't worry. This is going to be okay."

Ashes in my throat, I answered with a nod. Except nothing was okay.

Gideon returned with Em and Noah and, to my relief, a set of keys. "We should clear out this part and then check the opposite end of the castle next. There may be more there," he said.

Everyone set to work. Hands shaking, I began unlocking doors and then moved in to help lift one of the sleeping prisoners.

Ronan held a man by his ankles, and I grabbed his wrists. "Thorne, we can do this. Go and wait with Kianna."

"I will not sit idle as my people are devoured by a curse they had no part in causing." I glared at him, daring him to argue, but without hesitation, he said, "On the count of three, then."

It was backbreaking work. There were close to two hundred people living in the castle, and only about half were already in the throne room. Thankfully, the cavernous space was more than adequate as we filed everyone in.

We worked through the night, and it was morning by the time we were done. Exhausted, we all sat quietly, surveying the bodies lying in neat rows like the wounded victims of war. Kianna slid down the wall next to me and took my hand.

"Thank you. All of you, for your help tonight," I whispered, the knot in my throat like fire. "The people of Ravalyn won't forget your kindness, nor will I."

As I stared at the sleeping people, I felt the erosion of all my naïve intentions. The game I was trapped in had more rules than I'd ever imagined. Sobs devoured my body as I fell against Kianna, silently begging her for strength. Her arms wrapped around me, and we stayed like that for a long time as I wept an endless, winding river of my failures.

Strong arms scooped me up, and Ronan cradled me to his chest before he carried me through the halls. With my forehead pressed to his throat, my tears soaked into his skin. I took a deep inhale, filling myself with his warm and comforting scent. Gently, he placed me on my bed and Kianna scooted in, banding an arm around my waist. Cocooned in her shield, I drifted off to sleep.

CHAPTER SEVENTEEN

20 DAYS LEFT

"DON'T GRIP THE BOW; let it rest in your hand," Noah said, squinting at a glass bottle that sat almost two hundred yards away. It was a nearly impossible shot, but I was becoming more comfortable pushing myself, testing the limits of the box that had once shaped the rigid corners of my life.

"I know," I said, clenching my teeth. "You've told me that a hundred times."

"Then do it right, Princess," Noah said, his expression daring me to argue.

With a shake to loosen my shoulders and an irritated huff, I focused on the bottle, trying to erase the image of the decaying prisoner. After replaying it over in my head too many times to count, I'd begged Noah for an archery lesson as a temporary distraction. It was only partly working.

Em and Ronan were busy behind us, swords clanging.

"Easy," Noah said, softly. "Remember—use your back to draw the bow. Not your arms." He hovered close enough to touch the weapon and send it off course, trying to throw me off. Slowly pulling on the taut string, I let the arrow fly. It hit the bottle dead center, and it shot off the log, crashing to the ground in an explosion of glittering shards.

"Yes!" I screamed and jumped up. "I did it! Did you see that?"

Ronan and Em were both clapping, and I blushed at their attention.

"Did you see?" I flashed a smile at Ronan. He returned it with an appreciative rake of his eyes that had me flushing about more than just my archery skills. A flush that had nothing to do with the fact he was bare from the waist up, a sheen of sweat highlighting the curves and angles of his flawlessly carved torso.

"Impressive, Princess Thorne. Woe be upon the man who ever tries to win your heart," he said, a hand pressed to his sternum.

Noah clapped me on the shoulder so hard I stumbled. "Yah, he'll get his balls ripped off anytime he opens his mouth."

I glared at him, and he laughed.

"It's true," I admitted and flicked my hair over my shoulder to a round of laughter from everyone. I snuck a glance at Ronan, whose admiring smile pleased me far more than it should have.

"Again," I announced, stalking over to the barrel to retrieve another bottle. For the next hour, I continued practising, only missing a handful of times until I'd broken every single one.

"I think I've done all I can here," Noah said, finally. "I've created a monster." He scrubbed his hand over his face, and I threw out an evil cackle. The lesson had done the trick and relieved my burdens for a short time.

The sun was beating warmth on the ground, the sounds of melting snow serenading us with a symphony composed of drips and gurgles. Ronan and Em were circling each other. He was mesmerizing to watch, as graceful and fluid as melted sugar pulled into ribbons.

Blades flashing and grunts echoing, Ronan and Em moved in bursts of precise energy and a sequence of motions, every thrust controlled and practised with years of impeccable training. After a valiant fight, Ronan knocked Em to the ground and pointed his blade at her heart with an adoring smile.

"One day, I'm going to beat you," Em snarled from her position on the ground, but I could hear the respect in her voice.

Ronan reached out a hand and helped her up. When he moved, I tried not to notice the way his back and arms and stomach flexed and rippled. My mouth going dry, I was failing miserably.

This close, I took the opportunity to study the scars on his back. Thick ridges crossed his skin like a poet scribbling an anguished sonnet. Some wrapped around his sides, where the whip had curled around his ribs. A hard knot of rage formed in my chest, wanting to deliver a tenfold avalanche of punishment to whomever had caused him such pain.

Noah and Em were taking a turn now, facing off across the courtyard as my mind wandered to last night and the dungeon. How much time had passed since the curse's suspension of time had failed? Had it been happening all along? The likely answer was that it had started when I'd woken up, and that meant we might not have much time left before it consumed the entire castle.

Time. It had become my most formidable foe. One I couldn't stop, even with an army of a million hardened warriors.

Ronan had been right to stop me before I'd stepped over the threshold. I didn't know how the magic would affect me. Would I also have dissolved into a pile of nothing? I shuddered. In an increasingly long list of problems, this was another for which I had no solution.

Ronan drifted over to stand next to me, arms crossed and accentuating the curves of his biceps. His bared torso was so utterly distracting that it took a prodigious effort not to reach out and trace a finger along the planes of his stomach. I shook my head, silently admonishing myself.

Stop it, Thorne.

A bead of sweat slid down his neck, slipping through the well of his pecs. My eyes tracked it, like a wolf stalking prey, as a thousand variations of me leaning over to lick it sprinted through my mind before they went straight to the space between my thighs.

Squeezing my eyes shut, I averted my gaze. These were useless thoughts. Tomorrow was Valentus. I'd get what I needed for my tincture in Tenby, Kianna would have her fun, and then Ronan would leave. My secret would be safe. I couldn't afford any more distractions.

"How are you feeling?" he asked, leaning in close, dispelling every notion of ignoring the way the sun reflected off his skin and how good he smelled, even when covered in sweat. I let out a long breath of air.

"Like I'm zigzagging for cover under a barrage of flaming arrows?" He offered me a concerned look. "I'm scared. And worried. And I don't know what to do." The admission felt ripped from my spirit, like I was offering a piece of myself to be weighed and packaged. I'd been trying to hold it together, but Ronan made me feel safe enough to let go, just a little. But I had to keep a better handle on myself. I kept forgetting who he was, and that was going to get me in trouble.

He shifted closer—so close, I only needed to tip forward an inch for my breasts to brush against his chest. Blood rushed to each of my limbs and pooled low in my stomach.

"I wouldn't let anything happen to you, Thorne. Ever." There was such sincerity in his voice that a tiny spring bud bloomed in my chest, bursting to life in a riot of petals. I studied his face, wondering why he was so intent on helping me.

"Thank you. But I can take care of myself." My problems weren't his to solve. He had enough of his own.

Ronan laughed softly, leaning down so his mouth brushed the shell of my ear. I closed my fists against my thighs, resisting the overwhelming urge to sink my teeth into his flesh and taste him. To trace my tongue along the hard lines of his body.

"I have no doubt about that, Little Lion," he said, his voice smothering me in shadowed silk.

An involuntary smile crept to my face as a shiver rippled down my back.

This felt too good. He was too tempting. Too...*distracting.* So I pulled away. "I'm going to see how Gideon is doing with dinner."

After all the times he'd done it, it was my turn to give Ronan the once-over. I let my eyes sweep slowly from his feet, up his thighs and narrow hips, to his chest and impeccable face. His glittering green eyes met mine with such open rawness, I felt like a melon split in half, my insides oozing out in a wet and shapeless heap. The intensity compressed my lungs, forcing me to turn away first.

A low, dark chuckle told me I'd just lost our stand-off, and I huffed in irritation. "Put some clothes on," I snapped. "It's winter, for god's sake."

Before Ronan could notice my blushing cheeks, I hurried to the castle, more laughter following in my wake.

Later that night, I tossed and turned, unable to sleep. I couldn't stop seeing the man in the dungeon, half of him eaten away. The image forever tattooed on my brain, I'd carry it with me for the rest of my life. I'd let him down. I only hoped I could do better for the rest of the people in this castle.

Giving up on sleep, I roused from my bed, tying my robe over my nightgown.

Kianna's door was closed, and I held up a fist, about to knock, when I stopped. I shouldn't disturb her just because I needed company. Instead, I made my way to the throne room. At the top of the dais, I placed a soft kiss on my mother's forehead. Every night, I hoped for something. Every single time, I hoped for some flicker of consciousness. For some sign that she heard me or knew I was there. But of course, it never happened.

After I smoothed the black curls that hung around her face, I moved to my father. His unruly nest of hair had a life of its own, even in sleep. I tucked it under his crown, wishing I could see his eyes. I pressed a kiss to his cheek, touching his face. "I wish you'd wake up," I whispered. "I miss you so much."

Normally, the cadence of sleep worked like a balm to soothe my tightly wound nerves—the murmurs and snores, the softly exhaled sighs of peaceful slumber. But tonight, the sounds were less comforting. They reminded me more of the clock that kept ticking, an incessant buzz in my ear winding down with a high-pitched drone.

Feeling no desire to linger, I moved in the kitchen's direction, the one spot in the castle where I always felt safe now. As I descended the stairs, silent on slippered feet, I heard Em speak.

"Noah, remember those twins we met when we were campaigning in The Red Canyon? They dressed as cooks to sneak into the camp?"

"Remember them?" I heard Noah reply. "I thought I found the gods that night." There was a burst of laughter.

"What I remember is how eager you were to attack Yagomond's forces so we could get back to our tents where they were waiting," Noah said.

"Damn right," Em replied, and I smiled as I heard the clink of glasses.

Not wanting to disturb their conversation, I turned to head back up the stairs when Noah spoke again. "How about you, Ronan?" I stopped and waited, blood rushing to my ears. "I suppose it's time to get back to her royalness, the Lady of Elsenmoor, soon?"

Everyone laughed again, and then someone groaned, followed up with another round of laughter.

"She's not so bad," I heard Ronan reply.

My legs melted out from under me, brackish sludge bubbling in my gut. Gripping the wall, I backed up the stairs, blocking my ears from overhearing more. Gods, I was such a fool. I'd been making such an ass of myself. No matter what he said, he was a prince and the most beautiful man I'd ever seen. Of course, he had someone waiting for him in Estria.

I hated how disappointment filtered into the fractured chinks of my bones. How it burrowed so deep it would take years for me to unearth it. It didn't matter. Technically, we were enemies. Heirs of rival kingdoms. I had no right to this misplaced emotion.

I killed his father.

And in twenty days, Mare would come for me, and I wasn't one iota closer to figuring out how to break this curse.

Ronan was leaving the day after tomorrow. This time, I would make sure of it. I'd been throwing myself at a man who could never be mine.

Even if we wanted it, there was no future for us.

CHAPTER EIGHTEEN

19 DAYS LEFT

KIANNA WALKED INTO MY room and made a sound of disgust. "What is that?" She pointed at me, her lip curled. I'd donned a simple green dress and pulled my hair back at the nape of my neck. Currently, I was tying up my warmest pair of boots.

"What?" I looked down at myself. "Do I have a stain?"

"You are *not* going to Valentus dressed like that."

She pranced to my wardrobe, throwing open the doors.

"What's the matter with this?" But even as the words left my mouth, I understood. Kianna was stunning in a floor-length gown made of dark green silk, studded with sparkling crystals. Her deep brown skin had been dusted with gold, and even her wings were decorated with iridescent hand-painted stars.

She threw me a withering scowl.

"Kianna," I said, my hands on my hips. "I am not yours to control anymore."

The words hit the ground between us, slapping like wet cloth against river rocks. Kianna stopped thumbing through my closet, her posture stiff.

It was an unspoken wedge between us, leaving just enough space to examine it from every incongruent angle. Though we'd grown closer, I hadn't let go of the misery she and her sisters had caused. Nor the way they had always made me feel like a shriveled grape left too long in the sun.

But I snapped at her too often. Was short with her, even when she didn't deserve it. I was sure it was why she'd invited Ronan and the others to stay, so she wasn't stuck here with only me for company. They provided a much-needed buffer against my diluted patience.

"I know, Your Highness." She was having trouble meeting my eyes, and I dropped my hands. I wanted to bridge the chasm of our severed relationship, and I sensed she wanted the same.

"I suppose you're right," I said, finally, wanting to dispel the tension in her back. "This is rather drab."

Instantly she transformed, a smile lighting her face as she clapped her hands and returned to the wardrobe. The truth was, I missed my beautiful clothes. It was the one perk of being a princess I'd never minded. Silk and jewels, and always the latest fashions right at my fingertips. Always the best things money could buy. None of it had seemed important lately, though, when so many other things were competing for my attention. Besides, it was harder to kill a man while wearing a skirt.

Kianna pulled out a bright red dress, and I started to protest, but shut my mouth. Once in a while, I could accept what was in front of me. When no objection came, she clawed at my offending garment, and I slipped it off to replace it with something far bolder and more festive. Snug around my waist, the skirt flared into a cascade of red bits of silk and chiffon and lace, layer upon delicate layer. The neckline sat low, exposing the top swell of my breasts, framed by a soft trim of red petals.

Kianna led me to the dressing table. "Sit down."

With a wave of her hand, my hair twisted into a thick braid, loosened strands carefully framing my face. Scarlet flowers bloomed from her fingertips, and she wove them into the plait. Cherry-red lipstick and a swoop of black around my eyes completed the look. I had to admit, the dress was perfect with my brown skin and midnight hair.

"So much better!" Kianna declared, her eyes shining.

I smiled at her through the mirror. "It is. Thank you. But am I allowed to wear my boots?"

Kianna nodded. "Yes, a lady still needs to manage through the snow."

I laughed and donned my black wool coat with its wide collar of silver fox fur. It was sunny, so I left it unbuttoned as we made our way to the stables. The others were already waiting with their horses. I scanned the forest, wondering where Slumber, the horse, had ended up after I'd left him in the trees.

Ronan had his back to us, arms resting on the saddle of his mount. I bit the inside of my lip, staring at the way his pants stretched over the molded lines of his ass and his shirt skimmed up his sides and broad shoulders. Noah let out a low whistle as we approached, severing my single-minded thought.

"Look at you two. Don't you clean up nice?" He regarded me and Kianna with an approving nod.

Ronan turned, my cheeks flushing as he stared at me, those evergreen eyes focused on my mouth as he lifted a hand to rub his chin.

Stepping forward, I patted Ronan on the cheek. "Stop staring. You're making a fool of yourself." My tone was light and teasing, but I'd be lying if I said his reaction didn't please me.

He blinked and then grinned as he stepped back, an arm sweeping out to his horse. "Your carriage, Highness."

Damn.

There were four horses and six of us. A conflict of emotions bound me in hesitation. While being so close to Ronan wasn't an unwelcome thought, the conversation I'd overheard surfaced to the top of a weed-clogged lake, reminding me of Lady whatever-her-name-was, and I wasn't eager to put myself in a vulnerable position.

"Kianna can ride with you."

"Too late," she said, already sitting with Em, her slender arms wrapped around the other woman's waist. "Besides, I could fly if I needed to." She twitched her wings as if to illustrate her point.

"I'll ride with Noah," I said, feeling a little crazy.

"Your Highness," Ronan said, leaning down as if to ensure no one else could hear. "Between you and me, he is not as skilled a rider as I am. He is liable to let you fall and break that enticing neck."

Conscious of everyone watching me, I hesitated. I looked like a fool making such a big deal about this. I could ride with Ronan. This was for the sake of convenience.

"Fine." I threw my bag at Ronan's chest and then grabbed the saddle, pulling myself up and arranging my skirt around me. As he joined me, I felt every whisper of his hard body against mine scattering my pulse in a thousand directions.

"An excellent choice, Your Highness," he said right in my ear, so close his lips ghosted my skin. His bottomless baritone trickled down the exposed lines of my throat and the top of my breasts before a shiver ricocheted down my spine. "I'll try not to be too distracted by how good you smell." His words tightened every inch of skin like the tuning pegs of a violin.

I glimpsed him over my shoulder, and our eyes held for a prolonged breath, a flare of heat singeing me between my thighs. A moment later, the horse sidestepped, jolting us both, and the connection broke, much to my relief and disappointment.

As we rode for Tenby, I did my best to limit contact between Ronan and me, while also acknowledging I didn't really want to. The task was futile, anyway, because the pace of the horse made it impossible, and I suspected he was moving with me to ensure we remained in contact.

Maybe I didn't mind though. Maybe I *should* have minded remembering all the reasons this was a terrible idea. But the feel of him pressed to my back was thrilling, and it was hard to remember why I should put a stop to this. When his hand slid to my hip, fingers digging in with the slightest pressure, my thoughts jumbled like pieces on an upended chessboard.

Soon, entirely too soon, if I was being honest, we saw the lights of Tenby. We entered the city and headed for the White-feather. The celebration was already in full swing, festivities spilling into the streets. White lights and red paper hearts hung across streetlamps while flowers in shades of pink and red burst in every direction. Silently, I thanked Kianna for insisting on the red dress.

We dismounted at the inn, where tables sat arranged on the cobbles. More garlands of lights and red hearts hung overhead. Small lamps flickering with flames lined the perimeter, warming the air and chasing off the chill. People filled the tables—laughing, drinking, and eating. Thankfully, Maida and Alban, the blood Fae, were nowhere to be seen. We sat down as Gideon went to secure our rooms.

"Welcome to the night of love!" Verna bustled over, dropping tankards of ale in front of us. She looked at Ronan and me and winked. Bowls of venison stew materialized, and Noah and Em attacked them with relish.

"What exactly is Valentus, anyway?" I asked.

"It's a very old Fae celebration," Kianna said. "Intended to celebrate love, fertility, and all the things that go along with it. It's held at the start of winter as people tend to spend more time indoors." She gave me a coy smile, and I became increasingly aware of Ronan's ever-distracting and heart-fluttering presence.

Someone was passing around a giant glass orb, filled with slips of paper.

"Hey!" Noah jumped up, a folded square in his hand. "I want in." He deposited it in the bowl, followed by a grinning Em.

I frowned. "What is that?"

Em turned her grin to me. "That's the bowl of love. You put your name in, and it pairs you up with someone."

"What do you mean, pairs up?"

Em raised an eyebrow. "I know you were asleep for a while, but surely you know what goes on between two people seeking some amorous attention?"

I glared at her. "That's not what I meant."

She laughed and took a swig of her ale. "Then I suppose it means whatever you want it to mean. A bit of fun tonight, or someone to keep you warm all winter."

"I see." I turned to Ronan. "And are you putting your name in?"

"Should I?"

"You can do whatever you want." I feigned as much disinterest as I could, even though I'd never been more intent on hearing the response to a casually uttered question in my entire life.

"In that case, I think I'll take my chances and keep my name out of the bowl." His gaze dipped to where I was spilling out of my dress, and a molten thread raced up the center of my body.

Before long, the food was finished, and all but me and Ronan had drifted off in search of the night's entertainments.

"Will you walk with me?" Ronan stood and picked up my jacket, holding it open so I could slip my arms into the sleeves. As I shrugged it on, he wrapped it over my body, his hands lingering for longer than was perhaps necessary.

Warm and inviting, his large hand captured mine, leading me through the tables. He didn't drop it as we entered the street, and I kept my gaze on him. Dressed in a pale gray tunic, the cut showed off every sharp cliff of his hard-earned physique. The braids running along the sides of his head marked him as a warrior, as sure as the sword hanging from his side. After nearly stumbling on a crack in the pavement, I tore my eyes away with no small amount of reluctance.

More tables and chairs lined the sidewalks, full of people eating, drinking, and laughing. Fire breathers belched out plumes of flame into the night sky. Acrobats twisted around rings floating in the air, their sinewy bodies bending and folding like they were made of cooling honey. String quartets sawed with their bows while dancing women in long ruffled dresses and black-heeled shoes stomped in rhythm. Couples swayed in a small square, their bodies pressed close, lost in the music and the crisp evening air.

"Will you dance with me?" Surprising myself with the question, I bit my lip and chanced a peek at Ronan, worried I had been imagining the mood of the evening. I'd forgotten about his friend, Lady Elsenmoor. "Never mind," I added. "That was a stupid thing to ask."

I was about to pull my hand away and find a rotting log to crawl into until spring, when Ronan tightened his grip and pulled me back. His eyes were alight, that dimple on his cheek blinding me with its radiance.

"Where are you going?" He tugged my hand, drawing me toward the other dancing pairs. "I would love to dance, Princess." As he wrapped an arm around me, pulling me close, I let out a sigh that felt like it had been held too long.

My head fell against his chest, where I could feel the thrum of his heart. It dug into the fortress I was trying to erect, but the walls kept falling and I wasn't fast enough to repair them. A deep inhale of forests and cinnamon chipped further away at my crumbling façade.

"You look beautiful tonight," he said, his chin resting against the side of my head. "I almost had a heart attack when you and Kianna came out to the stables."

I smiled against the cut of his collarbone. "You're beautiful too."

His chest rumbled as he laughed, and his hands slid under my unbuttoned coat, finding my back where his roaming fingers burned lines of heat against my bare skin. His touch felt decadent, its warmth melting deep into my stomach before it pulled tight. My arms wrapped around his waist, I explored the dips and valleys of his muscles, the taut ridges interrupted by the scars I knew were there. I looked up, my hands lying flat on his chest. His arms stayed around me, the gentle swirl of his fingers threatening to undo me.

"Who did that to you?" His hands went still, but it was an answer I desperately needed at that moment. A fierce desire to protect him took root, gluing me to the earth.

Who brought this indomitable warrior to his knees?

"You really know how to kill a mood, Thorne." There was no anger in his words. They were part grim resignation and part patient exasperation. "My father."

My breath wilted. Echoes of the scars the king had scratched into me, twisted with the ones he'd carved into his son.

"When I was twenty-four, I led my father's army in battle against our enemies to the east, just beyond The Red Canyon. It was a small but wealthy kingdom that controlled access to the Salt Seas. It should have been a straightforward task, but I made a costly mistake and was captured and taken behind enemy lines."

As he paused, I touched his cheek, stubble rough against my hand. He covered it with his large palm.

"You don't have to tell me," I whispered, feeling like an ass for forcing him to relive this. "I'm sorry. I shouldn't have asked. I don't know what I was thinking."

"I don't mind sharing with you." His words felt like a confession, something profound in the beat between syllables. "They kept me captive and used me to blackmail my father into better terms, into gold—you name it. They held me for months. As far as being captured by your enemy, they were actually quite good to me. They only beat and tortured me a little."

My mouth dropped open, and he laughed.

"That's war, Princess. It is brutal and ugly and mean. I came to respect the commander of their army. We held a lot of similar views. Eventually, my father relented to their terms, and they sent me back to Estria only a little worse for wear.

"My father was furious. Blamed me for what he'd lost in the negotiations. The gold, yes, but more importantly, the position of power he'd been hoping to gain in the Salt Shore. He also blamed me for getting myself captured. He was right. It was an error made by a young soldier, and I should have known better."

"But you were... You *are* so young. Commanding an entire army at that age."

He shrugged, but the movement was strained. "I'd been schooled my entire life for it. That wasn't an excuse in his eyes. As punishment, he had me whipped before my entire army. It is the worst fate for a commander—letting my men see me like that. Broken. Vulnerable. Almost destroyed. My father knew it would be much harder for me to lead them after that."

Ronan's eyes were distant, his mind trapped in memories.

"The healers said it was a miracle I didn't die from my injuries, but it took months to heal. Even now, almost three years later, the scars still bother me."

"That is—I'm so sorry. You didn't deserve that."

He shrugged again, something raw and fleeting in his expression. My fingers flexed against the firm wall of his chest, wishing I could shovel into his soul and take away this pain.

"Did it work? Did you lose the hearts of your men?"

His smile was wan as he shook his head. "I didn't. They rallied around me. An act for which my father never forgave them. He can do nothing because replacing an army is no small task, but my father underestimated the character of his soldiers."

"I think he underestimated the man leading them," I said, and his gaze shifted as though something essential had just occurred to him for the very first time.

"Thank you," he whispered.

Fingers cradling my chin, his thumb swept my bottom lip. Despite every misgiving, I wanted him to kiss me. I wanted it like I wanted more cream on my scones or an extra cherry on my ice cream. I wanted it like I wanted sunshine in summer and the warmth of a fire in winter.

He leaned closer, and my breath expanded to fill the space between us, my soul departing my body. My heart thundered in my ears and my limbs, down to the tips of my fingers, and pulsed into an achy wet throb. Hands curled into the fabric of his tunic, I leaned in. His mouth hovered so closely I could taste the air from his lungs.

BOOM.

A giant red plume sparkled overhead, the sound startling us both. Another boom echoed, and a huge white burst lit up the starry sky.

"Fireworks," I breathed.

The sky flashed in purple and green and blue and pink. My mother once told me they had lit fireworks the day I was born.

Ronan and I turned to each other, regret painting a canvas between us. Our almost-kiss had been stolen away, leaving me stewing in a pot of unrequited longing. Kianna and Em approached, their body language suggesting something more than a casual relationship. Noah stood a short distance away, eyes cast toward the sky, a content smile on his face. Catching sight of us, he walked over, and we found a table to share ale and a large carafe as more fireworks rocked overhead.

A ripple of mixed emotions burrowed into the well of my chest. Mare's constant threat hung dimly like a lamp covered in cloth, but tonight the shadows seemed more distant, held at bay by the lightness Ronan drew into my limbs. Across the small table, our gazes snapped together, the barest hint of a smile curving on his lips. Imbued with fire and heat, it sang with the promise of a future that slid through me like silken ribbons.

CHAPTER NINETEEN

I T WAS TIME TO draw names from the bowl of love. All of us were now a little tipsy, and I followed Noah and Em to witness the outcome, curious to see how this would play out.

A man stood on a raised platform, the giant glass bowl on a table in front of him. He reached in and pulled out a piece of paper, shouting a name. A woman jumped up, hands gripping her skirts, her eyes wide. The man grinned and shouted out another name. This time, a man called from the other end of the crowd, unmitigated joy on his face. The woman ran toward him, and they embraced, tears on their faces, as if this had been the only thing they'd been living for.

"Wow, the bowl really works," I said, and Kianna giggled next to me.

The man reached into the bowl again.

"Em!" he shouted. "And... Christianna!"

Em cast her gaze about, body tense, as a stunning girl emerged from the crowd. She had piercing blue eyes and golden blonde hair, her snug pink dress leaving little to the imagination. Em broke into a huge smile, and Noah thumped his friend on the back with enthusiasm. It made my heart swell to see how much they cared for each other.

Conscious of Kianna, I watched her, but she only stood with her hands clasped in anticipation. Whatever she had going on with Em was none of my business, though a nosy part of me desperately wanted to pry.

"Kianna!" the man shouted next, and I gave her an incredulous look.

She broke into a small smile and raised her hands in a gesture of supplication. "I thought it might be fun."

"Indeed," I said as her partner's name was read. "Liam!" A man with close-cropped black hair and kind eyes stepped forward. He was irrefutably handsome.

With an elbow, I nudged Kianna. "Enjoy yourself, my friend." We both appraised Liam with a satisfied nod as he bowed to Kianna and held out an elbow. They melted into the crowd without a backward glance.

"Meredith!" the man shouted next. A woman perked up, searching the crowd as if she could pick out her partner before the bowl had its say. At least ninety years old, she was barely the height of my shoulder, and I didn't know how she could see anything past the press of bodies.

"I guess we have needs, no matter how old we get," I said to Noah. He gave an audible snort.

"Noah!" cried the man, and it was my turn to snort before I clapped a hand over my mouth. Noah had turned pale, his mouth opening and closing like a puppet.

I slapped him on the back. "The bowl is never wrong. Have a good night," I said, trying to keep the mirth out of my voice.

With a shove from me, he shuffled forward as Meredith approached, crooking a finger and batting a set of come-hither eyes. She dragged Noah off, and the last thing I saw was his wild mane of hair disappearing into the crowd.

Laughing so hard, my face hurt, I wondered if Ronan had seen this. As I scanned the plaza, my stomach plummeted like a star shot from the sky. He was sitting at our table with a very attractive and very busty blonde on his lap.

Their noses were nearly touching, her hand on his face and her breasts practically pressed to his throat. His manner easy and relaxed, he was laughing at something she was saying. My throat tightened, and air lodged in my windpipe as I attempted to swallow. Tears of amusement morphed into poison, my eyes burning with the attempt to hold them in.

Turning away, I shoved through the throngs of milling people. They pressed in, stone columns taking root, unyielding to my jostling. I needed to get out of here. What a fool I'd been, imagining all of this. Building a fantasy in my head. What did I think? I'd already heard about another woman last night. Did I think I was special?

Panic rose in my chest as I maneuvered through the thick crowd, ale-soaked bodies lurching in my path. The noise became unbearable, the white lights and paper hearts mocking me as I shoved harder, not heeding where I was going. Finally,

I burst through the edge of the crowd and picked up my skirt, running as fast as I could over the snow-covered pavement.

Inside the inn, I dashed for the stairs, ignoring Verna's greeting. I needed to get to my room and be alone. I didn't want anyone to see me like this. My breath tight, I slammed the door and pressed my back against it.

For a few minutes, I allowed my emotions to spiral unchecked, sinking into a well of unfulfilled wishes. Eventually, I forced myself to calm down by throwing open the window and sucking in deep breaths of clean winter air.

He was only a man. An exceptionally beautiful one who made me forget my own name, but this would never work. Even if he shared the same feelings, this could be nothing more than a hope. There was too much between us—too much he didn't know. There were lies and secrets and an ostensible ticking clock hanging over us like a jagged rusty blade.

I'd allowed myself to indulge in the distraction of his presence, but this holiday had come to an end. I had to break this curse. I had to save my family from Mare and then, somehow, save myself. The last thing I needed was to wallow in thoughts about a man who wasn't interested.

Too weary to change out of my bright red dress, I flopped on the bed, face pressed into the blanket. Footsteps thudded outside my door, and I went still, holding my breath. There was a knock.

"Thorne?" Ronan called. "Are you okay? What happened?" The concern in his voice was unmistakable, but I steeled myself against it. It was childish, but I refused to answer, hoping he'd go away.

Hands clenched in the quilt, I waited as he stood silently on the other side of the door. I could almost feel his indecision seeping through the wood, but after a few moments, his boots scraped the floor, and I heard him walk away.

A scream jolted me awake, my heart racing. I'd dozed off after Ronan had left, my dress puffing in a cloud of red around me. Another scream pierced the air, frantic and desperate.

"Get away from me!" It was Kianna, and it was coming from outside. Without thinking, I pulled out the dagger strapped to my thigh and pounded down the stairs, red lace and tulle whispering along the floors and narrow halls.

The common room held only a few stragglers passed out at tables. I raced out of the inn, trying to discern the direction of Kianna's screams. The sky was still dark. I heard another loud plea and took off.

Behind the inn was an alley, about six feet across. Neatly stacked crates lined the walls, the ground covered in a thin layer of trampled snow. Four figures stood in the gloom, cast in the glow of the early morning sky.

Kianna perched on her tiptoes, back pressed against the wall. Her wings beat against the brick, thumping like a bumblebee smacking into a window.

Maida, the blood Fae, stood in front of her. Waxing light glinted from his dark silver hair while his companion, Alban, held on to Em, both arms pinned behind her back. Her teeth were bared as she tried to free herself from the blond Fae's grasp, her eyes never leaving Kianna.

"Let go of me," Em snarled.

Alban threw Em to the ground with such force that she let out an agonized cry, and then he stalked for Kianna. "Come on, precious little doll. We just want a taste. I've heard so many tales about the pleasures of winged Faerie blood. It will only hurt a little."

A memory came unbidden, rearing up like the head of a hungry dragon.

I just want a taste.

My vision went dark and shrank to a point, remembering that day when King Goldraven had pinned me against a stone wall and snarled those words in my face. I felt the grip of his hand on my throat like it was still there, choking me and stealing my air.

Em was on her feet now, but something held her back. *Magic,* I realized.

Coming back to myself, I focused on Kianna and the blood Fae. "Get away from her!" I attempted to fuse steel into my voice, but it came out like shredded cotton. Four pairs of eyes swung to me.

The Fae were nearly painful to look at this closely. The way they moved, as if made from molten silver. The vivid intensity in their eyes. The glow of their skin was so bright, it was as if the very sun burned in their hearts. How could creatures so cruel be so beautiful?

I was absurd in my puffy dress, my hair disheveled and my face tight. Blinking to clear my sleep-addled brain, I pointed my dagger and hoped I was a more menacing sight than I imagined. Maida's glittering black eyes burned even hotter when his gaze swept over me.

"The sleeping princess." His voice was silky and mocking. "I wondered when we'd see you again."

"I don't know what you're talking about."

"Oh, but you do." He prowled slowly toward me. "All alone, asleep inside your castle. The cursed princess and her faithful Fae companion."

"How do you know that?" I cursed as soon as the words slipped out, knowing I'd just confirmed his statement, but surprise had taken hold of my tongue.

He tipped his head to the side and gave me a bland smile. "It is my job to know, Princess."

"What should we do with her, Maida?" Alban had closed in on Kianna. As he ran the tip of his nose along the column of her throat, she whimpered.

"Leave her alone!" I shouted, teetering on the verge of tears.

Maida laughed again, and I glared at him. "When we're done with her, maybe you can have a turn. If you're lucky." With a movement so quick I missed it, he stood directly in front of me.

It threw me off balance and I took a step back, almost stumbling to the ground. Body inches from mine, his expression was a mixture of smug condescension and heat. A full head taller, his honed form rippled with muscle covered in silver dyed leather, no doubt meant to make his shining head of hair even more glorious. The effect was flawless. Terrible and beautiful. Horrible and stunning.

Maida sniffed, lowering his head toward me, a finger stroking my collarbone as I held completely still. I wouldn't let him see me cower. "You *do* smell delicious for a human. I wonder why that is?"

A scowl pinched my face.

"Don't look at me like that, Princess. Not only would you enjoy it, but I'd have you begging for it by the end." He dragged his finger across my skin, curving it over my shoulder and down my arm. "Have you burning with need as you crawled on your hands and knees, pleading for release over and over again. Until you're a hollow, thoroughly fucked husk of the woman you were, my name fused to your lips."

His words swept through me on currents of spiced air. Burning and sinuous, they were edged in a forbidden darkness that had me aching to sink into them and swallow up every last drop. For a shameless moment, I *wanted* to give into him. Was this some trick of his kind? There was a pull from the center of my chest, and I almost leaned closer until the tether snapped, and I took a step back, hurling an angry snarl. He smiled as though he knew exactly what had gone through my mind.

"That will never happen. I'd rather die than let you touch me. Or her."

To my astonishment, he backed away, his eyes pinned to me. "We'll see about that. Though I do prefer a willing plaything. We will meet again. Let's go, Alban. This has become...tedious." He gestured to his companion, who peeled away from Kianna.

She sagged against the wall, her shaking legs no longer keeping her upright.

"Get away from them!" A voice floated from the end of the alley. Ronan careened around the corner, sword in hand. Hair mussed and loose, his clothes were askew and unfastened as if he'd just tossed them on.

Maida turned to face him. "Well, well, it seems everyone is at the party tonight. What are you doing here, Ronan?"

"That's *Commander Goldraven* to you," Ronan replied through gritted teeth. "Step away from them, Maida. I knew it was a mistake to let you two out of Estria."

Maida let out a low, guttural sound. "We are not under your command, *Ronan*." He paused, his expression feral, while he scanned Ronan from head to toe. His full lips stretched into a languorous smile. "Don't think I've forgotten what *you* taste like." Challenge entered both men's eyes as they stared at each other, and I pondered what history they shared. "But we were already leaving. Such a daring rescue, several moments too late."

Amusement had returned to Maida's face. He studied me with a long and questioning look before gesturing to Alban. They stalked off down the alley, disappearing from view.

I rushed to Kianna, who was now sobbing on the ground. "Are you okay? Did they hurt you?"

"I'm fine, Your Highness. Just shaken."

Em shuffled nervously in front of us. Whatever magic had been holding her back was gone.

"What were *you* doing?" I snapped. Guilt and defeat sagged in her shoulders as she said nothing, unable to meet my eyes. I wrapped my arms around Kianna and helped her stand. "Let's get you inside." I wondered what had happened to the man from earlier this evening and why she was out here with Em.

Ronan tried to help, but I waved him off. "Thank you for your *assistance*, but as you can see, I had everything under control."

"I can see that." Brows knitted, he stared down the alley in the direction the Fae had gone. "I'll kill those bastards."

"*Commander Goldraven*," I said, my eyes drifting down to his hips while I lifted an imperious brow. "Your pants appear to be undone."

With that, I dragged Kianna away, leaving him standing there, watching after us.

CHAPTER TWENTY

18 DAYS LEFT

AFTER A FEW MORE hours of sleep, I slipped off the bed, taking care not to disturb Kianna. She'd been too shaken after her encounter with Maida and Alban to return to her room alone, so I'd brought her here to get some rest. I changed into a black tunic and leggings, tied my hair back, and scrubbed off the makeup from last night. Some of the cherry-red lipstick stained my fingers, and I thought longingly of the kiss with Ronan that almost had been and now would never be.

Smothering that notion, I found Noah and Em eating breakfast in the common room, both looking like they could use three more days bent over a bucket.

"Good night?" I asked Noah, sitting down across from them. Verna hustled over with a mug of tea and a stack of pancakes dripping in syrup and butter. In response to my question, Noah groaned, his forehead hitting the table.

"My head is going to explode," he mumbled into the wood.

"I guess Grandma was wilder than you expected?" I suppressed a smile, remembering the look on his face when he'd been matched. His eyes bloodshot, he raised them to me.

"She is a witch." The words were uttered with a small bit of wonder, and then he flopped his head back down. I wasn't sure what to make of that statement.

I glared at Em, annoyed she'd done such a poor job of protecting Kianna. "And you?"

"How is she?" she asked.

"Sleeping." My tone softened when Em propped her elbows on the table, cradling her head in her hands in misery. This wasn't her fault. The only ones to blame for any of this were Maida and Alban. "She'll be okay, I think. She's been through a lot lately."

Em offered me a grateful nod before she ventured a bite of her breakfast.

We all fell silent, Noah and Em nursing their aching heads while I polished off my stack of pancakes, grateful I'd gone to bed before I'd had too much wine. "I'll meet you here in an hour to return to the castle, so you can gather your things, and then it's time for you to leave. Tell your commander your welcome has been overstayed, and I don't want you in my home any longer."

Their expressions wary, they watched me as if they weren't sure how their commander would respond to that news, but I didn't care. Ronan's feelings were no longer my concern.

Something Maida had said this morning had been weighing on my mind, sparking the seeds of an idea. He'd known who I was and known my history. Maybe he knew other useful things, too.

"Verna?" I asked, knocking on the bar to get her attention.

"What can I do for you?" She tucked her hands into her apron and wandered closer.

I leaned in, not wanting anyone to overhear me. Something told me Noah and Em might try to stop me if they knew what I intended. Or worse, they'd tell Ronan.

"You know the two blood Fae? Maida and Alban?" I asked, and Verna's eyes widened.

"Of course I do. I'd have to be living in a shoe not to."

"Do you know where they live?"

Verna threw back her shoulders, her mouth flattening in an arrow-straight line. "You shouldn't get involved with those two. They are nothing but trouble."

"I'm not getting involved. I need to speak with them. They might have information I need."

Verna hesitated, her eyes darting about the room.

"Please," I said. The desperation on my face must have convinced her because she dropped her shoulders and let out a dragging sigh.

"Fine, but be careful. They are vicious creatures who will destroy a beautiful young thing like you."

I bit down on the retort at the back of my throat, insulted she thought me so fragile, but arguing with her would do me no good, so I nodded.

"I'll be careful."

With reluctance, she told me where I might find them, and I thanked her before leaving.

I headed into the quiet streets, evidence of the night's celebrations everywhere. The garlands that once hung merrily had been torn down, ends dragging in the muddy snow. People lay on the road, and my heart seized until I realized they were just passed out from too many glasses of ale—the normal sleep after a night of revelry, not the endless slumber of an unbreakable curse.

Following Verna's directions, I made my way to the city center, finding an elegant stone townhome. Not giving myself a chance to change my mind, I knocked on the door and asked to see the Fae.

The servant who answered led me into an enclosed courtyard, where Maida was seated at a wrought-iron table sipping a mug of coffee. The servant was about to announce my presence when a pair of burned onyx eyes whipped in my direction. Maida's stare was so hard it fossilized me in place, my muscles and tendons going rigid. This was a terrible idea. What had I been thinking?

"You may go," Maida said, waving the girl away. I wanted to escape with her as Maida rose from his seat and regarded me with a licentious sweep of his eyes. He wore a dark gray tunic and leggings that molded to every muscled curve of his arms and chest. His features were savage—angled brows and razored cheekbones set against a thick pair of lips designed for cutting words and cruel intentions.

"What brings you here, Princess?" A smug sense of satisfaction twisted up the corners of his mouth, the weight of his gaze so heavy it felt like he could see straight through my clothing to every inch of my flesh. "Didn't I say you'd come to me begging?"

My words stuck, so I cleared my throat and gathered the particles of my courage into a minuscule pile, lifting my chin and meeting his pitch-dark glare. "That's not why I'm here."

He huffed out a laugh that said he didn't believe me, and maybe a small part of me was lying. Maida was pure smoke and raw sexual energy, and I'd be lying if I said I hadn't thought about the things he whispered to me in that darkened alley.

"Then what do you want?"

"You said it was your job to know who I am. What did you mean by that?"

His charcoal brows furrowed as he rolled his neck. "I don't share my secrets with humans, darling."

"But you know about the curse? You know who I am?"

"I do." The words were clipped, broken off at the ends like he was trying not to say too much. I wasn't sure how much to reveal to this ferocious male, but I had eighteen days left and time was draining away. I was rapidly running out of options. What was the worst that could happen at this point?

"Do you know what happened when I woke up?" I kept my question vague enough, wanting to keep the king's presence in my castle a secret. Unless Maida already knew.

"Why would I know that?"

"Didn't you say it's your job?"

He rolled his eyes as though I were miles beneath him. Either he didn't know or he was lying, so I forged ahead, throwing away my caution.

"I need to break a curse," I said in a rush, like he might not really hear me if I spit the words out fast enough.

"Why should that be my concern?"

This I had anticipated. Maida didn't seem like the sort to offer his help for nothing.

"I'll give you anything you want. Anything in my power to give."

A smile, one at half-measure, crept to his face, glee flaring in his eyes. "Oh, Princess. That is an exceedingly stupid thing to say to a Fae. What could have you so desperate?"

"Something went wrong and my family fell asleep too, and now I can't wake them up."

It was so slight I nearly missed it, but there was the barest widening of his eyes. That I'd caught him off guard with my admission unnerved me more than anything.

"So that's what happened. Fascinating."

He said nothing further, just kept staring at me like he was trying to figure something out.

"I'm asking for your help. Do you know how to break it?" My voice dropped to a whisper. "Please, I'm going to lose everything." A ball of tension bobbed in my throat, threatening to unravel at my feet.

Maida circled me with slow, measured steps as he assessed me from every angle. His tall leather boots clicked on the stones as he came to a stop in front of me, close enough that I had to crane my neck to see into his eyes.

"You have nothing I want," he said, his voice devoid of emotion, and hope crumpled in my chest.

"I'm begging you. Gold, jewels, anything."

He let out a derisive snort. "Be more original, Princess." He cocked his head, the gesture animalistic. "Perhaps there's *something* that interests me."

He gave me an extended once-over that plummeted straight to the core of my soul. The heat in his look told me exactly what he was suggesting.

"Now who lacks originality?" Instead of the anger I expected at my retort, Maida expelled a burst of laughter that seemed to shock us both.

He then lifted a shoulder. "It was worth a try."

"I'll think of something to give you. You have my word. Just help me, please."

He shook his head, pewter locks sparkling in the sun. "I can't."

"Can't? Or won't?"

He settled back into his seat and folded his hands behind his head. "Does it matter? It amounts to the same thing."

Anger curled like rotting leaves in my stomach. "I should have known you wouldn't help me."

"Yes, you should have." There was no hint of apology or remorse, just that haughty, smug expression.

"This was a waste of my time. I thought—"

"You thought what? You'd bat those pretty eyes at me, and I'd scramble to do your bidding? You may have the commander eating out of your hand, but I am harder to persuade." He picked up his cup and took a sip, watching me over the rim. "If you'll excuse me? You've already wasted enough of my morning."

"You're such a prick," I said, no longer interested in holding back. No longer trying to stay on whatever sliver of a good side he possessed.

He smirked and drained his cup. "I've been called far worse."

"Fuck you." The vehemence of my response surprised me. It wasn't until that moment that I realized how much I'd been counting on Maida to have an answer.

"You wish. Now go away." He made a shooing motion with his hand.

With a furious huff, I spun on my heels and spilled back into the street, blindly turning corners as I tamped down my anger. I should have known he wouldn't help me. This was another dead end. My salvation wouldn't come from an over-confident Faerie with a mean streak as wide as the sea.

As I turned a corner, I ran straight into a large group speaking in excited tones that pulled my attention.

"The king is a tyrant," a woman with a ruddy face was saying. "He can't be allowed to torture the citizens of Ravalyn like this anymore."

"They came and took my brother two days ago," a man said. "Claimed he was hunting on the king's private lands. Lies. My brother isn't a poacher."

"I heard those Fae of his chopped those men into pieces and then fed them to the Ritchers' pigs," said another woman, her eyes wide.

My heart sank. This was what my family's absence had created. Lives terrorized by a king who didn't deserve to rule them. As I listened to the litany of torments they'd suffered, I grew more determined than ever to break the curse so I could help my father reclaim what had been lost.

There were so many things riding on my success. So many people counting on it. It was better that things between me and Ronan weren't going anywhere. It was clear we could only be enemies.

How I wished I could tell these citizens of Tenby it wouldn't be this way forever. That I would do something about this, but I knew they wouldn't believe me. They wouldn't understand who I was. These people hadn't even been born when my family had gone to sleep.

Heart heavy, I hurried past the central market, hoping I could purchase the ingredients for the anti-sleep tincture, along with a pair of horses. Through the stalls, I browsed, picking up the mullein and betony I needed.

I found a horse vendor and negotiated a price for a reddish mare and a gray gelding. On my way back to the inn, I saw the same group of people still sharing stories. More atrocities committed by the king. That tyrant. I wasn't sorry I'd killed him. My only regrets came from worrying about my fate and what it would mean for Ronan. Despite everything, he deserved more than a father like that.

Kianna waited with my bag outside the Whitefeather as I passed the reins of the red mare to her.

"Where have you been?" she asked.

"Picking up supplies." I didn't tell her about my conversation with Maida, not wanting to upset her any further. "She needs a name." I gestured to the horse.

"Elinor," Kianna said, and I smiled. That was my mother's name. "And yours?"

"How about Curse?" I asked with a dry smile. She spit out a derisive laugh.

A moment later, Ronan and the others arrived, leading their own horses. Not making eye contact with him, I watched his gaze dart between me and the new horse at my side. He looked disappointed, but I didn't let the thought settle. I was done with whatever this was.

"You bought horses," Em commented.

"You are observant," I replied, hoisting myself on Curse. "Once you all are gone, Kianna and I need a way to get to the city."

Not waiting for anyone to respond, I kicked Curse into step and made my way down the street. The others fell in line behind me. As we rode, Ronan attempted to spark conversation, but I kept my answers short and curt enough to dissuade him. Eventually, he gave up and left me alone.

Kianna and Gideon rode with their heads bent, whispering about something. They glanced at Ronan and then at me, quickly looking away when they saw I was watching. I sighed. They were up to something again. I wondered what convenient excuse Kianna would come up with this time to keep them all here and why she was trying so hard to prevent them from leaving.

When we entered the forest, I noticed the tingle of magic in the tips of my fingers, and I frowned. It stole through my skin as it prickled over me with heightened awareness. But it felt wrong. Tainted. Like it had been bent and broken. Premonition dropped a burning coal in my gut as I nudged Curse, urging him to move faster. Too impatient to wait, I kicked him into a full gallop. I burst through the tree line, the castle's ramparts forming a jagged line across the horizon.

And then I saw it. Bodies.

Not just bodies, but parts of them. Legs, arms, heads, torsos. Ripped apart. Shredded and torn and defiled beyond recognition. Crimson streaks painted the pristine snow like an artist channeling her rage.

It was impossible to tell how many had died—the pieces of them scattered as if a giant hand had shaken them like dice and tossed them across the ground. I counted at least a dozen heads as my gorge rose, sour bile burning a line down my throat. Kianna and Ronan stood on either side of me, silent, staring, and in disbelief.

There were faces I recognized, and my heart ricocheted in my chest, thrashing against my ribs. My skin grew hot and cold all over, sweat breaking out on my forehead. "The throne room. They came from the throne room."

On wobbling legs, I dismounted from the horse as I kneeled in the snow, my hands pressed to the ground.

"Thorne, don't," Ronan said, wrapping an arm around my shoulders.

I shook him off with a glare and forced myself to bear witness to the massacre. Eyes open, their faces gaped at the sky as though they'd died in shock. As though they'd died in pain, screaming against the void. A sob erupted from my throat as my forehead dropped to the snow.

"How could she do this?" Kianna whispered, sinking to the ground and stroking the back of my head.

Kianna and I exchanged a look. Only one person could have done this. Only one Fae, with a heart so black that light could never find a way in.

Large, clawed footprints circled the area. The same ones we'd seen before. My blood went as icy as a windswept tundra.

"It's a warning," I said. "She's showing us what she can do and that we're powerless to stop her."

And that she had some kind of monstrous creature at her bidding.

Darkness took root inside me, sinking into my tissue and bones. These people had been innocent. They'd done nothing but be in the wrong place at the wrong time. Nothing but align themselves with *my* family. I might have bought myself and Kianna some extra time with my bargain, but I'd cost these people their lives. I was going to get more people killed if I didn't figure out how to break this fucking curse.

Tears broke through, sliding down my face and landing on my hands that were pressed to my knees. I wrapped my arms around myself, curling into a heart that was slowly cracking, slivers of it shedding away. I didn't know how to stop any of this. Mare was coming for us, and there was no way to stop her.

"Thorne." A large, gentle hand rested on my shoulder. But I didn't want this. Ronan wasn't for me, and this was a waste of my precious time. I shook him off, getting up and whirling on him.

"Get your hands off me." I was wild with rage as it burst out in a torrent of sorrow and confusion. It slammed into me, an axe biting into bark. I needed to be alone. Anywhere but here.

Before anyone could stop me, I dashed back to my horse and kicked him into a gallop. I raced to the trees, tears streaming down my cheeks. I needed to get away.

Find a way to separate myself from this.

Go back in time, to a riverbank deep in the forest where a childless mother begged for a gift attached to more strings than a marionette.

It was a bargain my mother should have never entered.

I had never been worth any of this.

Blind to my surroundings, I ended up in front of my grand-parents' chateau. The missing front doors were tall enough to walk Curse straight through. Cracked tiles clicked beneath his hooves, and I slid off. A grand staircase filled the foyer—a reminder of better days. I trudged up the steps, my tread heavier than iron. The wind howled through the halls, the song of the ghosts that haunted this place.

I paused in front of a large set of double doors, swinging one open. Inside was the bedroom where my grandparents had slept. An enormous bed sat against the right wall. The sheets were molded and stained. Beyond the bed, a set of windows lined the entire wall, their panes still miraculously intact.

A white stone fireplace dominated the far end, and a rotted rug sat drab and drained of life. My boots scraped along the cold stone, and I sank to my knees, pressing my cheek to the floor, trying to cool my burning skin. I inhaled a strangled breath, and then I didn't move for a very long time.

A delicate hand smoothed my hair as I blinked awake from a troubled sleep. Kianna sat next to me, her legs tucked under her, the skin around her eyes tight with worry.

"I didn't thank you for saving me this morning," she said. "What you did was very brave, if a little foolish."

Pushing myself up off the floor, I leaned against the bed frame behind me. "You don't need to thank me. I wish I could have ripped those bastards limb from limb."

Something sharpened in Kianna's expression.

"What?" I lifted my head. "Stop that. I am not the princess you and your sisters tried to make. I will never be her. I never was."

Kianna said nothing for a moment and then replied, "I see that now, and I'm sorry."

I raised an eyebrow at her.

"I'm sorry we didn't see you for who you were. I'm sorry we tried to force you into a box that must have felt like a cage. I'm sorry. You saved me without a thought for your own safety, as you've done over and over. You feel for the people of your kingdom in a way that a princess should. We were wrong. You *are* a princess, Thorne."

I stared at her and blinked as a tight knot unfurled in my chest. My throat was tense as I swallowed. It was the first time she'd ever said my name or spoken to me like a friend.

"Thank you," I whispered.

"And those deaths are not on your hands." She raised a palm when I tried to protest. "No, they are not. Those deaths belong to Mare and Mare alone. She started this one hundred and twenty-one years ago when she tricked your mother. This blood is on her. You are too young to have been given this burden."

"I'm a hundred-and-twenty-one."

Kiana let out a tinkling laugh. "Well, I guess that's true. In that case, I'm two-hundred-and-forty-seven." I gawped at her. "What? I know. I look young for my age." She fluffed her hair, and I smiled. She didn't look a day older than I did.

Kianna sighed, dropping her hands. "Honestly, you aren't the only one who found my sisters to be...a lot."

I said nothing as I waited for her to continue.

"I am the youngest and the least powerful of them. I don't want to speak ill of the dead, and I miss them and love them, but they didn't respect me very much."

As we looked at each other, something shifted. Sand rippling along the desert floor. For the first time, I saw Kianna in a different light, and whatever was between us was changing.

"I'm sorry. That must have been hard." I took her hand, and she squeezed it.

We sat quietly for a moment, lost in thought.

"Why is she after me? What did I do to her?" I asked finally. The question wormed its way under my fingernails. The random senselessness of Mare's hatred was more confusing than anything.

Kianna shook her head, wrinkling her nose. "I don't know. I hardly know her. We were borne of the same mother, but that's where our connection ends. I've only heard the stories about her, but we've spent little time together. I'm sorry. I wish I knew."

There was an apology in her expression, but I waved it off. Mare's actions weren't her fault either.

"What are we going to do, Kianna? I don't know how to break this curse."

Kianna studied the empty fireplace as she said, "You will find a way, Your Highness. I'm sure of it."

I let out a breath as heavy as marble, wondering why she had so much faith in me.

CHAPTER TWENTY-ONE

15 DAYS LEFT

Ronan and the others still hadn't left, and I'd given up trying to make them. As angry as I was with him, I had to admit their presence was comforting. I didn't relish the idea of being alone with Kianna in the castle if Mare and her creature returned.

We'd burned the dead, the ground too frozen to bury them, honoring their memories as best as we could. Em, it had turned out, was a beautiful singer, her voice carrying across the snow-covered landscape, more perfect than any avenging angel's.

As for Ronan, I did the mature thing and avoided ever being alone with him. I still took advantage of his presence, training until I nearly collapsed at the end of each day, my muscles liquid and my clothing dripping with sweat.

If I couldn't break this curse, the combined heft of iron and the potency of my rage would be the only defenses I had against Mare. I rebuked his attempts to divert the discussion to anything other than my training and, outside the ballroom, I evaded all conversation.

In the kitchen, I got to work on the tincture. There were numerous steps, and I spent whatever time I wasn't swinging my sword, chopping and mixing. Gideon helped me, stirring the pot whenever I was occupied with a lesson. His steady, kind presence brought warmth to the castle that made it feel like a home. Maybe I could convince him to stay when everyone woke up, but I knew how fiercely loyal he was to Ronan.

Kianna moved into my room through an unspoken agreement. At night, we lay on my bed and talked, sometimes about Mare and the curse and sometimes about nothing. Since the day of Mare's attack, we had found a quiet peace in our relationship. She had been so apathetic about breaking the curse, but now I realized it must have been a lack of confidence in her magic. There must be a way I could help her find it. I knew too well how difficult it was to bear the scrutiny of her sisters.

It was after supper when Gideon, Kianna, and I were exploring the castle, checking on the magic that was seeping away. We stood in a hallway; there was a clear demarcation between the warm and lit side where we stood, and the dusty, decaying side across the nebulous line of magic.

The two of them were sharing some kind of secret communication I didn't understand, looking at me and then at each other as though I was making them nervous.

"Is there anything you want to save, Your Highness?" Gideon asked, peering into the darkness.

"Save?"

"There may be things other than people you want to rescue."

Right. We still didn't know what would happen if anyone crossed the line of magic. Kianna thought the curse might be protecting the two of us since we'd been able to leave the castle without harm, but it was only a theory, and no one wanted to test this barrier.

"I suppose the vault?" I'd need gold if I was to mount an army against Estria.

Gideon sketched a quick bow. "I will let the commander know there is work to do." As he turned to leave, I caught his wrist.

"Gideon, no. You don't need to do that."

He covered my hand, crinkles forming in the corners of his soft brown eyes. "Nonsense, Your Highness. They will be more than happy to help. Especially Master Ronan." There was a tweak of mischief in his expression before he walked off.

The vault was packed with jewels and weapons and coins collected over centuries of my family's rule. I picked up a slim velvet box and popped open the lid. Inside glistened a diamond necklace laced with jet black stones.

"Ooh." Kianna's eyes were as wide as a child's in a candy shop.

"Do you want it?" I asked, draping it over her collarbone.

"I couldn't." She turned around to face me after I'd snapped the clasp in place.

"You can. It's stunning on you. I want you to have it." She stroked the necklace like it was a beloved pet. "Kianna, if I don't make it, I want you to take it all."

"Your Highness—"

"Please," I said. "Do something good with it. Promise me." She took my hands in hers. "If it will make you happy, I will promise. As long as you promise not to give up. No matter what happens, you will keep fighting."

"I can do that," I said softly, earning myself a sad but determined smile.

Noah and Em stomped into the room then and filled the next crates, hauling them through the castle to the room I'd designated as the new vault. It wouldn't be as secure, but the dangers that lurked in these halls weren't the sort that cared about jewels or gold.

Something caught my eye. Another velvet box I recognized with a heavy heart. Inside was a crown made of silver so pale it was nearly white. Thin tendrils were molded to mimic vines that twisted into a circlet woven with delicate flowers and set with stones in shades of pink, blue, and violet.

As Ronan moved behind me, I studied it in the dim light.

"What is it?" His breath brushed the back of my neck, and I shivered as I inhaled his familiar scent of evergreens and cinnamon.

"It was supposed to be mine. For when I became queen. My parents had it made when my mother was pregnant. She was so sure I'd be a girl. It ended up here once we understood I would never wear it."

I rotated the crown in my hands, examining it from every side.

"Try it on," he said, his eyes soft and warm. He was so close I only needed to lean back a hair to be touching him. I shook my head.

"It wouldn't feel right. I haven't earned it yet. First, I need to save my people and get my kingdom back." *From your family.* The unspoken words stretched between us.

He placed a hand on the small of my back. It warmed me from head to toe like curls of steam wafting off freshly baked bread. Every tiny part of me wanted more. Wanted to let go and tell him how I felt. As much as I'd tried to convince myself I didn't want him, that was patently untrue and I was fooling no one, least of all myself. But that future was impossible.

"You will earn it," he said. "You will wear it one day. If there's anything I've learned about you in the time I've known you, it's that nothing will stop you."

The weight of those words was heavier than he understood. He meant them—the truth reflected in his face.

But he couldn't have known it was the first time anyone had ever believed in me.

Suddenly conscious of being alone in the vault, I moved, but he closed the tiny scrap of space between us. His hand was still on my back, and his fingers flexed against my skin, sending whips of fire wrapping around my hips and through my stomach. I gripped the crown in my hand and forced myself to look away. Placing it back in its case, I picked it up, holding it close.

"We'll see about that."

Instead of storing the crown with the rest of the castle's treasures, I put it in my room. Here, it would serve as a constant
reminder of what else I had to lose. Once it was safely stowed,
I helped haul up crate after crate until the room was finally
empty.

It was past midnight when I called a stop to the work. Swaying on tired feet, everyone dispersed back to their rooms. I was
wandering back to my own room when I heard my name.

Ronan approached from the end of the hall, and I checked
both directions, seeking an escape route. There was nowhere
for me to run or hide. Ducking into a bedroom not only seemed
childish, but he'd already seen me. Instead, I kept walking,
picking up my pace, but he caught my wrist and tugged me
back.

"Stop avoiding me," he growled.

I flipped my hair over my shoulder. "I don't know what you're
talking about."

He stepped closer, and I backed up, coming up against the
stone wall. A hand placed on either side of my head, he leaned
over me, caging me in. My breath hitched at his body hovering
so close that I could feel whispers of him against my clothing.

"Why are you avoiding me? Ever since Valentus...I thought we
were coming to understand each other."

I drew myself up, straightening my spine, attempting to
maintain some semblance of dominance as I was forced to look
up at him.

"I thought so too, but you seemed preoccupied when I came
back from the draw."

"I—what?" Confusion crossed his face.

"And besides, you wouldn't want to disappoint Lady Elsenmoor back in Estria, would you?"

He shook his head. "Who told you about Lady Elsenmoor?"

"So, you don't deny it?"

"Deny what? That there is a Lady Elsenmoor living in Estria?"

"I heard you talking with Noah and Em in the kitchen."

Ronan closed his eyes, definitely seeking patience, before peering back at me. "*That's* why you won't talk to me?"

I bristled at his tone. "I think it's a perfectly good reason. I have no interest in becoming another notch on your bedpost. What kind of woman do you take me for? I am *a princess.*"

My anger blazed white-hot at this line of questioning, but he was also so beautiful that it was taking all of my willpower not to yank on his collar and devour his mouth. Not to drag my fingernails under his shirt and over the planes of his stomach.

"Well, *Princess,* if you'd continued your eavesdropping, you would know Lady Elsenmoor means less than nothing to me. She has chased me for years, but I have never once returned her feelings. Em and Noah were being immature pricks. They know she's not who I want."

"Oh." My voice escaped in a squeak while my cheeks grew warm.

"Yes. Oh."

His face moved closer, our noses almost touching, as I despaired at the things my body wanted. The way he had me trapped between his arms sent tiny bursts of energy detonating in every nerve, heating me from the inside out.

"And," he continued, his breath warm on me, "that woman at Valentus helped herself to my lap without my invitation. I was simply trying to find a polite way to tell her to get the hell off me, because I am a gentleman and not a brute, no matter what you may think of me."

"What about your clothes? You were half dressed when you came to the alley."

He growled softly, the sound tapping every secret, locked-up place in my heart. "Because I was *asleep.* I went to my room after I'd knocked on your door, took my clothes off, and went to bed."

My eyes dropped to his body while a vivid and remarkably detailed image of him lying in bed naked leaped to my mind. He smirked as if he could read the thoughts that must have been plain on my face. I shifted against the wall, suddenly feeling very stupid.

"Oh," I said again, so quietly it came out as nothing more than a breath of humiliated air.

His gaze was intense and searing, like being dipped in liquid gold.

"*You* were the only one I wanted to be with that night. *You* are the only one I've been able to think about since the moment I saw you." Silk threads wrapped around my heart at his statement. "Say you want to be with me, too." His voice was rough. I nodded slowly, my eyes never leaving his. "Say it, my ferocious Little Lion. Tell me you ache for me as desperately as I ache for you," he whispered, his lips brushing the shell of my ear.

"I want to be with you, too." They weren't coherent words. They were ragged breaths and panting gasps and longing sighs sent into the night.

He pulled back, a cocky grin spreading over his face. "You've made quite the fool of yourself, haven't you, Thorne?"

I made an indignant sound and his laughter, low and dark, skittered across my bones. He was right, though. In my desire to keep him at a distance, I'd jumped to a catalog of conclusions.

"You are so infuriating and so beautiful and so utterly intoxicating." He dragged his top lip along the exposed line of my throat, and I gasped as my hands gripped the wall at my back. My head tipping to the side, I closed my eyes and lost myself in his touch.

"Do you have any idea how crazy you make me?" He continued, keeping an unhurried pace, as he dragged the tip of his nose in the other direction. Unable to stand it any longer, I grabbed his hips and he purred.

"How I can't stop thinking about you?" His hips pressed into mine, and I whimpered softly as he ground his body against me, the thick length of his rigid cock pressing into my stomach.

My blood was surging, racing, pounding like a thousand horses loosed upon an open plain. An ache bloomed between my thighs as he swirled his hips, and I arched my back, trying to get closer.

"How I can't stop thinking about what it would be like to peel off these clothes and drink in the sight of your naked body? How much I want to lick every last inch of you and make you moan until you're such a quivering mess you have to beg me to stop?"

Every reservation I had was thinning like jam scraped over toast until nearly translucent. I wanted more. More of him and his hands and his mouth. I wanted them on me. I wanted him in a way I hadn't been willing to admit, knowing this was only going to end in disappointment. But right now, I didn't care.

Right now, all I wanted was to forget about the threat at my back and the noose swinging over my head.

We both paused, our breath fusing into a helix of ardent desire and mindless want. Fraction by fraction, he lowered his head as I waited on the precipice of a leap I had fought to avoid. But right now, with Ronan in front of me, I realized how foolish that had been. That this moment had been inevitable from the very start.

"Oh my, isn't this cozy?" A voice floated from the end of the hall.

Mare sauntered toward us, sinuous and viperous as a snake. She was a blaze of darkness, her slinky black dress falling in thick velvet waves while her sable hair haloed in a wild and untethered tangle. Her blood-red lips shone in the flicker of the sconces.

"Thorne, you have been *busy*." A sneer marred her pale face while she swept her eyes over Ronan. As he looked between me and Mare, I could practically hear the clicking of the pieces as he fit them together. "Well done, my darling. *Well* done." With a flutter of her dark lashes, she simpered at Ronan, handing me another reason I would rip out her throat and feed it to a sty of hungry pigs.

"What do you want, Mare?" Ronan's hand, clasped around mine, squeezed harder as I addressed the harbinger of my doom.

"I wanted to see how you were making out." Her tone was flat and bored as she surveyed our surroundings and planted a hand on one jutted hip. "I see my sister's magic is starting to fade. Tick tock, Thorne."

For a moment, I was torn on whether I was more irritated by her pointless taunting or that she'd interrupted my kiss with Ronan. Either way, the hatred that burned in my gut was a blue-white flame.

"Get out. You aren't welcome here."

"You know what?" Mare asked, tapping her chin. "I don't care. Where *is* my idiot sister?"

"Gone. You won't find her."

"Oh, you are a terrible liar."

I ground my teeth, willing myself to stillness. None of my weapons were on me, and Ronan was also unarmed. We'd let down our guard. A fatal mistake.

Mare took a few steps closer, cocking her head. The movement was supple and fluid, with nothing comforting or natural about it. Every angle, every plane seemed wrong, like she'd been pieced together with leftover parts.

"Did you like my present? They screamed so loud. It was the most delightful sound. I play it over and over in my head when I need a boost." She cackled, and I squeezed Ronan's hand so hard I felt his bones creak.

Hot tears bit my eyes, but I willed them not to fall.

"Perhaps another demonstration is necessary to quell this endless ennui as I wait." She fluttered a hand to her forehead and then trapped me with her fiery golden gaze. "I picked out your cage today. You're going to *love* it."

Before I could think about what I was doing, I launched myself at her. My soul existed outside my body, no longer in control of itself. She would not take another life from this castle.

Caught off guard by my sudden movement, she stumbled as I rammed into her, my shoulder pounding into her chest. The hours I'd spent circling the ballroom with Ronan as my teacher came to me now, nearly as natural as breathing. Long skirts getting caught around her ankles, Mare tripped and almost lost her footing.

The bored smirk had been wiped from her face, and the only thing left was loathing and unfettered rage.

"You little *brat*." She spat the words with such vehemence a line of spittle dripped down her chin. With a shaking hand, she wiped it away, and I realized she was as much a slave to her emotions as anyone else. She was controlled by her hatred, too.

As she lifted her hand to retaliate, another shape flew past me. I blinked, and she was trapped under Ronan. His large hands circled her narrow wrists, holding her hands to the floor.

Screeching, she thrashed under him, but he was too strong. She flicked her hand, caught in his fist, but nothing happened. She let out a piercing cry of rage, so loud the foundations shook. Somehow, she flipped Ronan off her, but I didn't give her the chance to rise. Instead, I crashed into her from behind.

She spun, her hand buried in the fabric of my shirt, and a fist came flying at my face. When Mare's knuckles connected with my cheek, my head snapped back before light burst in my eyes. My vision swam as a wave of warm heat bloomed where her claws had broken my skin. My knees slammed to the floor.

In that split second, Ronan leaped on her again and the two rolled to the ground. Ronan let out a grunt before blood spread, bright and red, across his white shirt, soaking his entire side. I screamed, and Ronan clamped onto Mare's wrists, trying to hold her hands back while she aimed her sharpened claws at his face. Blood was everywhere, and I couldn't tell whose was whose.

Ronan wrestled Mare into a headlock and, though she kept flicking her hands to call her magic, still nothing happened. Ronan's shirt was a crimson stain, his black pants shiny with blood. Mare finally writhed from his grasp, squeezing out of his hold. She shoved him, and Ronan slammed against the wall.

Footsteps stormed from the other direction as Noah, Em, and Gideon all ran up, fully armed.

Caught between all of us, Mare's eyes flashed as she focused her rage on me, a sneer gracing her lips. Blood slipped from the razor-sharp points on her fingers. More was smeared on the milky white skin around her mouth and dripping down her bony chest. She wiped her nose with her forearm, brimstone burning in her gaze.

"Tick tock, Thorne." With a bloody claw raised, she bared her teeth and snapped her fist shut. "When you are finally mine, I will tear you apart and crush your very soul until it's nothing but a memory. I will make your heart fucking *bleed*." Her words were spiked in a thousand needle-sharp pins, and if she'd hated me before, it was nothing compared to what she felt now. In a pooling whirl of blackness, she disappeared.

With a shout, I lunged for Ronan, who lay motionless, blood pooling beneath him where he'd slid to the floor. "Someone get Kianna. We need Kianna."

I tried to staunch the bleeding, tearing a long strip from my tunic and holding it up to the wound.

"It's going to be okay," I said, not sure which one of us I was trying to convince.

Ronan was awake but weak, his eyes fluttering. "That fucking witch. I'm going to cut off her head and feed it to the demons of hell," he groaned as I smoothed the hair from his face.

My throat was tight as I nodded, tears stinging my eyes. Kianna kneeled next to me. "Let me see."

I pulled away the soaked bit of reddened cloth as she examined the wound. Four long gashes sliced from above his hip and across his ribs.

"It doesn't look like she hit anything important, but they're deep. I don't have a strong affinity for healing." She bit her lip, wringing her hands.

"Kianna, look at me." My hands gripped her shoulders, and I stared her in the eye. "You can do this. You're stronger than you think. Your sisters were wrong about the kind of Faerie you are. I have every faith in you and your power."

Kianna's watery gaze reflected back at me, and she nodded. Ronan was blinking hard, trying to resist unconsciousness. He was pale as ice and I ran my hands over his head, trying not to look as scared as I felt.

Lips held in a thin line, Kianna pressed a hand to his side as a small yellow light flared. Her nose scrunched in concentration while she maintained the connection. Our collective breaths held, we all watched quietly as she worked.

A few minutes later, the light winked out as Kianna wiped her brow with a forearm. "We should get some stitches in him. This won't hold for long."

Ronan had fainted, his skin clammy to the touch. As Noah and Em lifted him, I clung to his limp hand. They carried him to the unused dining room table while Gideon left to ransack the infirmary. It was truly a miracle that we hadn't needed it before today. He returned with an armful of supplies and began preparing a needle and thread.

"How does he know how to do that?" I asked Em.

"When you're Ronan's manservant, it goes with the territory." I waited for her to crack a joke or break into an irreverent grin, telling me not to worry and that they'd all been through much worse before. But her face was grim as she watched with her arms folded tightly across her chest, her foot tapping impatiently.

Gideon worked quickly, sewing neat lines along each gash and then covering them in clean white bandages. Kianna stood by, handing him tools and bits of wrapping.

"We'll have to make sure it doesn't get infected," he said. "He lost a lot of blood."

"I think my magic can help with that," Kianna said as she placed her hand on Ronan again. Already, she seemed more confident.

"Will he be okay?" My throat was raw, as if I'd been screaming for hours.

Gideon's eyes widened as he took in my appearance.

"Woah," Noah said. "Did she punch you?" The memory surfaced—that bitch *had* punched me. My cheek gave a painful throb. Too caught up in Ronan's injury, I'd nearly forgotten. My skin was hot and tight, the entire left side of my face aching.

Noah held my chin in his fingers, examining me. "That is going to leave an impressive bruise, Princess."

"I'll get some ice for that," Gideon said, bustling off.

"Ronan is going to eviscerate her." Em flicked a look at his prostrate form, and I shuddered at the menace in her tone.

Kianna placed a gentle hand on my cheek. Light flared, and a hint of the pain subsided. "I'm sorry I can't do much more. I've used up a lot of my power for now."

"You did great, Kianna. Thank you."

She smiled, and I noted the proud set of her shoulders.

Gideon handed me a rag filled with ice and then cleaned the blood off Ronan with a second wet cloth. Cutting away his bloody clothing, he worked with practised efficiency. Em ran to his room and returned with a fresh pair of pants that the men helped put Ronan into. My eyes averted, I tried not to look, with little success. I scolded myself. Now was not the time to be ogling him.

"Let's get him to his bed," Noah said, moving to lift his top half.

"No," I said. "Take him to my room." Every pair of eyes turned to me, and I willed myself not to blush, but I couldn't stand the idea of him being all the way at the other end of the castle right now. My bed was larger and more comfortable, anyway.

"I can keep an eye on him then."

The expression on Noah's face made my heart clench—it was a combination of pride and happiness and relief. He dipped his head and then gestured to Em to grab Ronan's ankles.

As carefully as possible, they carried him to my room and placed him on top of the covers.

Noah pulled up a chair and dropped into it. "Go clean yourself up, Your Highness. I'll watch him while you do."

I gave him a small smile before heading to my bathroom. My clothing was soaked with Ronan's blood. As I stripped off my garments, Kianna filled up the bath. Once I'd washed, I pulled on a pair of leggings and a soft tunic. Combing my fingers through my wet hair, I left it loose and peered in the mirror to study my face.

There was a thin angry line across my cheek, the skin already turning various shades of blue and purple. I padded back to the bedroom, my feet bare. Noah was leaning back in the large armchair, snoring softly, hands folded over his stomach.

I found a thick blanket and placed it over him, brushing a lock of golden hair off his forehead. My chest ached at seeing how much they all loved each other. Siblings, even if not by blood. Not for the first time, it made me wish I hadn't been an only child.

Ronan's breath was even and slow as I crawled into the bed. Like this, he looked younger and softer, the usually fierce lines of his face smoothed by sleep. I traced his lips with my finger, remembering the heat under my skin before Mare had interrupted us.

My hand traveled lower, tracing the lines of his bared chest as I pressed my mouth to his forehead.

"If you don't wake up and finish that kiss, I'll kill you," I whispered in his ear.

Maybe I was imagining it, but the ghost of a smile formed on his lips.

CHAPTER TWENTY-TWO

13 DAYS LEFT

A FTER TWO EXHAUSTING DAYS, Ronan finally awoke, blinking up at me while I watched over him. Kianna had worked around the clock, staving off any hints of infection, and he was healing rapidly under her vigilant care.

"Hi," I said, lying on my side, hands pillowed under my head.

He reached out to touch my cheek with a frown. "Your face." His expression darkened. "Who did that to you? Did Mare do that?"

I hesitated, knowing the answer would set him off.

"Tell me." His voice was soft, but there was a command in it.

"Yes," I said as thunder flashed in his eyes. "But she's gone." I placed a hand on his chest, knowing he was about to get up and, sure enough, he tried. As soon as he sat up, he let out a sharp grunt and I gently, but firmly, shoved him back down.

"You aren't going anywhere." I leaned over him. "Stay here and rest. You lost a lot of blood."

"I will fucking kill her. I will rip her limb from limb and make her watch. I will—"

"Yes, I know. You will do all that. But first, shut up and lie down." I smoothed a strand of hair away from his face.

"Did you just tell me to shut up?"

My casual shrug was rewarded with a dazzling smile. How could he still look so good after nearly dying?

"How do you feel?" I asked, experiencing a strange little twist in my heart at seeing him alive and awake. I never wanted to relive anything like that again.

"Like I was stabbed."

I rolled my eyes before I gave him a serious look. "I was so worried."

"A little wound can't kill me, Princess. Good to know you'd miss me, though."

I snorted. "I didn't say that."

He smiled again, and his eyes fluttered closed. "I feel like shit."

Running the back of my hand down his face, his bit of stubble was rough against my hand. "That feels nice, though," he said with a sigh. His eyes still closed, I continued to touch him, admiring the thick fringe of lashes forming shadowed crescents at the tips of his cheeks. I explored his face with my fingers, tracing the bridge of his nose and the curve of his lips. Pale from his injury, he was still the most beautiful man I'd ever seen.

After this incident, Mare's threat had drawn closer—I could feel it perched on my shoulder like a gargoyle sharpening its claws. I needed to tell him everything, but there were thirteen days left until Mare returned one last time, and he wouldn't be able to help me. I knew, with the certainty that the sun would rise each day, he would take it upon himself to solve this riddle that had no solution. That he would tear apart the world to find it, only to come up empty-handed. I couldn't let him do that. He'd already brushed too close to death because of me.

He let out a soft sigh of contentment as I continued my exploration, trailing my fingers along the line of his jaw and down the curve of his throat before placing my hand flat on his chest, where his heart beat a steady, comforting rhythm. I'd lost two more days here at his side, but nothing could have kept me away.

My thoughts wandered, for the thousandth time, to the moment in the hall. His lips on my skin and the things he'd said. I couldn't stop fantasizing about what might have happened next.

"What are you thinking about?" He'd opened his eyes and was looking up at me, his expression clear and unguarded. "I hope you were daydreaming about something tall, dark, and fascinating."

Good gods, was I that obvious?

"I, uh..." I pretended to pick a piece of lint off my leggings. "That's none of your business." I could practically hear the roll of his eyes. My gaze flicked to him, and I grinned. Was there any reason to pretend? He'd cracked open my paper-thin shell, and now there was no going back.

He shifted, leaning up on an elbow as he pushed me flat to the bed. "I was thinking about how we were interrupted the other night."

"Oh? That?" I waved a hand in the air. "I remembered right this very moment. Haven't thought about it at all."

His arm snaked around my waist, and he pulled me toward him, crushing me against his solid chest.

"Liar," he said, kissing the delicate spot where my shoulder met my collarbone. I shivered from the top of my head to the tips of my toes as he placed more featherlight kisses in a row, stopping at the hollow of my throat. "You smell so good," he said, inhaling deeply. "Like flowers and mint and furious rage, bundled up in a perfect package."

I snorted out a laugh and gave him a playful shove on his shoulder.

He buried his face into my neck deeper as he echoed my laughter. "If Mare had killed me, my only regret would have been not being able to do this."

His mouth brushed mine softly. My lips parted for him as he took my bottom lip between his teeth, tugging on it gently. But it wasn't enough, and I was done waiting. I wrapped my arms around his neck and pulled him down, crushing my mouth to his. He let out a small grunt of surprise, recovering immediately before he claimed my mouth, angling my head to drive his tongue against mine, seeking and plundering.

Our breaths became a mingled wash of feverish pants and ragged gasps as heat melted every bone in my body. Ronan shifted, rolling on top of me, pinning me down with his delicious weight as his hips settled between my thighs. He tasted like sunshine and lightning—the two halves of his nature coalescing into the flavor of a summer storm.

Grabbing my wrists, he held my hands over my head as he sucked a hot wet trail of fire down the slope of my throat. My legs hitched around his waist as he thrust his hips against me, his savage groan vibrating right to the tight, aching apex of my thighs.

"Your injury. You're going to tear your stitches," I gasped, fingernails digging into his back as he took my mouth like I was an ocean to swim or a mountain to claim.

Not that I ever wanted him to stop, but I really should be more responsible.

"I'm fine," he bit out, his voice as rough as sun-bleached wood.

I moaned as we deepened the kiss, our tongues diving for each other. Tendrils of searing lust snaked through my blood, leaving a scorched trail in its path. Hands roamed along my sides, my back, my hips, and my thighs, as if he couldn't touch enough of me at once. When his thumb swept the bottom curve of my breast, I gasped into an arc, taut and intense with need.

"Ahem." A polite voice floated from the doorway. Ronan cursed as he pulled away, and I smiled against his chest as he looked over his shoulder.

"Gideon," he said, voice thick. "Your timing could be better, my friend."

"I'm sorry, Commander, but it's time to check your bandages. Kianna wanted to make sure you were healing properly." Gideon cleared his throat. "But I'm happy to see you're awake."

Ronan rolled off me, his face pale. This probably hadn't been the best idea, but I was finding it difficult to feel contrite about it.

Gideon and Kianna both entered, sharing a knowing look with one another.

After settling Ronan on his back, Kianna peeled away the bandage, her eyes going wide. "You're healing very quickly, Commander." She prepared a fresh layer of bandages. "One might think you have a drop of Faerie in you."

He snorted and then groaned. "This is all your doing, Kianna. You saved me. I don't know how I'll ever thank you enough."

Kianna's cheeks deepened to a crimson blush, and her eyes shone as she preened under the compliment. She pursed her lips and gave us both a pointed look. "Though it would be better if you refrained from certain...*activities* for a few more days, at least."

"We'll try to remember that," Ronan said, offering the Fae an innocent smile, and then winked at me. That won him an eye roll from Kianna, though her expression sparkled and she had trouble controlling her smile. If I didn't know better, I could have sworn she was up to something.

"Do you want some water?" I asked after Gideon and Kianna had left, and Ronan nodded.

Noah and Em knocked on the door, and I waved them in.

"He's awake."

"So we heard," Em said with a smirk.

"Those two are the worst gossips," I said.

Sitting on the armchairs where they'd spent much of the last two days, they leaned forward, elbows braced on their knees.

"Should we go after her?" Noah asked, getting right to the point. His eyes went to me and then to Ronan.

"Do you have any idea how to find her?" Ronan asked me.

I shook my head. "I assume she must live in the Faerie realms, but you two aren't going after her. She'll either kill you or lock you up, too." They all watched me with barely restrained fury. "I need to break this curse, ensure my family is safe, and then figure out what comes next. Please, if you do anything, she might hurt them."

Noah's hand balled into a fist, punching his other hand in frustration. "I'm going to rip her throat out."

"I think Ronan already has some more colorful ideas in mind," I said, and they all shared a grimace.

Ronan was pale again, his brow clammy.

"You should go back to sleep," I said, and it must have been a measure of how terrible he felt that, for once, he didn't argue.

CHAPTER TWENTY-THREE

11 DAYS LEFT

TIME MOVED IN A space of its own, the clock ticking in my head growing louder and louder until it echoed off every surface. There were moments I'd stop what I was doing, the sound so paralyzing it froze me to the spot. So deafening, all I could hear was the roar of my failure screaming at me in an endless loop.

As Ronan recovered, I continued my training with Noah and Em while I waited for my tincture to finish brewing. I wasn't giving up yet. I'd promised Kianna I would keep trying. Anything could still happen if I kept pushing forward.

Between watching over Ronan, getting battered in the training yard, and standing vigil in the kitchen, the strain slowly wore me down to a blunted nub. I'd never been more exhausted, but Ronan was healing, and I could at least untie that knot of worry.

My legs tucked under me, I sat in the chair next to Ronan as he slept when Gideon found me.

"I've prepared lunch outside, Your Highness. Come and eat with us. You've been wearing yourself thin, and you need some air. The commander will be fine for a short while on his own."

I looked at Ronan's sleeping form and then back at Gideon.

"And he wouldn't like it if you denied yourself anything to look after him."

With a small smile, I pushed myself up from the chair. "Okay, I am hungry."

Outside, the sun was shining. Gideon had set up a small firepit surrounded by benches covered in blankets and furs. Em handed me a bowl as I sat.

"Where's Kianna?" I asked, bringing it to my lips.

"Sleeping. She's worn herself out tending to the commander," Gideon said, pouring me a glass of wine while I made a mental note to check on her later.

The three of them chattered away as I listened, not feeling the need to say much, just enjoying their company. Their talk turned to life in the castle in Estria and their stories of fighting in the field.

"How did you end up with them?" I asked Em. "Are there many women in Estria's army?"

Em shook her head. "Only a handful. I was the first." She propped her knee on the bench, draping an arm over it. "I'm the youngest of nine brothers and sisters, so no one cared what I got up to. I was obsessed with watching the soldiers training at the castle, and I wanted to learn to fight like them. They either ignored me or chased me off when I hung around too long. Apparently, I was a distraction for the boys." She rolled her eyes, and I joined her. "The only person who ever noticed me was Ronan, and when he took command, he invited me to try. I was twelve—more than old enough to hold a sword. Noah and Ronan treated me like any of the boys, walloping me until there wasn't an inch of my skin that wasn't black and blue. But I kept coming back and, eventually, I found myself as his third in command." There was no arrogance in her statement, only a pride she'd earned and a profound respect for the men who'd trained and accepted her.

"Is it hard? Do the men give you a tough time?" I asked.

She grinned, the smile lighting up her sparkling gray eyes. "Sometimes, but since I can kick all their asses, it shuts them up pretty quickly."

"I think you're remarkable. I don't think I would have had the courage to learn how to fight if I hadn't met you," I said, and Em's cheeks turned a brilliant shade of red to rival the hue of her hair.

"Your Highness." She tipped her head forward in deference, her long braids spilling over her shoulders.

"And you?" I asked Noah.

"We've been inseparable since we were old enough to walk," he replied. "We grew up together with all the younger sons of noble houses whose fate was to serve in the king's army."

"And you've never resented that? Your future being decided for you?"

Noah shrugged. "We didn't know any different."

"How is it any different from being a princess?" Em asked, taking a bite of bread. "If you hadn't had that little problem with the curse, wouldn't you be married off to some prince or something? Shit, they probably would have married you to Erick!"

They laughed, and I did too, though the thought was unsettling.

It was true. Even without the curse, my life would never have been mine. With it, it had become something else entirely.

"I promise, Ronan thanks the gods every day he's the second son and not the first," Em continued. "Being king is the last thing he'd ever want."

"Why?" I asked.

"He belongs on a battlefield. It's what he was made for," Noah added. "Plus, he scares everyone in the castle. I think they constantly go to war to get him out of there."

"Us too," Em said, pointing a thumb at her chest, and we laughed again.

"You must be getting tired of this place?" I asked. It had been a while since I'd insisted they leave, but today, that wasn't the motivation for my question. "It must be rather dull and quiet compared to waging war across the continent."

"I think we all needed a break," Gideon piped up. "The last clash with the Faerie courts on the border of Estria was particularly bloody."

"And you've been stuck with these three all this time?" I asked, and Gideon beamed.

"He works for Ronan," Noah said. "We just tag along."

"I've attended the commander since he was a young boy," Gideon said, pride written in the shape of his straightened posture. "He's always had trouble with life at court. It is too much scheming and plotting and half-truths for a man of his nature."

"He's changed, though," Noah said. "Since coming here."

"What do you mean?" I asked.

"I mean, he's happy." Noah frowned. "He laughs more."

"Isn't that a good thing?"

"Of course it is. But we can't stay here forever."

All this time, I'd been petitioning for them to leave, but hearing Noah voice it felt like a star crashing to the earth. They *should* leave. And Ronan should not be asleep in my bed, but I'd kissed him and allowed myself the luxury of my emotions, and that had changed everything.

"Something troubles you, Your Highness," Gideon said before all eyes swung to me.

I'd gone inside myself again, thoughts leading me away from the present. "How much longer until the tincture is ready?"

"A day or two more," Gideon replied, gathering dishes and stacking them in a pile. "I am keeping a very close eye on it. I won't let anything happen."

Overcome with an emotion I had no name for, I nodded, my throat suddenly too tight to speak.

"Have you tried a hag hole?" Noah asked, popping an almond into his mouth and crunching it loudly.

"A what?"

"A hag hole," Noah said more slowly, as if that would help me understand.

"Noah, I don't know what that is."

He sighed. "When we were kids, and we'd get scared of evil Faeries coming to steal us, my mum would make hag holes. A wicked Faerie can't enter a room if there's a hag hole hanging on the door."

Em and Gideon were both trying to hold in smiles while I indulged Noah's story.

"How do you make one?"

"You find a bunch of stones, and you twist up some rope and tie them together until they make a wreath. Then you hang it on the door, and—" He clapped his hands together with a flourish. "—no more Faeries."

"And does it work?"

"All I know is we saw no evil Faeries in our rooms," he said with a nod of his head that suggested the matter was settled.

I covered my mouth as Em dropped her head into her hands.

"Noah, you're such a dolt," she said.

"Hey!" Noah threw an almond at her. "It worked for my mum!"

We were all laughing now, and I let out a long breath. "Honestly, I'm willing to try anything at this point."

Gideon stood up, the stack of plates gathered in his hands. "I'll gather the necessary supplies, Your Highness." Before I could protest, he turned and headed for the castle.

Later that evening, I awoke to Ronan curled around me, trailing kisses along my neck and over the back of my shoulder. I'd dozed off after spending the afternoon with Noah, Em, and Gideon, making dozens of hag holes. We'd hung them all around the throne room, reasoning if one was good, then surely thirty would be better.

"You brought me to your room," Ronan said, pressing his mouth to the curve of my throat.

"You've been here for days. You just noticed that?"

"No, I'm pointing it out. Why did you bring me here?"

"The new vault doesn't have a lock; I wanted to be sure you wouldn't steal from me." He laughed softly, breath grazing my skin like a warm coastal breeze. "Though this is an unexpected side benefit," I said as he shimmied closer and slowly slid his hand down my side, the heat of his fingers burning through my thin nightgown. "You should be resting."

He also shouldn't be here, but he was, and I was too weak to send him away. Too wrapped up in the feel, the scent, and the image of him to stop any of this.

"I'm tired of resting. I've rested enough." He bit my earlobe, dragging his teeth along the sensitive skin.

An involuntary gasp parted my mouth as I reached to cup the back of his neck. "Enough for what, Commander?"

"Wouldn't you like to find out?" His mouth returned to my throat as he pulled me even closer, his nose burying in the sensitive spot behind my ear. There must have been a clever reply on the tip of my tongue, but it dissipated in a puff of poplar seeds as his hand continued its exploration of my body, sliding across my stomach. "You feel so good. I could stay like this forever." His lips caught mine in a deep and soul-melting kiss. His hard arousal pressed into my backside, and I shifted my hips, causing him to groan softly. "I'm supposed to be resting, Princess...but please tell me you locked the door this time."

His mouth slid over mine, and I nodded as I flipped so we were facing each other. As we kissed, his hand drifted down my back and then up my side, dancing along my hipbone and then my ribs before his thumb swept over a nipple. My back arched as he teased it through the thin material of my nightshirt, and something unintelligible exhaled from my throat.

His hand continued its exploration, tracing circles between my breasts and then lower, stopping just below my navel. The gentle touch had me rocking into him, desperate for more. His hand slid down, pausing within devastating reach of where I craved release.

"I want to touch you, Thorne. I want to feel how wet you are and hear the sound you make when you come apart on my fingers. Sometimes it's the only thing I can think about."

My heart thumped against my vocal cords, nearly strangling my response. "Touch me, Ronan."

He made an approving sound in the pit of his throat, rumbling and full of masculine satisfaction. Green eyes bright, his stare spiralled into me with naked lust and longing. No one had ever looked at me like that, and heat dripped from my stomach and spread between my thighs.

He lowered his head, tugging down the bodice of my nightgown with his teeth, licking and then biting my nipple. I dissolved on a caramel-scented wind, my nails digging into his silken strands of midnight hair.

Continuing his exploration of my curves, his hand continued its journey, sliding along the side of my leg and catching the hem of my nightgown. As he dragged it up, cool air tickled my hot skin. It offered the barest hint of relief from the heat threatening to char me from the inside.

Hitching up my knee, he spread me wide and trailed a lazy finger up the inside of my leg—first one, and then the other. The heat of his arousal pressed against my hip, and I reached for him until he caught my wrist.

"You first," he said, placing my hand on my stomach. "I want you to experience this with no other distractions." There was a command in his voice that spread shivers over me before he continued his agonizing pace.

I whimpered, anticipating his touch. So close, but not close enough. My hips squirmed as he teased a path below my navel, looping swirls and twists like he was composing a ballad on my skin.

"So impatient," he drawled, but I cut him off as I pulled his mouth to mine. He moaned into me as his fingers drifted lower and lower.

I arched my back, hoping to encourage movement in the direction I craved. This was torture, a raw aching need more primal than anything I'd ever felt.

Finally.

Finally, his fingers slipped through my center, and he groaned. "Fuck, you're so wet for me. What a good girl."

At that, I crumbled apart like a puzzle dropped on the floor.

"Moan for me," he said as his fingers circled my clit, shock waves spreading out in every direction. "Tell me how you like it." He pressed harder and then slipped a finger inside me, and I let out a cry as his mouth devoured mine.

Oh, gods, I wanted more. I wanted all of him.

My head thrown back, he slipped a second finger inside me. I'd thought about him touching me more times than I could count, but nothing could compare to the reality of him now, bringing me closer and closer to the edge of a rocky cliff pummeled by a turbulent sea.

In that moment, my entire world became Ronan's skillful hand, his demanding mouth, and his muscular chest and thighs crowded against me as sparks exploded across my skin. Moving faster now, he nipped at my throat and my ear and my mouth as I rode his hand, repeating his name over and over.

And then release crashed through me as I cried out and exploded into a million ribbons of color. He kept his hand circling, his fingers moving inside me until I eventually found my fluttering way back to the earth.

After withdrawing his fingers, he placed them in his mouth, tasting my release with a satisfied gleam in his eye. I had never felt so wanted and needed and noticed.

When he was done, he pressed a kiss to the curve of my throat, eyes hooded.

"I'm so glad you didn't die," I said in a whisper.

He smiled against my skin. "Me too. Though now, I can die a truly satisfied man." As I blushed, he traced the edge of the bruise on my face with his thumb. "Does it hurt?"

"Almost as much as getting stabbed."

Ronan had gone pale again, our activity still too much for his delicate state. He winced as he shifted and collapsed on his back.

"I think I need to rest," he said, his eyelids fluttering closed for a moment before he peeled them open, desire in his expression. "As much as it kills me to say that right now."

And as much as I didn't want to stop, I knew he was still recovering.

"You're still healing." I pressed my hand to his chest. "I'll owe you one."

He clasped his hand over mine and stared at me. "You never owe me anything, Thorne. I'm just grateful to be in your presence, however you'll have me."

I tapped the tip of his nose. "Never turn down a favor owed from a princess."

He chuckled as he flipped my hand and kissed the palm. "I'll try to remember that." His gaze returned to my lacerated cheek. "And I will kill Mare for everything she has done to you."

"You're obsessed with killing," I teased, leaning over and pressing my mouth to his.

He pulled me down, wrapping firm arms around my waist. "I'll kill anyone who hurts you, Thorne."

"Don't make promises that might be too hard to keep, Ronan."

"I mean it. I will protect you with every breath in my body."

The declaration was bloody and violent, and a previous version of me might have shied away from it, but right now, wings as wide as the sea opened inside my chest. His words were raw and sincere, and no one had ever wanted to protect me like that.

"I'll protect you, too. With whatever I have, I will protect you."

The smile he gave me cracked my heart, releasing a warm river of golden light. It was so utterly disarming and earnest that I could do nothing but lay my head on his chest and listen to the steady beat of his heart.

CHAPTER TWENTY-FOUR

8 DAYS LEFT

RONAN RECOVERED IN RECORD time, partly thanks to Kianna and partly to some benevolent force that appeared to be watching over him. After a thousand more kisses in my bed, he was already back in the training yard with Noah and Em when I joined them.

My tincture would be ready to try this evening. As it bubbled on the stove, I was bouncing with excitement to test it, though I was also trying not to get my hopes up.

Noah and Em had also made dozens more hag holes to hang all over the castle, and while I was skeptical about Noah's claims, I couldn't help but feel touched they were all trying so hard to help me.

Ronan and I faced off outside, the sun high in the sky. I lunged, and he blocked me, so I tried again. He spun, evading me as I prepared for a counterattack that didn't come. I pounced again as he blocked me and stepped out of the way. Eyes narrowing, I fought harder, swinging left and right as he checked me with ease, but he didn't fight back.

Attacking with more fury now, I swung at him over and over. He evaded every one of my blows but didn't reciprocate, simply spinning away.

"What are you doing?" I hissed at him. "Why aren't you fighting back?" Wild now, I swung again and, this time, he didn't even attempt to stop me. The practice sword cracked against his shoulder, and he grunted but gave no other sign that I'd hit him.

"I don't know what you mean," he said, backing up. "I'm tired. I did just get stabbed, you know?"

"I just watched you flatten Em and Noah," I said with a swing that forced him to take a step back. He had never yielded an inch of ground to me—ever. With both hands pressed to his chest and a snarl that ripped from my throat, I shoved him with all my strength as he stumbled back into the stone wall of the courtyard.

"What are you doing? Fight me!" I screamed. He countered with a half-hearted swipe and glanced over at Noah and Em as he silently begged for rescue. They shuffled their feet, looking everywhere but at us.

Our swords crossing between us, I pressed myself against Ronan.

"Are you refusing to fight me?" A flash of guilt passed over his face, and fury tunnelled into my veins. "Are you kidding me?" Conscious of Noah and Em, I lowered my voice, seething with anger. "Are you afraid to spar with me because we kissed? Is that what this is about?"

Ronan leaned down, speaking into my ear in a gravelly voice. "Thorne, I can't knock you to the ground when I can still feel you hot and wet and squirming in my hand. When I can still taste the sweetness of your pussy on my tongue." His words were meant to disarm, and it nearly worked, because something equally hot and wet lashed through me. But I was also furious, and I pushed it away.

"Yes, you can! Why does this change anything? You said you'd teach me to fight. That was our deal from the first day I let you stay here. You don't get to back out on me now because we—" I looked at Em and Noah, who were finding the ground to be intensely interesting.

"Leave us," Ronan ordered, his eyes focused on me.

They practically tripped over each other in their eagerness to get away. After they disappeared into the castle, I retreated several paces and ran for him, swinging down my sword with every bit of strength I had. He blocked it but remained still.

"Ronan! Stop this! Fight me! You have a woman as your third in command, for gods' sake!"

"It's different," he snapped.

"Why? I need this! You promised!" Another wave of guilt crossed his expression, but he didn't seem inclined to budge. So I tried a different tactic. I lowered my sword and cocked a hip, offering him a small smile. "Fight me or I won't let you kiss me. Ever again."

I was bluffing, but he didn't need to know that. Regardless, the empty threat did what I intended because he narrowed his eyes at me.

"Did you blackmail me? With kissing?"

"I'm pretty sure I did," I growled, adding, "and more than kissing. There's plenty more where this came from." I swept my hand over my body, and he followed it, hunger flaring in his eyes. He wasn't the only one capable of disarming.

"If you recall, you owe me a favor." His smug smile suggested he thought he'd taken the upper hand.

"If *you* recall, we did not agree upon the terms of said favor." I pretended to check my nails. "I'll brush your horse for you."

His green eyes went dark, jaw hardening. Finally, he stepped forward and took a proper swipe at me.

"Ah-ha!" I said, leaping out of the way. I swung again, and he blocked it, but this time he countered and hit me in the ribs with a dull thwack. I grunted in satisfaction.

"Better." I graced him with a feral smile, launching myself at him as we became a blur of movements. His training had been impeccable, and I had been a motivated student. I still couldn't beat him, but I could at least hold my own for a few minutes.

He knocked the sword from my hand and swept a leg behind my knees, sending me flying onto my back. Ronan landed on top of me, pinning my wrists over my head.

"Was this what you wanted, Little Lion?" His gaze was full of fire and heat, and I was a spitting viper of fury, but I also kind of wished there were fewer clothes between us.

"Yes!" I willed myself to stillness, intensely aware of every place he was touching me.

Face lowered to mine, he said, "Don't you dare blackmail me again."

With my heels, I drew him close, wrapping my legs around his waist. Smirking, he stretched over me. But I used the distraction to flip him on his back, straddling him under me, wrists trapped over his head. He could have freed himself from my grip in a heartbeat, but I could tell he was very interested in where this was going.

Tracing the curve of his throat with my tongue, I ground my hips into his, feeling the thickening length of his cock and letting him think he'd won. Ronan shivered under me and moaned as I sucked on the tender spot behind his ear. When I felt the hard proof that I'd gotten to him, I lifted my head and conjured my fiercest look. Though I desperately wanted to continue what I'd started, he needed to be reminded of something.

"Then don't you dare treat me like some delicate flower ever again. I've had enough of that in my life, and I won't accept it from you. I have no problem with you wanting to protect me, but don't you dare stop me from learning how to protect you or anyone else I care about. If you think I'd ever be okay with that, then you don't know me at all."

I pushed myself up and stood. Dusting my pants off, I turned and stalked away, leaving him lying in the snow.

I stood with Gideon in front of my parents, studying them closely.

"Do you think this will work?" I asked, looking at the vial of dark liquid in my hand and then at their peaceful, sleeping faces.

"I hope so, Your Highness."

"Thank you for this. You've all been so kind."

He tipped his head, giving me that comforting smile I'd come to trust. "It was no trouble, Your Highness. Would you like some help?"

Holding the vial to my heart, I took a deep breath. If this didn't work, then I didn't know what I would do. "No, I'll do it."

At that moment, Ronan entered the room. He was as beautiful as always, dark hair hanging around his shoulders, the top half tied back. His tunic stretched over his frame in a way that left me breathless. Hands stuffed in his pockets, he gave me an apologetic smile that almost shook my resolve, but I wasn't quite ready to forgive him yet. Instead, I scowled and returned to my task.

With a heavy sense of foreboding, I approached my father and gently tipped up his chin. With the other, I unstoppered the vial and held it to his lips, drizzling the tincture in.

When I'd added enough, I closed my father's mouth. Hands braced on the armrests of his throne, I watched his face intently for any sign of movement. Endless seconds ticked by, but there was nothing. I waited, willing something to happen. I waited and waited, seconds turning to minutes, but the longer I stood there, the more I shook.

Until finally, I dropped my head with an anguished sob and stared at the bottle in my hand. Frustration rising like a cresting wave, I hurled the glass at the wall behind my parents' thrones. It smashed against the stone, thick dark liquid dripping like congealed blood. I cradled my face in my hands.

"Fuck," I muttered, my whole body trembling. I couldn't stop this. I couldn't break this. Time kept ticking, and everything was slipping away.

Strong arms circled me, and I pressed my face into Ronan's chest while I sobbed.

"It's going to be okay, Thorne. We'll figure this out." He ran a hand up and down my back, soothing me. I held on to him tightly, like he was my salvation. He didn't let go, murmuring reassuring words and blanketing me with comforting touches until my breath eventually returned to normal.

"Come, sit down." He drew me to the side of the room, where I leaned against the wall. Ronan sat down, taking my hand and sitting quietly as I continued to sniffle. He understood I couldn't talk about it, but his quiet, solid presence was exactly what I needed. Gideon had left the room, probably to tend to whatever meal he was preparing next.

"I just want to talk to them," I said.

"What would you tell them?" Ronan squeezed my hand and wrapped his arm around my shoulders.

I collapsed into his embrace as his chin rested on top of my head. "That I woke up. That we could finally be the family we'd always wanted. That maybe this was a second chance."

"You'll get to," he said, rubbing my arm. "Somehow, we'll figure a way out of this." I didn't miss the 'we' in his statement, and part of me was grateful while another only felt an ocean of guilt for what I'd dragged him into. Instead, I said nothing as I listened to his soft breath and his heart.

"I'm sorry," he said. Wiping my eyes, I looked up at him. "I shouldn't have treated you that way. I know you can take care of yourself and don't need to be coddled. I see how hard you're trying to save your family, and I was being an ass. Sometimes, I forget you are no lady."

I gave him a soft punch in the arm, a tiny smile creeping to my lips.

He took my face in his hands, a thumb sweeping over my cheek. "I'm in over my head, Thorne. I've never felt like this about anyone before. I don't know how to be normal around you. How to be anything but completely consumed. You've undone me, and the thought of anything happening to you, of anyone causing you harm, makes me crazy."

Well, I couldn't really argue with an apology like that.

"Oh, Ronan," I said, touching his cheek. "I've never felt like this either. I didn't even know *this* was possible." I gestured vaguely between us, as if trying to encompass the vast breadth of my feelings. Everything I couldn't find the words for. Another tear slipped down my face, but this one was for him.

"Why the tear, Little Lion?" he asked, kissing it away.

Because our days are numbered. Because I killed your father. Because I need to tell you this and can't bring myself to do so, and every day we're hurtling closer to the end of whatever this is, and I don't want it to be over a moment before it has to be.

I couldn't bring myself to say any of it, so I took the coward's way and didn't answer, squeezing him tighter. He tipped up my chin and kissed me with so much conviction that it pulled every breath from my lungs. He kissed me into heady oblivion, tugging me onto his lap so my knees straddled his hips. The gentle touches from earlier became more possessive, grounding me into a place where I could forget all the anxiety and worry, even if for only a minute. I wanted to lose myself in Ronan.

Our tongues clashed, sliding over one another, his hard heat pressing between my legs. I ground down against him, and we both moaned.

"Thorne," he said, momentarily coming up for air. "Have you ever—" He raised an eyebrow, and I bit my lip.

"Uh, yes." I laughed as his eyes went wide. "Why is that so shocking? You're not the first man to take an interest in me."

"No, I'm absolutely sure I'm not." Voice rough, his gaze swept over me like he was contemplating his favorite flavor of ice cream. "But you're a princess, and it's unusual, given you were so young and unwed when the curse fell."

With a shrug, I gave him a mischievous smile. "My days were numbered, and I didn't want to fall into an eternal slumber without a few formative experiences first."

He laughed, and I swore he was impressed with me right now.

"Who was it? Or was it a 'them'?" He widened his eyes again, and I smacked him in the shoulder.

"It was just one. One of my father's guards."

His jaw dropped, and I experienced a curious thrill that I'd thrown him off. "Is he here?" He looked around the room.

"He is." I shifted, wondering why he was asking me this.

"Where?"

"Really? Why?"

He smirked. "I want to see the man who first stole your heart."

"You're just going to tell me how you're better-looking than him."

His grin was confident. "Well, I don't need to see him to know that."

I rolled my eyes, but I pointed to where Adrian lay beyond my father on the third and fourth steps leading up to the dais. Ronan's expression softened, taking in the young man with the smattering of freckles on his nose.

"You would have been in so much trouble."

"I know. But no one paid much attention to me. It was selfish and reckless, and he would have been the one to suffer more if they'd caught us, but he never minded the risk."

Ronan laughed. "No, I don't imagine he did." He pulled me toward him, and I wrapped my arms around his neck and laid my head against his shoulder while his hands trailed along my back.

"Can I walk you back to your room?" he asked after a few minutes.

With a nod, I pushed away and stood. He took my hand in his large, warm grip, tugging me along as we paused to kiss along the way, pressed against walls and doors. I was drunk on him. It was euphoric and wonderful and distracting.

We stood at my bedroom door, where he pressed me against the door frame, one hand on my hip and the other bracing the wall behind us. After kissing me deeply, he pulled away and touched his forehead to mine. "Goodnight, Princess."

"What? You're leaving?" He'd moved back to his room once he'd recovered, and I'd missed his presence at my side.

"I'll see you tomorrow," he said in a way that sounded like he was trying to convince himself to leave.

"But what about...what we were just discussing?" I gestured toward the throne room. My face heated. *Did I really just ask him that?*

His smile was so irresistible it made my heart skip a beat. Tilting my chin up, he said, "If I stay with you tonight, things will lead to a place we can never come back from." His voice dropped so low I felt it tingle right to my core. "I can't keep my hands off you, Thorne."

"I want to go there," I said, breathless. "Don't keep them off."

He rewarded me with a dark and delicious laugh. "I'm thrilled you're so eager." He gently brushed his lips over mine. "But these things shouldn't be rushed. Not when it means this much. Soon, my beautiful princess." He pressed himself against me and brought his mouth to my ear. "I got a hint of how good you taste, and I can't wait for more. Soon, I'll spread your legs wide and fuck you until you touch the stars," he promised, and my heart performed an erratic leap in my chest.

Tick tock, Thorne. I shoved the reminder into a box and slammed the lid with a resounding thud.

Ronan stepped back and gave me a quick bow and wink before turning on his heel. I did my best not to pout as I watched him walk away.

CHAPTER TWENTY-FIVE

6 DAYS LEFT

"Will you come for a ride?" Ronan stood in the door-way to the kitchen, where I was helping Gideon wash up after dinner.

Lost in my thoughts, I gave a start. "What?"

My coat was draped over his arm, and he held it up. "Will you come for a ride?" he repeated as I wiped my hands on my apron. Kianna lounged at the long wooden table, polishing off her third lemon tart of the evening. Ronan furrowed his brow. "Are you okay, Thorne?"

"I'm fine."

Using the back of my hand, I pushed my hair out of my face. I'd been thinking about Mare and my parents. There was less than a week left before she returned, and unless Noah's hag holes actually worked, I was completely out of ideas. The only thing I had was a bit of training under my belt and my dwindling hope.

I also had to decide what to do about Ronan—either tell him the truth about Mare's deal or find a way to get them out of here within the next six days. Every time I spun up my courage to tell him, I stopped myself. I had no doubt he'd stay to confront Mare, and I couldn't ask any of them to fight this battle for me. That would be four more deaths on my hands.

"Where?" I asked, trying to stuff down my thoughts. I'd convince them to leave. There was no other choice.

"It's a surprise."

I narrowed my eyes, but his face gave away nothing. Kianna and Gideon wore twin smiles of collusion I couldn't interpret.

"What's going on?" I crossed my arms over my chest.

Ronan rolled his eyes and grabbed my hand. "Do you have to argue about everything? Just come with me."

"Yes, I do. It's what you find charming about me."

He laughed. "That may be true, but stop it."

He tugged me forward, and I relented. We exited the back of the castle, where his horse waited. Overhead, the sky was dark and swollen with thick gray clouds.

"Only one horse?" I peered at him, an eyebrow raised.

"I trust you don't mind riding with me this time?" I feigned nonchalance and shrugged, remembering how I'd balked at riding with him to Tenby. "Let's hope it's not too awful for you, Your Highness."

"Let's hope," I replied and grinned as I mounted the saddle.

Ronan settled behind me a moment later, and we slowly stepped through the trees, hooves crunching in the snow.

"When we went to Tenby, were you trying to get the horse to throw us together?" I asked.

"Absolutely." His mouth pressed to my ear as his hand slid from my waist into the crease of my thigh. "It was taking all of my willpower not to whisk you into the forest, rip off that sexy red dress, and fuck you against a tree so hard they could hear you screaming in the Faerie realms."

The sound that came from me was part laugh and part gasp. "You bastard."

A soft laugh brushed my neck as I leaned against him. His hand pressed to my stomach, he placed kisses along the curve of my throat. Eyes closed, I let myself sink into this moment of contentment, pushing away all the things that vied for my attention.

After riding for a while, it became clear we were on the path toward my grandparents' chateau. When we arrived, Ronan jumped down from the horse and then held on to my waist as I slid to the ground.

"What are we doing here?"

"You'll see." There was promise in his gaze as he took my hand, and we entered.

Debris littered the floor, broken glass snapping beneath our feet. I was truly curious now. We walked upstairs, toward my grandparents' once-luxurious suite at the end of the hall. The same room where Kianna had found me after Mare's gruesome warning.

Ronan dropped my hand to reach for the handles and then flung the doors open with a flourish.

Someone had cleaned up the room and lit hundreds of candles. They covered every available surface, lining the fireplace, mantle, and windowsills. A thick rug had been laid at the foot of the roaring fireplace, which crackled merrily. The massive wooden bed had been repaired and was covered in crisp white sheets and a mountain of gold and cream pillows.

"What? How?" Words failed me as I turned to Ronan.

"I wanted to give you some of the happy memories back. You said this place was important to you." Tears pricked the back of my eyes. It was such a wonderful gesture, ribbons of velvet wrapped gently around my heart. "As for the how, I had some help from Gideon and Kianna. Well, a lot of help." His grin sheepish, he rubbed a hand along the back of his neck. I realized he was nervous about my reaction.

"I love it. This is the most incredible, meaningful thing anyone has ever done for me."

He dropped his arm, visibly relaxing. "Kianna picked this out for you to wear." He held up a green silk dress that caught the falling light. It was a perfect match with Ronan's eyes. Kianna was such a clever Faerie. "I'll be back in a moment. You change."

Before he left, he pulled me close and kissed me. Despite every black cloud in my personal sky, happiness bloomed, obscuring them in a shower of rainbows. I ingrained myself into this moment, trying to forget about the future. There would be time for that tomorrow. I'd done this before. I'd done this every day of my life. A long time ago, I'd learned to separate the present from my uncertain future, building a wall so thick and so high nothing could cross it. It had been the only way for me to keep living and not dissolve into despair.

I took off my tunic and leggings and slid the soft green dress over my head. It was light and airy, with thin straps and a deep plunge that left my arms and my back bare.

Ronan returned, holding a bottle of wine and two glasses, and I flashed him my brightest smile. He deserved only the pieces of me that still shone, even as they grew tarnished. He kicked off his boots and took off his jacket, leaving him with a white shirt that fit every artful curve of his arms and his chest. Soft black plants stretched over his strong thighs.

"No dress for you?" I asked as he approached.

"I could never hope to be as beautiful as you in anything I wear." He cupped the back of my head with his large hand and tipped it back, drawing me into a deep kiss.

Dragging a finger down his chest, I leaned in and asked, "Have you arranged all this to cash in on your favor?"

Eyebrows drawing together, he gave me a puzzled look and then broke into a smile. "Am I that obvious?" I lifted a shoulder and tipped my head, wondering what I'd done to deserve all this. He leaned down, pressing his mouth to my ear. "You never brushed my horse like you promised."

A laugh burst out of me, and he captured the sound, kissing me until the room spun.

"Come, sit." He pulled me down on the rug and we leaned against the sofa, where we could enjoy the warmth of the fire. The wind howled through the trees, rattling the panes, the temperature dropping as snow fell from the sky.

"Did you order that? Because the only thing that could make this more romantic is a storm."

"Yes," he deadpanned. "For you, I did. I heard you love them."

Popping the wine cork, he poured us each a glass as I laughed.

Leaning together, we watched the fire, listening to the snapping of logs and the song of the wind. He traced a finger down my arm, making small circles up and down, sending a delicious shiver to the base of my spine.

"Ronan," I whispered. "This is amazing. You're amazing, and I don't know how I got so lucky that it was you who found me here and then *refused* to leave." I tried to look angry about it, but I hadn't felt that way in quite a while.

"It's me who's the lucky one," he said. "What were the odds of finding my very own fairy-tale princess in a rickety inn miles away from Estria?"

"Rickety? Verna will slit your throat in your sleep if she hears that."

He chuckled, and we kissed—softly at first, and then more fiercely—as our tongues touched and danced like snowflakes caught in the wind. Getting up on my knees, I pulled at the hem of his shirt, and he lifted his arms so I could yank it over his head. Everything about him was so impossibly beautiful. The planes of his face. The curves of his muscles. The wild intensity in his astonishing green eyes.

My dress followed his shirt to a pile on the floor.

He wrapped his hands around my hips and didn't move, his gaze learning every inch of my skin. "I knew you'd be breathtaking, but not even my most vivid dreams could ever compare to this perfection."

He pulled me down, flipping me onto the carpet. His pants went with the rest of his clothes, and he stretched his warm, powerful body over mine.

The lines of my control were fraying, and I tipped my chin up, inviting him to touch me everywhere. His rough palm slid up my thigh and along my ribs as he lowered his head, planting open-mouth kisses along the tops of my breasts. Taking one of my nipples between his teeth, he bit down gently, sending a shivering bolt of lightning to the aching throb between my thighs.

Distantly, I registered the gale battering the windows, its howls shaking the room as the sky erupted into a fall of thick, white flakes.

Ronan settled against my hips, his scalding cock brushing through my center. As he kissed me, he thrust against me, and I moaned. His tongue drove deep into my mouth, our kiss fueled with a need that went beyond the layers of my skin, beyond the blood in my veins, digging deep into the heart of my soul.

Mouth sliding lower, he returned to my taut nipple, biting and sucking until I was a helpless, mewling puddle of unrequited lust. He moved lower, lying between my legs, fingers sweeping over my sensitive skin.

I inhaled a sharp breath. My legs quivered as he ran his hands along the inside of my thighs, and I whimpered, desperate for him to touch me.

"Always so impatient." His voice rough, he was staring at me like a man contemplating the entire sum of his mortality.

"Ronan, please."

"I love hearing you beg, Little Lion." He flashed me a cocky half-grin and then lowered his head, sweeping his tongue where I needed him so much. A surge rushed through me as he flicked the bundle of nerves between my legs. I cried out, burying my hands in his hair.

"Do you like that, Thorne?"

"Oh gods, yes." I gasped as he moved back and forth, nipping and licking and biting, until I became a life raft, tossing in a tumultuous sea.

Hips lifting off the carpet, I pleaded for more and he increased his pace, his tongue making rough circles against my clit. He groaned and slipped a finger inside. Coaxing and insistent, he drove me to the edge, my fingers gripped in the carpet beneath me. As I cried out his name, I plummeted into nothing and everything as a wave of pleasure, bright and sparkling and brimming with hope, ripped through me.

Ronan pulled back and stretched out over me, capturing my mouth with his. He tasted like sex and the sheen of my longing.

"You have no idea how much I've been wanting to do that," he said, voice thick. Stars danced in my vision, and I pulled him down to me. "I'm never going to stop wanting the taste of your sweet, wet pussy on my tongue."

"I could live with that," I said, breathless, and he let out a low chuckle, his mouth against mine.

He stood, pulling me up with him. The assessing sweep of his gaze was full of yearning and heat. "You are perfect, Thorne."

My eyes roamed across his body, taking in every hard line and chiseled crevice. Impatient and hungry, he yanked me toward him, lifting me up as I wrapped my legs around his waist.

He walked me to the bed, laying me down.

"I think it's time we gave you eleven new gifts fit for a princess," he said. "Because I think we can officially declare the chastity one void."

I let out a bubble of laughter. "Definitely." I drew him closer. "What do you have in mind?"

He slid his cock against my wetness, and I groaned at the lusciousness of those hard ridges against my soft skin.

"How about bravery?" He placed a gentle kiss on my neck. Bravery—it was one of the first things Kianna had said when we'd woken up. That it wasn't one of my gifts. But maybe that wasn't true anymore. I nodded, a lump growing in my throat.

"Brilliance." He dropped a kiss on my collarbone. "Kindness." A kiss above my breast. "Loyalty." A kiss between them. He trailed his lips lower and lower, kissing me slowly as he bestowed these new gifts like drops of crystal hung from sparkling chandeliers.

"Strength. So much strength." I liked that one. "Selflessness. Generosity. Humor. Wit." His mouth below my navel, he swept his tongue in lazy circles, and my hips came off the bed, savoring this wonderful torture. He pulled back to look at me.

"Ferocity. Definitely that." I gave him a sated grin. "And how about sensuality?" He waggled his eyebrows, and I laughed.

"I like those very much. Thank you, Commander."

"Don't thank me, Thorne. Those are yours. You took them. You didn't need me or anyone to give them to you. You've had them all along."

A light awakened as the weight of his words slid under my skin, taking root like a hundred-year oak. "Then thank you for helping me realize it," I said, my voice soft.

He flashed that crooked grin I loved so much, and it felt like my heart tripled in size. We kissed again, his body crushing mine, and I ached deep in the furthest reaches of my battered soul.

"Fuck, I'm so hard," he whispered into my skin. "I want you so much."

"You have me, Ronan. Take me." Among the shredded tatters of a ruined life, a piece of me had been found, and I wanted every part of him.

With a thrust, he was inside me, and I cried out as I dug my fingers into his back. "Thorne," he breathed. "You're so beautiful. Gods, you feel so good." Another thrust stroked into me, slowly filling and stretching.

As wind and snow coalesced into a blank white canvas of sky, its ferocity echoed the swirl and storm inside the room. With Adrian, our love had been sweet and warm and new, but this was something entirely different. Wild and breathless, it was layered with curtains of smoke and heat and wonder. It felt ancient and gilded with the permanence of time, rich with a lifetime of stories yet to be written.

My hands slid along the expanse of his skin, exploring the dips and ripples of his muscles while they bunched and contracted as he moved into me.

"I love it when you touch me," he growled, the guttural sound so raw I clenched around him. As he moved faster, he clamped a hand on my hip, a gesture that claimed me as his. I opened myself up, wanting to give him everything. With a bruising kiss pressed to my mouth, he thrust harder, his long and firm strides building friction.

He pushed up on his hands, piercing me with an intense look that thickened the air between us. My hands scraped over the hard planes of his chest and stomach, and he closed his eyes and groaned, his head falling forward. An arm sliding under my waist, he lifted my hips and drove into me harder, his hips churning as curls of smoke and silk and ribbon gathered us into a tangle. He thrust once more, and I cried out as I fractured again. He followed soon after with a ragged moan that thrashed through the air.

Mouths meeting in a wash of elusive breath, we descended back to earth in a frisson of panting, sweat, and immutable satisfaction. Propped on his elbows, he collapsed on top of me, trailing kisses along my neck before he pressed his lips firmly to mine.

Not sure I could form words, I stared at him, tracing his lips, cheekbones, and jaw with trembling fingers.

He offered me a crooked smile. "Are you okay, Thorne?"

With my head tipped back, I blew out an extravagant breath. "My gods, yes."

His answering smile was lit by the stars and, right then, the only thing I wanted was to make him smile like that every day for the rest of his life.

Arms wrapped around me, Ronan lay down and pulled me in close, twining his legs with mine.

Outside, the snow whipped across our view, reflecting in slivers of moonlight like glitter tossed in handfuls up to the sky. As we snuggled into each other, the room flickered under a curtain of shadowed light. Embers glowed in the fireplace, casting a rosy glow that matched the flush of my skin and the color of my restored heart.

For tonight, I let myself be pulled from the brink of loneliness. Tonight, the darkness would remain outside and, here, I would only think of the good.

CHAPTER TWENTY-SIX

5 DAYS LEFT

S LEEP WAS IN SHORT supply for the rest of the night as we reveled in the touch and taste and feel of each other through the hours. By the time we awoke, sunlight streamed in through the curtainless windows, warming bare skin and mussed cotton sheets. The storm had broken, leaving everything covered in a fresh layer of snow.

Ronan was already awake, looking down at me as my eyes fluttered open.

"Are you watching me sleep?"

"Yes," he said with a grin. "Is that a problem?"

"It's a little weird," I said, and he yanked me into him as I giggled. *Giggled*. Who had I become?

Already kissing him frantically, I pushed him on his back and climbed on top, straddling his body. I clasped his already hardening cock in my hand, and he moaned as I slid him into me. Guiding my hips, he rocked me back and forth, my hands pressed against the planes of the chest I had spent hours touching, licking, and biting. We came together in a heaving burst of sweat and light that left me dizzy with wanting.

When we both stopped panting, the sweat on our skin cooling, I asked, "Gideon didn't send breakfast, did he?"

Ronan smirked. "Of course—he'd never let you go hungry."

He got out of bed, and I admired the view of his round, muscled ass and powerful thighs as he retrieved a basket.

"He assured me it's all your favorites." He unpacked cheese, crackers, salami, and fresh bread.

"This was great and all," I said through a mouthful, "but I'm running away with Gideon."

Ronan laughed. "You're getting crumbs in the bed."

"No longer fastidious, remember?"

"I remember." He kissed me, licking away a crumb at the corner of my mouth, and I sighed and shivered all at once.

After we'd eaten, we laid on the bed facing one another, Ronan's hand running along the curve of my back and my hip in a hypnotic motion.

"I want to stay like this forever," I said. "I feel so many things when I'm with you, Ronan."

He lifted a dark eyebrow. "Good things, I hope."

"The best things," I said, fusing the words with as much conviction and earnest truth as I could.

"We can come back soon. Whenever you want." He tucked a strand of hair behind my ear, but his words sank into me like drops of rain soaked up by a dying field of wheat.

There were five days left until Mare returned, and I needed to get him out of here.

"What's wrong?" he asked, noting the shift in my mood.

"Nothing. I wanted to say thank you for being here. You've all been so helpful. The castle has felt so safe."

"Well, I had ulterior motives," he said with a wink as his hand found the flesh of my ass and gave it a healthy squeeze.

I snorted at his joke, but I knew he would have helped me, anyway. He would have helped anyone in my situation.

"But why does it feel like you're trying to tell me something I don't want to hear?"

This was my opening. I willed myself to say it. Willed myself to ask him to leave, for his sake. But after last night, I worried he'd feel rejected. Like I'd regretted this when that was the very last thing I felt.

I shook my head and pressed my mouth to his. "No, not at all. I just wanted you to know how much I appreciate you."

"You're sure? No second thoughts about what happened here?"

"No, gods no. Of course not. I'd do it again a million times."

A wolfish grin stretched over his face. "With pleasure, Princess." And then we were kissing again, and I vowed I'd tell him later.

Cowardice. Selfishness.

After another hour in bed, we dressed and rode back to the castle.

"I'm going to take him to the stables," Ronan said, wrapping his arms around me. "Thank you for everything. That was—"

"Magic," I finished for him, and he nodded, giving me such a long look that it felt like he was trying to capture a glimpse of my soul.

"Yes, exactly. Better than magic. I—" He shook his head and then kissed me on the nose. "I'll see you inside."

As I watched him walk away, he cast a glance over his shoulder, the smile on his face like sunshine reflecting off a crystal-clear pond.

When he disappeared around the corner, I rubbed my face. I had to tell him it was time to leave. When he came back from the stables, I would. No more excuses.

Inside, I found Kianna waiting in my room.

"Hi there." She was bouncing up and down in anticipation.

"What?" I asked, pulling off my coat.

"How was your night?" She clasped her hands in front of her, and I gave her a quizzical look.

"It was wonderful. Thank you for helping him."

"I'm happy for you, Your Highness." There was something so raw in her voice that I frowned.

"Is everything okay?"

"It's so wonderful you and the commander have found each other against all the odds. That he came here, and now you can break the cu—" Fear sparked in her expression before she looked at the ground, not meeting my eyes.

"What did you say?"

Hands clenched in the green folds of her dress, she didn't raise her head, wings twitching in obvious agitation.

"Kianna." My voice sharpened to a dangerous edge. "What...did you say?"

Finally, she looked up at me, indecision wobbling in her eyes. "Nothing?"

I marched closer. "What aren't you telling me?"

She hedged again, looking around the room as if someone would help her.

My hands balled into fists. "Kianna, what were you going to say? Tell. Me."

Now her hands flew up, clasping under her chin. "The curse," she whispered, eyes wide as sunflowers.

"What about it?"

"I've known all along how to break it." She winced, her shoulders drawing up to her ears.

My entire body went numb. My neck grew hot and my fingers tingled, blood stilling in my veins. I said nothing. I couldn't speak as I waited for her to continue with whatever valid reason she had for keeping this from me. But she was frozen, and the yawning silence stripped away the little patience I had. "How?!"

Kianna's bottom lip quivered, and a strangled breath wheezed out of her throat. "True love's kiss. You can break it with true love's kiss."

A fist punched me in the chest as every molecule of air was sucked from the room. I couldn't breathe.

True love's kiss.

It was so simple. The ending to every fairy tale I'd ever been told.

"You've been lying to me all this time?" My words weren't an accusation. They were the pained whisper of utter betrayal. She'd been deceiving me. Letting me run around like a fucking idiot, picking herbs and making potions, when she'd known this all along.

She nodded, eyes filling with tears. "I'm so sorry."

"How could you do this to me? Why? Why didn't you tell me?!"

Voice pleading, she dropped her hands to her sides. "Because what difference would it have made? There was no one else here, and I thought if you knew, it wouldn't help. You wouldn't have been able to do anything about it, and that would have driven you mad.

"But then, by some twist of fate, the commander showed up, and I saw the way you looked at each other. I thought a miracle had been sent."

"But you still didn't tell me?"

"Would you have fallen in love if you *had* to? That would have been too much pressure. It might have ruined everything. Love doesn't work that way."

I glared at her, but what she was saying made sense.

"That's why you never seemed interested in breaking it." She nodded. "And why you kept finding reasons for them to stay. And got Gideon's help." I remembered the two of them conspiring more than once.

She nodded again. "He said he's never seen the commander this happy, and if we could save you both, he wanted to do everything he could to help."

"Why a kiss? Why would that break the curse?"

Kianna shrugged. "I was working quickly when I cast it. There wasn't time for creativity, so I relied on an old standby."

I pressed my hand to my throat and sank down on the edge of the bed, emotions swelling in my chest.

"Do you love him, Your Highness?" Her question was strung in the air between us like a tentative garland.

"I...don't know." I saw the apology and the regret in her eyes. She thought she had been doing the right thing. "I think I could. I think I very much could." She allowed herself a hopeful smile. "But I've been lying to him, Kianna."

"Your Highness, he will understand about the curse and why you couldn't tell him everything."

I shook my head. Kianna may have lied, but I was no better. I'd told so many lies they threatened to bury me. "No, it's not that."

"Then what?" She sat down next to me, and I stared at my hands clenched in my lap.

"The man I killed. That day we woke up." Kianna took my hand. "That man was the King of Estria. Ronan's father."

Kianna gasped, fingers pressing to her mouth. "What? That can't be."

"It is. That's why Ronan and the others were in Tenby in the first place. They were searching for him in secret. They're afraid of what will happen if anyone discovers he's missing."

Standing up, I paced the floor, touching my lip as I remembered the feel of Ronan's kisses. He'd made me feel something profound. Something I never thought I'd have. And I'd betrayed his trust.

I had done a terrible thing. Not in killing the king, but in keeping it from Ronan all this time. Why had I let this go on for so long?

"I have to tell him. I think I could love him, and I think he could love me, too." Hands pressed to my middle, I tried to calm the nest of wasps buzzing in my stomach. "But we can't be anything if I don't tell him the truth. I just hope I haven't ruined everything."

Kianna nodded, lines creasing her forehead.

Grabbing my coat, I yanked it on and ran outside to the stables, but they were empty. Circling around the side, I searched for him, but he was nowhere to be seen. Then I saw his footprints in the snow. A set of hoofprints ran alongside them, both prints leading into the forest toward my graveyard.

Dread morphed into a coiled serpent, sharp teeth and venomous fangs scratching under my skin. Following the footprints, I picked up my pace until I was sprinting through the trees. The horse came into view first. That fucking horse I should have dealt with when I still had the chance. I cut through the trees into the clearing.

Eleven neat squares burst with colorful flowers, but the twelfth was the only one I had eyes for. A light dusting of snow covered the clearing, the dense canopy of royal birch shielding the ground. I knew the hole hadn't been deep enough. Ronan crouched next to the king's grave. His head was bowed, and a scrap of rotted red material hung from his hand where the Estrian sigil stood out clearly on the cloth.

At my approach, he stood slowly.

My steps were tentative, like I was walking a tightrope, and one wrong move would send me plummeting off. The mask on his face was pieced from sorrow and pain and confusion.

I wanted to throw up. I wanted to die for making him feel this way. Last night, I'd made him smile like the sun lived inside him, and now, it was like I'd stolen every happy thought he'd ever had.

"Tell me this isn't what it looks like, Thorne. What is my father's horse doing here? What is this?" He held up the cloth, like blood dripping through his fingers. His eyes were wide and rolling as he lost control. "Tell me this isn't what this looks like!" My strong, self-assured warrior was descending into panic, and it was all my fault.

I walked closer. "I can explain."

"Try," he said, and I swallowed the flicker of fury in his eyes.

I'd been a fool. I'd irrevocably destroyed something between us. "He woke me up."

His brows knitted. "I don't understand."

With tattered breaths, I told him the story of waking up to the king leaning over me. About what he'd done to Kianna and every one of her sisters. About how he had chased me through the castle and my only choices had been to kill him or be killed myself.

As the words spilled around our feet, they thickened, rooting us in the quicksand of my lies as something in his expression shifted from anger to horror. When I was done speaking, I shook, tears tracing lines down my face.

"That can't be—he wouldn't. He *couldn't*."

"But he did. Why would I make that up?" I asked as I built my defenses. "Why would I have killed him? I didn't know who he was. I know you don't want to believe your father could do this, but you told me yourself what kind of man he was."

An unsettling light burned in his evergreen eyes as if he were really seeing me for the very first time. Something fractured, his expression draining out, leaving only an empty burned plain of nothing.

With measured steps, I walked closer. "I'm not sorry I did it—he deserved it and much worse, but I'm sorry I lied. I should have told you. But I thought you'd arrest me or worse, and I had to stay here. I had to break the curse. I knew nothing would go in my favor if anyone found out. No matter what he had done, I killed a king. Then I got to know you, and the guilt ate away at me because I could see you aren't like him at all. You are nothing like him, and I—" My voice cracked. A shuddering breath warped in my chest, and my eyes wouldn't focus. I couldn't look at Ronan. It hurt too much to witness his fury. "I couldn't break your heart like that. It was selfish, and I was a coward, but I didn't want this to end. Whatever this was. I didn't want it to be over. I didn't want *us* to be over. I'm so sorry. I shouldn't have lied to you."

My soul laid bare, I dragged my gaze to meet his. When I saw only shadows and violence, the pieces of my heart severed and fell away.

I'd lost him. This betrayal had been too much.

"I trusted you," he said with barely controlled rage. "I was falling for you. Last night—that meant more to me than anything ever has. I've never felt this way about anyone."

"I'm sorry," I whispered. "I'm so sorry. I will do anything to make this up to you, Ronan. It meant everything to me, too. Tell me what I can do. Anything. I'm falling too." I reached for his hand, but he pulled away and I sensed him go somewhere deep inside himself, lost to me forever.

"No. I can't do this. I need to get out of here."

My answering nod was heavy and bruised. Before brushing past me, he gave me a prolonged look that crushed whatever dim light still dwelled inside me into cold, lifeless embers.

After he'd gone, I dropped to my knees and then to my hands, lying down in the snow, the bite of frost seeping into my clothing. My soul shattered, the shards scraped beneath my skin, scarring me forever.

I wondered if I would ever see him again, and then I sobbed and sobbed and sobbed until I couldn't feel anything at all.

A gentle hand brushed the hair from my forehead, and I opened my eyes. Kianna leaned over me, concern in the angle of her shoulders.

"Ronan?"

"Gone," she said. "They're all gone."

A dry sob sliced the back of my throat. "It's over, Kianna. I've lost him forever."

"You should come inside, Your Highness. It's going to snow again."

Some irretrievable part of me appreciated she wasn't trying to tell me everything would be okay. She helped me off the ground. My clothing was damp, and my fingers were stiff with cold. Dimly, I registered the king's decaying corpse as nausea swelled in my gut.

We needed to deal with that. But later.

"I'm sorry, Kianna." My voice was a raw whisper, dragged thin from crying. "I've failed you, too. She's coming back in only five days, and I don't know how to stop her."

"We'll figure something out, Your Highness."

"No, we won't."

"No, we won't," she agreed, and a weight fell away.

I couldn't fix this, and I could finally stop trying.

Kianna's lips were set in a stiff line as we made our way back to the castle. Falling on my bed in my dirty wet clothes, I buried my face in the pillow that still smelled like Ronan. Like dense forests and sun-warmed cloves.

A fresh wave of tears engulfed me, pulling me under and drowning me in the turbulence of its undertow.

CHAPTER TWENTY-SEVEN

2 DAYS LEFT

FOR DAYS, I LAY in bed, somewhere between conscious thought and the brittle pieces of my sanity. Kianna brought me food, but everything became ash in my mouth. Snow fell in thick flakes, wind screaming through the halls as if it, too, were mourning the bottomless depths of my loss.

The ticking countdown of Mare's return throbbed through the walls and the floors of the castle. In my ears and in my head, a constant insistent sound pounded against the inside of my skull. But I no longer dreaded the checking of those last boxes on the calendar. Now I counted them down, minute by minute, because when Mare came back, I'd make sure she killed me.

When I finally got up, I was driven only by the need to say one last goodbye to my family. My limbs were hollow, like tarnished flutes that only played off-key. The castle was dark, and I couldn't tell if it was day or night as the snow streaked in horizontal lines across every window.

My body achy and stiff, I grabbed my father's sword sitting propped at the foot of my bed. The cold iron felt solid in my hands. Dragging the tip along the ground like an anchor, I entered the hall, passing Kianna's bedroom. It sat empty as I shuffled past. My stomach growled, and my throat was dry from neglecting food and water.

The halls were so quiet, devoid of Em's jokes and Noah's laughter and Gideon's patient caretaking. And Ronan. His absence felt as if every drop of blood had been sucked from my heart. As if every star had fallen from the sky. As if every ocean had been drained of water.

With slow, measured steps, I stumbled toward the throne room, the scrape of the sword on stone echoing off the walls. Darkness spread beneath my feet like spilled tar. It slid along the stones, sticky and viscous. A tang seeped into the air, tickling a memory I couldn't place. The blackened pool grew under my boots as I ventured closer. Not a pool—a trail, winding its way like a steady mountain stream. Lights flared ahead of me, and I squinted against a sudden brightness that revealed a spooling river of crimson.

Confusion blurred my thoughts, one piling on another in a jumble.

Why was there blood on the floor?

As my vision cleared, a nail hammered into the meaty, pulsing center of my heart.

Everyone was dead.

I stared and stared, unable to process what I was seeing. Slits in their throats. Hearts ripped from their chests. Heads torn off and discarded on the floor like they were nothing but useless trinkets.

Dead. Dead. Dead.

Viciously. Violently dead.

My mother slumped forward, blood coating the front of her pristine white gown. My father's head lay at her feet, eyes still closed in an enchanted sleep from which he would never awaken.

Blood was everywhere.

In the haze of my thoughts, all I could see was a thick red crest, like a tidal wave drowning me. I blinked, willing the image to change. This wasn't real. This was only a nightmare. This was an oil painting hanging in a vengeful god's living room.

This wasn't real. *This couldn't be real.*

In my grief, I was hallucinating.

But Mare stood in the center of the room, a cruel twist on her lips. Kianna lay at her feet, crumpled and still.

"No, no, no," I said, surprised I was capable of sound. "No, no, no." I was shaking. "No, what did you do?"

No. No. No. No. No.

Mare placed a hand on a jutted hip. "You didn't break the curse. We had a deal, Princess."

"I still had two more days," I whispered, my heart pounding against the iron bars in my chest. "I still had two more days."

"Oh please. You weren't going to break it, and we both know it. Your darling prince is gone."

She knew, too. Knew how to break it and let me dangle on a fraying string. I didn't even get to say goodbye. I knew I'd lost and Mare would come, but I didn't get to say goodbye. At the very least, I deserved that much. After everything, she owed me that.

"I had two more days," I whispered. The words felt heavy in my mouth. Like something I could dig up from the earth and salvage in my grasp. "I had two more days," I said again, my voice gathering volume. "I had two more days!" I screamed it so loud, the flames in the sconces seemed to shudder with the force of my rage. "I had two. More. Fucking. Days!"

Engulfed in a torrent of grief so deep it would take an army to cross, I flew at Mare, not caring what happened to me. I had lost everything. Every single person I'd ever loved was gone. My death was the only way to escape this twisted nightmare.

I knocked Mare off her feet and landed on top of her. To block her from using her magic, I grabbed her wrists and ground them into the floor, remembering when Ronan had done the same. Mare was smaller than me, all spidery limbs, and I was strong from my hours of training. She hissed and spat, bucking her hips, trying to dislodge me.

My sword lay by my knee, but I couldn't let go of her hands to reach for it. I had only one heartbeat of time. Instead, I let go of one wrist and punched Mare in the face with a satisfying crack of retribution. She shrieked and speared a blast of power at me, sending me flying. I landed on the blood-soaked floor, my back tearing open on the rough stone. This time, she leaped on me as she snarled with the unrestrained fury of a roaring tiger.

But it was then I stopped struggling. This was what I wanted.

I wanted her to kill me. There was nothing left for me here.

She raised a thick, dark eyebrow. "Giving up, Princess?"

"End it, Mare. You win." There was no mistaking the complete and utter defeat in my voice.

Her eyes flashed. "I don't think so," she hissed, digging her hand into my hair and yanking up on it. "You aren't getting away from me. You haven't suffered enough. I promised to make your heart bleed. This isn't over yet." She flicked her wrist, but still, nothing happened. She did it again, and a hope I had no claim to flared in my chest. She still couldn't take me. Maybe Kianna was still alive.

Mare must have realized it too, because she made a sound of frustration and got off me. A metal claw fisted in my hair, she dragged me to where Kianna lay in a pool of blood, her wings limp and dull.

My eyes watered as I saw her chest rise and fall, and I offered a silent thank-you for Kianna and her nine lives. Preparing to bring down her wrath on Kianna, Mare raised a hand when, suddenly, she went flying.

Astonished, I watched as she screeched and hurtled through the air, slamming into the wall. A sickening crack vibrated off the stones as her head snapped against the surface. Knocked out, she slumped to the floor.

"Thorne?" said a deep voice I knew. A voice I'd turned over and over in my head, savoring its cadence and notes since he'd left. I was splitting apart, my body a collection of skin cells and tears, barely held together.

I was hallucinating again. This wasn't real either.

But there he was, kneeling before me, hands smoothing over my limbs and my hair. "Did she hurt you?"

"Ronan." His name came out like a prayer I'd just learned and wanted to remember. I blinked over and over, waiting for this image to change too.

I was dreaming. My mind had finally broken.

My face cradled in his hands, he looked at me like he would slay every monster in the universe and serve them to me on a silver platter.

"Are you real?" I asked, touching his brow.

"Thorne, I'm so sorry. I should never have left you. It was all too much at that moment. I understand why you did what you did. I'm sorry I left. I'm sorry I left you here with her. Please forgive me."

"Really? Are you really here?" I touched his ear, marveling at its simple perfection. How could an ear be so beautiful?

He grabbed my hand, pressing it to his face. The stubble on his cheek scraped my palm, and I closed my eyes as the sensation traveled the length of my body.

"Really. And I'm never going anywhere, ever again." His gaze flicked to where Mare lay against the wall. "But we should probably deal with this."

He pressed a long, deep kiss to my palm, then stood and walked over to where Mare stirred. He raised his sword but didn't get the chance to attack as she sent him flying halfway across the room. Like a four-legged demon, she leaped, landing on him and knocking him to the floor.

"Oh, isn't this delightful?" she crooned. "He came back for you. How utterly noble and how utterly stupid."

Busy tormenting Ronan, she didn't notice me stand. Watching her threaten him awakened the devil that had found a home in the darkest halls of my spirit. I would not lose him again. With a roar, I ran toward her with my father's sword and stabbed her through the back, sliding the blade into the chambers of her shriveled black heart. Body arching, she screamed and writhed. Ronan slammed a boot into her stomach, and she flew back. As she crashed to the floor in a snarling twisted heap, there was a flash, and she disappeared in a hazy black cloud of magic.

For a few silent moments, we stared at the empty spot where Mare had landed. She'd escaped us again, but this was only a temporary reprieve.

Then I looked over at Ronan, still unable to believe he was here. I had been so sure I'd never see him again. But he was up and striding over, the weight of a million moments yet to be lived in his eyes.

He swept me into his arms and kissed me with the light of a thousand fires burning across a dry desert plain. "Can you forgive me?" His hands cupped my face. "I shouldn't have reacted that way. I'm so sorry I left. I should have been here to protect you."

"I shouldn't have lied to you."

"No, of course—it was too hard to tell me. He deserved it. I've always known what kind of man my father was, but some boyish hope always clung to the idea that maybe I'd misunderstood him. But hearing what he did to you and to Kianna's sisters was the confirmation I needed to understand it had always been a foolish wish. And I didn't handle that well."

Our foreheads pressing together, I inhaled his warmth and his scent. "There's nothing wrong with wishing your parents were better than they are. And of course, I forgive you, Ronan. You're the brightest spot in my life. I can't believe you're really here."

Eyes searching, the force of his gaze chained me to the earth.

"I love you, Thorne." He whispered it, but its strength and truth resonated as clear and solid as the ringing of crystal chimes. "I love your fire and your heart. I love your courage and every inch of your invincible spirit, my ferocious Little Lion. You have made me whole when I feared a piece of me would always be broken."

"I love you too, Ronan. Oh, gods, I love you too."

Of this, I was sure. I had never been so sure of anything in my life. His lips found mine in a kiss that folded, stretched, and filled every splintered crack and gaping crevice of my heart.

A moment later, that tingle of magic I'd come to recognize zipped through my body. It swept from the top of my head, down to my toes, shivers scattering down my back.

"The curse. We broke it." My eyes floated shut. "But too late. I was too late."

His arms wrapped around me, and I pressed my face against his chest as tears fell again.

Kianna moaned from her spot on the floor, and I ran to her. My arms wrapped around her, and she hugged me back, both of us sobbing. I didn't want to think about how close I had come to losing her, too.

She surveyed the room, and I watched as the horror of it reflected in her posture, a hand coming to her mouth.

Suddenly, I couldn't breathe. They were all dead. I'd lost them all. I'd failed everyone.

Air. I needed air.

I turned and ran for the front door, bursting into the cold. My legs pounded the snow-packed ground as I slipped on the ice, catching myself before I continued running. Snow and wind lashed against me as I sprinted, holding my breath as my lungs burned.

Sliding to a stop, I stretched out my arms and hurled myself into the void as I screamed and screamed, needles carving against the back of my throat. The wind whipped my hair and my clothes, but I kept screaming, railing against fate and the world and every moment I'd been made to suffer through this cursed existence. My heart pounded as my soul came unmoored from itself, tumbling and turning, to be lost forever.

Everything spun. Around and around, the world spun. I waited for none of this to be real. To finally wake up from this nightmare.

But it was real. It hurt too much for it to be anything else.

Ronan turned me from behind, hands on my shoulders, and pulled me in.

"None of it mattered," I said as I crumbled. "They were never going to survive. I failed them all."

"You failed no one, Thorne. This isn't your fault."

My legs gave out, my knees striking the ground. Ronan came with me, his arms never leaving. I was sobbing so hard there was no sound, just the choked breath in my mouth. The weight of a kingdom gone forever crushed my chest, wrenching out every last drop of feeling.

"They're all gone. I've lost them all." The words tumbled to the ice, freezing there for eternity.

Ronan pulled me on his lap, where my head rested on his shoulder, snow gathering on us. "You have me. You haven't lost everything. You will always have me. Forever. I am never leaving you again." He smoothed the hair on my head, lips pressed to my temple as the snowfall twirled.

Eventually, Ronan scooped me into his arms. Our clothing was icy and wet, and I was shaking so hard my teeth felt like they'd crack.

He carried me back to the castle and lay me on my bed. "We need to get out of here," I heard him say. "I don't know if that sword killed Mare. If not, she's going to come back. We need to run. Get Thorne away from here."

"I'll pack a bag. We need to change her into something dry." Kianna tugged off my waterlogged boots. "Where will we go, my lord?"

"Estria. It's where I can protect her best." He paused. "I'm going to deal with my father's body. It can't stay there like that. Someone is going to find it."

"What are you going to do?" Kianna asked.

"I'll burn it. I'll say I came across it in the woods and animals had mauled it. We'll say he was knocked off his horse. No one else knows but the three of us?" A moment of silence. "Then this secret dies with us. No one can ever know what happened, for Thorne's sake. Regardless of her valid reasons."

"Yes, my lord," Kianna replied.

Ronan pressed his lips to my forehead. "If you hadn't, I would have killed him myself for what he did." He said it softly, but his tone was savage, like he'd rip apart the world, piece by piece, with nothing but his bare hands.

Then I heard his footsteps walk out of the room.

CHAPTER TWENTY-EIGHT

G ENTLE HANDS GUIDED ME to the bathroom, where a hot bath awaited. My teeth chattered violently, my skin a mottled blue. Cold had seeped into every crevice. Kianna helped me from my clothes and into the bath. My fingers and toes were so numb, the water scalded them like I'd been dropped into liquid fire. The pain helped my mind focus while my surroundings continued to tilt and spin. After the burn subsided, I lay back, closing my eyes.

Over and over, I saw my mother's curls soaked in her blood. My father's severed head lying at her feet. The hole in Adrian's chest. The slice across Isabelle's throat. Images branded into my mind forever, playing on a loop until the world turned to nothing but cinders and dust. A constant reminder of how I couldn't save any of them.

Footsteps clicked on the tiles, and someone crouched next to the tub. Ronan said my name quietly. My heart seized at the concern on his face when I opened my eyes.

He had come back. He loved me, and he was right—I hadn't lost everything. Not completely.

Arms braced on the edge, he leaned against the tub. I wanted to tell him so many things, but the words stuck, trapped in an opaque orb of grief.

Ronan reached for a towel. "The water is getting cold. We need to get moving. You aren't safe here."

I felt nothing as he helped me dress. He, too, had changed into dry clothing. Kianna brushed and braided my hair. They both moved softly around me as if I were made of porcelain. But they needn't have bothered. I had already shattered into a thousand dry, dusty pieces. No sudden movements would make any difference. Ronan helped me into my coat, pushing gloves onto my hands. The horses waited in the high castle entrance, but the snow was still falling. We wouldn't stay warm or dry for long.

"I need to do something first," I said, dropping Ronan's hand and walking to the throne room. Blood coated the floor, and I stopped at the threshold. Though I didn't want to go in, I needed to see them one last time.

As I looked across the space, I finally understood my parents had never truly been mine. That we had never been given the chance to belong to one another. Mare had poisoned our relationship, ensuring every day had been imperfect and complicated. Right then, any blame I still harbored for how they had treated me deflated and floated away. We had been set up to disappoint each other from the very beginning. I couldn't hold on to it anymore.

They had been given a child and then, almost immediately, had it taken away. It would have been better if I'd died then, rather than haunting their lives for twenty-one more years. That couldn't have been easy, either. None of this had been their fault any more than it had been mine.

"Goodbye," I said to the dim room. "I forgive you, and I love you." I didn't know when I'd be back here. It felt wrong to leave them like this, but Mare would return soon. And they didn't need my protection anymore. One day, I'd come back to give them the end they deserved. I hoped.

I joined Ronan and Kianna, and we stepped outside into the snow. He shut the door behind us, as if that would keep anyone out. It certainly hadn't so far. But why would anyone ever want to go in? I'd spent my life haunting the halls and, now, they were filled with more ghosts than any one castle could possibly handle.

We mounted our horses and rode into the night. Before we ducked into the trees, I looked back. My castle sat forlorn and tired, a gray stain blotting the horizon. A monument to blood and death and tragedy.

"Let's go," I said, turning forward to yet another uncertain future.

Ronan claimed it was a two-week ride to Estria, traveling on the open road. We would risk it, hoping Mare hadn't recovered yet. It would give us time to regroup. The only thing we could hope for now was the safety of Estria's army and its walls.

CHAPTER TWENTY-NINE

A FTER A WEEK OF traveling in a haze, we stopped for the night in a small city. It had been snowing off and on the entire time, and sleeping on the cold, hard ground had worn us all down. We needed a warm bed for a night.

Seated in the inn's common room, Ronan placed a hearty stew of venison in front of me. I had hardly eaten for the last week and noticed the worried glances Kianna and Ronan shared. For no other reason than to ease their minds, I forced myself to swallow a few bites.

I was fine. I would be fine. Somehow.

"What are the chances she's still alive?" Ronan asked Kianna.

Kianna sighed, though it wasn't in irritation. He'd asked this many times already, but I understood why he had to keep questioning.

"I don't know. I'm sorry Commander."

"You have no idea?" he pressed.

"A sword to the heart would kill me, but Mare has always been special. Capable of more than the rest of us were."

"Why?"

She shrugged. "We have many fathers. Fae are a fickle bunch until we find our mates. We take many lovers through our lifetimes. Our pedigree determines what powers we possess and how strong they are. Only our mother was the same. I'm still surprised my spell held out against Mare all these years, to be honest."

"She's not dead," I said, and they both turned to me with surprise. As silent as a specter, I had said little this past week. Even I was surprised to hear the sound of my voice. "It can't have been that easy. She's not done with me."

Kianna nodded. "I think so too. She's never let go of anything."

"Why is she so fixated on you?" Ronan took my hand between his.

I shook my head. "I wish I knew."

We fell into silence. Another storm had driven everyone indoors, and the room was loud and full of boisterous chatter. It almost felt normal. Like life actually could go on and this state of perpetual emptiness had an ending somewhere.

Something chipped away at the numb shell I was encased in.

"Is it safe in Estria?" The question had been at the back of my mind for days. I was now the queen of a rival kingdom. A small one comprised of no one but me, but it was a kingdom, nonetheless. There were people still loyal to Ravalyn out there.

Ronan shifted, clearly not comfortable with the question. "I don't know where else you'll be safer right now."

I nodded. It wasn't entirely an answer, but it would have to do. "You could be inviting something very dangerous into your home because of me."

He took my hand, pressing it to his heart. "It's yours now too. Everything that is mine is yours. If I have to call on every man who has pledged their life to me and my army to protect you, I will do it."

I didn't want anyone else dying for me, but it was no use arguing with him. For now, Estria made the most sense.

We finished our meal in silence, Ronan never letting go of my hand.

My small room was cozy and dark. Dominated by a large bed pushed up against the far wall, it was covered in a cheerful blue and white quilt, stitched with hundreds of tiny squares. A fire crackled against the opposite wall, chasing away the chilled edges of travel.

I changed into my robe and warmed my hands by the fire.

Someone knocked, and Ronan popped the door open a crack.

"Are you okay? Can I get you anything?" He had taken a separate room. I hadn't asked why, but I assumed it was to give me whatever space I needed.

But looking at him, I didn't want space. Not from him. He loved me and I loved him, and nothing had felt more right or true in my life. I took his hand and pulled him inside the room, shutting the door.

His expression was part sadness, part concern, but all of it was brimming with hope and love.

Arms circling his neck, I rose on tiptoes and kissed him. "Stay with me, Ronan."

"Are you sure?"

"Yes, if you want to."

"I want nothing more. I only want to be with you. Tell me what you need. I'm here for you." His hands circled my waist, and I kissed him again.

My skin let out a sigh as his hands ran down my back. I hadn't lost Ronan.

Our kiss started out tender and sweet, but his hands fisted into the fabric of my robe, and it shifted into ribbons of fire, searing and untamed, whipping around us like a winter squall. I pushed him against the wall, devouring his mouth and his throat and the smooth golden skin bared by the open collar of his shirt.

As I reached for the laces of his pants, he grabbed my hands. "Thorne."

"I need you," I breathed. He held onto my wrists, desire and longing sparking in his eyes. He was practically vibrating, but he was being so careful. It only made me want him more, and I didn't want him to be careful. "Make me feel something other than this endless despair, Ronan. Please."

Slowly, I untied my robe and slipped it off my shoulders, letting it pool on the floor. The heat of his gaze traced every one of my movements, a hand absently rubbing his chin as though he was imagining every thing he planned to do to me. He was pure hunger and raw energy, and I knew then I'd never tire of him looking at me that way.

"You make me insane," he said so low that it was nearly a growl.

He closed the space between us, his lips crashing into mine, his tongue entering my mouth like a man desperate for his last sips of water. I returned his kiss, but it wasn't just a kiss—it was a promise and a wish and the sum total of my love for him.

I slid my hands under his shirt, moaning at the feel of his fevered, muscled skin. After pulling it over his head, my mouth pressed to the center of his chest and I dragged my tongue down, tracing the carved lines of his stomach. My nails scratched the cut of the angled muscle that dipped under his waistband as I fell to my knees. His head tipped against the wall while I unlaced his pants and pulled out his erect cock.

As I stroked him with my hand, he moaned. "Fuck. That feels amazing." When I placed the tip of him into my mouth and sucked, I felt the exhale of his entire body shuddering in response. Slowly, I dragged my tongue up the back and then drew as much of him into my mouth as I could, his hips thrusting and his cock hitting the back of my throat.

He moaned as he drew out and slid back in, one hand gathering my hair at the back of my head. He gripped it tight, his dark eyes burning and his hips pumping.

"That's it. Take it all like a good girl."

He thrust again, letting out a rumble that shot straight to the dampness gathering between my thighs. As he used my mouth, I slid my hand between them, touching myself as the ache in my core grew bone-deep.

A moment later, Ronan pulled out of my mouth and drew me up. He flipped me around, my back against the wall as he pressed himself against me. "I'm going to fuck you against this wall," he said, the rumbling growl of his voice making my thighs clench. "I'm going to make you come so hard you can't breathe."

My back arched as I whimpered out an unreserved agreement, his blazing kisses branding my throat and the tops of my breasts. A moment later, he discarded the rest of his clothing and crushed me against the wall with his lean, hard body.

Ripples of heat ignited, sparking in the air that surrounded us. I ached to feel him inside me. Grabbing the back of my thighs, he lifted me up, and I wrapped my legs around his waist. Being the opposite of careful, he thrust inside me, and I cried out. One hand wrapped around the back of my neck and his face buried in my hair, he said my name again and again as he drove his hips into me. I shivered as pulses raced over my skin and he filled the hollow chambers of my heart.

I hadn't lost everything. I hadn't lost this.

My body pressed between his solid chest and the unforgiving wall, he thrust harder. Both of us clung to the knowledge we'd almost lost one another, and the heat was raw and edged in tendrils of smoldering flame.

"Harder," I gasped, wanting to feel only him mining into the deepest reaches of my body. Behind me, the wall shuddered as I clutched at his shoulders, fingers digging into chiseled muscle. The entire inn could probably hear us, but I was too consumed to care. Moans escaped me as he planted searing, desperate kisses over every inch of my skin.

"You make me feel whole," he said between ragged gasps. "Like anything is possible." His drives grew faster and more insistent, slamming into me with a ferocity that sliced and peeled away what had died inside of me.

A jumble of limbs and tongues, his hands gripped my thighs as I came in a glowing blaze of starlight, and he rocked into me again and again until he also tumbled into his release. A growl burst from his throat, the sound spearing me with lightning.

We stayed that way for a few minutes after, clinging to one another. Our breaths were short and fevered, our eyes locked and foreheads pressed together. Pulling away from the wall, he dropped me on the bed and slid in next to me, cradling me against him.

"I love you," he murmured, lips against the curve of my throat. "You have no idea how much."

I traced the lines of his beautiful face and offered him a tentative smile. Grief still weighed in my chest, but he had tamped down the roughest edges.

Green eyes bright, relief was visible all over his face. "It's good to see you smile. Even if it's a hesitant one," he said. "I missed that. And your light. I see your light."

"You are my light, Ronan." And there it was. That smile borne of sunshine I had vowed I'd make him feel every day.

My love burned with brilliance as it settled into my heart.

"What happened after you left that day?" I asked, feeling like I finally had the strength to do so. My fingers trailed along the faded scars that marked his arms and chest. I touched the one that crossed his right eyebrow, tracing the arc of his bone. It was my favorite.

"We rode for two days, and I was a complete ass to everyone. I think Noah was ready to stick a knife in me and cheerfully leave me on the side of the road."

Fingers trailed along my back, and I arched at the tingling it sent down my spine.

"Do they know?"

He shook his head. "No, I said we'd gotten into an argument. They were so stunned when I told them we were leaving. I thought Em would die when she said goodbye to Kianna, and Gideon was running around like a madman trying to make sure you had enough to eat. He's grown very fond of you." He stopped, a shadow crossing his face, and I pressed my lips to his. "I'm sorry I overreacted, and I'm sorry I left when I knew Mare was coming. If I'd been there, maybe—"

"Stop feeling guilty. There's nothing you could have done. If you had stayed, she might have killed you too, and that would have broken me for good. Can we accept we both made mistakes? The only person to blame for any of this is Mare. I don't want this lingering between us. I forgive you. I love you."

He gave me a small smile.

"I like that idea." My thumb traced his bottom lip. After barely touching him for the past week, it was now the only thing I wanted to do. "As long as you'll allow yourself the same forgiveness."

"I'll try," I whispered, aware of the burden in my chest.

"After two days of riding, I realized I'd made the biggest mistake of my life, so I turned back," he continued. "I told the rest to travel on to Estria and raced out of there. They didn't like it, but I ordered them to go. I didn't want them to get wind of what happened to my father. They would never tell, but the fewer who know, the better. It would have taken me half the time if that damn snow hadn't slowed me. And then I found you with Mare." His expression darkened.

"Ronan, what are we going to do? If Mare is still alive, this isn't over, and I don't know how many more times I can stick a sword in her and hope she goes away. When she strikes again, it will be with all her might, and she *will* have her reward after so many misses. The curse is broken—there is nothing to stop her anymore."

"I don't know." He rubbed a thumb over my cheek. "But we will stop her. I promised you I would kill anyone who hurts you, and I meant it. We'll find a way. We'll go to the Fae for help if we have to. You are my roaring lion, and no one is taking you away from me. It feels like I've waited so long for you."

Softly, I touched my mouth to his. "I hope it was worth the wait, Commander. I'm not exactly free of drama."

"Nothing has ever been more worth it," he replied before I pushed him back on the bed and asked him to take me away again.

CHAPTER THIRTY

O N THE OUTSKIRTS OF Estria, we stopped for the night. Another week had passed with us peering over our shoulders, but there had still been no sign of Mare. The weather
was warmer here, touched only by the first blushes of winter.
Kianna found us a glen covered in a canopy of golden trees, the
ground softened by fallen leaves.

We sat in front of a crackling fire as the sky grew dark. Kianna
lay in the grass, wrapped in a blanket, staring at the flames
with sleep-heavy eyes. I huddled next to Ronan with his arm
wrapped around my shoulders.

I was nervous about entering the city, and I could sense he felt
the same.

"Thorne," he said eventually, looking at the fire, "do you want
to stake your claim to Ravalyn and the kingdom my father
stole?"

"I don't know. I mean, yes, I want to, but I can't go in there and just ask for it. I understand I'm going to have to fight for it. Against your army."

Mouth in a determined line, he looked at me. "I won't fight against you."

"Will you have a choice? My army consists entirely of me, and maybe Kianna, if I can talk her into it." The Fae had fallen asleep, her diminutive frame curled into a tight ball.

He closed his eyes, clasping my hand. I considered what it would mean to walk away from my claim and accept Estria's rule. It would be so much easier.

I was so tired. So burned out from fighting for every tiny scrap of happiness that never lasted, anyway. Maybe it would be the smart thing to do.

Did I want to start a war? It would be the shortest one in history.

"I need you to be careful. Erick and my father have always been fond of taking the things I love," Ronan said, a bitter grind in his voice. "My father tried to take the loyalty of my soldiers and failed. Erick tried to take Noah once, and he failed at that too."

"What happened?" I asked, my eyes widening.

"My brother has always been jealous of our friendship. What he's never understood is that when you stand on a battlefield covered in another man's blood, it forges an unbreakable bond. Noah and I have had each other's backs since we were old enough to hold a sword. He is my brother in all but blood. And Erick has always hated us both for it. He wouldn't understand loyalty if it slapped him in the face. He saw our friendship as a threat, always convinced I was plotting to kill him and take the crown for myself." He scoffed and shook his head. "He'll never understand there's nothing I want less than to be a king." My head on his shoulder, I burrowed closer into him as he continued.

"We had just turned fourteen when one of the high noble families came to stay with us. They had a daughter around our age. Margaret. Noah fell instantly in love." He laughed softly at the memory. "Of course, my brother saw an opportunity. One afternoon, my father took me and Erick hunting with Margaret's father. There is a small house in the woods we use as a base camp for longer hunting trips, and after a long day outside, we headed there to spend the night. Erick had Margaret smuggled into the house, locking her in a room."

I sat up, making an indignant sound, as Ronan's bright eyes flashed.

"He had one of his guards rough her up and then procured several so-called witnesses. They claimed Noah had dragged her there, thinking the house was empty. Noah was at the castle the whole time, but everyone believed my brother. What was a future king's word against a lowly soldier? I don't know what Erick said to Margaret to convince her to go along with the lie, but when I demanded answers, she refused to speak. I didn't believe it. Margaret's father flew into a rage and demanded Noah's head. My father acquiesced immediately. Margaret's family was powerful, and my father would never let his conscience get in the way of securing an advantageous ally. We went back to the castle, and Noah was dispatched to come speak for himself. He denied it, of course, but was sent to the dungeons, and they slated his execution for the next day."

A hurt that ran deeper than an ocean trench blazed in Ronan's eyes. Maybe I'd stick a knife in Erick too.

"I confronted Erick and told him to tell the truth, but he claimed ignorance. He thought it was all a joke. I was beside myself. Gideon tried to calm me down, but I wasn't having any of it. I was young and furious, and I wanted to destroy everyone and everything. The next morning came, and they dragged Noah into the courtyard. I tried again to make everyone see reason, but it was no use. My father's guards had to hold me back as the executioner walked up to the beheading block. I was crying so hard, and my brother stood there with that smug look on his face. I swore then I'd kill him, and not because I wanted his fucking crown. Then at the last second—" He chuckled at some long-held recollection.

"What?" I asked, shaking his arm, impatient to hear the rest.

"Gideon. I don't know how he did it, but he got the man who actually beat Margaret to confess. There he came, dragging the man by his ear, and made him tell everyone what he had done. The man was actually sobbing. Well, that stayed my father's hand. Erick played it off like he was going to come clean at the last moment all along, and it was only a prank among friends. Nothing happened to him, but any kind of relationship we had broke forever that day."

"I don't understand it," I said, and he raised his brows in question. "How did you grow up with that—with *those* men and you're...you?"

"Maybe I'm good at hiding it," he said with a derisive laugh as he tossed a twig into the fire.

"You're not, are you?" I feigned terror and then laughed when he seemed genuinely worried I'd believed him.

With a roll of his eyes, he wrapped me in his arms and gave me a kiss. "Are you okay?" he asked, pulling away. "I mean, all things considered, of course."

"Not really, but I have no choice but to keep going."

He touched my cheek and then ran his thumb over my bottom lip. "Your strength and resilience are the most incredible things about you. What I love about you most."

A swelling of pride bloomed in my chest at his heartfelt words. "I wish my parents could have met you. They would have loved you."

"I wish I could have met them, too. I would have been able to tell them I was the single luckiest man in the world that you fell in love with this humble soldier."

I rolled my eyes. "Please. There is nothing humble about you." He threw his head back and laughed before I captured his face in my hands. "But that's something I love most about you." I settled against him as he wrapped his arms around me. "Can we stay here forever?" I asked. "I don't need anything but you and this fire and this blanket we're sitting on."

He planted his lips on the top of my head and nuzzled his cheek in my hair. "That sounds like a wonderful dream, Thorne."

As we approached Estria, the road grew clogged, forcing us to slow our progress.

"Is it normally this busy?" I asked as we dodged an oncoming cart traveling at breakneck speed, people scattering out of its path. I turned to watch it barrel away, and Ronan shook his head.

"Not quite this busy."

Ahead, tall buildings made of stone and brick rose beyond the wall. A series of white and gold banners lined the tops, their embroidery sparkling in the sunlight.

Ronan frowned. "The royal wedding."

"What?" I asked.

"I've been gone so long, I forgot it was coming up. My brother is engaged to marry Lady Perrand of Galin. My father has always coveted their gold mines."

"Why do you look upset?"

"I'm not," he said, rubbing a hand down his face. "I just loathe the endless scheming and plotting of my father's court." He reached out a hand across the space between us, and I took it.

Kianna rode in front, smiling at the children, who were whispering behind their hands and pointing at her shimmering wings.

As we entered through the gates, the guards nodded at Ronan. Before my eyes, he transformed into the warrior I remembered from Tenby the first time I'd seen him. Gone was the

softness in his eyes, to be replaced by the hard flint of a bat-
tle-trained warrior returning home. Though I cherished the
tender version of Ronan I'd fallen in love with, there was something thrilling about this one that sent a tendril of heat curling down the back of my neck and spiraling into my stomach.
Hopefully, we could find some time to be alone again soon.

The city was a tempest of activity, markets sprawling in every
direction as hundreds of vendors sold fruit, cloth, weapons,
and every manner of trinket and bauble one could conceive.
Four- and five-story townhomes rose on every side of us, their
neat rectangular windows lined with flowering window boxes
and framed with tidy curtains. Bustling taverns, restaurants,
and patios lined the street, music and chatter spilling from the
windows.

Even the clothing was more regal. Less homespun cotton, and
more silk and leather and brocade, even on the shopkeepers
and servers. The cobbles beneath our horse's hooves gleamed
like they'd been polished on hands and knees by the rays of the
sun.

As we rode down the main road, all eyes were on us, many
people placing fists over their hearts as Ronan passed. They
eyed me with guarded curiosity while they showered Kianna
with wide-eyed gasps and admiring whispers.

"Do they not see many Fae here?" I asked.

"Most Fae stick to their own lands. Magical folk have little use
for humans."

Kianna overheard and grinned at him. "I have plenty of use
for you, Commander."

His expression remained serious, but there was a hint of laughter in his eyes.

As we traveled through town, Estria's castle appeared up ahead, the sight knocking me into a reality I wasn't entirely ready to face. It was at least three times the size of Ravalyn's and constructed from elegant white stone, shaped into slender towers and wide swooping arches. As I took in the wealth and enormity of Estria, I suddenly felt very small and foolish. I could never hope to defeat this kingdom in my wildest dreams. They had money and an army, and a century of practise in the art of warfare.

I was one lone princess with absolutely nothing.

"Are you okay?" Ronan asked, sensing my unease.

A lump forming in my throat like a rotten apple, I shook my head. Perhaps this was a mistake. Perhaps I should have stayed home and been content with the sliver of kingdom I had left. I could rule over my broken tomb of sorrow, shrouded in a cocoon of gray.

We entered the courtyard, the guards silently acknowledging Ronan's presence as we slid down from our horses.

A gray-haired man wearing a guard uniform strode over. "Commander," he said, bending at the waist. "Welcome home. It's good to see you."

"I have news of the king, Averill. Where is Erick?"

"In his council chamber. He wanted to see you the moment you returned. Will your companions be staying in the castle?" He glanced over at me and Kianna, an inscrutable expression on his face.

"Yes, but first, they should accompany me to see Erick."

"Very well, Commander. Follow me."

Ronan clasped the sleeve of my coat and pulled me back. He looked like a man being dragged to his own execution.

"What is it?"

"Stay strong. My brother is unpredictable. Whatever happens, we will find a way out of it. I swear, I will follow you wherever you go."

"Ronan, you're scaring me."

"I don't mean to, but be on your guard."

I nodded, and he let go.

We followed Averill into the warmth of the castle. Moving through a series of corridors, he ushered us into a high chamber with windows that stretched from the floor to the ceiling.

A long wooden table, surrounded by tall chairs, sat in the center of the room while a lit fireplace lined one length of the wall. A man sat at the end of the table, fingers steepled in front of him. He eyed us up and down with all the pleasantness of a cat assessing a mouse for dinner.

Ronan threw me one last grim look and then turned to a pillar of iron as he approached his brother.

As I drew closer, a kick landed in my stomach, and I nearly missed a step. Erick was the mirror image of his father. Where the king's hair was gray, Erick's was dark blonde. He was slimmer, with a smoother face, but there was no doubt whose son this was. That face leered over me in my nightmares, blood spurting from his neck as I twisted my dagger. My nose flared as I sucked in a breath.

Kianna must have realized it too, because she caught my hand and stroked it. In gratitude, I squeezed her fingers.

Forcing myself to stay collected, I met Erick's calculating gaze as it rattled me from the precarious foothold of my composure.

"Ronan, it's nice to finally have you home. Tell me you located our esteemed father?" His voice haughty, the man was one giant sneer.

"I found him," Ronan said, his own voice emotionless.

Surprise flickered in Erick's expression as he studied his brother. "You did?"

"In the forest on the outskirts of Estria. He was lying in the dirt, already dead. Wolves had gotten to him. There was almost nothing left."

"And what did you do with the body?"

"I burned it. He wouldn't have wanted anyone to see him that way." Ronan held a small box he'd taken from his saddlebag when we'd arrived. "We should prepare a memorial immediately." He held out the box to Erick, who curled his lip but didn't reach for it. Instead, Ronan set the box on the table.

"On the outskirts of Estria?" Erick asked, looking at me and Kianna. "And who are you?"

"Allow me to introduce Princess Thorne of Ravalyn and her Faerie companion, Kianna." He gestured to us, tension written in every line of his body. His anxiousness was wearing at my own anemic defenses.

Erick assessed me again, his gaze shifting from curiosity to satisfaction. "So, you *do* exist."

"Excuse me?" I asked.

"My father spoke often to me of the cursed kingdom at the edge of Estria. He believed suppressing the rumors of your existence was imperative to the future health of our lands."

"What are you talking about?" Ronan's voice was hard.

Erick turned to Ronan. "Nothing, Ronan. Only it seems our father's wish went unfulfilled. Come here, Your Highness." He crooked a finger at me. "I want to get a closer look at you."

I narrowed my eyes, but I did as he asked, apprehension twisting hard in my gut.

Erick peered at his brother and then at me, a secretive smile on his thin lips. "Well, aren't you a lovely little thing," he crooned. My skin crawled as if ants had infested my clothing. "What brings you so far from home?"

"I've come to reclaim the lands you stole in my family's absence." The words slipped out on their own, dropping between us like a decaying carcass rotting in the sun. Until now, even I hadn't known what I'd do when faced with Estria's next king.

To cover my surprise, I squared my shoulders, feigning a confidence I didn't feel. I wasn't sure if confronting Erick was really what I wanted, but this was a bell that could no longer be unrung.

Erick laughed, the sound as crisp as the snap of frozen branches. "Yes, your family's *absence*. That is one way of putting it. A curse, was it?"

"It doesn't matter. I am back, and I have come to reclaim what is mine."

"Yours? Are you the Queen of Ravalyn, then? I understood you were a princess."

"My parents have both passed," I said, willing myself not to crumple. "So yes, I am now Ravalyn's queen."

My bluff smelled as rancid as horse shit. I was the queen of nothing.

"Well, that *is* interesting." Erick tapped his chin. "Do you know I am still quelling uprisings in the eastern townships? They are still loyal to Ravalyn, even though you abandoned them." I could see how angry it made him to admit this.

"My family was beloved. We were good to our people."

Erick raised an eyebrow. "So good you disappeared and left them to be conquered by my family. My great grandfather fought for those territories and won. What makes you think you have any right to them?"

"Because they were taken unfairly."

"Well, I suppose *that* is a matter of perspective." Erick stood, pressing his palms to the table. He wore long red robes adorned with scrolling borders of gold. "Very well. I implore you to remain in the castle as a guest of Estria. We are nothing if not civilized, even when faced with our enemies. Especially ones of such might and ferocity."

It was obvious he was mocking me, and I allowed myself the briefest fantasy where I'd cut off his cock and feed it to him. As if hearing my thoughts, he pelted me with a suspicious look that I returned with an acerbic smile.

"Erick, I see wedding preparations are underway," Ronan interjected, changing the subject. "The Lady Perrand will make a beautiful bride, and it will be a fitting opportunity to celebrate your coronation as well."

Erick offered his younger brother a shrewd glance that assessed him from head to toe before returning his gaze to me. "Yes, we will see about that."

CHAPTER THIRTY-ONE

"**Y**OUR HIGHNESS," A STOUT elderly woman said, entering the room with a silver tray suspended between her hands. After the meeting with Erick, Kianna and I had been escorted to guest rooms that did nothing to diminish Estria's obvious advantages over my kingdom.

The bedchamber was enormous, the walls lined with pale blue silk adorned with creamy filigree. Ornate rugs of fine luminous wool covered the blue marble tiles where I stood.

The woman curtsied and placed the tray on the low table in front of a blue velvet sofa that faced a massive four-poster bed also draped in blue silk. Sunlight poured in through tall windows that opened to a long balcony stretching the length of the room and curving in a delicate arch.

The tray bore a pot of tea and a plate topped with cookies, candied fruit, and thick slices of white cheese. My stomach grumbled in acknowledgement.

"You are invited to dine with Prince Erick as his guest this evening. I am to help you get ready."

"And you are?" I reached for a cookie.

Aghast, she snatched one from the platter, depositing it onto a small plate before thrusting it toward me.

"I am Luella," she said with a tip of her head, hands folded in front of her stomach. "Should you require anything, I am at your service."

Parched, I reached for the teapot, and she jumped as though someone had prodded her with an iron hot poker.

"Your Highness," she said in admonishment. "Please, you should allow me to do that."

She gestured for me to sit on the sofa and poured the tea, handing me the cup with a confounded expression.

I'd forgotten how little I was supposed to do for myself, all those weeks alone in the castle. Here, I was a princess again.

With a sharp clap of her hands, three more women entered the room, each holding a stunning dress. Their style was distinct—the cut low, and the silhouette tailored with trim sleek lines. Something about their simple, understated nature appealed to this version of me. Less window-dressing and more to the point. More practical and definitely less innocent.

"Which do you prefer?" Luella eyed me, wringing her hands.

I pointed to a dark green one on the far left. Made of shimmering emerald material shot through with veins of silver, the color reminded me of Ronan's eyes.

"Splendid." Luella clasped her hands under her chin and grinned. "Let's get you out of those traveling clothes."

After a bath, her team of helpers buffed and plucked me, twittering around me like a cheerful flock of hummingbirds.

It felt like a completely different life from the last time I'd undergone such ministrations. I mourned for the girl I'd been, but not because of the pretty hair and fancy dresses. I could feel how much I'd changed in the past month—how much I had grown.

They braided my hair, coiling the plaits and pinning them to the back of my head, mimicking a crown. The effect was impressive, making me look like the queen I hoped to be someday.

The dress was a perfect fit, skimming over my hips and flaring into a wide skirt made of long layers sliced at various angles. A ladder of black lacing cinched my waist and pushed up my breasts to accentuate the low scooping neckline. Form-fitting sleeves stopped above my elbows, and a pair of glittering diamond and emerald earrings dangled so low they nearly brushed the curve of my neck.

Luella beamed as she circled me like I was a prized sculpture in a museum. "Oh, you are beautiful, Your Highness."

After a spin in the mirror, I had to admit it was a vast improvement over the damp and dirty clothing I'd trudged around in for the past two weeks.

A knock rattled the door, and a girl ran over to open it. A breathy squeak pumped from her lungs as she bent into a curtsy so low she nearly toppled over.

Ronan stood at the threshold, so beautiful and flawless I almost joined the poor serving girl swooning on the carpet.

Clad in polished black leather armor adorned with golden trim, it fit him like it had been painted on, highlighting the breadth of his shoulders and the strength in his arms and thighs. Braids neatly redone, the sides of his head and his jaw were both cleanly shaven.

He cleared his throat as he took me in, appreciation stoking in his gaze.

"What do you think?" I twirled my skirt around my legs.

He took a step closer. "I think—" The words chopped at the roots, he glanced at the row of open-mouthed women all staring. Instead, he graced me with a lift of his eyebrow and the tease of a devious smile that suggested the thoughts on his mind were not ones to be uttered in polite company. "I came to escort you to dinner." Transforming into a model of gentlemanly formality, he held out an elbow, which I entwined with mine.

"I missed you today," I said once we'd left my room.

"I'm sorry. Erick had me in meetings all day. I missed you too."

"Is everything okay?" I asked, the unspoken knowledge of the king's demise weighing heavy on my mind.

Ronan's sharp nod assured me I had nothing to fear and that my secret was safe.

"What did you think of our future king?"

I pulled a face. "He looks just like your father. I wasn't prepared for that."

Ronan nodded. "I should have warned you."

"It was just a shock."

"You look stunning," he said, giving me an extensive once-over. "I love seeing you in the style of Estria. It suits you."

"I picked the dress to match your eyes." I dragged a finger down his shoulder. "What were you going to say in the room?"

With a rapacious smile, he stopped and pressed me flat to the wall. Elbows braced on either side of my head, he trailed his lips along my neck and said in a thick voice, "I was going to tell you how delicious you looked. How I want to lick and taste every inch of you and then fuck you until you're screaming my name." He crowded his hips against mine, and I bowed against him like a sail caught in a warm southern breeze.

While he kissed me, voices floated down the corridor and he backed away, his expression telling me we'd be picking this up again as soon as we were alone. We turned a few more corners and approached the dining room, the wide hallway filled with guests arriving for dinner.

The guards nodded at Ronan as we passed through tall doors into the room, already buzzing with activity. Walls covered in pale gold shimmered in the glow of half a dozen large golden chandeliers that ran the length of the room. The long mahogany table was set with gilded plates, cups, and flickering votives.

As the prince's guest, I was seated at the head of the table, next to two large empty chairs I presumed must belong to Erick and his bride. Ronan was seated on my right, and I said a silent thank-you. Perhaps that would make being next to Erick more tolerable. I trusted nothing about the man or his intentions.

Maida and Alban floated through the doorway like the clouds in the sky were their willing servants. Maida's midnight stare found me at the front of the room. My wine glass paused at my lips, and I shot him the coldest glare I could conjure.

I wasn't over the way he'd dismissed me in Tenby, nor the way he'd propositioned me for his own twisted amusement. As if recalling the same memories, he offered me a cunning smile that writhed several inches under my skin.

Hushed whispers accompanied their appearance as they strode through the room like a pair of vipers. A gorgeous, sultry woman clung to Maida's arm while Alban escorted an angelic man and an equally stunning woman, one on each arm. They radiated a dark aura that drew every eye in the room their way.

Kianna also entered, flanked by Noah and Em. She wore a pale green gown, her black hair braided and coiled similarly to mine. After giving me a small wave, she lowered herself into the chair Em pulled out for her. Noah cracked a wide grin as he sat down, and I resisted the urge to run over and hug him. There would be time to catch up later.

I took a sip of my wine, and Ronan sat down, having finished the conversation he'd been drawn into. A moment later, a beautiful woman with dark hair and bright green eyes was escorted over. The guard holding her arm pulled out the chair next to Ronan, and he rose with an enormous smile on his face.

"Mother," he said, embracing her.

"I'd heard you were back. This place is never the same without you here." She beamed up at him, a hand on his cheek. "And you've been on quite an adventure." She lowered her voice. "Is it true about your father?"

It was clear from the devotion on her face she adored her son and that made me love him even more. "I'm sorry, Mother. I would have told you myself, but Erick insisted on monopolizing me all afternoon."

She waved him off. "It doesn't matter. Though we'll need to make an official announcement tonight. The nobles have been getting restless, but we can shut them all up now that Erick is officially eligible to take the crown." Her words were perfunctory and pragmatic, with no remorse at the news of her husband.

I couldn't fault her. As his wife, she was likely more familiar with his cruelty than anyone.

Ronan sat down, an arm sliding across the back of my chair.

"Allow me to introduce you to Princess Thorne of Ravalyn. Thorne, this is my mother, Vivian."

"It's a pleasure to meet you," I said. "Thank you for welcoming me to your home."

Vivian smiled as she sat. "The castle is abuzz with mention of you, Your Highness. Welcome to Estria." Her eyes turned to her son, something knowing in them, before she smiled at me again. "I hope you'll be staying with us for a while."

"Thank you. I hope so too," I replied as all eyes turned to the front of the room where Erick and a woman with icy blonde hair and bright blue eyes, wearing a sparkling gown, entered.

"The Lady Perrand, I presume?" I asked Ronan as they paraded through the crowd.

"The one and only." His hand slid onto my thigh and squeezed it gently.

"That's not very discrete, Commander," I teased.

He leaned in closer, his lips brushing my ear. "If I had my way, we would never have left your room tonight. Forgive me, Princess." My breath hitched as his hand slid higher.

Ronan cleared his throat and pulled his hand back as Erick and Lady Perrand arrived at the end of the table. We stood to welcome them, and they sat down, with Erick taking the seat next to me, his bride on his far side. To her left sat another woman with auburn hair and light brown eyes. She struck me with a hostile glare.

"Who's the redhead, and why is she looking at me like she wants to build a tomb with my bones?"

Ronan glanced over and said quietly, "That is the notorious Lady Elsenmoor. You might remember her from a conversation you eavesdropped on and then entirely misunderstood." He lifted an eyebrow, and I flattened my mouth, giving him my best imitation of disapproval.

Erick stood again, and the room fell silent. "Thank you, everyone, for joining us here this evening. While I know many of you have arrived in Estria for the joyous occasion of the royal wedding, we also mourn the terrible loss of my father. We received confirmation today that he met with his end, traveling the road on the borders of the kingdom."

Erick continued speaking about the king for several minutes as a murmur ran through the crowd, heads bowing and prayers falling from lips. "But now is a time for celebration, and my coronation will take place one week from today—two days before the wedding."

A smattering of applause followed, and Lady Perrand nodded to Erick as he resumed his seat. He gestured for the food to be served, and a din of chatter overtook the room. The mood wasn't especially grave, given they'd just been told of the loss of their king.

"How are you enjoying Estria, Your Highness?" Erick asked me.

"It is impressive. I've never been to such a large and prosperous city." Surely flattery never hurt, and there was no need to outright antagonize him.

He popped a piece of roast chicken in his mouth and chewed thoughtfully. "I should very much like to see our kingdoms working together," he continued. "I do not want my rule tainted by rabble-rousers in the eastern regions."

My voice as cool as the inside of a satin purse, I replied, "I think they are more than rabble-rousers. It seems to me they are quite organized. For your father to send blood Fae to administer gruesome public executions in the center of town, suggests they aren't only a nuisance?"

So much for amiable niceties. Maybe I didn't have the diplomacy to be a queen.

Erick pursed his lips and glanced past me to Ronan, who was deep in conversation with their mother. A pea-green shadow crossed his furtive expression.

"Yes," he said, looking back at me. "But I'm sure we can find a suitable way to ensure everyone gets what they deserve." Erick took a slow sip of his wine, calculation written on his face like a backwards riddle. More transparent than glass, he wasn't even trying to hide he was planning something. I only wished I knew what he was thinking.

Mercifully, I made it through dinner after a round of endless speeches about the king and the future of Estria. When dessert had been devoured and guests started finding their way back to their rooms, I descended the dais and headed for Noah and Em.

Forgoing all appearances of decorum, I hurled myself at Noah as he swung me around. Next, I embraced Em, holding on to her so tightly she grunted.

"We missed you too, Princess," she said, fondness in her voice.

"I'm so sorry, Highness. Ronan told us what happened with your family," Noah said, his face bent close to mine.

"The hag holes didn't work," I whispered.

"Ay. My mum was a wonderful woman. Loving and kind and brilliant, but she was also full of shit."

I snorted and wiped a tear that had escaped down my cheek. "Thanks for trying anyway. Both of you. For all of your help."

"It was my pleasure. I'd have made a thousand more if I thought it would have made any difference."

He wrapped an arm around my shoulders, giving me a one-armed hug as Ronan made his way over.

After we'd all caught up for a few more minutes, Ronan escorted me back to my room.

"So how bad was that?" he asked after we arrived.

"He's plotting something," I replied, biting my bottom lip. "What? Why are you looking at me like that?" Ronan's heavy-lidded gaze set my heart galloping.

"You're beautiful when you do that," he said, brushing my mouth with his thumb. He drew me in, kissing me, and thoughts of Erick washed away like footprints at high tide.

"Come inside. I think you had some very specific plans you told me about," I said with a wink as I dragged Ronan into my room.

After a glance behind him, he turned to me with a wolfish grin, kicking the door closed with his heel. We made quick work of our layers of clothing, not even making it to the bed before we fell to the floor and lost ourselves in each other.

CHAPTER THIRTY-TWO

S UNLIGHT STREAMED INTO THE room as I awoke to Luella and her helpers holding a silver tray bearing a pot of tea and a plate of toast, eggs, and strips of bacon.

"Rise and shine," she trilled, placing the tray on the table and opening the heavy curtains.

Ronan was still asleep, and it was at that moment the women all noticed him. They stopped their chatter instantly, wide-eyed glances shifting between them.

"Luella," I said, willing authority and calm into my voice. This was fine. I was a grown woman. I was allowed a man in my bed. "Could you give me a moment? And perhaps knock next time."

"Yes, of course, Your Highness. I apologize." Eyes on her feet, she dipped into a hasty curtsy. Then she shoved the other three women out the door, their feet tangling beneath them. None of them took their eyes off Ronan, who had woken and was sitting up, the golden expanse of his muscled chest filling the room with masculine energy. The door slammed shut, and I flopped down on the bed.

"Well, that was mortifying." I covered my eyes with my hand, and Ronan leaned down and kissed me. Luella and her flock became a memory as his tongue slipped against mine. Lips trailing down my body, he kissed my stomach and the skin below my navel, spreading my legs and trailing more kisses along the inside of my thigh.

"They're waiting outside," I said, breathless and squirming with need.

"Do you want me to stop?" He asked in a dangerous voice and then did something with his tongue that drove every thought from my head. All I could do was whimper as he chuckled quietly and moaned, "Fuck, you taste like strawberries dipped in chocolate. I want this every day for the rest of my life."

His words were like stars woven from satin, and it took only a few minutes for Ronan to turn me into a panting mess, hands fisted in bedsheets, his name a benediction on my lips. After I'd stopped shuddering, he crushed me in a long kiss and then groaned as he pulled away.

"While I want to spend the entire day here doing this,"—his eyes roved up and down—"I have to go to a council meeting."

As he slid out of bed, I made a sound of disappointment and rolled to my stomach, hands propped under my chin. "Does that mean I owe you another favor?"

"Oh, I definitely think it does."

"I think you gave those young ladies quite the thrill this morning, Commander," I teased, fluttering my eyelashes.

I admired the view of his body as he hunted down his pants and tunic, our clothing scattered all over the room. After putting himself back together, he kissed me, touching his forehead to mine. "I love you, and I'll find you later to continue where we left off," he promised with smoke in his voice.

More than a little drunk on his affection, I gave him a half-grin. Four women toppled into the room as he opened the door. I covered my face as I held in a burst of giggles behind my hands. Luella had turned bright red after being caught in the throes of eavesdropping.

Ronan offered them a quick bow, pretending he hadn't noticed a thing. "Ladies," he said, before turning to me with a wink and making his exit.

One woman watched him leave, her eyes following him out the door.

"Marie!" Luella snapped. "Put your eyes back in your head and come here." The girl jumped, scurrying over with her gaze pasted to the ground. Luella barked orders, and her birds rushed to obey.

"You have been invited to join Lady Perrand for lunch, Your Highness."

A groan sat perched on the roof of my mouth. *Fantastic.*

A short while later, I was dressed in a pale gray gown of a simple but elegant cut, the material thin and airy. My hair hung loose down my back in thick curls—courtesy of Marie.

I followed the guard through the winding halls of the castle to a blooming solarium, where a small wrought-iron table sat surrounded by pots and boxes bursting with flowers. The sky was gray, a dusting of snow falling on the browning grass. Two

women were already seated—Lady Perrand and, to my agonized delight, Lady Elsenmoor. A smile cranked on my face, I
approached and offered a tip of my head.

An attendant pulled out a chair, into which I settled with as
much grace as I could.

"Welcome, Your Highness," Lady Perrand said. "We didn't
have time to speak last night. I am Esme, and this is Angeline."
She gestured to the auburn-haired woman, who raked me with
an imposing glare.

"It's a pleasure. Please, call me Thorne."

"What an unusual name," Angeline said, her voice smooth
and sultry. "Rather prickly, isn't it?"

"I had an unusual upbringing," I replied as a servant filled my
wine glass with sparkling liquid. "More, please," I said when he
stopped only halfway. I had a hunch I would need a full serving.

"Yes, do tell us—a curse? You were really asleep for a hundred
years?"

With a mute nod, I took a sip.

"How did you break it?" Esme asked, her icy blue eyes open
and curious.

Angeline was sizing me up as she waited for me to answer.

"True love's kiss," I said, and Esme went wide-eyed while
Angeline scowled.

"True love?" Angeline said, her lip curling. "And who did you
fall in love with?"

About to reply, I stopped. That wasn't any of her business,
and I assumed my answer wouldn't win me any friends at this
table.

"That isn't important. What matters is that it's broken, and I'm here to claim what was taken from my family."

"I see," she replied, eyeing me with a different kind of interest.

"Erick told me about how you've lost your lands. I hope you can come to a fair and amicable resolution," Esme said, laying a gentle hand over mine. There was only genuine concern in her expression. "Erick was very amenable to working something out with you."

I hid my shock at this news. Though he'd said something to that effect last night, this seemed too easy. He couldn't possibly intend to give my kingdom back. However, I sensed no cunning or guile in Esme—her belief in her fiancé was genuine. Either she was naïve or entirely too willing to see the good in Erick.

"That makes me very happy to hear." I returned her smile, and she beamed.

"So, it was Ronan who found you?" Angeline asked, returning to the subject of her interest. She was looking at me like something she'd scraped off her shoe.

"And Noah and Em and Gideon," I replied, knowing she was panning for information I wouldn't give. "They happened upon my castle in their search for the king's whereabouts."

"And it was there they found him?"

I nodded. "In the forests on the outskirts of Ravalyn. Such a terrible tragedy. Wolves have always been frequent in the area. It's dangerous to travel alone in those woods."

"I wonder what the king was doing out there in the first place?" She was attempting to unravel something, and I kept my hands loose in my lap, trying not to let my nervousness show. There was no reason for anyone to suspect anything. And there was certainly no way to prove it.

"I overheard Erick talking," Esme said, looking around to check if anyone was listening. She leaned in closer. "He thinks the blood Fae offered the king a way inside the castle, and that's what brought him out there."

I shivered, the hairs on my arms standing. The king *had* come looking for me that day. Only he hadn't gotten what he had expected. I was even more glad I'd killed him.

Maida had also lied to my face, but that had hardly surprised me.

Esme was watching me, her expression sympathetic.

"I guess he didn't make it," Angeline said.

"Yes, I suppose not." Keeping my voice even, we exchanged a look.

But it was time to change the subject, so I asked Esme about her wedding plans. Thrilled, she dove into the myriad details of the nuptials and, mercifully, I sat back only half-listening as I tumbled this new information like rocks, polishing them to uncover their truth.

While I listened with one ear to Esme, I formulated a plan. She'd said Erick was open to finding a solution to unite our two kingdoms, and I was determined to do just that.

Protecting my family's legacy was my only goal. I had to save it. For their memory, and for their honor. I'd failed them for the last time.

A pair of guards marched ahead of me as I followed them to Erick's council chamber. I'd asked to speak with him hours ago. Inside, I found Erick seated at the head of the table, along with several other men, taking my measure. Ronan stood near his brother while Esme's hand rested on Erick's shoulder.

Ronan appeared impassive, but I caught a hint of worry as his gaze flicked to me.

"Your Highness," Erick said, pressing his fleshy palms to the table as he stood. "Welcome. Please, come in."

He gestured to the front of the room, and I came to rest a few feet from where Ronan stood with a hand on his sword hilt, giving away nothing.

"I have been considering the matter of your kingdom," Erick said, the word 'kingdom,' drawn out as if it were the punchline to a joke. "The council has been talking in circles all day but has come to no conclusion that satisfies me."

I stepped forward, my courage lodged in my throat. "Your Highness, that's why I requested to see you tonight. I have given it some thought and would like to discuss my plan. I have some ideas on an arrangement that is mutually beneficial."

Erick dropped his glittering eyes on me. "Is that so?"

I nodded, swallowing the sourness of my indecision, suddenly unsure of what I was doing. The room in the air expanded with tension, though I wasn't sure why.

"Yes, I propose—"

Erick cut me off with a slice of his hand. "I'm not interested in your solutions, Princess. I have made up my own mind and invited you all to hear my decision."

Something cold—a clawed hand of doom—raked gouges along my spine. A warning, like a delicate world rendered in crystal about to shatter.

"Given the situation of the former people of Ravalyn and their desire to see the return of the Ravalyn line, it only makes sense for our kingdoms to form an alliance."

An alliance. This sounded promising, but the warning blaring in the back of my head wouldn't settle. Ronan's gaze clashed with mine.

"A marriage," Erick said, offering me a magnanimous smile. I frowned as that delicate city of crystal formed hairline cracks. "Between the new Queen of Ravalyn and the King of Estria, forming an unshakeable bond between our realms."

Silence thundered through the room as everything shattered, releasing an army of misery, leaving nothing but scorched earth in its wake.

Esme gasped, clutching a hand to her stomach, the other flying to her throat as if trying to stop her soul from leaving her body. The council sat open-mouthed like a row of frogs croaking in a pond.

"But, sir, what about the gold mines of Galin?" a councilman asked.

Erick waved a hand. "That was my father's desire. I am far more interested in quelling these uprisings and consolidating what is left of Ravalyn with Estria in a decisive manner. I've had enough of their protests. This should shut them all up, for good."

Ronan's jaw turned hard enough to split mountains. Brother against brother, their eyes met in the raw arena of a lifelong blood feud. Erick was doing this to punish him, confirming all of Ronan's fears.

"Your Highness," I said, trying to tamp the hurricane inside me. "While I'm certainly flattered by your proposal—"

"This isn't about flattery. Don't be ridiculous," Erick said, a sneer on his face.

My sweaty hands clenched in my skirt. "I don't think this is necessary. You're already betrothed to Lady Perrand, and I have no interest in marrying you. We can find another way to unite our kingdoms."

Erick rose from his chair. "I think you misunderstand me, *Your Highness*. I am not requesting your hand in marriage. You will do this,"—he turned to Ronan and then back to me, a slow smile spreading on his thin lips—"or he will die."

On cue, two of Erick's guards seized Ronan by each arm.

"Do you think I'm a fool?" Erick asked, stalking closer to his brother, who strained against the guards' hold. "That I wouldn't see how you look at her? That you can carry on inside the walls of *my* castle and keep it from me? What did you think? That *you* were going to marry her?"

My heart withered and died in my chest, ashes clogging my throat and stinging my eyes. I had no choice. I would do anything to keep Ronan alive.

"But why?" I asked, searching for any answer that would stop this. "You can't want me."

He shrugged. "That is hardly the point."

"No," Ronan said through clenched teeth. "You don't have to do this. Not for me."

Esme sobbed quietly in the corner. I wanted to beg her forgiveness—I didn't want this.

Erick nodded to a third guard standing in the room, who stalked forward, punching Ronan in the stomach so hard he folded in half, nearly collapsing to the ground.

"No!" I tried to reach him, but yet another guard held me back. Erick had orchestrated every move of this play.

"Do we have a deal?" Erick stalked so close our noses were almost touching.

Eyes filled with tears, I nodded.

"Thorne, no," Ronan said as he tried again to shirk off the guards holding him. A blade found its way to his throat as he nearly ripped from their grasp.

"Take him away." Erick gestured as I freed myself from the man holding me, running to Ronan.

Pressing my face to his throat, I felt the force of his hard swallow.

"Don't do this, Thorne."

"I told you I'd protect you, too. I can't let him hurt you. I love you, Ronan."

"We'll find a way out of this. I promise," he said before he was jerked away, and I didn't know if he believed those words or if I did, either.

Erick gestured to his guards, and they took me by the arms.

"So, I'm to be your prisoner, then?"

"For now, yes. After the wedding, that will entirely depend on you."

With that, they dragged me away.

CHAPTER THIRTY-THREE

Locked in my room, I paced as I unraveled like snagged cloth. Ronan had been the only thing keeping the demons from my family's death leashed under my skin. Now they slithered over me, their touch numbing and cruel as a bitter winter wind. If Erick killed Ronan, there would be truly nothing left for me. Everything and everyone I loved was already gone, and he held all the pieces of my shattered heart.

A knock pummeled the door and Kianna flew in, followed by Noah and Em. At the sight of their concerned faces, I cracked, the last of my resolve lost in a pile of shards. Kianna wrapped me in a hug, and I cried on her shoulder as she made soothing noises. I hadn't lost her yet, though it felt as if it was only a matter of time before someone took her away, too.

"It will be okay, Your Highness," she said over and over.

"It's not okay. We're right back in the castle and as lost and hopeless as ever. I couldn't break the curse then, and I don't know how to stop this now." I turned to Noah. "Have you seen him?"

He nodded. "He's holding up."

"Tell me the truth."

Noah's shoulders sagged. "He's a total wreck. I've never seen him like this. One moment he's raging, and the next he's just staring into nothing."

Pressure squeezed my chest, my heart ballooning into thin walls ready to pop. "This couldn't have all gone more wrong. We should never have come here." I sank down on the bed. "How can Erick get away with this?"

"He's walking the line of his authority," Noah said, rubbing his chin. "But it seems the nobles agree on the need to consolidate with Ravalyn. And there is no love lost between Ronan and any of them."

"We'll get him out of there," Em said, crouching down next to me. "Don't worry, Princess."

"Oh, Em, and then what? Erick will kill Ronan if I don't marry him. The only thing we can do is run, and what kind of life would that be?" We all fell silent for a few moments. "If I had been a regular child..." I said, quietly. "If Mare hadn't shown up and cursed me, I would have been forced to marry a prince in line for a throne, anyway. This was always going to be my fate." A tear tracked down my cheek. "I just didn't count on falling in love with someone else first."

"Erick is scum," Noah said, fists clenched. He had more reason than most to despise his future king. "He *won't* get away with this. He's been torturing Ronan their entire lives, and why? Because their mother always loved Ronan more."

"I suspected as much," I said, remembering the jealousy I'd seen on Erick's face at supper. "But he would never admit that."

"No, he wouldn't," Noah agreed.

"It doesn't matter why," I said. "Just that he's done it."

Someone rapped on the door, and a guard told the others they had to leave.

Kianna gave me a big hug, her wide, dark eyes finding mine. "You are strong, Your Highness. Don't forget that. I've never known anyone with as much courage as you." She peeled away a lock of hair pasted to my forehead, tucking it behind my ear.

"Thank you. I don't know what I would have done without you."

We hugged each other tightly before they forced her to leave.

As the door closed, I collapsed on the floor in an inconsolable puddle.

The days blurred into one as I did nothing but stare at the ceiling and think about my family and Mare. I wondered what had become of poor Esme, rejected for Erick's petty revenge. Mostly, I thought of Ronan and the raw, cavernous hole in my heart.

My nightmares were blood-soaked walls and gaping wounds... My mother and father alive and screaming for me as Mare stood behind them, an evil, twisted grin on her face. Me and Isabelle playing as children, happy and secure, when her head flew from her body and blood gushed over me, covering my clothes and my hands and my hair. I dreamed of Adrian. He leaned in to kiss me in the garden when, suddenly, Mare reached into his chest through his back and ripped out his heart. I screamed and screamed and woke up in an ocean of sweat, panting and breathless.

Kianna visited regularly, but I barely registered her presence as she smoothed my hair from my forehead, murmuring words of comfort. Words that meant nothing and everything. She couldn't fix this. No one could, but she was here, and it was more than I deserved.

The day of the wedding arrived, bells clanging across the city. Estria celebrated a royal union, none the wiser about what was happening within these walls. Their kingdom was prosperous and whole. They had lost a king, but a new one waited in the wings, and this marriage would help secure their futures. They were safe, and I was trapped.

Luella and her birds arrived to ready me for the ceremony. They had been quietly attending to me the past week, helping me change, keeping their voices low. Numb to my surroundings, I saw nothing as they bathed me and helped me into my wedding dress.

It was thick and itchy, covered in jewels and embroidery so heavy it felt like wearing a coffin. Someone had found my crown—the one my mother had made when there had been hope in her heart and promise in her womb. Kianna must have packed it when we'd fled Ravalyn. Another misplaced dream and unfulfilled wish to add to the midden heap of my life.

Kianna came in once I was ready, clasping my hands in hers. "You look beautiful, Your Highness."

I offered her a small, sad smile. How I looked didn't matter. I'd broken one curse only to be trapped by another, and Mare was still out there somewhere. But true love wouldn't save me this time. Perhaps once this was over, Erick would leave me in peace to mourn my family and find some way to sew the pieces of myself back together. There would always be seams about to split at the slightest bit of pressure, but I had to learn to shoulder this patchwork of a life.

"Kianna, you should go home."

Her forehead pleated. "What do you mean, Highness?"

"I am grateful for everything, but you don't need to keep doing this. It isn't your fight. Ravalyn was never your home, and I'm not your family. You don't owe me this loyalty. You never did. All I've ever been is a burden." The words were an offering, culled from my chest like a still-beating organ. I didn't want to say them, but they had to be said. For twenty-one years, I had been an obligation. A chore. She had never been beholden to me.

She blinked so slowly, it was as if she'd been partially frozen.

"You're right," she said, and my spirit caved in on itself. "We aren't family by blood, and I don't have to be here, but if you think I'd leave you now—after everything we've been through—then perhaps I haven't been clear enough. Perhaps I once viewed it that way. Perhaps duty kept me in that castle for as long as it did. But you *are* my family now, Thorne. I've watched you grow up, and I am so proud of the woman you've become."

Her words were hard to grasp, like trying to scoop up mist that slipped through my fingers. So I tried again, pushing her, wanting her to snap and admit the truth of my words.

"But I've done nothing but mess this up at every turn."

"No," she said, holding my hands tighter. "You have fought and fought for your family and for yourself. And for me. Don't think I took your sacrifices lightly. You tried to save me, even when our relationship was different. And you will fight now. I know this feels like the end, but you will make the best of this. If there's anything I've learned about you, it's that you are strong enough to face anything. Remember when you promised you'd never give up? I'm asking that of you again."

"Do you really mean it? That I'm your family?"

Her answering smile was kind, constructed of the fleeting bits of love left in my life.

"Of course, Thorne."

"You too," I said. "You're my family. Thank you for not leaving me, too."

She wrapped me in a hug. "Don't cry—you'll ruin your make-up."

"I don't give a fuck," I said, and she laughed.

"Fair enough." Letting go, she stepped back and gave me a nod that signaled the beginning and ending of everything. "Shall we?"

Vivian Goldraven waited outside to usher me into the chapel, her expression inscrutable. Acting as my escorts, Kianna and Vivian stood at my sides. Did Vivian approve of this union with Erick? Did she know what he'd done to Ronan?

My heart was broken, but I reminded myself of what I still had left. The people of Ravalyn. Those who remained loyal, despite everything, for one hundred uncertain years. It was for them I forced one foot in front of the other as the music swelled to a lilting crescendo. At least now, no one else would have to die defending me or my family. It wasn't much, but it was something.

The chapel was enormous, hundreds of eyes falling on me as my footsteps padded softly on the thick rug running down the center aisle. Digging into the furthest caverns of my perseverance, I made myself look up to where Erick awaited.

My breath stopped, and I stumbled at the sight of Ronan standing to Erick's left. Attired in his gold and black armor, an angry red slash stood out on his cheek. Our eyes met, and a scream bubbled in my throat. Erick had done this to punish him further, twisting the knife as deep as it would go, forcing Ronan to bear witness as he took me away with unequivocal finality.

Curious eyes watched me. I'd stopped walking, my breath shallow and my vision blurring. I couldn't do this.

Kianna fastened her hand to my elbow. "Come, Thorne," she whispered. "You must keep moving. For his sake."

My eyes burned with a volley of flaming arrows, but I nodded, facing the front of the room. One foot trudging in front of the other, my eyes never left Ronan. Let them all wonder why I wasn't looking at my husband-to-be. My heart split apart into a million jagged, rusty pieces. But there was nothing to be gained by torturing either of us like this, so I forced myself to look away.

Erick's smile was generous as I stepped up to the altar, as if he'd done me a favor. While the officiant spoke, a dull roar filled my ears, drowning out all sensation. I repeated what I was told to repeat, my voice as flat and wooden as a chessboard. The only thing I registered was the moment we were declared married. I closed my eyes as something cold and dead rushed through me. It was done. Ronan had been wrong—we hadn't found a way, and right now, I couldn't bear to look at him.

Erick and I turned to the guests. They clapped and smiled, and I forced my chin up. Esme sat near the front, silver lining her eyes.

I'm sorry, I tried to tell her, wanting to drop to her feet and beg her forgiveness. I would give anything to trade places. What would happen to her? Would she be sent back home or married off to another nobleman in Estria? I was far from the only victim here.

Erick held out his hand high in front of me, and I had no choice but to place mine in it. We walked down the aisle—a king and his queen—my soul shredding to ribbons.

The celebration continued with dinner in the banquet hall, where Erick and I arrived before our thrones. My new throne. Erick's cruelty continued unchecked—Ronan sat in the chair directly to my left. Stiff as cardboard, I sat down, not looking at him or at anything, my vision unfocused.

There were speeches and toasts. They placed food and wine before me, and I went through the motions of eating and drinking, but it was all dirt in my mouth. I remembered nothing from one moment to the next. This was both the most memorable and most forgettable day of my life.

As the evening wore on, the party grew louder—at least someone was enjoying themselves. Erick excused himself to confer with a group of men dressed in the silks and furs of noblemen.

Beside me, Ronan was as still as a statue. Neither of us had moved much this evening, trapped in the pause of our grief. I risked a small glimpse, and his eyes found mine instantly.

"I'm sorry," he said, so quietly I wondered if I'd heard anything at all.

"This isn't your fault," I said.

"I shouldn't have brought you here."

"You had no choice, and you aren't responsible for Erick's actions."

"You shouldn't have gone through with it." His large hands balled into fists against his thighs.

"And let him kill you? I'd rather die. I'd marry him a thousand times if it kept you safe, Ronan. At least you're alive."

"I am not alive without you. There is no purpose to any of this without you."

"I know," I whispered.

We were both staring forward, our mouths barely moving.

He placed a hand on both of mine, clasped in my lap. "I love you," he said, with so much agony it snagged in his throat. "You are the air I breathe and the blood in my veins and the stars in my sky and—"

I squeezed his hand. "Don't. This is pointless. It's only going to hurt more. Forget me. Move on."

"I can't do that. I could never forget you."

"You have to try." I glanced at Erick's back. "He will kill you, and if that happens, then I really won't be able to go on. If you can find a way to be happy, that will be enough for me. I can endure anything if you are happy."

"Thorne," he breathed, and the sound ground what was left of my heart into nothing but fine powder. It sifted through the cracks in the floor to be lost to the wind forever.

Erick finished with his discussion, and Ronan pulled his hand away.

"Well, then," Erick said, resuming his seat and wringing his hands. "You'll be thrilled to know, little brother, Markus Hammond is going to help fund our campaign against Galin. We'll get our hands on those gold mines after all."

My eyes widened at his calculating heartlessness. First, he'd dumped Esme, and now planned to wage war against them?

"You'll need to prepare the army to leave in one week. I imagine this will be a long and bloody battle." He dropped a stern look on both of us. "It should keep you away from Estria for quite some time. I can't have you two making a cuckold of me, can I?"

Erick was as cunning as a freshly honed blade, more so than I'd given him credit for. He would get both his mines and Ronan out of the way with one tidy maneuver. It was one crippling defeat after another.

"I'm tired," I said. "I'd like to be taken to my—*our*—room." I shuddered at the final act yet to come of this farce, but I couldn't look at Ronan. Any longer, and I would throw myself on him and cling to him and never let go.

"I will join you soon," Erick said.

I stood and offered him a shallow curtsy. "I will see you short-ly, husband." I tried out the unwelcome word. It felt thick and sour in my mouth, like curdled milk.

When I arrived at Erick's bedchamber, Luella and Marie were already waiting. They eased me from my heavy gown, replacing it with a thin, white nightgown and a navy robe. Deft fingers smoothed out my braids, and Marie brushed my hair.

Before bidding me goodnight, they both eyed me with un-derstanding—I was a queen and they were servants, but the language of a woman forced to bed a man was a universal one.

The room was twice the size of mine, decorated in jewel tones of blue, red, and violet. Every surface gleamed with marble, while the fabrics were rich and sumptuous.

Seated on the edge of the king's enormous bed, my feet dan-gled off the floor. Maybe I could pretend I was sleeping when he arrived, but I already knew this would be his final insult to Ronan. He would leave nothing open to interpretation or division, and for that, we must consummate our marriage.

Erick entered the room, slithering in like an overconfident weasel. I focused on my feet as his attendant helped him un-dress and redress into his nightclothes. I was still staring at my toes when the bed settled as Erick sat next to me. The door closed firmly, locking me in, the sound like the snap of the reaper's fingers.

"Can I assume you are no maid, and my little brother has already sullied you?" His tone was dry. Finally looking up, I gave him a sharp look, and he scoffed. "Oh, I hardly care, *wife*. In fact, that makes things easier. I really don't have the patience to coax a trembling virgin into bed tonight. It's so utterly tedious." He reached out and picked up a lock of my hair, twisting it in his fingers. A pungent churn spun in my gut. "You *are* rather striking, aren't you? I can see what my brother finds so intoxicating about you. It's a shame you have to talk so much. You'd be much more beautiful if you remained as silent as you were today."

I wanted to rip out his throat. I wanted to tear out his heart and feed it to him. I wanted to smash his face into tiny shards of bones and blood and snot and brains.

"Oh, don't look at me like that. Get over it, my *queen*. It's going to be a long and odious life, otherwise."

Still holding my hair in his fingers, he slid closer. As he placed a hand on my leg, I closed my eyes and took a deep breath. I wasn't frightened, only broken. My soul had already departed my body, and I wouldn't feel a thing.

Erick slid my nightgown up my thighs, an eager look in his eyes. Whether that excitement was for the use of my body or simply the offence to his brother, I couldn't be sure.

"Lie back," he ordered, standing and shucking his robe. A sharp vibration of memory shuddered through me as I thought of Ronan on a very different night, just weeks ago, in a very different life.

Shifting to the middle of the bed, I did as I'd been told, seeing myself as if floating from above. I was not here. My mind crawled into itself, hiding from the shadows that enveloped me. Erick clamored onto the bed, straddling me, and I willed myself to relax. To enter some other place on a distant plane of awareness. I would have to keep doing this. We would need to produce an heir. Probably more than one. To get through this, I'd build up an arsenal of weapons crafted for my survival.

I tried not to think of Ronan. Of how little time we'd had together before we'd been torn apart. I missed him so much that it felt like a rusty dagger piercing my heart.

Erick's breath washed over my skin, clammy and warm. He looked so much like his father that I was transported to yet another day in yet another life. A day when I awoke, after a hundred years, to a man with murderous rage in his eyes. Panic broke out over my skin like a rash.

I was wrong. I couldn't do this.

But it was happening anyway. Erick pushed my nightgown past my waist, and I felt the unwelcome sear of his manhood hard against my stomach. I squeezed my eyes shut as tears painted my cheeks in watercolors of endless resentment.

My fists were clenched into the bedspread, and spots darkened my vision as I pressed my cheek to the sheets, trying to look away. My chest drew so tight I couldn't breathe.

But then, with a breathy whoosh of confusion, Erick flew off me.

A crack shattered the air as he crashed into the wall. His body hung suspended, pinned for a moment as if even gravity had been caught off guard. As he slid to the ground, a thick trail of blood followed him to where he collapsed, his head drooping forward, his chin resting on his chest. A gaping wound in the back of his head oozed blood and brains and viscera.

Too shocked to move, I blinked once, twice, three times, and then let out a bloodcurdling scream.

CHAPTER THIRTY-FOUR

CRUEL LAUGHTER FLOATED FROM the doorway. From where I kneeled on the bed, I spun around to find Maida and Alban. The pewter-haired Fae leaned on the frame, his muscled arms folded and one ankle crossed behind the other. Dropping his stance, Maida's gaze scraped over me as he crossed the room and crouched over Erick's body. He tipped an appreciative nod, as if impressed with himself.

"What have you done?" I asked, pulling my robe tight and backing toward the headboard. The door ricocheted open, and Ronan's towering form filled the doorway, sword out, all fury and brimstone.

"I heard you scream," he said, confusion in his expression as he took in the two Fae in the room.

Alban had plonked himself on the bed, leaning against the headboard, legs crossed and arms bent behind his head. He rolled his eyes at Ronan. "Your princess is fine," he drawled.

"That one, on the other hand..." He flicked a wrist at Erick's prostrate body and, at that moment, eight more figures of varying heights and ages appeared. The heads of the noble houses filed into the room like a row of petulant ducklings.

"What is the meaning of this?" one nobleman demanded, eyes darting around the room. He wasn't much older than I was, and there was an uncertain tilt to his shoulders. A new head of household, unused to the bloody affairs of kings and kingdoms.

This certainly wasn't the wedding night I'd envisioned, though I couldn't be sorry that Erick's plans had been interrupted.

I was now trapped between Erick's dead body, Alban lounging on the bed, Maida with his vicious sneer, and a gaggle of nobles all eyeing me with mounting suspicion.

Cinching my robe tight, I stood and leaped to the floor, positioning myself next to Ronan—the only person I trusted in this room. He took my hand, pulling me close.

"Is there a problem?" Maida asked, leaning against the bedpost, loose and lithe as a jaguar.

"I don't understand," Ronan said, sword pointed with his free hand. "What did you do to my brother?"

"Arrest him!" a nobleman shouted. This one gray and lined. "These Fae have terrorized the castle and the city, and now they've murdered the king. Commander, call for the army!"

Maida raised a hand. "I wouldn't be so hasty," he said, turning on the fuming nobleman. "Do that, and I will call down a legion of Fae to wipe out every man, woman, and child in this castle."

Uncertain silence collapsed in the room.

"What is going on?" Ronan demanded. "Explain yourself, Fae, or I'll kill you myself."

"It has been the desire of King Nictis to see a Fae placed on the throne of Estria for many years. Well, all human kingdoms, but he's had his sights set on the largest of them for a while. And *he*," Maida said, pointing to the dead king on the floor, "is not Fae."

"If you presume to place yourself on the throne, we will meet you with the force of all of Estria's army!" Another nobleman stepped forward, eyes blazing.

"Not me." Maida's face split into a slow, menacing grin. "Him."

"Me?" Ronan asked, his brow furrowed.

"Haven't you ever wondered why you're a bit faster? A bit stronger? Why you heal so much quicker than others?"

It was true. The cut on his cheek that had stood bright red during the ceremony earlier today was nearly healed. I thought of how quickly he'd recovered from Mare's attack. The way Ronan moved and fought had always bordered on preternatural. I had always put it down to training, but perhaps it was more than that.

"A dampening can only suppress so much. It's enough that one might never suspect the truth, but some of one's true Fae nature always slips through."

"A dampening?"

"The Fae place them on children they want to hide amongst humans. A glamour to conceal your Fae appearance, and a dampening to restrict your power and access to magic."

A question flickered in Ronan's expression. Uncertainty, but something else, too. "You're lying. This makes no sense."

"Someone find the queen dowager," Alban said, snapping his fingers. He pointed to the young nobleman who'd spoken first. "You, go get her. And be quick about it."

The man opened his mouth to object, but Alban hissed, his sharp Fae teeth snapping. The nobleman blanched and scurried from the room. We all watched him leave, and Maida's gaze shifted to where Ronan held my hand. With a jerk of his chin, he indicated I should look at Ronan.

I gasped when I took him in. It seemed impossible, but he'd become even more beautiful. The glamour was gone, revealing delicate, pointed ears and glowing skin so bright it almost hurt to look.

"How do we know this isn't a trick?" I asked, narrowing my gaze on Maida.

Ronan was shaking his head, and my breath disintegrated in my chest. "I can feel it," he said with no small bit of wonder.

At that moment, Ronan's mother came into the room and paled as she took in her son, the truth written on her like a prophecy hammered into stone.

Reaching up to touch his cheek, Vivian trembled like a wind-blown petal. "He promised," she said, addressing Maida. "He promised to keep him safe."

Maida gave a shrug of his wide shoulders. "You knew this day was coming, and King Nictis tires of waiting. With your husband out of the way, the time had come."

"Someone explain what is going on," Ronan demanded, his initial uncertainty giving way to steel and anger.

Maida raised a slate-gray eyebrow at Vivian and said in a bored tone, "Would you care to do the honors, Your Majesty?"

Ronan swung his gaze to his mother, who quailed under the fierceness of his expression.

After a coarse swallow, she finally spoke. "Many years ago, I fell in love with a Fae noble who is close to the king, but I was already married to Winston. We had an affair, and you were the result."

Ronan swayed on his feet.

The man I had killed was not his father.

"To keep us both safe from Winston's wrath, we agreed to keep it quiet and raise you as his son. Your real father performed the dampening and glamoured you to look human. I've always felt differently about you, Ronan. That was no secret. You were created out of the greatest love I've ever known, unlike your brother, who grew up to be so much like his father I sometimes couldn't bear to even look at him. I hated that man," she said, her voice catching like silk on a thorn.

Ronan said nothing, a disbelieving look on his face.

I wanted to comfort him, but there were no words to soften this. "What does any of this mean?" I asked. "Why are you telling us all this, and why did you wait until now to reveal it? You knew the king was dead weeks ago. Why wait until tonight?"

Maida canted his head. "I only received my orders after Erick surprised us by deciding to marry you instead of Lady Perrand. I was curious to see how things played out," he said with a wicked laugh. "Oh, that was a delicious bit of irony. But even I couldn't stomach him heaving and panting over you any

longer. I needed to end that obscene display. You're welcome."
He made a sickened face.

Shame flushed my cheeks, knowing Maida had watched Erick about to force himself on me. Ronan's hand tightened
around mine, fury coiled and ready to strike like a caged viper.
Maida's slow smile spread again as he turned to the noblemen
who had been listening in stunned silence. That snapped whatever spell they had been under because they all broke out in
a chorus of denials and refusals to accept a half-Fae prince as
their king.

Maida silenced them with a slice of his hand.

"You're under the delusion you have a choice here. King Nictis
will invade Estria should you refuse him. Your pitiful human
army will be nothing against a legion of trained Fae warriors."

No one could deny the truth of that.

Maida crooned at me. "Don't look so devastated, Princess. I
did you a favor."

A few hours later, I was back in my guest room. As night blan-
keted the city, I sat on the balcony beneath a thick quilt before
a firepit crackling with flames, with my legs tucked under me.
The cold air opened my lungs.

Ronan approached, his shirt sleeves rolled up, displaying the
corded muscle of his forearms. He looked human again, with

rounded ears and standard canines. Like Maida and Alban, he still glowed faintly, but it wasn't as hard to look at him.

"Maida showed me how to control my, uh...otherworldliness," he said, sitting next to me. "He says it makes humans uncomfortable to be around our true forms."

"How do you feel?"

"Different. My sight, my hearing, my speed... It's all so different. The world looks nothing like it did before." I didn't think he meant just physically.

"What about the noble houses?"

"They've agreed to King Nictis's terms. Me on the throne to form an alliance between Estria and the Fae. My father would be turning over in his grave. He loathed the Fae."

"But at least it means security for your kingdom."

"Yes." Ronan rubbed a hand down his face.

"What is it?" I unspooled from my position, scooting in next to him and draping the quilt over both of us.

"I've never wanted to be king. It's the last thing I've ever wanted to be."

"I know. But you will make an excellent one. You are a better man than your father or your brother could have ever hoped to be."

His answering smile was tight and sad.

Taking his face between my hands, I stared into his dark green eyes. "But this isn't all bad. At least now we can be together. That is what I wanted from the moment I saw you, Ronan. You light all of my darkest corners and fill them with sunshine. I want to be by your side forever. You have a chance to bring peace to your kingdom. No more warring with the Fae.

It could be a bright and wonderful future, and we could make it happen. It's the only thing I want."

That smile I loved so much lit up his face. "That's all I want too, Thorne." He opened his mouth as if preparing to say something else, but instead, he scooped me up and took me to bed, where we made love until the sun came up.

For the first time since I'd awoken in that cursed castle, my second chance felt so close I could trace its outline with the tip of my finger. I allowed the barest sliver of hope to leap from its place at my feet and lodge like a spark inside my chest, flickering faintly. Once, I would have tried to suffocate it, denying it the air it needed to breathe into fire.

But I was done believing in darkness.

I wanted light.

I wanted salvation, and I was ready to burn.

CHAPTER THIRTY-FIVE

A FEW DAYS LATER, we gathered for Ronan's coronation—a celebration hastily stitched together with fraying strings and threadbare cloth. Luella and the girls had put me in a simple white dress that trailed along the floor, a stole of pure white fur wrapped around my shoulders. My hair down, Marie had curled and adorned it with winter blossoms before placing my pale silver crown on my head.

In the castle garden, Ronan stood with his mother, the noble heads bearing witness. Snow fell gently, settling on our shoulders and dusting our hair. With Kianna at my side, we waited near the dais. Noah and Em, dressed in their ceremonial armor, beamed proudly at their friend. Their brother. Their king.

Nearby, Maida and Alban lurked, their presence a reminder to everyone of the consequences of rebellion.

Watching Ronan, I was struck like a bell. Again, he wore his black and gold armor—a king and warrior. Now I was his, and he was mine. This was more than enough. After everything, it was more than I could have ever hoped for.

After Ronan was crowned, he took my hand, and we exchanged a smile that conveyed a myriad of emotions wrapped in paper and string. A promise and an oath. To love and protect until the very end of our days, as we had once sworn to each other in a cursed castle on the edge of a decaying kingdom.

Ronan pressed his forehead to mine. "I love you," he said. "We will be happy. I promise I will do everything to make you happy."

"I already am, Ronan. How could I not be with you?"

At that moment, everything seemed possible. For a brief, glittering second, I allowed myself the luxury of dreams. To tread sands of joy, kicked up on sun-warmed winds.

But I should have remembered that was never meant to be my destiny.

A noise like the tearing of souls ripped through the garden, and every thought in my head sharpened as the devil came crashing in.

After all, happy endings were only for the hallowed, and fairy tales weren't real.

The ramparts of the castle exploded as stone shattered, and something large and scaled and so black it drank the light, landed in the center of the garden. Legs bent to cushion its descent, it stretched to its full and terrible height. A demon, a monster, the lord of the underworld itself stood before us, leathery wings spread wide.

Chaos erupted.

Screams filled the air as it stalked toward me and Ronan. His sword out, grim determination set in his posture like hardened clay. The demon's feet scraped the stones, three long toes tipped by even longer claws. The same tracks that had surrounded the mutilated bodies of a dozen innocent people sacrificed at my door.

Ronan was shouting orders at the guards who attempted to wound the demon, their arrows and blades futile against its thick hide.

But I already knew it was no use.

The demon didn't fight back; it only stared at me, and I understood why it was here. The gleam in its eyes was intelligent, almost human. This was no rabid beast. No mindless minion. It was a servant, an unholy messenger sent to deliver me to my inescapable fate.

Why I thought I could ever run from this, I'd never know.

One of its great clawed feet lifted, and it prowled toward me.

Holding me behind him, Ronan acted as my shield. My protector. My true love.

But he would not die for me—not today or on any day.

"Ronan," I said, wrapping my arms around his neck. "I love you. I am so grateful for every moment we had together. I'm sorry we didn't have more time, but I've always belonged to a different fate. Your memory will keep me whole when I am broken. Thank you for everything." I kissed him and filled it with every ounce of joy and light he had brought to my dark and bewitched life, though it could only be a shadow of all he had given. "Goodbye," I whispered. And before he could react, I ran.

He shouted my name, giving chase, but even with his new speed, he couldn't catch me. I was already gone. This was our ending.

On wings of ruin, I leaped for the demon, and it snatched me in its taloned grip. Wings already beating, it rose into the air, and then there was nothing but a spiraling whirl of darkness.

CHAPTER THIRTY-SIX

Light seared my eyes as they watered from the sudden on-slaught of sensation. Golden bars wavered in my view, forming a cell. Not a cell—a cage. They surrounded me on all sides, parallel lines enclosing me in every direction and running overhead, revealing a clear blue sky.

A groan escaped my lips as I moved, my hip throbbing from sleeping on a bed of unforgiving marble. My memories were foggy after I'd jumped into the demon's awaiting claw, his talons so tight I had blacked out. That might have been days or weeks or hours ago.

"Welcome back, Princess," a voice said. The back of a dark silver head leaned up against my prison.

My response was to groan even louder. "I should have known you'd be part of this," I hissed.

Maida swiveled his head to meet my gaze, a silvery eyebrow climbing his forehead. He wore a simple gray tunic that clung to his chest and back, revealing every dip of his sculpted skin.

Strangely, I was dressed in pale yellow layers of sheer gossamer, dotted with winking crystals. It reminded me of the dresses Kianna always wore. Only this was shorter, my brown legs mostly bare against the cold marble. Wherever this was, the landscape had yet to be touched by the creep of winter. Given my attire, I was grateful for this small mercy.

Head spinning, I pushed to a seated position, my hair loose and tangled. With a sickening feeling, I watched as a well-dressed Fae couple approached my cage, staring down their noses with twin sneers.

The female had pale skin, shiny black hair, and bright violet eyes. She sniffed as she leaned closer. "They do smell dreadful, don't they?"

What?

"And look at her eyes," said the male. An aristocratic face was set with bright blue eyes and topped with rich brown hair. He pulled on his companion as if to protect her...from me? "So devoid of any signs of intelligence. Nothing but animals. Feral. Someone ought to put them all out of their misery."

Excuse me?

Rage formed a black ball in my throat. I lobbed it at them, lunging for the Fae, gripping the bars and baring my useless human teeth. They jumped out of arm's reach, laughing nervously.

"Sometimes they bite," Maida said, still reclined against my cage.

The Fae couple regarded him with mortification as if we'd ruined their innocent Sunday stroll. The male shielded the female, and they hurried away, moving toward another cage set along a carefully manicured path. Butterflies fluttered between the blooms, along with tiny sprites who hopped from stamen to stamen.

The next cage held another woman, who was so still she could have been made from stone. Blank eyes stared ahead, seeing nothing.

Finally, I took in the magnitude of my surroundings. It couldn't have been more jarring or horrifying. An array of golden cages dangled overhead. Women filled these, too. Slumped against their bars, thin legs dangled as their prisons swayed in the breeze.

Fae strolled in every direction, dressed in their finest, pointing and laughing. Almost idyllic in their nonchalance, they laughed with the careless hilarity of the privileged, sauntering amongst the flowers and human shells.

"What is this?" I asked Maida, his back still turned to me. "Where am I?"

An arm swept out. "Welcome to Mare's human menagerie." As he stood, Maida dusted off his pants and tilted his head. "Where every princess is a plaything." Something sharp moved in his gaze, and his jaw ticked.

"This is why she wanted me?"

I picked out your cage today. You're going to love it.

"On the surface, it looks that way," Maida said, "but she does seem to take a special interest in you."

"Why? Why is she so obsessed with me?"

"I don't know. Mare is...obsessive."

"Why are you here? Did she put you up to the entire thing with Ronan?"

Maida's eyes flashed. "No, that was not Mare's plan. I was working for the king."

"So you just bounce around, doing the bidding of the most evil Fae of the moment?"

"I don't work for Mare, Princess. Consider me an interested bystander."

My gaze narrowed at him.

Maida's attention was drawn to another group of Fae wandering past my cage. I growled at them, and they jumped back, squealing with glee. A menagerie. This was exactly what they came for. To see me behave like a wild beast. I slumped against the bars, the cold metal biting into my bare skin.

My insides were cracked, empty pools of nothing. Mare had taken everything, and now I was trapped here, completely at her mercy. I thought of the look on Ronan's face when I'd kissed him goodbye, but I wouldn't let him die to protect me. That demon would have ripped him limb from limb. Enough people had died for me already, and I would not be responsible for one more drop of spilled blood.

Was Ronan looking for me? If it had been the other way around, I would look for him forever. I'd never stop. But I hoped he couldn't find me and was forced to give up. That Mare finally killed me, and he had no choice but to turn away and find happiness some other way. In time, he'd get over me. I'd meant what I'd said—I could endure anything if he was happy.

Maida watched me like I was a trunk full of secrets.

"What?" I snapped. "If you're done gloating, feel free to fuck off. I'm sure you have someone else to torment."

Tinkling music drifted over, and a large cart covered in candies, macarons, and sugared fruit rumbled past my cage. My stomach growled, and my mouth watered at the honeyed scent. Women in their cages looked down at the cart, their shadowed eyes hungry with longing. While they were clean, all wearing pristine floaty dresses like mine, they were also overly thin, their hair hanging limp and their cheeks hollow. Fear clutched my heart and stomped on my tender organs.

Fae strolled to the cart, handing over glittering coins as they filled paper cones with bejeweled treats. The woman in the cage next to mine gripped her golden bars so tightly her knuckles turned bloodless.

"What is this place?" I whispered, tears burning my eyes. I was going to die here. There was no question this would be the last place I'd ever call home.

Still leaning on my cage, Maida looked off in the distance, where the menagerie spread for miles beneath a clear blue sky.

"You'll find out soon enough, Princess." The words bore an edge of apology and that, more than anything, twisted my insides into something entirely unrecognizable. With one more look, he pushed himself off my cage and walked away, hands stuffed in his pockets.

That night, it rained. Huddled in the center of my cage, I tried to keep away from the splashes of water hitting the ground. Thunder rolled overhead. Shivering and cold, it was too dark to see the others. Above, cages creaked as the strong winds buffered the bars and, suddenly, I was grateful for my relatively sheltered place on the ground.

Tears mingled with drops of rain as I curled into myself, longing for Ronan. Longing for Ravalyn and my family. Longing for some other existence where none of this was real.

Ronan didn't want to be a king, but at least we had been together. Just the two of us against the world. I thought of the first night we'd spent together in my grandparents' chateau, letting the memory ignite the tiniest spark of warmth. Curling into it, I held on to it so tightly that my body ached in every corner. It was the only thing I had left.

CHAPTER THIRTY-SEVEN

O N THE MARBLE FLOOR sat a small white plate with gilded edges, piled with colorful cakes and glistening morsels of fruit. Next to it was a large glass filled with pale yellow liquid, drops of condensation forming on the outside.

The storm had abated overnight when I'd drifted into a restless sleep and woken up damp and shivering. Pushing myself up, I scanned the world past my bars, sensing a trick.

The woman in the cage next to mine was still asleep, a similar meal lying next to her. My throat was raw with thirst, and I reached for the glass, gulping its contents, and then choked. Salt. As salty as a dead sea. Spitting and gagging, I spattered the front of my dress, soaking it in brine.

Desperate for something in my stomach, I reached for the plate of treats. Taking a tiny nibble of a purple frosted cake, I retched. It tasted of death and rotting, forgotten things. Like unhappiness mixed with flour and eggs, baked, and then served with ill intentions.

This wasn't food—it was a game. My stomach rumbled and roiled, so I chanced another bite, just to have something in my body. I was so hungry. But as it touched my tongue again, I vomited up the scant contents of my intestines. Bile running down my chin, I wiped it away with the back of my hand and sank on my knees, dropping my head into my hands.

Other women stirred in their cages, and I watched when one shoved her meal between the bars as food and glass crashed to the stones below, shattering the quiet morning.

A cry of triumph erupted from the cage next to mine, where the woman was stuffing cakes in her mouth so fast she nearly choked. She chugged the glass of liquid, closing her eyes in ecstasy. Perhaps sensing my curious gaze, she glanced over, clutching the glass to her chest as though I could walk through my bars and take it.

"Once in a while, it's real." Her voice was dry and thin like autumn leaves. Tears shone in her eyes. She descended onto the food again, making noises like an animal, licking every last speck and every last crumb that had fallen to the floor. Unable to take my eyes off her as she wallowed in this ephemeral pleasure, I wondered how long it had been since she'd last eaten.

"Don't worry, there are ways to earn it." Maida stood before my cage again, large hands circled around my bars and head angled to the side. Glittering black eyes read me up and down. In his non-glamoured state, he was glorious—light brown skin, bright and gleaming as polished brass; the perfect lines of his face creating a vision the greatest artist in the world would spend his entire life trying to capture.

"How?" I asked, despite my better judgment.

"So eager, Princess? You think it will be easy? Or fun? Mare rewards those who give up something in return." Malice laced his words, and my hands balled against my skirt.

"Give up what?"

He straightened his neck, pelting me with his gaze. "Your dignity, your morality, your humanity. Perhaps all of the above."

I glanced back at the woman, wondering what part of her soul Mare had forced her to cut away for table scraps. She'd finished her food and was lying on the floor of her cage, arms wrapped around her body, rocking back and forth.

A moment later, two Fae guards stomped up behind Maida.

"Lucky for you, Princess, you're about to find out," he said as the guards unlocked my cage. They took me by each arm, and we wound through the manicured pathways.

An oval stadium loomed ahead, rising from the landscape like a squat mountain, where hundreds of elegantly dressed Fae filled the stands. Small crystal glasses filled with champagne dangled from their fingertips. Human women in gossamer dresses wandered between the spectators, handing out delicacies nibbled by razor-sharp teeth.

They were here for a show, and I feared I was the entertainment.

Those fears were confirmed when I was handed a sword and a dagger. Polished steel gleamed in the sunlight. A guard shoved me, and I stumbled through a gate, landing in the dirt, weapons scattering.

The noise crested at my entrance, chatter racing through the stands. I forced myself to look up. Directly ahead was a raised platform, where Mare sat surrounded by a group of vicious-looking Fae. Maida and Alban lounged amongst them, like pieces of a matching set.

I picked up the weapons and stood. Slowly, I walked to the center of the ring, wincing at the sting of gravel scraping my soles, my bare feet kicking up dust. Mare and I watched each other, enemies facing off to the death, but the odds of this fight were decidedly uneven.

"Welcome, Princess Thorne," she said, her voice ringing clearly across the arena.

I straightened my spine, feigning a confidence that was nothing but a lie. "Do your worst, Mare." I spat the words like bitter regret, and the crowd went wild, cheering and clapping as Mare's gaze narrowed at me.

"I know you all came for a show." She smirked, a wicked gleam in her eyes. "And I'm thrilled to present the inaugural performance of my latest addition to the menagerie." She tipped her head. "I did this all for you, Princess. What do you think?"

I had no idea what to think. Did all of what for me? I said nothing, not wanting to give her any more ammunition to destroy me.

She lifted her chin, once again addressing the crowd. "I think I've quite outdone myself with this one." With that, she spread her arms wide and levered them up as four doors, one in each corner of the stadium, slid open.

I spun on my heels, trying to fit them all into my vision at once, wondering what atrocity waited for me. What wild, many-fanged beast I must defeat not only to survive, but to earn my supper.

Out of the darkness emerged four slight figures. Four women like me, in short, gauzy dresses, leaving little to the imagination and offering even less protection. One carried a sword like mine. Another a battle axe. One, a long broadsword she gripped with two hands, and the last, a bow and arrow, a quiver slung on her back.

They approached and surrounded me, forming a ring of hunger—both physical and mental—written into every line of their skin. The crowd let out a collective hush. They seemed as surprised by this as I was.

"A fight to the death," said Mare. "The last one standing will live another day and earn herself a special treat." She grinned at me with a blood-red smile. "Begin!" She clapped her hands, and the crowd lost control.

As the stands vibrated, the women circled me. It was clear they meant to go for me first. The one with the sword and dagger held them like someone unused to weapons. With a cautious shuffle, she swung, missing me by a mile. Evading her with ease, I was suddenly stupefyingly grateful for all those hours I'd spent training with Ronan, Noah, and Em.

Instinct kicked in, and I stalked toward her and knocked her to the ground. Both weapons fell from her hands, and she scrambled back, trembling from head to toe. I raised my sword, ready to deliver a blow.

But I couldn't do this.

The woman with the bow waited, an arrow notched and aimed at my chest. Long red hair clung to her scalp, sweat running down her face.

I stopped. I didn't have to do anything. I could let them kill me and escape.

My hands raised in supplication, I dropped my sword and dagger, leaving myself unarmed, my arms spread wide like an offering to the angels. This was the promise I'd made. There would be no more blood under my watch. Not a single drop spilled by my hands.

The women exchanged uncertain glances as they continued to circle, unsure of what to make of me.

"Stop!" Mare shouted from the stands. Her hands gripped the railing in front of her while her nostrils flared. "Pick up your weapons, Princess. I warn you right now—you *will* fight back. I know what you did during those days in the castle. I know you thought you could best me. Let's see how proficient a student you are." She laughed, nails scraping down my spine. She had done all this for me. Built this stadium to prove nothing I did would ever be enough. "If I think you are not trying, if I think you are not doing your best, they will all die anyway. And I assure you, it will be far slower and more painful than the swift death you can deliver. Their blood is on your hands, regardless, but you can at least make it clean."

She had me cornered in every conceivable way.

Panic set in as the wall I was keeping against my emotions sloughed away like soil on a drought-ridden landscape. My choices were few—kill them or watch them be tortured. The woman holding the axe seemed familiar with its grip, but that was one weapon Ronan hadn't taught me how to defend myself against.

A joyless calm stacked itself on my shoulders as the roar of the stadium rattled my bones. My only choice was to end this quickly, for their sake and mine. Maybe I'd even be lucky enough to die in the process.

Before any of them could react, I dropped down to grab the dagger from the ground and flipped it at the woman with the bow and arrow—a trick Noah had taught me. It spun, end over end, and caught above her left breast. Striking bone, it bounced off, but it was enough to send her crashing to her knees. I lunged, grabbing the bow and snapping it over my knee. Scooping up my dropped dagger, I grabbed her by the hair and slit her throat. She was gone.

It all happened so quickly; none of the others had even moved, but now the woman with the battle-axe screamed, running at me. I dodged her swing, and she spun, caught in a circle of momentum created by the weight of the weapon. My sword struck, biting through skin and bone, so deep into her arm it forced her to drop the axe, blood staining her lavender dress. The first woman with the sword and dagger was still on the ground, wide-eyed and shaking. She had never fought anyone in her life.

Eyes cast heavenward, I whispered a prayer for her soul and for mine. For the helpless woman I had been once, too. Then I ran her straight through her heart, and she slumped over, dead.

The woman with the broadsword trembled as I faced her next, clasping the weapon in her hands. Helpless as a blind kitten, she didn't even try to stop me as I knocked it from her hand and ended her life swiftly. The crowd screamed in ecstasy while stinging tears streamed down my face.

Finally, it was just the woman in lavender who had once held the axe. She clutched her ruined arm, swaying on her bare, dirty feet. I made quick work of her, slitting her throat and gently lowering her to the ground at my feet.

Covered in blood and corrosive shame, I dropped my weapons and sank to my knees with my face in my hands. It had been so easy. Too easy. They had never stood a chance. I was still alive, but I'd rather be dead. I looked up at Mare and the cruel satisfaction on her face—this was exactly how she'd planned it.

Guards lifted me from the ground. My legs were hollow and wooden, and they dragged me along, a trail of blood staining the dirt. Something heavy hit me in the head, and then there was darkness.

When I woke up, I was back in my cage, cleaned, and wearing a new dress. It shimmered in pale pink, covered in a rainbow of crystals. On the floor was also my reward: a large platter laden with an entire roasted chicken, plump golden potatoes floating in maroon gravy, and thick slices of bread with butter. Expecting another trick, I took a nibble, but even a drop tasted like heaven. I descended on the food, my chin and fingers running with juices. Nothing had ever tasted so good.

The other women watched me. They knew what I'd done to earn this bounty. There was judgment in their eyes, and the breath in my lungs twisted. More had died because of me. They might have washed the blood off, but I could still feel it staining my hands, running hot and red as I'd stabbed and sliced those women apart. Nothing could forgive what I'd done.

My appetite curdled, and I pushed the food away, attempting to hide from their accusing stares by scrambling to the back of my cage.

The rest of my day was spent lying on the floor of my prison as Fae ambled by, tossing lewd comments I tried to shut out.

Thanks to my performance, I was now the star attraction.

That night, I was further rewarded when I was once again dragged from my cage. Two guards marched next to me, but they didn't restrain me this time. I was no threat to anyone, save scared young women in flimsy dresses. We wound our way past the cages and fountains and seating areas, all of them shimmering and beautiful—a place for the Fae to play while we suffered in the dark.

Up ahead was a small castle. Same as everything else, it was delicate and intricate, like the frosted layers of a wedding cake. A wall surrounded the castle, and we approached a gate that gleamed silver in the waning light. More guards nodded to my keepers as they opened the gate, letting us through.

"I suggest you stay close," one of them said to me, his voice flat and emotionless. "If you get lost, I can't guarantee we'll ever find you again, and I assure you we're friendlier than what you'll find in there."

I swallowed, wondering what fresh terror hid around the corner next.

We passed through the gate and entered a long hallway lined with mirrors. Crystal chandeliers dangled overhead, so everything blazed with blinding light. The guards marched down the hall, not waiting for me. Cold tiles numbed my feet as I scurried to keep up.

We turned a corner, and more mirrors stretched in every direction. Hundreds of them reflected back on themselves, bending light and shadow into unrecognizable puzzles. The effect was entirely disorienting. Already, I couldn't tell where we'd come from. I hurried after the guards, understanding their warning now. One could get lost here in the space of a sigh.

They turned another corner I hadn't even seen, my reflection following me. There were dark circles under my eyes, and it looked like I hadn't slept in a hundred years. *Oh, the irony.* Scratches covered my face, matching the maze that covered my arms and legs. The pink dress was even shorter than I'd realized, and I tried tugging it down to no avail.

Turn after turn, the brightly lit halls stretched into forever. We flipped another corner, and I gasped.

Ronan lay dead on the floor, sliced from throat to groin, entrails spilling, a pool of blood spreading under him.

With a cry, I rushed to him, only to be greeted by a solid barricade. I bounced against it, my forehead striking the mirror and knocking me back as I landed on my backside. The image was gone. Just an illusion. One so real, terror lived in my skin like sandpaper.

As I gathered my wits, I noticed the guards had disappeared. Scrambling to my feet, I spun around and around, finding nothing but a labyrinth wrought from silver and flung into eternity.

"Come back!" Only silence answered after my echo, the guard's warning about what else lurked in these halls scattering gooseflesh over my skin. "Please, come back!"

After a few tentative steps, I hesitated, worried I'd get even more lost if I continued. Was it better to stay where I was in the hopes someone would find me?

I didn't like it here. It felt wrong in this place, like square pegs hammered into round holes.

Something slimy and vicious licked in my gut. I twirled, trying to find the source. A hand grabbed my arm, and I screamed, jumping away.

"I told you to stay close," growled the guard, yanking on my arm with such force I stumbled. Not letting go, he tugged me down the corridor. I averted my eyes from the mirrors, looking down at my feet. We spun through more halls and corners until, finally, we stopped before a large set of doors and entered a sprawling chamber, the ceiling soaring high overhead.

Frosted white walls rose up, covered in thick swirls of marble that looked almost good enough to eat. Or maybe I was just really hungry.

The guards jostled me through another set of doors, and we entered an even larger circular room. Here, the walls and floor were inky black, all perfectly smooth and shiny like the skins of ripe cherries. Hundreds of glittering crowns hung from pegs set in the wall, spreading from the floor to the ceiling.

Fae filled the room, dressed in lustrous fabrics, laughing and drinking as trays of food and colorful cocktails were passed around.

My jaw clenched hard enough to crack walnuts. It was a fucking party.

More women like me, dressed in filmy, barely there dresses, dotted the room. Some sat quietly next to the Fae, who had their arms slung around their shoulders. One sat on the lap of a male Fae, who was mostly ignoring her as he conversed with another male, but she looked terrified.

Other women stood with trays in their hands, not moving as Fae drifted past, depositing empty glasses and picking up new ones. I quailed at the sight of two women standing at the center of a group of onlookers. They were testing their magic, turning the women into various beasts, forcing them to sprout feathers and hair and hooves, rendering them into grotesque hybrids of woman and animal.

Horror wove a thick noose around my neck and tightened. The guards dragged me to a throne that sat against the back wall. Black and gleaming, it reminded me of a spider protecting its web. A nest of sharpened points rose up behind Mare as she lounged, her hand dangling over the side of the armrest, the other fisted under her chin. She perked up as we approached, sitting up and leaning forward.

"Ah, Princess Thorne. So nice of you to join us." She scanned me from my wild, unbound hair to my red, freezing toes. "That was quite the performance today. I'll have to make it harder on you next time."

Next time. Of course, there would be a next time. Mare was far from done with me.

"How do you like my little home?" She gestured, purposely drawing my attention to the crowns hanging from the walls. Some were gold, some pewter, and some silver. Some were plain and severe, and some engraved and adorned with dozens of jewels of varying size and grandiosity.

"I see you are admiring my collection," she said, a lilt to her lips. "I am rather proud of it." An elbow braced on the arm of her throne, she leaned her chin on her fist.

"Have you figured out what you and the other girls all have in common?" She raised her eyebrows and flicked her eyes to the row of crowns directly to her left. When I saw my own pale crown hanging from a small wooden peg, I sucked in a breath.

Princesses. We were a collection of human princesses.

Mare's lips stretched in the approximation of a smile. "That's right. I've been collecting them for centuries. It's my little hobby. Princesses are so delicate and breakable."

The acidic contents of my stomach rose.

So many lives gone. So many girls and women taken from their homes. Mare was far worse than I'd ever given her credit for.

My attention snagged on two crowns close to mine. Dark silver, set with red and black stones. A memory kicked at my brain. *Carissa and Madeline.* The sixth and eighth princesses of our neighbouring kingdom. The reason Captain Andrick had taught me to protect myself.

Mare caught my stare. "I often have to settle for the younger princesses," she said, her tone indicating how put out she was by that fact. "Heirs are more closely guarded, and their disappearance raises too much fuss. But the last ones born—no one cares much about them."

"Is that why you wanted me? As the only heir?" I croaked, my vision turning gray.

"Oh no, you are far more special to me than that." She stood and approached me, stepping down from the dais with care. Free of her metal claws, a red fingernail tracked down my cheek.

"Why? Why do you hate me so much?" My throat was so dry, the words burned like flames.

As she circled me slowly, the din of the party carried on, everyone oblivious to our interaction. The only people bearing witness were my two guards, who waited as still as statues.

"Let me tell you a story of a Fae who fell in love with a human king. He was handsome, with black hair and dark eyes that reminded her of the night sky. He promised love and eternal devotion to that Fae and, in return, she pledged to love and protect him for all of her eternal days. She even offered him the rarest gift a Fae can give a human—immortality. It would mean linking her life to his and giving up a piece of herself, but she was willing to make that sacrifice for him."

Premonition shrieked at me, screaming at the top of its lungs in a never-ending circle. I swayed on my feet. Where was this going?

"Then one day, the handsome king met someone else. A fair and beautiful maiden, with hair like spun midnight and eyes as deep as the sea. Being a fickle and foolish human, he declared his love for the maiden and broke his promise to the Fae. She begged and pleaded for him to reconsider, to see the error of his ways, but he told her the love he had for the Fae wasn't as pure. It wasn't *true love*." Her voice dropped dangerously low on the last two words. "He spurned the Fae's gift of immortality, saying he would rather die a human than live forever with the Fae. Spurned her gift, like it was nothing but a worthless bauble." Rage flashed in Mare's eyes, so fierce it distorted her pupils until they were wide black holes, full of nothing. "The king and the maiden were married to much rejoicing in their kingdom. Of course, where comes marriage, must soon come an heir. And the king and his queen tried and tried to have a child, but the queen could not conceive."

The blood in my veins froze, slowing to a glacial pace as my heart beat on in sluggish rhythm. Mare stopped circling, halting in front of me. Pinching my chin between her thumb and forefinger, she squeezed hard enough to make tears drain from my eyes.

"So, one day, the queen was sobbing on the riverbanks near her castle when the Fae just happened to walk by. And the kind and generous Fae told the queen she would grant her wish and deliver her a child. But of course, nothing is given without a price, and the queen would have to give up something too. The queen was understandably wary, but she agreed that after the birth, the Fae would return and demand a price. The queen was so blinded by her need to have a child that she asked no more questions and went on her stupid, foolish way. Of course, I don't need to tell you what happened next."

She bared her teeth, and I wrenched my face from her hand.

"No. My father couldn't have loved you."

"If it hadn't been for *that woman*, he would have loved me. We would have been happy. We would have been together forever."

"So you did it to punish them?"

She shrugged her narrow shoulders. "They had to pay. So I gave them everything they wanted, and then I took it away. I wanted them to suffer. I wanted them to feel the sting of losing you over and over again. I wanted it to hurt."

"But it wasn't my fault. I haven't done anything to you. And now they're dead. Why are you doing this to me?"

Her eyes turned hard as she stared into me, peeling away layers as if she was tearing into an onion. "Because it wasn't enough. Because they fell asleep and never had to go through the pain of actually losing you. Because my sister cast a curse she didn't understand, and I was left unsatisfied for one hundred years."

She was shaking now, wrath rolling off her in opaque sheets.

"They were miserable for twenty-one years." My voice caught. "We were never truly happy. The curse lived with all of us. They suffered. They suffered so much." It was the same truth I understood the day they had all died. I laid it before her, my soul naked and exposed. "I swear to you—they didn't get away with anything."

Mare cocked her head as if considering my words, and then she laughed. It was a dead sound, something tossed to the bottom of a pit to be buried forever. It was awful and hateful, and I knew then, with the certainty of the stones cold and hard beneath my toes, that I was lost. That nothing would ever convince her my parents had suffered enough. That I'd suffered enough. She would keep me here, a living, breathing jewel in her collection until I died at her will.

"Take her back to her cage." She gestured to the guards, who began to haul me away. "And Princess? I'll see you in the ring."

CHAPTER THIRTY-EIGHT

A ND SO IT WENT. Night after night, they dragged me into the arena barefoot and barely clothed, starving, thirsty, and freezing. The patrons all knew me now and chanted my name.

Some were rooting for me, but most were not. They booed when it was over too quickly; they screamed in ecstasy when I was injured; they called for more blood as I slashed down these women, one by one. Princesses, just like me. Every night, I prayed it would be me who died. Every night, I prayed one of those women would murder me as I'd murdered them all.

My only consolation was the hope this *had* to be over soon. I couldn't possibly last much longer. Either through steel or starvation, something would release me from this hell.

My rewards varied from fight to fight. After the first one, my meals were far less grand. Sometimes it was scraps. Sometimes only a little more. Whatever it was, it was never enough. They healed the worst of my injuries but left me tired and aching, weak and hungry. During the day, I fell into a fitful sleep, trying to ignore the Fae that visited my cage.

The other caged women eyed me warily from behind their bars, probably wondering if I'd kill them next. My conscience weighed on me like a ceiling of sandstone. I'd been given no good choices—kill them quickly or let them burn in agony. I didn't seek their forgiveness, nor did I expect their absolution. We were enemies, divided by lines none of us had drawn.

Mercifully, I wasn't invited to any more of Mare's parties. I watched as guards took away women and led them toward the palace through the maze of mirrors. It was of little comfort, but I'd have rather fought for survival than face the humiliation of that black throne room, drowning in its trophies of misery.

I lost track of the days and weeks when, one night, I was again deposited into the arena and handed my sword and my dagger. There was no question they were mine now.

The crowd was edgier than usual, more ravenous. Already they were cheering so loudly, a frenzied mania hung in the air, thick enough to form clouds in the sky. Maybe it was only me who felt it. Maybe they were as bloodthirsty as they were every night, and I was losing my tenuous foothold on reality. I was told I'd been making Mare a lot of gold with my performances.

As if this were all a game. As if it were merely a transaction. As if I gave a shit about that.

Tonight, only one door opened at the corner of the arena, and a woman almost twice my size stepped out. Dressed in polished metal armor, she looked as though she could single-handedly snap me in two. I looked down at the useless, delicate dress I wore every night. The same dress all the princesses wore, giving no one an advantage. This was a new test, then, and Mare had changed the rules of our game.

My opponent's steps were heavy, boots thudding in the dirt. Her straight blonde hair was cropped short and her clear blue eyes stared through me. She believed she'd won this already, and I was inclined to agree. Perhaps this was my chance to end this.

Without preamble, she swung, and I ducked as her blade whistled so close I felt the breath of it on my skin. I thrust my sword, and she blocked me, our blades clanging against the din of chatter and cheers. My arms were already aching. This woman was much stronger and well-fed, and had probably slept in a proper bed last night. I wouldn't last long.

Still, I tried.

For what it was worth, I tried anyway, remembering the lessons taught by my beloved prince in a cursed castle ballroom. But I couldn't best her with my sword, and I couldn't win at hand-to-hand combat. I needed another way.

She was so tall I barely came up to her chest. Stance wide, she faced me, and I took a risky gamble. As I charged for her, she smiled. I was a flea, easily flicked away. An annoyance. An irritation. I ducked and slid between her legs.

She wasn't expecting that. Before she had a chance to recover, I jumped and launched myself onto her back. She wasn't expecting that, either.

With my forearms locked around her throat, I squeezed her windpipe with every bit of strength I had. Dropping her weapons, she grabbed my arms, trying to pry me off. I wrapped my legs around her torso, hanging like a child off her mother. It took every reserve of strength I had, but I didn't let go, and the crowd was losing its mind.

They loved a surprise ending. They weren't expecting this, either.

My opponent spun in circles, trying to dislodge me, but I hung on. She clawed at my arms, drawing blood, leaving deep gouges in my skin. The walls were too low for her to slam me into them—something I'd realized only after making this desperate attempt—and it felt like fate had finally thrown me a fucking bone.

Bent at the waist, she attempted to flip me off, and she danced around the arena as I clung on like a stubborn crab. Instead of my arms, she went for my legs, clawing and scratching at them. Blood dripped off me in rivers. Next, she tried to reach for her dropped weapons, and I panicked, knowing I would be in trouble if she got a hold of them.

I squeezed harder, hoping to make her black out, and she stumbled. It was working, but I was tiring, and my leg slipped from her waist. That was all the leverage she needed. She grabbed my thigh and pulled it with all she had. My arms snapped from her neck, and she flung me halfway across the arena like a bag of bruised plums.

My dress offered no protection as I skidded against the hard dirt, skin tearing across my back and ribs. Blood pooled beneath me, creating a reddish sludge. I gasped, trying to catch my breath, pinching it like motes of dust. The crowd screamed louder. They were stomping in the stands. The wind knocked out of me, I couldn't move. But it didn't matter because I had lost. I groaned and waited for her to come.

She took her time, pandering to the crowd. They fed off her energy, switching sides. Fickle and entirely disloyal, they'd already abandoned me. They wanted to support a winner.

Finally, she approached and hovered over me, a smile stretching in a grim specter. With her sword pointing at my twisted heart, a peace as wide and calm as a still blue lake spread through my limbs. This pain, this wretched agony, would all be over soon. I closed my eyes, my face bent to the sky, offering myself to infinity as I waited for the end.

"Stop!" The command rang through the arena, pinging off every surface like a kernel in a steaming pot. Everything went silent as my eyes popped open. My opponent was looking away, her sword still primed above me. "This match is over!" Mare declared, followed by boos and hisses from the crowd. They'd come for blood, and she was denying them.

No. Don't stop.

The gate opened, and Mare was striding along the floor of the arena, black skirts swirling. The large woman lowered her arm, confusion furrowing her brow.

"Get rid of her." Mare gestured to the guards who'd emerged behind her. Without hesitation, they seized the woman, slit her throat, and dropped her to the floor in a thundering crash of metal plates and armor. Even the crowd recoiled in shock at this casual infliction of death.

Mare prowled closer, grabbing me by the back of the head, her hand fisting my hair. I arched in pain as she lifted me, and I reached for the hand clamped to my head.

Mare hissed in my ear, "I am not going to make it that easy for you, Princess. I am not finished with you yet, nor am I done with your suffering. When you do finally die, I promise it is going to be *spectacular*."

She let go and threw me to the ground, where I landed face-first, coughing in the dust.

"Please, let me go," I whimpered, hating the sound of it, but this had become the only language I knew anymore. Mare had carved out my dignity, bit by excruciating bit. "Please, I want to die. I want it to be over. I'll do anything." Wracking, shuddering sobs ripped through my body, tears mingling with blood and sweat and dirt. "Please." I writhed on the ground.

The crowd had gone quiet as the blonde woman's corpse cooled next to me. There was no joy in this, even for them. I was a pathetic bug, smashed on the sidewalk, with nothing left to give.

Mare leaned over me—a towering black inferno—her voice laced with lethal calm. "Be careful what you wish for, Princess."

CHAPTER THIRTY-NINE

T HIS TIME, THEY DIDN'T heal or clean me. Instead, I was left
alone in my cage for several days, filthy and covered in
blood, my dress torn and hanging as limp as my hopes. Mare's
final words in the ring had suggested she was working up to
something, and now she was leaving me here to wait and stew.
I couldn't imagine what else she had left to throw at me.

Maida's footsteps came into view where I lay with my cheek
pressed to the marble. He dropped to the ground, leaning
against the bars. His arm held out, he procured an offering—a
jug of water, passed through the bars as he peered over his
shoulder.

I eyed him with suspicion.

"Go on. It's fine. I promise."

I crawled over and snatched it, taking a careful sip. It was
sweet and cool and clear as a mountain stream. I tipped it back
and began gulping it down.

He reached out and clasped the bottle. "Slow down, you'll make yourself sick."

Bottle pressed to my chest, I scrambled back, snarling. I had become the animal meant for this cage. Maida's dark eyes widened in a flash of pity before it was replaced with something I couldn't name.

"You shouldn't have let her see you like that," he said. "Knowing how much you want to die only makes her want to keep you alive."

I knew it was true, but the fight in me now languished in a deep, dank cellar.

"What does she have planned for me?" I asked, afraid of the answer. "How will she torment me next?"

Maida lifted his powerful shoulders. "I don't know, Princess."

I took another sip from the bottle and groaned. My ribs ached where the giant woman had crashed into me, and a massive blue and yellow bruise was visible through the rips in my dress.

"Come here," Maida said, waving me closer, but I shrank back. He raised his eyes skyward. "What's the worst I can do? You want to die anyway. Maybe I'll do you a favor."

Unable to argue with that logic, I inched over to him.

Reaching between the bars, he placed a hand on my ribs, his palm so large and my body shriveled from malnutrition, it engulfed my torso. I exhaled a rough breath at the first warm and gentle contact I'd experienced in weeks.

His face softened as he concentrated. A soft golden light flared beneath his hand, and the pain in my side ebbed. "I can't do too much, or she'll know. But that should help."

The bruising was still tender, but it no longer hurt to breathe. "Why are you helping me?" I leaned my head against the bars.

Maida went to pull his hand away, but I grabbed it and held his forearm against me. I didn't care who it was—I just needed to feel something that wasn't cold steel in my hand, or hot blood from a wounded princess, or the unforgiving hardness of marble beneath me. I needed warm brown skin and a heartbeat to remember what it was like to be alive.

Finding whatever sliver of pity resided in his corrupted heart, he didn't pull away. So I clung to his arm like it was a parachute and I'd been shoved off a cliff. His warmth seeped into me, nothing but this tiny scrap of kindness anchoring me to this life. Tears flowed down my cheeks, and I sobbed quietly, burying my face in the crook of his elbow.

After a while, I pulled back and let go, too beaten to be embarrassed. "I'm sorry," I said, looking at the stained sleeve of his pale gray tunic. It was covered in tears and the dirt and blood that painted me like a stain.

"It's okay, Princess. I hope it helped," he said softly. Without another word, he stood and walked away.

CHAPTER FORTY

THE CROWD WAS ROARING so loudly I could hear it from my cage. What had them so worked up already? Maybe Mare had found another mouse to trap in her maze, but I knew I couldn't be that lucky.

Guards lined up outside my bars, and dread climbed into my throat. Whatever the crowd was screaming about waited for me.

I wasn't sure how many days it had been since my brawl with the large blonde woman. My rewards had evaporated long ago, and I'd eaten only sporadically. I'd finished the water from Maida yesterday, nursing the contents like a deer with her foal.

Nothing but snarled hair and shivering skin, I ached with a bone-deep exhaustion. I couldn't fight anymore, even against a princess who didn't know which end of the sword to hold. Maybe whatever Mare had plucked from the dark recesses of her imagination would finally be my undoing. She had promised me a spectacular finish, and I prayed she had finally grown tired of me.

The guards unlocked my cage and hauled me to my feet.

"Please, I need something to eat." My voice was cracked lines in the pavement after an earthquake.

They ignored me, and my tears flowed freely as I stumbled between them. My legs were covered in dried blood, and my side throbbed even after Maida's healing. He never came back after that day.

As we approached the arena, the noise was a living thing, ferocious and snarling. Only something monstrous could have revved the crowd up in this way. Pressure built behind my eyes, in my limbs, and in my chest. I wasn't sure I could look.

They handed me my weapons. My arms were so weak I could barely hang on to the hilt, the tip dragging on the ground. They opened the gate and shoved me inside, where I tripped, landing face-first in the dirt. Upon spotting me, the Fae chanted my name amidst the usual chorus of boos and hisses and jeers. They both loved and despised me.

Pushing up onto my hands and knees, I willed myself to stand, knowing Mare was watching. And that's when I saw what had whipped everyone into such a state of excitement. A hand punched through my chest and ripped out my bloody, withered heart.

Ronan knelt on all fours in a cage, chains around his neck, wrists, and ankles, preventing him from standing. Our eyes met across the dusty floor of the arena, and I coasted on a sea of nausea.

No. Not this. Anything but this.

As we stared at one another, the look in his eyes broke what was left of me to be broken. Mare had finally found a way to make me suffer enough.

"Look what I found," Mare trilled in a sing-song voice, projecting it across the arena. "We caught him trying to rescue you, but he wasn't quite fast enough." She laughed, delighted with herself.

I closed my eyes and took a deep breath. I'd lost all sense of time and the world outside in this place, but of course, he'd come for me. I would have come for him, too. Nothing would have stopped me until I'd torn apart the world to find him.

Ronan strained against his chains, fury and fire and rage roiling off warm, muscled skin. His cage wasn't golden—it was iron, strong and solid. Tired, but thinner than I remembered, he appeared unharmed. At least for now.

Mare took her time, enjoying the crowd's reaction. They knew who Ronan was to me. It was then I noticed Kianna seated in the chair next to Mare, her eyes wild with terror as her gaze met mine. Mare was going to take the only two people I had left. Again.

"I have another surprise for you, Thorne," she said, raising her arms in the now-familiar gesture that haunted my dreams. The door in the arena's corner slid open. The same door that had revealed countless young women, night after night. Women I'd murdered over and over. Only this time, it was not a young woman who walked out.

It was Noah.

I sank to my knees as he stumbled into the arena, blinking at the brightness. Beaten, his face was swollen and bloody, his clothes torn. He saw me and stopped. The world spun out.

"You know the rules, Princess," Mare said. "A fight to the death. If I suspect either of you isn't giving it your all, you'll first watch the other one die in a slow and exceedingly painful way." Her lambent gaze turned to Ronan. "And then he'll be next." Mare tapped a finger against her chin. "The new king's true love or his oldest childhood friend. Who *will* win? *Who* is he rooting for?" A wicked grin crept across her face, and the crowd screamed wildly.

Ronan's eyes darted between me and Noah.

I'll kill anyone who hurts you. Protective words whispered to me in a darkened bedroom, once upon a time.

Don't make promises you might not be able to keep, I'd told him.

And this was the promise. Me and his best friend. I couldn't beat Noah. Even if I were fed and healthy, I couldn't beat him. He towered over me, all muscle and warrior breeding. I was a hungry, weakened princess with a month of training. Ronan's gaze met mine and if an entire lifetime of regret could have been folded and flattened into a basket, I would have offered it to him now.

Noah ran a panicked hand through his wild mane of blond hair as Mare clapped her hands once over her head. "Begin!"

The crowd swooped into a bellowed chant, shouting my name with their spittle-coated lips. Right now, they were on my side. They knew me, and our love was a complicated thing. But as soon as I faltered, they'd defect, betting on the horse with the steadier gait.

Noah watched me as I stood and started to circle him. He looked to Ronan and then to me, and I understood with the clarity of chiming silver bells the choice he was being forced to make.

"I said 'begin'!" Mare screamed.

"Attack me," I said to Noah. "Do it, or none of us will walk away from this."

"I can't do that," he said, his sword up.

"You have to," I hissed. "There is no choice. She will see to that."

We continued to circle. Mare would tolerate this for a short while, but her patience was thin. I glanced at Ronan and hoped he could see the apology in my expression. When I swung for Noah, he dodged me with ease, stepping out of the way, leaving me unharmed. Fury shook Mare, so I lunged again, more viciously this time. Noah had no choice but to shove me off.

And then I lost my mind. Mare had finally broken me. She had broken my bones. Broken my mind. Broken my heart and torn apart every piece of my fucking soul.

A tangled mess of teeth and nails and hair, I launched myself at Noah. He wrestled me to the ground, trying to protect me from myself, but I was a storm, untethered and lashing against the waves. In my frenzy, I kicked him in the stomach, and he went flying. It shocked me enough that cold resignation replaced my raw fury.

I jumped up, scooping up my sword, and raced for Noah. Finally, he understood what had to happen, even as remorse consumed us both. At the last possible second, he picked up his own sword and blocked me, jumping up and advancing. Adrenaline was the only thing keeping me standing.

I bent down to pick up my dagger, but that was a mistake because then Noah was on me. An arm clamped around my waist while another wrenched the sword from my hand. A heartbeat later, he had his dagger at my throat, my back pressed against his chest. This was the end, and I wondered if Mare would stop him from killing me. But no, this had been her plan all along—to ruin as many lives as possible.

Noah hesitated.

"Do it!" Mare hissed. "Do it, or there will be far greater consequences."

"Do it," I said, sobbing. "Please, do it. She'll make me watch him die. Please," I begged. "I don't want to live anymore. Give me peace, Noah. She'll never stop."

"He'd never forgive me," Noah said, the sound so anguished it sliced my flesh into strips. The crowd roared around us, enveloping us in a chanting cavity of white noise. The world constricted down to only the two of us. I felt his tears as they fell against my neck.

"Noah, please," I whispered, and felt him shake his head.

"Do it!" Mare shrieked at a fever pitch. She was going to destroy us all.

"You'll get out of this," Noah was saying, now. "You're one of the bravest people I've ever met. It's no wonder he fell in love with you."

"What?" I asked, bewildered. There was no way out of here. "Please, Noah. Do it. I'm begging you."

I felt him inhale a deep breath against my back, and then he pressed his lips to my temple and whispered, "Take good care of him, Thorne. Have a good life. You both deserve that."

In a movement so fast, I didn't even see it, he let go of me and spun around to face me. He grabbed my hand in both of his, wrapping them around his dagger, and then plunged it into his heart. Blood gushed hot and red over my hand, and I screamed. Noah slumped down as he slid off the blade and landed face-up in the dirt.

I kept screaming. I couldn't stop screaming. The crowd was screaming. Mare was screaming. The universe became one loud, endless scream, echoing against the dark for a thousand years.

And then the world exploded.

CHAPTER FORTY-ONE

T HROWN OFF MY FEET, I flew into the air and landed on the hard ground, my already ravaged skin tearing on the gravel and dirt. Hard objects pelted from the sky, and panic swelled as screams filled the stadium. But it was no longer the frenzied bloodlust of the cheering crowd—it was fear and pain and confusion.

One moment, Noah had sacrificed himself, and the next, there was nothing. Just the ringing in my ears and the stinging of my skin as if I'd been pushed down a hill inside a barrel full of tacks.

My face buried in the nest of my arms, I lay on the ground. Whatever had caused that explosion could come and find me. I'd once promised Kianna I'd never give up, but she was gone, and Noah was gone, and Ronan was gone, and I had nothing left to give. I let out a sob that bundled the fear and the hope, the anger and the joy, the love and the loneliness that had all been my prison for the past one hundred and twenty-one years.

But then, strong arms scooped me up, and I was pressed against a warm body. My mind registered a familiar scent that filled my veins and fortified the collapsing walls of whatever fight I had left. My eyes fluttered open to find Ronan speeding us away from the arena. He leaped over the gate in one stride, and I must have finally succumbed to death because this couldn't be real.

"Ronan?" I croaked, my throat rubbed raw from screaming. My heart seized. I had missed him so much that I almost snapped in two. We were racing through the menagerie, twisting around cages and down the pathways.

"Stop," I said. "Ronan, you have to stop."

"What?" he asked, coming to a halt.

"We can't leave them here." The princesses were looking toward the arena, the noise drawing their attention. But some watched us, their eyes pleading and judging.

Without a word, Ronan put me down and started wrenching on the doors of the cages closest to us. His newfound Fae strength made quick work of the bars and locks. Screams and dust still hovered in the air over the arena.

"Where's Kianna? Mare had her!"

"She flew away," Ronan said. "She was okay. We'll find her."

"What happened? How did you get out of that cage?"

"I found my magic," he said, breaking the lock on the cage that sat next to mine. The woman cowered in the corner, and I knew most of them were too scared to run. Where would they even go? "I discovered it when we came after you. I guess maybe

I've always known. Metal. I can manipulate metal. Not just iron or steel, but anything. I've been practicing with smaller items. I've always felt an affinity with weapons, but I thought it was something that came naturally to me. I think this is why. I've never done anything like that before. When Mare put those chains on me, I felt a vibration in them, and the whole time you and Noah were fighting, I was trying to figure out a way to make sure my escape took out as many of those fucking Faeries as possible. I tried to shield you from as much of it as I could. I'm sorry if it hurt you."

"Ronan, I'm sorry. Noah, he—" I broke off, unable to continue.

He took me in his arms. "It wasn't your fault," he said, pulling me in for a hug.

I couldn't hold on to him tightly enough, his touch restoring the breath in my lungs after I'd been living on nothing but sips of borrowed air.

There was a shout in the distance and Ronan looked up, his face turning white at the cages dangling overhead. With his magic, he popped open the doors, but there was no way for the women to get down.

"We can't help them all, Thorne. I knocked Mare out, but she's going to come after you," Ronan said, grabbing my hand. "We'll get the rest of them out of here, I promise. But we have to get you away from here."

My gaze trapped on the swinging cages, I let him tug me away. "Okay," I replied and ran with him, our hands clasped as I tried to corral my guilt. We'd come back for them. If we survived.

Ronan flew across the ground so fast I couldn't keep up, my feet tripping under me. Without missing a step, he scooped me up again, carrying me at a dizzying pace toward Mare's palace.

"The gate—we can lose them inside the maze." I pointed to the silver doors. Two guards flanked them, but Ronan didn't hesitate. Using whatever magic now ran in his veins, he drew their swords from their sheaths, and in a flash, they plunged straight into the heart of each guard, gutted by their own swords. I turned to Ronan, wide-eyed, and he offered me an uncertain look.

"Nice trick," I said.

As we approached the entrance, he put me on the ground and pulled the swords from the guards' chests, wiping them on their cloaks. He handed me one and held the other in his grip as we entered the maze of mirrors.

"Don't let go," I cautioned, and he squeezed my hand.

We moved as one, around corners and down hallways, our mirrored selves mimicking our strides. I was obscured in so much dirt and blood, it was hard to tell where I ended or began.

The mirrors toyed with us. Suddenly, my reflection turned and ran away, and I stumbled, unable to catch myself. The next moment, it came back at me—teeth bared, hair flying, and leaped. I shielded my arms around my head, but nothing happened. Only an illusion.

Ronan wrapped his arms around my waist. "Don't let go," he reminded me.

We ran. Up ahead, the castle of Ravalyn burned, and I lay dead and slashed through the heart. This time, it was Ronan who stumbled. He cried out, crashing into the mirror, cracks appearing like spiderwebs.

"It's not real," I shouted. "I'm here. I'm fine."

"Gods, it feels so real," he breathed, his chest heaving.

"I know."

Seeing the fissures in the glass gave me an idea, and I rammed the wall with the butt of my heel. The cracks grew, spreading over the surface.

"Not with your bare feet—you'll hurt yourself," Ronan said, picking up on my idea and smashing it with his boot.

The mirror shattered, the sound echoing through the halls. Shards crashed to the floor, leaving an opening, but there were more mirrors behind it, stretching in every direction.

We were trapped here. Every time I broke free, there was another door, another lock, or another cage. I became a whipping tornado of anger and frustration, all howling wind and spinning debris. Screaming echoed in my ears as I pounded the mirrors with my fists and my heels, eventually realizing the sound was coming from me. The glass splintered and cracked, the shards embroidering my skin with cuts and currents of blood.

I felt nothing. I was nothing.

"Thorne!" Ronan grabbed me and pressed me to him, pinning my arms. "Calm down." I fought against his hold and then slumped against him. "You're hurting yourself."

"We'll never get out of here. She'll never stop. I wanted to die. You have no idea how much I wanted to die." Sobs wracked my body as I pressed my face into Ronan's chest.

"We are going to stop her, and I am going to get you out of here." He sounded so sure, I wanted to believe him more than I'd ever believed in anything. "But I need you to hold on a little longer. You've been so brave, but we need to keep moving. Don't look in the mirrors. Just look ahead. Can you do that, my lion?"

I nodded, and he took my hand.

We ran again. Visions flashed in the corners of my eyes. Of Ronan and Kianna and my parents. Of them covered in blood. I saw Noah and Em and Gideon. Isabelle and Adrian. Kianna's sisters and Ronan's father, looming as large as a giant. I shut my eyes and ran. I saw Ronan's mother and Esme, and even Angeline and Erick.

Kingdoms burned, and buildings collapsed, and the earth cleaved in two.

We rounded another corner, where a silver-haired, black-eyed sentinel waited at the gates of hell.

"Maida," I said as we skidded to a stop. "Don't try to stop us."

He dropped his folded arms, gaze shifting between us, and then shook his head. "Follow me," he said, but we didn't move.

"Why would we trust you? You're probably going to take us straight to Mare."

"Didn't I help you?" He raised his hands in surrender.

"Yes, but I'm sure it was only because you had something to gain."

His shoulders slumped. "I suppose I deserve that. I won't take you to Mare. I want to help you get out of here."

"Why?"

Maida ran a hand down his face. It wasn't quite remorse, but there was something tormented in the action. His dark gaze fell on me. "I'm the one who helped the former King Goldraven find you. He made me an offer, and I gave him the sword that allowed him to cut the brambles that protected you. But when humans use Fae objects, it sometimes messes with their heads. Often, they become the worst versions of themselves. And that day... Well, I'm not proud that I helped him do what he did."

"You knew what happened."

Maida nodded. "I told you it's my job to know these things." He cocked his head and let out a sigh, as if he was already regretting what he was about to say. "I'm also sorry about how I treated you when you came to me for help. You've impressed me, Princess. Not many could have survived what you did in this place."

The admission surprised me enough that my response stuck to my tongue. Our gazes met, and if Maida had meant anything to me, I would have forgiven him then.

Somehow, he understood what I couldn't say. "Just let me help you."

I still didn't trust him, but we also didn't have many options. We could wander in here forever or take our chances.

"Fine. Help us."

Maida returned my nod with a sharp jerk of his chin and spun on his heel, leading us through the halls. Only our reflections followed us now, mirrored a million times into the distance. We turned a corner, and ahead lay the doors to Mare's castle.

"There is an exit out the back, where you can escape," Maida said as we entered the black throne room, pointing to a door almost hidden from view by Mare's throne. "There is a tunnel that will take you outside the walls of the menagerie. Once you're outside, run and don't stop."

"Thank you." After a moment of indecision, I threw my arms around his neck. I didn't know why I did it, except for the need to convey my gratitude for the small kindness Maida had shown me. He stood stiffly and then wrapped his arms around me. "I won't forget what you did. Whatever your reasons."

I was about to turn away, when he stopped me, his fingers grabbing my chin before he tipped up my face. With his endless black gaze, he stared down at me, something foreign, but also strangely familiar passing between us. I blinked through a haze, the world tilting ever so slightly.

"You should go. Before she finds you," he said, finally.

I nodded slowly and turned away, noting another strange look that passed between Maida and Ronan before Ronan looked back at me and held out his hand.

Our fingers clasped, we sprinted for the exit. We'd only made it a few steps when the ceiling above us shattered. Splintered glass accompanied a sonorous roar, raining down shards like deadly rain.

Mare's demon flapped its wings, dropping with a thud into the center of the room. Gaze anchored to me, it stretched to its full height and let out a huge burst of fire.

CHAPTER FORTY-TWO

"**M**ARE," MAIDA HISSED, DRAWING the sword at his hip and baring his fangs.

Cunning malice shifted in the demon's eyes. This creature didn't belong to Mare. It *was* Mare.

I was struck by how vastly Kianna had underestimated her sister's power.

"Run!" I screamed, but it was too late.

Something heavy hit me across my stomach, and I flew several feet, crashing into the wall. An agonized scream ripped from my throat as my skin tore against the stone, sending shocks of pain deep into my bones. I felt like a cadaver, my skin flayed to expose muscles and tissue and bone.

Blood gushed from my stomach, anguish exploding in sharp, stabbing waves.

With a burst of flame, Mare aimed another attack at me, but Ronan dove in front, shielding me with his body. Heat singed every pore like I'd been wrapped in a curtain of lava. Sweat ran in rivulets down my skin, the fire blasting and burning for what felt like forever. The fear of losing Ronan again wrapped shackles around my wrists and my ankles, numbing my limbs. Finally, the flame receded, and he pulled back, miraculously unharmed.

"How?"

"Fae blood," came his reply, and I almost passed out from relief.

Maida shouted, and Mare swung her giant, black head. Though he was trying to distract her, there was nowhere to run. Fallen debris and Mare's thick, muscled body blocked our only escape routes.

Ronan stood and surveyed the room, glancing over at me with a determined look. He closed his eyes, shoulders tensed. Pain scoured my body, my vision going dark. As I pressed my cheek to the ground, a strange rattling noise sharpened my focus.

It was the crowns. They were vibrating and twitching, jolting to life. Jittery and impatient, they danced on their pegs, like restless children fed too much sugar.

'I found my magic.'

Metal. Rivers of it. A veritable wall of it.

Hundreds and hundreds of crowns made of every variety of gold and silver and pewter and iron had been enshrined in this room. They hopped and scooted, shuddering and shaking. And then, as if in slow motion, they began to slide forward. With the precision of a trained artillery unit, they moved together in unison as every crown shot from the wall and slammed into Mare's demon hide.

Ronan twisted his hands, and they buried themselves into her thick skin like drills penetrating rock. Mare threw her head back and screamed so loudly that the entire room shook.

My head spun, the wound in my stomach gushing crimson.

Blood, black and oily, oozed and dripped as her macabre trophies buried deeper and deeper, snapping bones, piercing blood vessels, and popping organs like over-inflated balloons. The sound of Mare being shredded apart echoed in the screams of every princess she'd tormented for centuries.

A massive claw swiped at Ronan, but he jumped back and didn't falter.

With a bellowing screech, Mare tipped over, collapsing on top of her throne. Dozens of spikes drove up through her head as she landed, her roars cut short forever.

Silence dropped over the room, and I fell back, staring at the ruined ceiling. My eyelids were so weighted down, I couldn't stop blinking. My body was numb.

Arms circled me, loving and warm. Ronan pressed a hand to my stomach, trying to stop the blood. But even I could see there was too much of it. A flutter of green caught my eye, and Kianna appeared above me.

A Faerie godmother, fallen from the sky.

"Thorne," she whispered, tears shining in her eyes. "I found you. I was so worried."

"Can you help her?" Ronan asked, panic rolling in his eyes.

"I'll try." There was a rustle of fabric, and a gentle hand rested on my midsection.

At first, I felt nothing, but then there was warmth, the same as when Maida had healed me. I gasped as the wound slowly closed, the process almost as painful as the injury. Tears ran down Ronan's cheeks, and I swept one away. Whatever Kianna was doing must have been working, because he exhaled an audible sigh and dropped his head to my shoulder.

Several minutes later, most of my cuts and bruises had healed. Though I still ached everywhere, it was enough for now.

Kianna was sobbing as she collapsed against me, her arms circling my waist. "I'm so sorry," she said. "I'm so sorry for everything she did to you."

"You saved me, Kianna. You saved my life." I stroked her head as I whispered the words.

For a long time, none of us moved. Our arms and bodies entwined, I basked in the sound of their breaths and the beats of their hearts, like I could distill them down and infuse them into my veins.

"Marry me, Thorne," Ronan said, breaking the silence. Kianna and I both looked up, our eyes wide. "I love you. Be my wife and my queen and be with me forever."

"I've never wanted anything more," I said as I floated on a golden river of light.

I had been broken.

I had been beaten.

But I had not shattered.

Finally, after every baptism by fire I'd walked through, I would get my second chance.

Kianna let out an ear-splitting shriek and threw her arms around us both. "You're getting married!"

Ronan kissed me and stood with me gathered in his arms.

"I think I can walk," I whispered.

He shook his head, dropping his forehead to mine. "No. I am never, ever letting go of you again."

CHAPTER FORTY-THREE

W E FREED THE PRINCESSES, reuniting them with their families, knowing the memory of their captivity would be etched into them forever. But they had survived and could now begin to pick up the pieces of their future.

For those who hadn't—for those whose crowns had become the weapons that had destroyed Mare—we vowed to honor their memory.

Camped outside the menagerie's walls, Em and the rest of the Estrian army filtered into the compound. Enchantments had blocked their entry after Mare had captured Ronan, Noah, and Kianna for her cruel games. Together, we tore it all down. Every golden cage was stripped and broken. The stadium was toppled, its empty stands collapsed to the bloodstained floor.

We burned the wedding-cake castle, smashed apart Mare's labyrinth of mirrors, and destroyed every shred of misery and anguish that haunted this place. While it didn't cleanse away the stains forever inked on my heart, it did finally release the claws that had found a permanent place around it. When all that was done, we finally went home.

We arrived in Estria quietly, only a handful privy to the full weight of the truth. When I laid myself bare for Kianna, reliving every painful detail, she broke down in tears. Together, we would heal against what Mare had done to us both. After one hundred and twenty-one years, Kianna and I had finally become friends. So much more than friends. She'd saved my life and shed the weight of her sisters' scrutiny. We were both changed forever.

Gideon was so happy to see me, he nearly crushed my ribs in his enthusiastic embrace. Then he promptly turned bright red, let go, and offered me a formal bow. "It is good to have you home, where you belong, Your Majesty." His eyes shone as he cleared his throat and emotion stuck in mine. I might have lost a father, but maybe I'd gained something else.

Ronan and I were married quietly, under a starry night sky. Only those who meant the most were there. We both agreed it was the most perfect wedding in the history of weddings. To the most perfect man I could have ever dreamed of.

Ronan and Em didn't blame me for Noah's death, but a part of me would always shoulder the burden of his last moments as his innocent blood gushed over my hands.

"He told me to take good care of you," I told Ronan. "I begged him to kill me, but he said you would never forgive him."

"That was Noah," Em said. "Faithful to the very end."

We fell silent, each lost in our thoughts.

"I will," I said, taking Ronan's hand. "Take good care of you. I promise."

He gave me that smile that had kept me warm in my darkest moments in the menagerie. "I know that, Thorne. You changed everything. Who would have thought a cursed princess in a castle would be my destiny?"

"Speaking of the castle," Kianna said, "what are we going to do with it?"

"I think I have an idea," I replied.

On the edge of a small kingdom, a princess had been born, but hers had not been a fairy-tale beginning. She'd grown up in a castle haunted by her own ghost, and all that remained now was a tomb of countless shattered lives.

This, too, we took apart brick by brick.

My family, my parents, Isabelle, Adrian, and every other person who'd slept in the castle were buried on the grounds. Side by side they lay, finally at peace. The Fae graveyard was now overgrown with flowers. A carpet of them covered the once-grassy clearing, including the space where Ronan's father once lay.

Every trace of his crime, and mine, erased. At least to those who didn't know the truth.

Where the castle stood, we had built a garden to rival the heavens. Kianna's magic flowed through the paths and beds, showering everything in flowers teeming with life and wonder. Stones had been placed for every princess who'd lost her life, and in the center, the largest one of all for Noah and the sacrifice he'd made.

Promoted to Estria's new army commander, Em stood before Noah's tomb, her head bowed. Ronan and I waited as she approached, stopping to place a fist over her heart and then cracking a smile.

"To second chances," she said. "And to a new king and queen. May you be happy forever."

I hugged her, and she turned to leave, taking her army and Kianna with her.

Finally, it was just Ronan and me. We rode to my grandparents' chateau, restored to its former glory. It was our place to be alone, away from the politics and whispering walls of Estria.

Hand in hand, we walked through the grand doors and paused with the overwhelming weight of all we had endured.

Once upon a time, a cursed princess had woken up in a castle and, though it had taken a while, she had finally gotten an ending. A chance at the life that had always been waiting.

I looked at Ronan, and with an explosion of love bursting in my heart, we kissed.

For now, we were happy.

Continue Thorne and Ronan's journey, and order To Save a Kingdom today!

Get your free copy of Wicked is the Reaper, a prequel novella, by signing up for my newsletter at:
nishajtuli.com

Want more fae romance, hot love interests, and girls with attitude? Then order Trial of the Sun Queen, the first book in the Artefacts of Ouranos Trilogy.

Continue with Thorne & Ronan's journey!

TO
SAVE A
KINGDOM

Never miss a release!
Get your free copy of Wicked is the Reaper, a prequel novella, by
signing up for my newsletter at:

nishajtuli.com

COMING DECEMBER 2022

Looking for more fantasy romance featuring strong heroines,
hot Fae love interests and all the action you can handle?
The Bachelor meets the Hunger Games in the *Trial of the Sun
Queen*, Book One in the Artefacts of Ouranos Trilogy, coming
to Kindle Unlimited.

ACKNOWLEDGMENTS

This feels silly to say, but how do I do this? The last two years of my writing journey have brought a lot of new and wonderful people into my life. Ones I didn't expect at all. (No one supports you like a friend you've met on the internet and you've never actually met.)

The pandemic was both a weird time but gave me the gift of finding myself. I don't know if any of this would have happened otherwise.

Melissa, my writing spouse, I don't know what I'd do without your enthusiasm and your humor and just your wild and lovely spirit.

Bria, you've become one of the first people I go to when I've got another book done. I appreciate all your insight and advice and I just know your 'yes' is coming any day now.

Shaylin, I feel like I found a writing soulmate in you. You're so talented and brilliant, and I can't thank you enough for putting your mark on this manuscript.

To Ashyle, Raidah, Christine, and Jenna, thank you so much for being my last eyes on this book!

Thank you to the slew of beta readers that helped me make this book everything it could be. Maricota, Laura, Shiloh, Lisa, Alison, Emma, Lucee, Kaila, Rebekka, Jessica, Alanna, Lauren, Drea, and Keshe.

To Pine, Irene, Sunyi, Al, Frances, Hana, Gabi, Zippy, Marco, Liz, (those of you I already mentioned above!) and everyone else in WMC. You are all the best and I'm so lucky I found all of you.

To my agent Jennifer Herrington. I know we didn't make it out on sub with this one but I'm still grateful for your input into making this book so much stronger and for always being such a force of support and positivity, even though things have been tough.

And... I hope we're not done with this book yet.

To the reading community on BookTok and Bookstagram, thank you for being so enthusiastic and supportive of a brand new author who still had to prove herself. You're honestly the ones who made this all possible.

To my mom who was the one who always read books and looked at me and said "couldn't you write this?" Yah, I guess I finally did.

To my kids, Alice and Nicky, you are a never ending source of joy in my life, even when you're driving me crazy. It's a good thing you're cute. Thanks for being patient with me when I get distracted writing stories in my head when you talk to me sometimes.

And of course, to my husband Matthew, who's support and belief in me has never wavered a single day since we met all those years ago. Thank you for giving me the space and the freedom to pursue this and for allowing me to be the dramatic one. I'm not exaggerating when I say I couldn't do this if I didn't have a partner who gets it.

ABOUT THE AUTHOR

Nisha has always been obsessed with worlds she cannot see. From Florin to Prythian, give her a feisty heroine, a windswept castle, and true love's kiss, and she'll be lost in the pages forever. Bonus points for protagonists slaying dragons in kick-ass outfits.

When Nisha isn't writing, it's usually because one of her two kids needs something (she loves them anyway). After they're finally in bed, she'll usually be found with her e-reader or knitting sweaters and scarves, perfect for surviving a Canadian winter.

Follow Along For More

Website and newsletter: https://nishajtuli.com
TikTok: https://www.tiktok.com/@nishajtwrites
Instagram: https://www.instagram.com/nishajtwrites
Twitter: https://twitter.com/NishaJT
Pinterest: https://www.pinterest.ca/nishajtwrites

Made in the USA
Middletown, DE
11 August 2022

71097319R00246